POOR M

D0539841

Jonathan Falla

POOR MERCY
A NOVEL

First published in Great Britain in 2005 by Polygon
an imprint of Birlinn Ltd

West Newington House
10 Newington Road
Edinburgh

www.birlinn.co.uk

ISBN 10: 1-904598-28-5
ISBN 13: 978 1 904598 28 2

The publishers acknowledge subsidy from

Scottish
Arts Council

towards the publication of this volume

British Library Cataloguing-in-Publication Data
A catalogue record for this book is available on request
from the British Library

Typeset by Palimpsest Book Production Limited, Polmont, Stirlingshire
Printed and bound by Creative Print and Design, Ebbw Vale, Wales

For Kit, my boy

ACKNOWLEDGEMENTS

The author would like to acknowledge the support of the Scottish Arts Council who, with a generous award, made the completion of this book possible.

Sections of the novel have appeared, in slightly different forms, in *Cencrastus*, *Signals (London Magazine Editions)*, *New Scottish Writing 1998* and *Macallan Shorts 2001*.

CONTENTS

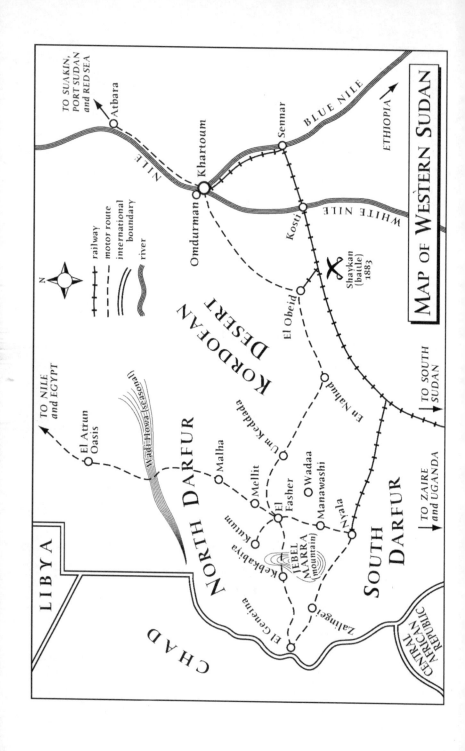

PREFACE

This novel was loosely inspired – or perhaps 'provoked' is the word – by events that took place in 1991 in the Darfur region of Western Sudan, where I was employed by a British charitable agency. As I write this foreword, in 2004, Darfur is once again in crisis. It may be thought that I have written the novel in response to the current situation. In fact I have been working on the story, in one format or another, off and on for more than a decade.

The events of this year 2004 are a direct development of conflicts we observed in 1991. Even then, the tensions and the dilemmas were already old. One evening in Darfur I was invited to the house of a local government official, a sophisticated and thoughtful man who had obtained a video tape of a BBC *Panorama* programme concerning famine in Sudan. We watched it together. The film was not new; it had been made at the time (1988) of a previous Sudan famine in which many things were going wrong with the international aid effort. The programme in its turn looked back at *another* previous famine (1985), concluding that lessons had not been learned and mistakes were being repeated. But, as we watched on that evening in 1991, we had the chilling realisation that we were repeating those old mistakes yet again. And now, as I read the news in 2004, I hear those echoes once more.

Darfur has had a hard history. The famines of recent decades stem in part from present politics and also from a protracted drought that began in the 1970s. But Darfur has been susceptible to hunger for as long as anyone knows; there was, for instance, a terrible famine in 1888. For centuries, the harsh landscape has been crossed and re-crossed by pilgrims, slave traders and soldiers. In this history, Britain has played a less than glorious role; the last Fur sultan was shot in 1916 – by the British army.

I wish to emphasise, however, that I am not writing history or a tract on aid programmes. This is a work of fiction. I have felt quite free to interpret and alter the minutiae of events. I recall Evelyn Waugh who prefaced his 1950 novel *Helena* with a note declaring (but not apologising for) his altering of facts concerning the early church in Constantinople, in order to better suit his tale. Finally, wrote Waugh, "the story is just something to read."

Glenduckie, Fife 2004

PART ONE

The Burnt Hands

ONE

Farah ibn Mashoud, a sweet-tempered young man of promise, was shot with a high velocity rifle on the road from Nyala to El Fasher – a work of some skill. Most travellers in Western Sudan move slowly, on camels swaying over the *goz*, the dune-lands, or in trucks and jeeps boiling and floundering for days on end along the soft sand trails. But for 200 kilometres from Nyala north to El Fasher there lies a gravel road that becomes faster each year as it disintegrates, for the rain runs off the pallid pink dirt cutting grooves and corrugations that set up a juddering in every bolt of a car and in the passengers' teeth and brains, so that you must make your vehicle fly, skimming the ruts from crest to crest with an odd sensation of only partial contact with the road.

Thus, in the Land Rover, Farah had his foot hard down, to keep his teeth in their sockets, to be swiftly home with his wife Farida, and because he was carrying a report on livestock prices in a plastic briefcase tucked behind his seat. It was his own work, and urgent, for Mr Xavier Hopkins was meeting the Americans on Wednesday. Farah felt proud, important, and anxious; he gripped the wheel hard and his back ached as he peered ahead. His elegantly boned face was set in a frown, the gentle black eyes specked with dust. Even with the vents wide open and the dry wind caressing him, Farah ibn Mashoud was sweating.

It was Monday afternoon, far too late in the day. He'd gone to retrieve a spare tyre "borrowed" by the Nyala police, but it was "not available". He'd agreed to transport the chief clerk from the Labour Office, but the man's female dependents must also be collected from their homes scattered across town. They were ready to depart, but Farah's aunt must first wrap a gift of orange cloth shot with gold. Farah had been eager to be away in the morning,

3

to avoid being caught on the road in failing light, but they did not leave Nyala until nearly three, by which time this dignified and courteous young man was near to losing his temper. When the aunt bustled across the compound to impress final messages upon him, Farah said nothing, but climbed into the white Land Rover and pulled the door shut with a slam. There was little conversation, for the turbocharger whistled loudly and the coachwork rattled as they scudded north over the ruts. Under the canvas back, the women jammed their slippers among the bags and bundles, brooding on a bad year, on the shortages, the unrest, the jostling of tribe on tribe in dispute over scant grazing and water. They watched the plume of dust they trailed, pressed handkerchiefs to their mouths and retched in miserable silence.

At five-thirty they neared the halfway souk at Manawashi, with Farah and the Labour Office clerk looking eagerly for the army post. The road climbed among late afternoon shadows cast by jumbles of heat-shattered rock. From the crest of the rise, the little market town and the camp would soon be distantly visible . . .

The first bullet drilled through the soft aluminium of the wheel arch and into Farah's ankle, exploding the bones. The second came through the door and smacked into the Labour man's tubby abdomen. The third smashed the driving mirror, and glass cut Farah's cheek. More shots: he was hit in the thigh, and he lost control of the vehicle. A tyre burst and shredded, heavy shards of rubber and steel cording whipping off. The Land Rover lurched to the right, banged over a pile of rocks and slewed to a halt on the shale slope. The racket of the car was replaced by a single obscene sound: a female shrieking. Farah opened the driver's door and tried to step down, but collapsed by the front wheel and fainted.

He was brought to his senses by pain, but he could not move. He opened his eyes, but saw nothing but a red fog. His cheek bled and stung sharply where grit had entered the cut. He felt fabric brush his cheek, heard heavy footsteps close to his face and the low whimpering of a woman. There came mutterings and soft thumps: the bags were being rifled.

4

Farah did not feel afraid. It was not a matter of courage; as he lay, stillness came over his mind, a merciful response to impotence. He knew the close proximity of murderous force, had no answer to it and so remained quiet, thinking very little except, regretfully, of Farida his wife.

A scratching sound began, at once tiny and very loud, close to his ear. He strained to see. In a lurid red light, shapes began to form; he made out strange pale patches, which at last he saw were the pages of his market report, stirred by a breeze and scraping over the ground. And he felt an absurd urge to protest: *Stop this at once! That report is urgently required by Mr Xavier Hopkins, who meets the Americans on Wednesday!*

Farah pushed himself up on his right elbow and looked into the cab. The portly Labour Office man sat there still, immobile, staring tearfully forward with an expression of astonishment and the hands clasped over his belly kneading feebly. Twisting his head, Farah could just glimpse, across his left shoulder, a gunman standing over two squatting figures: a woman who moaned and rocked, and another holding a cloth against her arm.

Then Farah was struck across the ear and temple, and slumped back onto the dirt. He was kicked on the back of his neck, his injured cheek scraping harshly over the gravel. He glimpsed the ellipse of a rifle's muzzle hanging close to his cheek. He heard a shout, and at once the men all round him jerked into motion, running. Farah had an instant of hope – but a sudden, tremendous roar and burning flash by his face ended that. Something struck his neck; he felt as though he'd been pinned through his throat to the ground – and that was his last thought.

The news that Farah was dead on the road from Nyala to El Fasher reached his employer, Mr Hopkins, that same evening.

*

Monday night and the lights were off: no diesel in town. Xavier Hopkins observed, through a fine haze of mosquito net, a night sky free of sodium. Just half an hour of rest, of silence, then he must work again but now, as he lay, Xavier felt so pinned and helpless that he thought himself the still point of a universe in which everything and everyone else moved about him in contorted and convoluted orbits. Peering up through the mosquito net, Xavier thought that all creation could get about the sky, but not he. For State Security would hardly let him move one inch.

The Field Director of the Action Agency lived centrally, near the souk. Broad *nim* trees with saw-toothed foliage shaded his courtyard; bougainvillaea planted in red-painted oil tins framed the latrine door; rudimentary brick parterres daubed with splashy whitewash were home to his white Land Rover. It was quiet save for the nearby mosque, but Xavier liked the call of the muezzin, which he found reassuring, an assertion (bizarre in the circumstances) that the world was orderly. He slept out in the open every night except in dust storm or downpour. His bed was a creaking thing of rough-hewn whitewood; its joints were spikes jabbed into sockets; its legs were crudely turned and appeared to twist in pain a little more each day. The whole was held together with thick, hairy string and topped by a lumpy kapok mattress. Over it was slung a box mosquito net tied to the tree above.

Here lay Xavier Hopkins, Field Director, charged with devising systems for forecasting and preventing ghastly famine in Darfur Province: thirty-eight years old, six-foot-two, pale skin and thin hair, fastidious, slightly Catholic, well-experienced in the realms of Aid, an MA in African history and terrified of going into the desert with insufficient drinking water. A poor linguist but a sharp mind, so it said in his employer's files. A gentle chap, people agreed. Out of his depth, he himself suspected. He'd been here two years. He lay thinking. Far from rest.

There was a famine now: at least, the World Food Programme in Rome had predicted one, USAID had declared it, American satellite images confirmed widespread crop failure and a catastrophic food deficit; Oxfam and Save the Children had launched a major funding appeal. Word was out, and the Darfur farmers had heard of their own disaster. The locals had seen the jeeps, the offices being opened, and so they'd done the decent thing: day by day, delegations came in from the villages with scores of names pencilled in Arabic onto scraps of paper, the lists of the destitute.

But was that famine? Xavier had worked in Uganda during a real famine, in '80–'81; he recalled the skeletons in the fields, revealed when the grass died back. He'd worked in the death camps of Ethiopia in '85. There, children had shivered to death and had lain unburied because no one could dig in the rocky ground. That was famine; Xavier knew about famine.

Every day the office radio hissed: *Is there a famine?*

Possibly, he replied, but the signs are inconcl . . .

There must be, if there's no harvest!

Yes, that's likely.

The Guardian says there's a famine. CNN says there's a famine. You're on the spot, you must be able to see. Has it happened yet? Has starvation begun? "I just don't know," Xavier radioed back, "Maybe. We're trying to find out. I've sent my people into the markets . . ."

He pestered the Ministry of Health but those poor gentlemen knew nothing: they'd not visited their own outposts for months. Behind the Ministry, their jeeps languished for lack of diesel and spark plugs, gathering sand in their bearings.

"Go and find out for yourself," ordered the Khartoum office with London HQ at its back, frantic not to be caught napping. Xavier had bitten back his anger, had retorted that it wasn't so simple in a province the size of France with scarce diesel, few roads . . .

"We're sending you a team," said London: a nurse, a doctor, a nutritionist, with a clutch of 'field staff' head-hunted from VSO and the language schools of Cairo and Nairobi, to measure, to survey, to be ready . . .

Xavier groaned; he already had a team, an excellent local team, built up over several years by himself and his predecessor. Besides, Sudan did not want to be surveyed. Was it embarrassment? Resentment? State Security insisted that the Tribal Situation was too dangerous, that the Border Situation was dangerous, that there were bandits, that foreigners must sit tight, that a Security officer must accompany each team, knowing that the villagers would see this man and say not a word. Xavier wasn't having that.

By sheer stubbornness, Xavier at last got questionnaires out to a few thorn villages.

"Excellent!" applauded Khartoum, "Splendid!" cried London, "At last!" yelled Rome, New York, Brussels, "So now, tell us: is there a famine?"

"We're not sure," he havered. "The people are thin as lizards, but they're not dead yet."

"What are they eating?" the ambassadors of the 'Donor Nations' demanded to know.

What indeed: roots and berries? Snakes and beetles?

Only night and his string cot in the cool yard gave Xavier relief. As he lay watching the stars rotate above him, he knew that as soon as day came the pressure would recommence and his anxious young field officers, as eager as London and Rome not to be caught out and blamed, would come by turns to Xavier's office to urge him: "We must get food to the villages, or the peasants will sell up and start walking to town, there will be camps, there will be cholera, you *must* give the go-ahead to Khartoum . . ."

Khartoum meanwhile was trying to jump the gun, to force the pace. The embassies announced that thirty thousand tonnes of Australian wheat and American maize was on its way, was now "in country", was warehoused in Port Sudan, was beginning to rot, to turn grey with mould while everyone waited for Xavier's say-so. If only he'd agree that there was a famine . . .

Until Xavier, on his grass-rope bed under the massy black night sky, found his head too heavy to lift, so full was it of worry. As this supposed crisis had developed, Xavier Hopkins had seen that he was a fall guy of peerless quality, Grand Master of the Most Illustrious Order of Patsies; it was, if nothing else, a steady position. For if the Government in Khartoum really had let its people slide into starvation, why then, an aid agency was the very thing to blame. Xavier was blamed already: for incompetence, for being set in old British ways, for being the stooge of Washington and the World Bank, for snooping, for being blind to suffering, for being reckless, for being over-cautious. The compliant Khartoum press editorialised to order, and the ambassadors with their indifferent Arabic heard of it a week later and turned on Xavier: *Is there, or is there not, a famine?*

Then they lost patience. The Donor Nations announced a mission, high-powered, American-led. Xavier's skin crept at the prospect.

He lay on his back and, as the constellations turned in stately derision overhead, he renamed them: the Scoffer, the Nine Bright Smirks, the supernova Incredulity and, somewhere, a sucking black hole full of Utter Bullshit.

He sat upright, gently lifted the edge of the mosquito net and swung his legs over the side. No sleep, not now. The Americans were coming, they'd be at the office Wednesday evening; he must be prepared, have his facts to hand, his arguments honed. He must not be cowed and browbeaten, he *would not*. He would tell the Donors, he'd spell it out: he'd act when and only when he knew the truth. He would not be bullied into turning this poor province into a sink for the surpluses of agricorporations, damn them, he would not! He would call for food shipments when and only when there was demonstrable need. Until then, he would survey, survey, survey, in spite of the risks, the reports of bandits.

The Americans were coming. Arrangements must be made.

There came a soft *Salaamalaikum* in a German accent.

"Xavier?" the woman said, calling through the dark. "The police have come with a message. There is very bad news about Farah."

The news gave Xavier a nasty headache, because he'd liked Farah and dreaded informing his family, and because he'd asked Farah to travel when, every day, the countryside was becoming more dangerous. And because he must make some arrangement to help the widow, which is not something aid agencies know much about. And also because he'd the Americans coming in two days' time and he badly needed Farah's evidence from the markets. And because, once again, his programme was short staffed.

Thus, when Mr Mogga turned up out of the south, there was a job waiting.

*

Xavier first set eyes on Mr Mogga this same Monday evening. But he hardly knew it, for the circumstances were most unhappy. Xavier had to speak with the bereaved family at once, of course. He could not shirk that.

His task was made slightly easier by Fauzi, a dapper young man on the Agency staff who wore fastidiously laundered clothes and sunglasses with amber lenses. Fauzi would not have been Xavier's first choice of interpreter, for he was a pompous young man who considered himself indispensable in all delicate situations, and in consequence irritated everyone. But Fauzi lived at Farah's home, lodged in a separate brick room. Xavier drove to the house, which stood in that quarter of town where the *jellaba*, the merchants from the Nile, had once clustered.

At the compound's side entrance, Xavier felt incipient stage fright, his legs trembling as he stood in the dark before the gate.

"*Salaamalaikum*," he called, pulling himself together.

"*Walaikum asalaam*," cried Fauzi, heaving open the clanging steel gate so promptly that Xavier wondered if he'd been waiting, poised, just inside.

Fauzi shone a little tin torch in the Field Director's face.

"Oh, Sir, you are welcome!" the young man gushed.

"But I'm afraid, Fauzi . . ." said Xavier, telling him the news.

Fauzi listened with silent attention and then looked over his shoulder, indicating a cluster of oil lights glimmering on the far side of the compound.

"She is there," he said, "she is just home from the souk."

A little group of women and children were gathered on the porch of a small brick house, chattering and preparing food, slicing something into enamel bowls with a steady snick of knives. Xavier saw the women smile, heard them cry, "Come now, coffee! Welcome!", saw the mother rise and take a step towards the chicken-wired kitchen house . . . then stop, and look back at Fauzi, her expression changing, puzzled, frightened, as Fauzi spoke.

Somebody was keening. There came questions, low and timid, to which Fauzi replied in a clear, steady voice, unhesitating. Fauzi turned to Xavier, who shuffled his feet in the warm sand.

"I think you must come again tomorrow. We must do something for these people," the young Sudani murmured.

Xavier had said not a word.

He left the compound, hurried out to the Land Rover by Fauzi's feeble torch. As he reached for the car door, Xavier glanced across the road following the torch beam, which, for a brief moment, lingered. There was a man in the shadows. He was small, very black, stocky in a busy way, with a bald head and premature grey tufts over his ears. He stood motionless, his arms straight by his side. He was gazing at the brick wall almost as though he could see over it and knew exactly what was within.

The man now looked straight back into the torchlight.

Xavier peered at this fellow and wondered: who is that?

"Good night, Sir," said Fauzi.

Xavier climbed into his vehicle and drove away.

*

The watchman had spotted Mogga already, some days past.

The watchman shared the Agency Resthouse compound with an ibis. Perhaps it was lame in the wing, or hard up or homeless. It should have frequented the *fula*, the town pool, or perhaps Wad Golu the irrigation reservoir, but both were dry. So here on Tuesday morning it paced about the dirty sand, slowly waving its naked neck and long, down-slicing beak like a sickle, striving for what little pomp it could muster in its destitution, waiting for the watchman to throw it scraps.

The watchman was an ancient, sullen cuss. He lived in the yard, his hut like an upturned coracle of branches covered with black polythene lashed down with orange plastic cord. There was a uniformity about the sheeting that smacked of *Reagan* – a generic term for all relief materials dating from a previous famine. The old man had been here in this compound since *Reagan*.

His condition was squalid, his manners bizarre. His wardrobe consisted of a single yellowing gown of old cotton. He neither washed nor shaved, and his face was fringed all round by a greyish white stubble. He seldom left the yard, but shuffled through the deep fine dust in sandals cut from old tyres, boiling his tea, slicing offal into his black pan, filling a water bowl for the ibis and feeding it bread. Though there was a latrine in the back yard, the old man preferred to defecate beneath the dining room window. He kicked sand over his excreta, and no one knew of his habit until the rains began. The landlord would admonish visitors to pity and respect the old man, who was of the Zayadiya tribe and twenty years ago had been in a furious battle of nomads, Zayadiya on Kababish, and had seen his three sons shot. Some nights, awful dreams possessed him and cries and groans rang out from under the black plastic.

When the foreigners were out, the watchman wandered the house. The Resthouse was old and stark, the walls whitewashed, the woodwork blue. There were four featureless rooms with concrete floors, and a netted verandah facing the walled back yard. There were no carpets or sideboards, bookcases, lamp stands or armchairs, no television; only the costly radios the *khowajas*, the Europeans, kept in their suitcases. There were no cupboards: around the bare walls of the rooms, those suitcases lay, doing wardrobe service. Someone had bought half a dozen string beds from the *souk*, with wooden frames that harboured bedbugs in their joints; no one had thought to buy one for the watchman. At night, even the wire-meshed verandah was suffocating, and the *khowajas* would drag the string cots out onto the sand of the back yard. By dawn everyone would be cold. The *khowajas* would eat dry bread with jam, and go unsmiling to their work. A minute of silence – then the screen door would open and the watchman would enter.

He would pass through in a slow, gritty shuffle, touching everything. There was a refrigerator, its rubber seals black with mould. He'd look inside: in Fasher town electricity was rare, and when the power died the refrigerator went into reverse and soaked up warmth, gently cooking the contents. In the back porch, a tall clay water jar oozed greasily: he'd finger it. Across the sandy yard was a kitchen shed where a charcoal stove of rusted steel stood on the concrete floor. A black-shrouded figure sat fanning the coals with a tin plate while stirring a pot of starchy noodles. If the watchman drew near, the woman stopped fanning until he moved on, grumbling.

Tuesday morning, however, he ignored her and returned to the front gate to peer into the street and nod with satisfaction. He was an old fool but he was a watchman too, and he had seen off that squat little black, a southerner, who for days had hovered in the street outside, but now was gone.

*

Before anyone else met Mogga, the Agency's senior nutritionist Rose Price had known him for almost a week. They had both frequented the tea circle of Farida, Farah's wife.

Shortly before the shooting, *sharia* law – its strictures, prohibitions and penalties – had been imposed on Darfur Province. The news took a day or two to percolate down to the Fasher tea ladies. The desert town was accustomed to menaces from the capital far away on the Nile, which regarded the western desert as a nest of delinquents. Now, it seemed, they were all to be flogged. For those already on the margins of ruin, there was nothing for it but to continue with their fragile trades, to wait and see.

Farida had not stopped taking her tea stall to the souk each evening, after the merchants had locked their booths and gone. A broad tract of dusty sand sloped away from the market's meat tables down to the dirt road and the broad town pool, the *fula*. As the light failed, a score of women would stake small claims. There, Farida would place her square iron stove, fan up a little fire of charcoal and plant her kettle. On a tin box she'd array her scratched but tough, thick tumblers, her glass jar of tea, her sugar and milk, her pots of sweet, cheering canella, uplifting cardamom and ginger, her rags, her plastic strainer.

Each woman had a red plastic strainer, trucked in over the desert from Libya. Each had a grass mat for customers, or a circle of tumbledown rushwork stools. A tiny oil lamp, and all was set. Farida made just one concession to the new Law: her daughters, who lugged the gear and fetched water and would then have skipped and chased in the cool awhile, she now sent home promptly.

For she had seen the State Security police put up their brown tent, a big, square tent by the mosque gates, and no one knew what they might do. They seemed to be biding their time, but what if you were dragged into that tent? There were rumours: that a merchant found with a false balance had been flogged unconscious; that a young man caught dealing in stolen jeep tyres had had his hand amputated in the town prison; that the cells were filling with prostitutes, awaiting sentence. As yet, nothing had occurred in the souk. But the atmosphere of peaceable civility was disturbed. Everyone was uneasy.

The customers still came, their voices a fraction lower. These were bankrupt, drought-ridden days when the *fula* stayed stubbornly empty when it should have been pleasantly, coolly awash and the towering *siyal* trees that ringed it should have been loud and swaying with a weight of water birds. This year, the *fula* was a parched expanse of cracked mud in the heart of town, good for nothing but parking camels. But still there was this simple evening pleasure left to the Arabs: the souk, the air like silk, the ground warm beneath the shoe, and a field of sand spangled with little lamps. Each pool of light rippled with mild conversation; gentlemen in white gowns, on mat or stool, sipped sweet peppery tea while behind the stove sat the proprietrix swathed in coloured robes drawn properly over her head. Nothing could be more decorous – though it was all now an obscenity under the Law.

Farida was less concerned for Law than for life: the family must eat, and her husband Farah's glamorous foreign employers were perpetually short of cash. They obviously meant to pay him, and Farah swore that they were good and honest people, but often the banknotes were simply unavailable. Maybe the cash had to come by truck across the desert from Khartoum, or by ship from Arabia; she didn't know. Farah and Farida had a lodger at home, a faintly ludicrous and rather lonely young man called Fauzi who worked with Farah for the foreigners, but if they couldn't pay Farah they couldn't pay Fauzi either, so the rent he could contribute was minimal. Selling tea in the souk barely earned Farida a living, but it fed the girls.

She occupied a low place, almost beneath the fierce new Law. The profits were small indeed, but Farida did not despise her occupation. She'd never converse with the men who drank her tea, but it was agreeable, an education to listen to their talk as the day cooled. The companionable little lamps glimmering on the sand were soft and pretty. A jeep might pass the *fula* and its lights would sweep the souk catching everyone in silhouette. Then you'd see unsuspected crowds, or tall spectral camels moving silently by, set about with headlight rays filled with luminous dust. All around was life, but quietly. It was not only trade for Farida, but a rare good hour in the burnt, anxious town. She had her customers ringed before her, patiently watching her deft hands move among the jars and glasses. She felt proficient, she was providing. She liked the soft voices indicating their appreciation of this civilised time. Farida shuffled her plastic slippers into the sand, drew her green robe across her throat and, in her pauper's way, held court.

And to this court there came two strangers.

Firstly, one evening, a solitary man, rather short and very black, with ears tufted like an owl. A southerner, she thought, although surprisingly he spoke some Arabic. He seemed to know no one. When he first sat himself by her stove, he seemed distracted, peering always into some sorrowful memory. He returned each night, and only slowly did he relax a little. But still he kept apart with his thoughts.

A southern black was unusual enough, but Farida was astonished when a *khowajiyah*, a foreign female, a gawky white woman, came to her tea circle. Sometimes this person came on foot, sometimes she drove (drove herself!) in a huge white jeep that she parked by the empty meat tables. But she always came, by clear preference, to Farida's stove. Who does not like to be chosen, and repeatedly?

One night, she described the newcomer to her husband Farah. "Miss Price!" he said at once, "Miss Rose Price."

He was impressed. Miss Price, he declared, was a senior figure in the Action Agency. She'd been in Africa many years. She was the nutritionist, which meant that she knew exactly how much food was good for you.

But, though Miss Price continued to frequent her tea circle, Farida did not mention the connection. She felt, a little vainly, that they had their own link that did not involve her husband. Also, if the truth be told, Farida was a little frightened of Rose.

For a start, it was not something a Sudani woman would do: going out of an evening to drink tea in public, still less to smoke a cigarette. When the *khowajiyah* first came alone, there were three Arab men already on the stools, and the little southerner who watched everything intently. Momentarily, Farida feared what might happen. But the Arabs scarcely reacted; only one long black hand, elongated and ring-heavy, gestured courteously towards a seat. Later, after she'd gone, someone recalled seeing this *khowajiyah* supervise a great weighing of children in the shanty settlements. Serious work, undoubtedly.

Well, they murmured, the very tall *khowajiyah* looked mannish enough for it, wearing trousers and her hair so short above the lined, bony face. She was a woman, no doubt: the trousers were of floral print, and small breasts pushed at the T-shirt. Such beings were known to inhabit the 'relief offices'. But her advent in the night souk was so odd that no one knew how to react; thus, the Arab gentlemen behaved as if nothing unusual had occurred.

She would appear at Farida's stove and take a stool in the semi-circle, her yard-long legs in their flowery trousers jutting across the sand at peculiar angles, her arms scrawny and freckled. Farida wondered if these were smallpox scars. The *khowajiyah* would ask for tea in stiltedly proper Egyptian Arabic – *Ashrab shay, min fadlak* – then light a cigarette.

The first evening that she came, Farida hardly heard another word from her. She would not have addressed the *khowajiyah* herself, and the Arab men spoke among themselves, studiously oblivious, while the little black southerner seemed absorbed in his thoughts as always – though Farida did catch his glances of curiosity. The white woman sat in silence, sipping and puffing.

She seemed content. Farida concluded that she was thankful for calm company and the field of gentle lights, that she was putting down the daily burdens of her job. And Farida was pleased; it was, after all, what the gentlemen also came for, a need that she, Farida, could answer. So a second tea might be indicated, those long speckled fingers tucking the empty glass onto the wooden box with a *Min fadlak*, 'please'. A second cigarette would follow, the ash dropping noiselessly to become part of the wide dust.

On the fourth evening, there came a change. Almost all the men had departed; only the silent little southerner remained, and the white woman. There came the soft *plop* of a camel hoof nearby. Then Farida heard a timid "Ma?" from the dark behind her, and found her daughter: some small complaint from home. "Now, get back with you, you must not wander out like this!" said Farida, glancing instinctively towards the Security tent that tonight stood empty. The girl trotted away.

The *khowajiyah* said:

"That is your daughter?"

Farida looked up in surprise.

"Zeinab, my eldest," she replied.

"How many do you have?"

"Three girls. One is a baby, at our home."

"And boys?"

Farida hesitated – and the foreigner hurried to retract.

"I'm sorry, it's no business of mine. I've no family myself."

None at all? Farida gazed at the stick-like woman sucking briskly on her cigarette. What, then, was her story? Had some tragedy driven here from her country to loneliness in Sudan? Farida noticed the little black southerner paying close attention, perhaps wondering those same things. For pity, Farida found herself telling her own tales to this strange gawky woman on the far side of the tin-can lamp, to help her feel at ease.

When Rose Price left that evening, they knew each other's names, and Farida was curiously thrilled. But then she noticed a solitary officer of State Security observing her from the shadows near the brown tent. She packed up her stove and left early.

Rose Price did not return for two days; then she reappeared, greeting Farida by name and explaining that she had been north to Mellit to ask the children there if they were eating enough. Farida nodded, a little awed – but before she could reply, another voice cut in.

"You can assist those children?"

It was the little black, the southerner, cradling his tea and studying her.

"If that is the wise thing," said Miss Price coolly.

"How could it not be wise to assist these poor people?" he demanded.

Rose Price was taken aback by his eagerness, his animation. But she would not be rattled.

"One must be careful," she replied. "If I give everyone in town free food, how will the trader in the market sell his grain, for which he is wanting money? That trader will close his shop and leave town. Then, when my free food is finished, there will be no supplies at all and the people will starve all the faster."

The little man was leaning forward and beaming at her with an unsettling intensity. She looked down, stirring her tea.

"Yes," he was saying, "yes, one must be so careful, one must think ahead . . ."

Stirring her tea, Miss Price did not see his sudden expression of alarm – until she herself glanced down, startled, at her own forearm. It was touched by the brass ferrule of a military cane. The tip lay there, moving upwards a little, stroking Miss Price as though its owner wished to know of what materials a *khowajiyah* was compounded.

At the far end of the stick stood an officer of State Security. Rose Price sat upon her rickety stool, puffing on her cigarette, disdaining to react. The man regarded her with a distaste that was evident even in the darkness. His cane touched, and then lifted slightly the loose collar of the pinkish T-shirt off her shoulder. Perhaps, thought Farida, he can now see the breast.

The officer said, "This is not a proper shirt."

Rose Price stood up, and was taller than the policeman. It occurred to Farida that a foreign woman could never sustain one

18

single day's work in El Fasher if she were not possessed of a great will. This defiance of Security, though, was giddy-making for this was not any officer; this was Colonel al-Bedawi, Chief of Security for the Province.

Rose Price continued with her cigarette, not troubling to prevent smoke drifting across the man's face.

"This shirt," she retorted, "is clean, and quite decent if not pulled about by ill-mannered persons."

The Colonel regarded her without flinching – but for a second he hesitated. He said, "Your vehicle should not be parked under the tree there. No one is permitted to park by the souk."

"The souk is closed," said Rose Price loudly.

"Remove the jeep," said the officer, turning away, his stick tight under his arm.

Farida gazed up at Rose Price: *What magnificent folly!*

Rose smiled down, seeing the woman's anxiety.

"Have they ever made trouble for you?" she asked.

"No trouble yet. But in *sharia* it is not allowed for women to sell tea to gentlemen in the dark."

"They've threatened you?"

"Not yet," said Farida, for whom every day was threatening.

Rose Price glared in the direction of the Security men as though she would shortly deal with them and destitution together.

She muttered, "I'd best move the car."

The Land Rover lamps turned across the stoves, dazzling everyone and for an instant illuminating the little southerner, who had not moved but seemed far away in his thoughts again.

At moments during the following day, as Farida battled with the grit and the labours of her home, with sweeping back the duststorms and getting her girls away to school, she thought with regret that she would not see Miss Price again; no one willingly tangled twice with State Security.

Then, late on a Monday evening, Fauzi the lodger crossed the compound to introduce a tall white man who brought news: her husband Farah had been shot by bandits with a rifle on the road from Nyala to El Fasher.

The ensuing hours piled one horror on another. Farah's poor bruised corpse was buried swiftly the next morning, Tuesday. Almost immediately afterwards, Farida was dispossessed. Farah's relatives met few problems and no legal obstacles in seizing all the property. They were educated; Farah's cousin, a bullying, sweaty man, was a government official. Farida was unlettered; she could put up no resistance. By midday, the steel kiosk in the souk, its battery of pans and ladles, its stock of oils and flours, tin plates and alloy spoons, everything with which she'd cooked good meals each day for labourers and minor functionaries – all this had been claimed and distributed by the pitiless in-laws. With a tremendous show of charity, the big cousin declared that Farida could stay on in the brick house – as long as she paid him rent. Otherwise, they left Farida only her stove and tea kettle – she could still sell tea, he announced magnanimously – and her three valueless daughters in whom they had no interest.

Farida had produced no son, and might as well be barren. She was not marriageable, and she had no gold. She had neither land nor gardens, no mule for hawking water through the lanes, only her tea circle and a place on the sand each evening. Widow Farida was twenty-nine years old, coal-skinned, beautiful and not quite beaten, but with few other options except perhaps prostitution.

In a state of shock, she returned to the souk that same evening.

That Tuesday night, several of the tea ladies were absent. Two had set up without lamps, hoping somehow to tempt customers and serve in darkness. Just one of Farida's clientele came by, taking a quick glass, leaving. Conversation stopped at hurried courtesies. The calm was fled – as was the income. With no one to serve, Farida waited apprehensively. She saw the knot of Security men by their tent, their guns and sticks pulled about in hands that seemed impatient for work. The camels passed by, their riders not stopping for tea.

And then he was hurrying towards her, the little southerner, as though he feared he might be late. He sat down quickly, saying at once:

"Has she been? She has not been already? Miss Price, I mean."

Well, thought Farida, he knows her name; he has been listening.

Farida was about to reply, to say that it was unlikely they would meet the *khowajiyah* again, when the souk was lit as a vehicle edged along the upper margin by the mosque wall only feet from them.

Rose Price marched down and sat with her usual abruptness, a grin in her voice.

"I'm not parked in the souk there, am I?"

Tonight, Miss Price had a light cardigan draped over her shoulders. She took out her first cigarette, examining it with close interest. She raised her face; Farida realised that she was being scrutinised, but that the scrutiny was not unkind. Does she know? About Farah, does she know? She must know, surely; she is something senior there, Farah had said.

But for a moment, neither the little black nor the gangling white woman spoke. Feeling this world to be quite unreal, Farida made them both tea, a little fearfully.

"Girls well?" said Rose Price brusquely.

"Thanks be to God."

"Studying?"

"All day they study hard. They are resting at evening."

"Excellent," said Miss Price.

"You are busy today?" enquired Farida politely.

"Always busy," replied Rose, "There's a bunch of Americans in town. I've to prepare reports for them."

The little man could not restrain himself.

"So – what will you report?" he cried.

Rose Price was startled and gave him a hard stare. She lit her cigarette.

"I shall say that there is no need for panic," she said, after a moment.

"No need for panic," he breathed back at her.

"But great need for vigilance," she added sternly.

The match's flare and the slow red cigarette lit deep lines in Rose's sand-scoured cheek. Not a face, thought Farida, that our fragrant Sudani oils have smoothed. It was a strong face, energetic. Regarding it, Farida felt her fears diluted. Rose Price jerked up her chin to blow away the smoke, and again smiled across the coals at the small black woman in her green robe. In tonight's tense and sparsely populated souk, Farida felt protected by this smile.

"So, what hopes do you have for them?" Miss Price enquired out of the blue.

"Hope?"

"For your girls."

Such conversations! Farida considered a moment.

"I hope that they learn . . ." she began.

She stopped, startled. Another cry came; she looked to her right, down the sand slope. At that moment, two jeeps by the Security tent fifty yards away turned their headlights full upon the scattering of women.

Instantly, the last clientele rose to their feet and vanished. A shrill of alarm went across the women on the sand: a line of a dozen or more police stepped in front of the lights, each framed in dusty silhouette. They fanned out rapidly, trapping the tea stalls against the wall of steel booths. Frantically, the women swept up their possessions, attempting to douse coals, stuff money into their clothes, retrieve glasses, spoons, spices. But the police were among them, reaching down, seizing on their arms hard, so that the women squealed.

Shame! snarled the officers, *Have you no shame? We'll teach you shame!*

Rose Price stood rigid with anger. Farida scooped and grabbed at her things, her last remaining property, but panic shook her grip and her hands were full. She tried to hold the wicker basket and the lamp with her right hand and to lift the tin box with her left but dropped it all . . .

"Into the car!" snapped Rose Price, sweeping up dropped crockery, pulling Farida to the Land Rover.

"In!" she commanded.

Farida hesitated.

"My stove . . ."

The precious iron stove, isolated on the sand, full of burning coals.

"Leave it," commanded Rose, "it'll be scorching."

She started the motor, gunned it, hauling the other inside.

"Oh!" cried the widow in despair: her assets, her very last goods! She almost clambered down from the Land Rover even as Rose began to turn the wheel, to pull away . . .

Farida saw the little black southerner step up to her abandoned stove and kick it over so that coals spilled out, angrily sparking. Then he picked it up. With his bare hands, he crouched down and seized the iron frame, ran with it to the rear door of the slow-moving vehicle, thrust the stove inside and slammed the door shut.

Rose Price accelerated along the bank of the *fula*. As they lurched and swayed over the ruts, Farida twisted about and saw her friends dragged into the brown tent, saw Security men pointing, expected to hear bullets slapping into the ponderous vehicle, expected to start screaming – but they were away, speeding across town.

"That is an outrage, that is a bloody outrage!" fumed Rose Price.

Farida had ridden on the back of trucks, but never before in a Land Rover. She sat rigid, gripping the dashboard. Through her fear, through her numbing grief, she was admiring the scrawny *khowajiyah* arms that mastered this enormous thing. Both women were silent a moment.

"Was he caught?" Rose said suddenly. "His poor hands."

*

That same Tuesday evening, Xavier got to meet Mr Mogga properly.

Xavier was picking his way through the unlit streets and hoping not to drop the Land Rover into one of the unmarked middens. Gripping the dashboard beside him, Christa his German field officer brooded; Xavier was not feeling conversational either. He tried to concentrate on tomorrow and the American visit, but he could think only of the impossibility of getting things done, and of being at the behest of distant powers, and of William Hicks Pasha.

Once, Xavier had been an academic Africanist. It doesn't follow that an aid programme field director would know the first thing about African history, but Xavier did. His grandfather had been Public Surgeon in Kenya Colony; grandson Xavier had chosen to anatomise the financial structures of colonialism. One idle graduate afternoon in Durham University Library, he'd come upon an archive of papers relating to Anglo-Egyptian Sudan, seventy foxed and fusty boxes of it. Ferreting through these was a scholar who was editing the letters of General William Hicks – or, to give him his very senior Ottoman title, Hicks Pasha. Xavier and the scholar conversed, took tea, became acquainted. And she told him an extraordinarily pathetic story.

For much of the 19th century, Egypt had claimed to rule all the Sudan from the Upper Nile east as far as the Red Sea, and west and south into the heart of Africa. But the tribes were unimpressed and in 1881 they flocked to the black flag of a rebel: Mohammed Ahmad, the Mahdi. They swelled his battalions of 'helpers', the Ansar, who, armed only with spears and swords but with a courage scarcely equalled in history, would rush towards regular troops equipped with rifles and heavy machine guns. The Ansar swept away garrison after garrison of Egypt's supine levies.

The frantic Egyptians hired a British officer, instructing him to lead a force from Cairo to Khartoum. From there, he was to crush the Mahdi. They made him a General and a Pasha, a high governor, and he went to the Sudan with 10,000 men, a million rounds of ammunition, rocket launchers, telegraph wires and a Nile flotilla. In 1883 Hicks Pasha marched westward into Kordofan to find the Mahdi and there, in the early morning of November 5th, he and his army were annihilated.

A brave but naïve man was William Hicks, though sufficiently astute to realise, on arriving in Khartoum, that his expedition was extremely hazardous by reason of the incompetence of the Egyptian Army. These were men who had recently been beaten in the field by the British, a fight celebrated in verse by the great William McGonagall:

I think that their leader should be ashamed of himself,
For I consider that he has played the part of a silly elf.

They were simple *fellahin*, poor peasants; they had neither desire
nor reason to fight in Sudan. Some had been sent in chains.
Though they took with them a battery of the latest machine-guns
designed by Nordenfeldt of Sweden, many of Hicks' men wore
chain mail and carried medieval iron caltrops to deter enemy horse.
They knew only one formation, attempting to march through thick
scrub in fully formed-up squares, 200 yards across. The best of
them were 350 bashi-bazouks from Albania. These, at least, were
fierce.

The Durham historian showed Xavier Hopkins a box of letters
written by Hicks to his wife who, poor woman, must have been
ever more dismayed. Hicks wrote of his despair of turning the
Egyptians into an army:

> I never in my life saw such a rabble – like a flock of fright-
> ened sheep. I could not believe such dolts and fools exist. I
> have no word strong enough to express my contempt for
> them.

But his contempt for the dozen or so Europeans seconded to
him was scarcely any less:

> My English officers are no help to me. They want judge-
> ment and increase my difficulties, and seem to think that
> they are to be merely ornamental.

His staff officers were corrupt, idle and clueless; they would do
nothing he asked:

> I have an English ADC, Brody, and 3 grooms all to look
> after 3 horses, and yet I discovered this morning that my
> horses have had no grass of any kind for 4 days . . .

As he laboured to organise his force, Hicks' anxiety grew, letter
by letter:

> Another day of worry and trouble . . . I am surrounded by
> intrigue, deception and liars . . .

At last they marched out of Khartoum, with guides who gleefully led them astray. They wandered southwest into a region
of waterless scrub where the Mahdi's men had blocked the wells.
By November 4th they were completely lost. They burned in
the sun, they sickened, they panted for water, unaware that there
was a large rain pool just fifteen minutes away. The Ansar were
on all sides; the snipers never let up. The camels were moaning from their wounds and the army lost hope. Hicks ordered
his band to play, but the musicians sank bleeding into the long
grass with bullet holes through their tubas. At dawn on
November 5th the army formed up in its ponderous squares and
began to move forward through the bush – and immediately the
Ansar tore into it. The Egyptian formations collapsed in upon
themselves, panicking, firing upon each other, and within
minutes it was over. William Hicks died fighting, hacked down
from his horse.

But it was not this last battle that haunted Xavier Hopkins.
Rather, it was Hicks' complaint, echoed over and again in the
sorrowful, bemused, hurt-filled letters: that his Egyptian colleagues
and counterparts seemed determined to obstruct his every step:

> No amount of orders will make the officials move! Why do
> they put all these obstacles in my way?

Why? Poor Hicks never found out why. A century later, Xavier
Hopkins often wondered if he himself was doing any better.
Perhaps these oh-so-important Americans could help? There was,
for instance, the peculiar loathing that Colonel Hassan al-Bedawi,
Chief of State Security in Darfur, seemed to have for all Europeans;
there was his transparent pleasure in delaying travel permits (now
so grimly justified by Farah's death), his delight in restricting
access, in the complaints and summons he threw at Xavier's team
at every opportunity. It was as though the Colonel had a personal
allergy; the mere sight of a European – even the very upright and

decent Miss Rose Price – brought him out in hives and rashes that could only be alleviated by a head-on clash.

Xavier did not yet know of his nutritionist's misadventure in the souk that Tuesday evening, but the German woman sitting in silence beside him in the Land Rover had caused trouble enough. They were now heading back to the house where Fauzi, that pompous dimmock with dark glasses, lodged with Farah's widow. It was here that Xavier would again encounter Mr Mogga.

TWO

Fauzi had a piano, which he lost somewhere in the sands beyond Tawila.

When, at long last, Colonel al-Bedawi gave his grudging permission for a first field survey, Fauzi was allocated to the team. The leader was Christa the German.

"I need answers," Xavier Hopkins urged her, "rather badly. How hungry are they? Have they got reserves in the villages or not? What the hell is going on?"

Xavier told her to take Fauzi as interpreter. She frowned.

"I don't know about this Fauzi. It sounds like Faust, but not so clever."

They departed for the bush in Land Rover No.8 with young Daud driving, together with three Sudanese assistants, boxes of provisions, pans and clay stoves, jerrycans of diesel and two spare tyres and Fauzi's piano.

It was not a large instrument, and could fit into his shoulder bag. It was a small electronic keyboard of two-and-a-half octaves, with a pinched little voice driven by three torch batteries. Some might have called it a toy; Fauzi had ambitions as a wedding entertainer, and called it a piano.

He kept it concealed in his bag for the first hour. Daud turned south into the scrublands, pushing cautiously over hard little dykes and across abandoned fields, skirting dry riverbeds and inching through gaps in old thorn hedges that cluttered the wide tracts of stony dirt between villages. It was slow, tedious going, hardly ever more than a crawl. Distances were almost impossible to gauge; from the hours travelled, you might think you'd soon see the Mediterranean – only to find that you'd covered barely ten miles.

So now Fauzi opened his bag and inched a few keys of the instrument into view, to let them glimpse it.

"What's that?" someone asked.

"It's a piano," Fauzi replied, smiling mysteriously. But the German woman ignored him, staring instead at the sun-shrivelled crops.

At each village, the Land Rover stopped under a tree and the team stepped down: Jemilla and Nahid, handsome young women tossing their pink and green *tobes* looser in the hot breeze; Ahmed, burly and keen. With clipboards and pencils, they dispersed among the thorn hedges and conical thatched roofs to begin their survey. The women would come from the shadows, replying with easy frankness to Nahid and Jemilla who asked about their families. The men's suspicions were soon disarmed by the open candour of Ahmed, and they spoke readily (if cannily) of their farms. But when Fauzi addressed them, they would frown, puzzled by his bookish, pedantic speech. They would screw up their sandblasted faces and say, "What?" rudely, then turn to Ahmed to have it repeated. This happened again and again, until Fauzi wanted to shake their shoulders and shout: "*I'm* asking the questions!"

So he stayed close to Christa, interpreting for her. But when she enquired of certain elders, "How many farms have been abandoned?" Fauzi turned to the villagers and asked, "How many farmers have been bandits?"

At the end of that long first day, they were dehydrated and weary of the Land Rover wallowing and scratching through scrub, rocks, riverbeds and thorns that could pierce even those massive tyres. They were sick of their own voices asking, "How many goats? How many daughters? How many dead?" At the end of nine hours of this work, when they were at last scudding across open country towards their overnight stay at Tawila, Fauzi suddenly clutched at his bag and called out that he had lost his piano.

The others barely looked at him. Fauzi raised his voice: "Stop the car!" and Daud the driver pulled into the shade of a tree, glancing uncertainly at Christa. No breeze entered the stationary vehicle. The German turned and peered at Fauzi, barely comprehending.

"You have lost a piano, Fauzi? Where was that?"

He thought it was in the village of Seifou, but Umm Rawq was a possibility and they must go back. Fauzi's colleagues stayed mute. Daud glanced at his watch rhetorically: the light was failing and this was bandit country; think of Farah, out late on the road from Nyala . . .

No one said aloud, "What sort of fool brings a piano on a field survey?"

Christa tonelessly ordered a short detour to Seifou. The piano wasn't there. Now Fauzi declared that the thieves of Rahad al Bardi, way behind them, had seized the piano through the window of Land Rover No.8 while the team had been about their humanitarian duties. The thieves must be confronted promptly, before the piano could be spirited across the border into Chad.

But the team sat exhausted and sullen; they avoided his eyes. Daud looked at his watch again: no roads, no maps, the light dying. Christa said:

"I'm sorry, Fauzi. Perhaps we can send a message tomorrow. Now we return to Tawila."

His mouth fell open in protest, but the others looked away and Daud restarted the motor.

Two days later, returning to town mid-morning, Christa went to the Director's office. She strode past the village deputations at Xavier's door and marched in to stand before Xavier. She put her shoulder bag in the centre of his steel desk and ranted:

"It's impossible. My staff have contempt for this man and he despises them. Also, sometimes he smells of drink. I don't trust him, he is spoiling my team!"

Xavier tried to stop her.

"Christa, I have people waiting to see me . . ."

But she barged on:

"I have seventy-four villages to survey, I have one hundred and twenty thousand people in my district for which I am responsible, I have no time to be dealing with this stupid young man's inadequacies, I have to . . ."

Xavier Hopkins only half-listened. He had slept poorly, had

woken sweating several times in the night. He let her talk herself out, savouring the cool passes of his oscillating fan. Then he said bluntly:

"Does he get drunk?"

"No, but . . ."

"If there are no grounds for sacking, there's no way we can get rid of him. There are laws even here."

"Then you must transfer him."

Xavier became angry: why should he antagonise another team leader by dumping a liability on them? But the German was implacable: she would not leave the room until she was freed of Fauzi. Xavier remembered that he was due at a meeting with the Provincial Agricultural Officer. He seized on an idea.

"We need a supervisor for the Seed and Tool stores; can Fauzi count?"

"He says he can play music. One two three bong, one two three bong, that is counting."

"Then I'll send him to Seed and Tools."

Fauzi came before the Field Director next morning. Xavier Hopkins examined the slim young Sudanese whose soft face and amber-tinted glasses looked faintly laughable under a limp cotton sunhat of militaristic green. He wondered how this figure could arouse such ire. Fauzi listened to his new instructions, lifted his chin and asked to which grade he would be raised. Xavier blinked, taken aback.

"Why do you think you should be upgraded?"

"Because I am promoted Stores Supervisor."

The meetings with the Agriculture Office were not going well; Xavier needed to conserve his energies.

"Very well; Grade Four."

The store was half a mile from the office, a discouraging trudge through heavy sands. It was an unfinished house; there were curlicue steel grilles in the windows but the brick walls were bare. When you entered, cement dust rose from the floor, with its unhealthful stink.

At Seed and Tools the responsibilities were not onerous. Bundles of hoe blades were stacked with ten-kilo bags of sorghum seed. There were green wheelbarrows that wanted assembling, and sacks of cement for the 'Food for Work'. From time to time a driver would be sent to collect: each item must be logged out. The old watchman slept on a string cot on the verandah, his knobbed stick lain on the floor by him. At a small wooden table to which gobbets of cement clung like molluscs, Fauzi sat drawing pencil lines in an exercise book and listing the hoes. When he had finished that, he walked to the tin gate, dragged it open so that he could stand in the shade of its brick archway, stared down the street full of nothing but sand, and considered resigning.

*

He was twenty-six and of a *jellaba* family, traders from El Obeid. Fauzi had none of the brashness that trade required, and he'd come west to El Fasher seeking Government service. Instead, he had fallen in with the foreign aid experts. Fauzi had escorted and interpreted for Dutch nurses, Brazilian hydrologists and a Welsh authority on marginal farming, all of whom had passed him on quickly; he now had a plastic bag full of references. As each new wave of advisors came to the province, he enquired after his departed international friends; occasionally he was rewarded with a card, a note, a photograph. He believed he had more friends and colleagues in the aid agencies of Europe and America than he had in West Sudan.

He had drunk deep of their conversation. His radio (its weedy, distant voice) told him of the great ant heaps of mankind, the vast landscapes of the globe, the industry and invention, the wars and romances, the science, spectacle and tumult of the continents – but to Fauzi, who had never seen the sea, the world paraded in the persons of Gina the Canadian doctor, Heidi the agronomist from Mainz, Pete the Irish logistician. Their casual talk was Fauzi's university; he drank it up as the desert soaked up rain, and if Gina or Heidi or Pete had come back a year later, he'd have astonished them; he'd have recited their most trivial chat back to them verbatim.

And now this German, this Christa, this most interesting and

much travelled young woman had banished him. The next morning they coincided in the office yard and for a ridiculous moment
Fauzi thought she would apologise for the slight. But Christa only
nodded to him, "Fauzi" – and passed by, saying no more.

So: Seed and Tools. How was he to be stimulated in a hot
cement room with only an illiterate, toothless watchman for
company, logging the ins and outs of hoes tied up with string?
How, content? He must demand better! Fauzi stared down the
street hoping to see not three sleeping dogs and a litter of dry
palm leaves but a car sent for him, to summon him back to the
office. But the street was empty.

He lived alone, although sharing a high-walled compound. The
widow Farida and her three small daughters stayed in two brick
rooms on one side; Fauzi rented a detached room on the other,
thirty paces away, but he rarely spoke with them and the family
came and went by another gate. Next to Fauzi's room was his own
latrine, and a 44-gallon drum for water, dented halfway down its
flank and pierced by rust. A small acacia tree rustled over the gate,
which Fauzi kept chained and padlocked.

Of an evening, Fauzi was delivered home by the office Land
Rover. He would bathe and change, walk to the souk to eat bread
and beans in oil, return home – and then what? As night fell, he
would pull his chair (white tubular steel and green plastic twine)
out onto the warm sand where the legs would sink lopsidedly. He
would pour a glass of sweet crimson hibiscus juice, adding a
measure of *arigi*, raw and forbidden date spirit. He would turn on
his radio, place it on the ground by him and try to fend off his
bewildered loneliness.

The evenings were very long. The piano was stolen. There
were women to whom one could go, but he had neither the income
nor the nerve for debauch. He did wonder, in this respect, about
the widow across the compound, but only one man ever visited
her, the landlord, an intimidating, bullying figure.

With effort he might read. In a tin trunk he had paperbacks
bequeathed by former international friends: Sven Hassel, Wilbur
Smith, an incontinent family saga from Cornwall. Some evenings

he would hear wedding celebrations in the neighbourhood. The crudely amplified voices, the buzz and boom of bass-heavy music, the thudding drums together sounded like a sweet promise of society – or a cruel jibe. He would drink rather more of the turpentine-scented *arigi* than was good for him.

Each morning, the Land Rover passed by his gate to take him to the office compound where he would linger for a quarter of an hour to feel part of the Programme, noting the departure of survey teams, or Miss Price the nutritionist going to her vehicle. Fauzi would smile familiarly at everyone, and drift across the yard to eavesdrop on discussions between Dr Maeve and the Field Director who would glance at, but not include him. Soon he would have to walk the fatiguing streets to Seed and Tools, to tighten the plastic over the windows and count the hoes again.

One day, to his astonishment, he had a late afternoon caller.

"Unng, hmmh, grmm," mouthed the toothless watchman by way of an introduction. Behind him stood a little black man with tufts of hair over his ears. They stood facing each other in the blazing heat of the gateway.

"Good afternoon," bobbed the intruder.

Fauzi glowered at him.

"Yes?" he growled.

"Oh yes," rejoined Mr Mogga courteously. "May I speak with you?"

For a moment, Fauzi considered the absurd option of saying no. Then he realised that this person *wanted* to speak with him, Fauzi.

"What about?" he demanded.

"You see," began Mogga, "I have noticed that you are engaged by the foreign experts . . ."

Fauzi prepared to bristle.

". . . in a position of responsibility."

Fauzi, just a shade, relaxed.

"True," he replied.

Mogga gave him a winning smile.

"Then you are the person to advise me. I am come to town to

seek a position but have little experience of foreigners, while you have much."

Fauzi rather warmed to this fellow.

"True, again," he said.

"They are remarkable people, no?" the little man asked. "Will you tell me all about them?"

Of a sudden, Fauzi's world seemed more congenial.

"I shall fill you in," he said. "Walk with me to my house. It is across town, past the *fula*, but we can take the time to discuss."

So Mr Mogga came to Fauzi's lodging, to drink *arigi* with him at dusk and learn all the names, ways and talents of the internationals. Though the little black was no substitute for real conversation, nonetheless Fauzi felt enormously gratified, noting the close attention that Mogga paid to everything. He invited Mogga to come again.

Hovering in the office forecourt at 8.15 a.m., Fauzi was startled to hear himself addressed by the German who had so rudely disposed of him. She was not unattractive this morning: she wore her thin blonde hair held neatly in a leather clasp, and had dressed her meagre body in fresh blue cotton. Christa moved through the dust and difficulties of Sudan in a ladylike manner. She was all smiles now.

"Fauzi? Would you like to help me out?"

Fauzi rose to the challenge. His utmost, he assured her, anything at all.

"You are so kind. Some visiting colleagues will come to our Resthouse this evening, and we like to offer them refreshment . . ." she hesitated slightly, "of a sort that you know . . ."

Fauzi stared in chagrin. This woman had discarded him, had discounted his professionalism, but had heard he could supply liquor! But then, here was a chance of conviviality. A deal was done; she gave him money.

"I shall deliver at eight tomorrow."

"Oh, that is a trouble for you. I shall send Daud to collect from your house."

"But I would be so pleased . . ."

"It is crazy, and so far. Daud will come."

In her blue cottons and court shoes, she stepped over the sand to join her team waiting in Land Rover No.8 outside.

He brooded all day and, on issuing a wheelbarrow, distractedly made an error in the exercise book. Rubbing with an old, perished eraser, he tore the page. He longed to share his grievance, but with whom? The watchman? He looked at the toothless old fool rinsing his shabby robe in an oil drum by the latrine and wondered whether this man had ever tasted *arigi*. Would he consider Fauzi damned? Fauzi was damned if he cared.

With *sharia* re-imposed, one must be careful. But he'd have taken his chance for an evening at the Resthouse, to sit under the stars with the German and her colleagues, holding a cigarette and a pungent glass. They'd have dissected the world with wit and penetration. Yes, possibly, State Security might have swooped; the experts would be acutely embarrassed and Fauzi flogged and jobless. But he'd have risked it. All day he brooded. That evening, dressing after his bath by the light of the streetlamp (working for once), Fauzi resolved to send word that there was no refreshment to be had.

But he had forgotten: first to arrive was Mogga, smiling and chatty. Even as they exchanged pleasantries, Fauzi sensed a terrible quandary. He was an Arab: an Arab does not withhold hospitality. Furthermore, if he were to deny Mogga a drink, the black might depart, and what would that do for his evening? But if Daud were to appear while they sat there quaffing, what should Fauzi say? Claim that they had that very moment finished the *arigi* that Christa had ordered? Was he to tell such feeble lies in front of a southerner?

As they stood there, a vehicle turned into the lane and halted. Both men looked toward the gate, Fauzi expecting Daud's jolly call. But, instead, there was a hesitant knuckling on the tin and the woman's voice, softly:

"*Salaamalaikum*, Fauzi."

He froze in surprise. Mogga glanced at him, interested.

It came again: "Fauzi?"

He stepped forward, tugged off the chain, and dragged the gate juddering open. The streetlamp lit her more than she liked, and she looked about nervously. Fauzi felt an unaccustomed advantage. He became expansive.

"*Walaikum asalaam!* Such a pleasant surprise."

"I won't come in . . ."

"Oh, but my house is open."

Christa glanced up and down the lane and shuffled her feet. Of course: Daud the driver had a name for piety. He could not be sent to collect liquor.

"Fauzi – our arrangement?"

"I have not been to that place just yet. I shall go now, I shall be quick. Will you wait here in my house?"

She peered past him through the narrow gate at the gloom of the yard.

"No. Where is the place? I shall come."

Fauzi was impressed. His international friends had never brushed with the low life of town. But at that moment, a voice came from within.

"Let us go to this interesting place, all together," called Mogga happily.

"Who is there?" hissed Christa in alarm.

"A friend!" cried Fauzi, cursing the black. He could think of no alternative, no way to get rid of Mogga. "Yes, let us go now, together."

They drove in silence: it was only a few blocks. Fauzi indicated a gate overhung by a froth of peachy bougainvillaea. Again, there was a streetlight, humming. Christa drove past quickly and rounded a corner into the deep shadows beneath a *hejlij* or soap-tree. She killed the headlamps. Fauzi sensed her tension, her straining eyes and ears: what if Security . . . ? He was about to suggest that she wait in the vehicle, but she opened her door and stepped down.

Even in the unlit back street, Land Rover No.8 loomed very white. The street was empty but, in a deep black doorway, Fauzi glimpsed leather-slippered feet and heard a man's soft whisper:

"*Khowajiyah*, a foreigner . . ."

They hurried past in silence, through the sodium light towards the bougainvillaea gate.

A gaggle of children and two young women were lazing on beds out in the cool watching an Egyptian soap on a foggy black-and-white television. Fauzi was recognised; they scrutinised Mogga and nodded warily to Christa who was looking about her, all curiosity.

Behind a rush screen, the distillery: a round, thatched hut, infernally hot. In the centre was a circular brick fireplace; sitting over the low charcoal glow was a grey aluminium pan one metre across. A fat matron streamed sweat and reeked and bulged from a wringing blouse. She waddled around the fire to where more pans stood on the sand, stirring these with a wooden paddle. The soft light gleamed on the contents. Christa gagged: the pans seethed with glittering, struggling cockroaches – until she recognised dates, kilo on kilo of dates mashing, fermenting, shining like oiled wood in the lamplight, then foaming and hissing softly as the ponderous, fleshy woman stirred. Fauzi beamed at Christa, delighted by her interest. Then they heard laughter.

Outside by the television, Mogga was perched among the sprawled girls, chattering merrily.

They came away with small plastic jerrycans oozing a turpentine-scented spirit. They dropped the bottles into a plastic bag and hurried to the Land Rover.

Fauzi said, "This is interesting for you? This lady makes fine wine."

Christa did not reply, but started the motor quickly. A moment later they were back at Fauzi's gate. He tried again:

"Won't you come in for a moment? We can have some talk . . ."

But she would not.

"Thank you, Fauzi, my guests are now coming."

All that evening, in the dark outside his bachelor's bedroom, he could think of nothing else. In his mind's eye they gathered under the thatched *rakuba* at the Resthouse: Xavier, Toby, Miss Price, Freddy, Lorna the nurse and Dr Maeve and all their guests, quick-witted and cosmopolitan: the International Programme. Talking: he could just hear them. Talking.

"I think I might have joined them for an hour, don't you?" Fauzi exploded to Mogga in indignation. "Who else can I talk with in this backward town?"

Listening quietly, there in Fauzi's yard, Mogga nodded, pondering.

She would be wanting more, of course she would. Fauzi went back to the bougainvillaea gate.

"So, I have stocks in hand for Miss Christa," he assured Mogga, showing him the two new bottles that he had obtained. To seal the relationship, he had written with a Magic Marker on the plastic:

Always – Best Kwality of Refreshment!

But she didn't collect, not from the office, not from his house, nor from Seed and Tools. When Fauzi saw her across the compound on Friday, Christa gave him a quick, cold look and moved away.

Fauzi did not go to prayers. He was dropped at his lodging by the Land Rover, which slewed noisily away down the street. A small boy with a water-donkey approached, leaving in the dust a trail of drips from the swollen black skins slung across the animal's back. The boy tapped a stick on a plastic funnel – *tock, tock* – and Fauzi gestured from the gate. The expressionless donkey ignored him; in silence, the boy untied the skins and water sloshed into Fauzi's oil drum. Paid the standard price, the boy turned back towards the town wells. The entire transaction had required only: *Shukran, thank you. Shukran.*

As he rinsed his shirts in a tin bowl under the tree, there was a *rat tat* on the steel gate. It was Mogga come to call. Fauzi opened the *Best Kwality of Refreshment.* He felt defiant and expansive.

"Drink up!" he cried, "there's plenty more where that came from."

"Oh, yes," smiled Mogga. "They are distilling tonight, in fact."

Fauzi peered in surprise.

"How do you know?" he asked.

Mogga gave a diffident little grin.

"Well, you know, I am living there."

Fauzi froze, his glass halfway to his lips.

"Yes," continued Mogga, "I have moved in. My former lodgings were not pleasant, and very far away. So I mentioned to our friends that I was seeking a room."

Fauzi was profoundly shocked. He whispered.

"But they are low people. They make wine. And the young ladies, they . . . receive gentlemen."

Mogga grinned.

"I think so," he said.

An hour later, when Mogga rose to leave, Fauzi jumped to his feet also.

"Let me walk with you!" he exclaimed. There was anxiety in his voice.

Mogga studied him sympathetically.

"I should be glad of your companionship," he replied.

So they went together through the dark lanes. One turn away from the distillery, Fauzi stopped short. There was the spiny *hejlij* tree throwing its shadow across the wall. And there, under the tree, was a dim white bulk.

Astonished, Fauzi approached the Land Rover. As Mogga watched, Fauzi reached out, half-believing that his hand would pass right through a phantasm. But even in the gloom he could read the small red number 8 on the driver's side. Incredulous, they rounded the corner heading for the billow of creamy peach-coloured bougainvillaea – but the gate opened and the German woman emerged. Fauzi jerked Mogga into a black doorway as Christa, unseeing, walked past them toting a heavy plastic bag.

*

Fauzi took a day off sick. Mogga came to enquire but Fauzi would not open his gate. It was a protest: he sulked, he brooded, but was vanquished by loneliness. He returned to work next day, resolved to say nothing.

Fauzi disembarked from the staff car, intending to set off at once on the fatiguing walk to Seed and Tools. At that moment,

Mr Hopkins the Field Director appeared at the office door; a Sudanese visitor was departing. Fauzi recognised him as an agent of State Security, a minion of Colonel Hassan al-Bedawi. The Director's eyes drilled loathing into the man's back. Another figure emerged from the shady office: Christa. Without a word she hurried to her vehicle. Her professional cool was gone, she looked red-faced and flustered. She was, Fauzi saw, close to tears.

It all came out: the tea boy had heard everything, the secretaries spread the tale. The German had been reported, Land Rover No.8 had been seen in a certain back street, she had entered a house known to State Security. They weren't having it; under *sharia* law she could be flogged. If it were reported again, expulsion would be swift: Colonel al-Bedawi wished Mr Hopkins to be in no doubt about that. The humiliated Director had bitten his tongue.

When Mogga appeared at his lodging that evening, Fauzi sang of vindication, of comeuppance. With a mug of spiked hibiscus lodged in the sand by his feet, Fauzi turned over and over this small, bright gem of justice.

*

There was one further twist. Important Americans had arrived in town, and on Wednesday there was to be a meeting: this seemed to be a source of great worry to Mr Xavier Hopkins; in fact the whole team was on edge. Something extraordinary was in the air. Fauzi saw Daud in his smartest clothes and No.8 newly washed. In the office yard he saw the sweepers in overdrive, the wilted flowerbeds watered and weeded, a crate of Libyan Fanta bought in from the souk.

Back home on the Tuesday evening, Fauzi pondered the possible imminent changes. Perhaps the Americans would take over altogether. They'd be less surly and serious, less sour than these Europeans. He'd done well with Americans before, they were happy to talk! Jobs were bound to shuffle and switch: it must be to his good. He'd not be sorry to be done with Europeans, with their wretched Seed and Tools.

Another surprise: there came a familiar knock at his gate and he bustled over to welcome Mr Mogga but the latter did not smile and bob with his usual genial courtesies. Mogga said at once:

"My friend, can you assist me?"

Startled and alarmed, Fauzi turned on the torch he carried (the streetlights were off as usual). Mogga stood there with his face running with sweat and his arms held out before him.

"My hands . . ." murmured Mogga.

Fauzi shone the torch onto the outstretched hands. Across both palms and the pads of the fingers were angry, red-brown weals.

"Oh!" gasped Fauzi, and for a moment stood helpless. Then he said:

"The woman, we must call the woman, she will do this!"

He went scurrying across the yard calling out to his landlady; a moment later he was back with Farida in his wake. When she saw Mogga, she halted abruptly – and to Fauzi's astonishment took Mogga's wrist and went down on her knees before the visitor. She was murmuring a prayer of thanks.

They bathed the scorched hands in cold water dipped straight from Fauzi's oil drum, then Farida wrapped them in clean rags, politely instructing Fauzi as she worked. Fauzi had always considered himself the soul of compassion but had never seen himself as a ministering angel before. He rather enjoyed the role, even as he listened intrigued to the tale from the souk.

Lights swept the side street. A diesel cut by his door and that voice that he'd thought never to hear at his gate again came clearly:

"*Salaamalaikum*, Fauzi. Are you there?"

Two of them! The German and the Director, as shifty as could be. "May we have a word, Fauzi?" the woman said as the Director looked at her anxiously, and for once there was no wheedling: they pushed inside.

Only then did they notice the others present. Seated on low chairs of blue wooden slats, Farah's widow Farida was speaking in a low voice with a man who, after a moment, the Field Director realised he'd seen yesterday, in the street outside. He was short, and chubby faced. Age indeterminate, but not old. Skin very black, nose rather squashed: he was no Arab. His head was almost completely bald, save that over each ear bobbed a thick tuft of black-and-silver hair. He gave Christa a smile, a quick nod of his head and a flash of bright eyes. For some reason, both his hands were wrapped in rags.

"This is Mogga," said Fauzi. "My acquaintance."

"Yes," agreed Mogga.

Fauzi went straight to his room before they could stop him. He came out with more steel chairs, setting them in formation on the dark sand.

"We can't stay . . ." the Director began, but Fauzi ignored him. He offered proper Sudanese hospitality, and even Europeans knew not to snub it. Before there could be discussion, they must be seated, with large tumblers of *karkadeh* and another jugful between the chairs. Beaming, Fauzi treated them to the full protocol of courtesy and enquiry. Until he concluded:

"And you have guests from America; they are very well?"

Startled, Mr Hopkins glanced at Christa who tidied her nice floral dress over her closed knees and looked into her *karkadeh*. She said,

"Xavier meets with them tomorrow. That is why we're here."

"Ah, yes?" said Fauzi, sweetly.

"We hope to persuade them to offer help," Xavier began, "very substantial help but of the right sort, not food. With their aid, we can perhaps embark on important projects, reconstruction, new facilities, animals, boreholes, that type of thing."

There was, Fauzi noted, peculiar emotion in the Director's voice, as though a pressure of water was building behind a weakened dam. His chair legs had dug deep into the sand; bending forward to cradle his glass, Xavier was all askew.

"We're very grateful to them for coming," the Director continued, sounding extraordinarily ungrateful.

"We want them to know this," asserted Christa.

Fauzi understood completely: "You wish them to have a good time."

"Yes, that is important."

"You wish to offer some refreshment?"

"It would help."

Of course it would help, thought Fauzi. The point would not be lost on Americans: the Agency in touch with the unofficial pulse and still able, amidst distress, to conjure gaiety.

He said, "How about entertainment? Some piano music? I could borrow an instrument . . ."

"I think they are not musical . . ." said Christa hurriedly.

"I'm sure they're not musical!" Xavier Hopkins clamoured in agreement. "And it's a working party, with discussions, if you follow me . . ."

"Discussions? Also, conversations?" said Fauzi.

"Exactly," said the Director, "Wide-ranging and important conversations that we are keen to have go well."

Fauzi regarded them, weighing things. He glanced at his friend Mogga, and saw in the little black's gentle face something that calmed and reassured him. Fauzi felt a little inward sigh of realism.

"So, Fauzi," said the woman, "Can you help us out? With refreshment? As only you know how."

Fauzi looked at her straight. He allowed himself a curt, ironic laugh.

"But I think you know where to obtain *Best Kwality of Refreshment*," he teased.

"The thing is, Fauzi . . ." began the Director.

"You, however, should not be seen there," said Fauzi sternly, "that would be an error. Beg your pardon, but I think that no one in your position should risk being seen in such a place."

Christa glared into her *karkadeh*, her face ablaze.

The Director murmured, "Of course not."

Fauzi continued, "As it happens, there is no need to go. You see, I have stocks, ordered previously but not collected. I like to keep myself in stocks; such is my vocation as Storekeeper. I daresay I am in sufficient stocks for a dozen thirsty Americans."

The Director looked at him, hopeful.

"It would be such a help."

"Then rest assured. Let us have some more juice."

"I'm not sure we have much time . . ."

"I have made a big jug, and your visit honours me. Look what a large jug of hibiscus I have made you, and with it we can have some conversation. Just five minutes of conversation."

So they made conversation with Fauzi, as Farida replenished their tumblers of cordial and Mogga sat quietly, noting, not interrupting. Xavier enquired about Fauzi's work for other agencies, and Fauzi expressed some opinions he'd developed over long afternoons at Seed and Tools. Next, it was gratifying to have the Director give him, Fauzi, a personal briefing on the priorities of the Programme, with enquiries after Fauzi's plans.

At last Mr Hopkins looked at Christa.

"I must be getting back," he said, "to prepare for the Americans."

As they got to their feet, Mogga sprang to his also.

"Allow me," he said.

He hurried to open the gate for the visitors, escorting them into the street. Fauzi heard, a little to his surprise, an exchange of a few sentences outside. A moment later, Mogga returned, thanked his friend warmly and said a polite farewell, then departed also.

After they'd all left, Fauzi finished the *karkadeh*. He settled himself to replay the entire, fascinating conversation, word for word, and he enjoyed as never before the sinking of his chair into the evening sand.

*

Wednesday morning. When Xavier reached the office, he immediately ordered a cover-up. For there, in the Agency compound – at the office they had never quite pulled out of from one bad year to the next – there was a terrible reminder of old humiliations. Terrible, and laughable.

It was a boat. Five hundred miles from the nearest bend of the Nile, leaning up against the compound wall: an unlovely grey aluminium tub. It had been brought here in a previous crisis year. Someone had said that the rains would flood the wadis, making it impossible to truck food to distant villages. Someone had sent a boat, in sections, by air and at enormous expense. How many

45

bottle tops and blouses had been donated by Middle England to send that metal boat to the desert? There in the office compound, it rested among drifts of sand and dust. There had been no rains, no water at all in the wadis that year. The boat's bottom had not been wetted.

In his worst moments, the image of that boat would rise up in Xavier's mind to mock him. *You're out of your depth*, the dry boat laughed. It must be put away, it must be concealed, lest the Americans gawp and demand, *What in God's name is that?*

"Fetch a tarp!" he cried to the gatekeeper and the usual knot of drivers. "From the truck, from the store; maybe there's one in Seed and Tools, but wrap that thing up."

He saw them jolted, alarmed by the tension and irritation in his voice. He could hear it himself. He did not want these high-level visitors. They would be pressing for clear answers, and Darfur was not a land of clear answers. The Donor Nations still urged him to declare a famine – how the young hotheads in Xavier's team would cheer! – but any half-wit could see how things got out of hand. The markets flooded with free food, the farmers bankrupted, trade grinding to a halt because they'd have to commandeer all the trucks . . . The Sudanese authorities had not welcomed this mission any more than Xavier, and when a dust storm seemed certain to close the Fasher airfield, people said, "The Governor has spoken to Allah and He has sent a fine *haboob* to keep the Americans away." But an hour later the dust subsided and people said, "The Americans have had a word with Allah and He has changed His mind."

Fauzi was fetched from Seed and Tools, bringing a large sheet of blue plastic, taking charge of this important task, ordering the gateman and the drivers about and exasperating them. By mid-afternoon, the boat was swathed, and Xavier was as ready as he would ever be.

"Sir," said the gateman, irritable and disbelieving, "there's a man to see you. He's a black, a southerner. He claims he has an appointment."

Xavier looked. In the gateway, a short, balding fellow stood.

He had a red nylon bag over his shoulder and his hands were wrapped in rags. He smiled genially at the Director. For a moment, Xavier could not place him.

"He claims," continued the scornful gateman, "that he spoke with you last night."

*

Rose Price, London-trained tropical nutritionist, had a recurrent dream. It was a memory of her childhood, of the day her dog had caught a mole in her parents' lawn. The amiable old retriever had hoiked the blind thing out of its hole, had lobbed it playfully into the air, had beamed at little Rose in a cheery way: "Here's a new friend; shall I break every bone in its pretty body before sweetly biting it in half?"

Rose had screeched at her bemused dog who did his best to please the child by tossing the helpless mole against the pear tree. Rose had run to the garden shed and come back with a huge, battered old shovel that Dad used for snow and leaves, a bent and jagged thing. The dog backed off, uncertain. Rose had hefted the shovel above her head and had thwacked it down as hard as she could on the mole, *thwack thwack thwack!* But when she stopped and looked down, the silky brown creature lying on its back was not dead, was not grateful, but opened its tiny mouth and screamed at her: a miniature howl of agony, outrage and reproach.

It was this that came to Rose in her sleep: the little gaping mouth, that terrible reproachful scream.

Often it had visited her, this memory, throughout her long years of field experience – Botswana and Senegal, Eritrea and Nepal – usually when work was not going well and she was stressed and exhausted. When things were especially bad, the mole would come to her by day also: just the open mouth, the tiny sound. An atrocity for which she was somehow responsible, and a remedy that inflicted agony. She was thinking of this just now, sitting in silence on a bed, alone in the Resthouse.

The flimsy mesh door flew open against the wall. The Resthouse trembled: the team was back, heads throbbing from surveys and inspections and meetings, hurling their work satchels onto the beds, scooping water from the jar, pushing the scum aside with a finger before drinking. They sat at once, slicing the Spam, pulling apart the stiff white noodles, covering everything with damp grey salt.

Taciturn Rose Price came to the table and drained a smeared tumbler of water. Dr Maeve carefully wiped the table around her own plate and nibbled delicately at the tough dry bread, twittering of this and that. Toby Kitchin, a half-Ghanaian coloured boy from Colchester, sat brooding and frowning, his eating youthfully greedy. Next to him sat Freddy from the Nyala office, his green shirt sweat-darkened, the heavy black-framed glasses blurred with grease, his lank hair swinging over the noodles. His feeding was vigorous, his complaints loud.

Why, Freddy demanded, weren't they all meeting this circus of Yanks? If they were such big shots, maybe they could sort the shambles. Where were the new vehicles? Impounded by customs. Where was the diesel? 'Borrowed' by the police. Where were the money and the computers, the ink, the calculators, the spare tyres, the air filters, the water filters? How could one work like this? Where were the travel permits for village surveys? Security were prevaricating. Xavier bloody Hopkins was prevaricating. Why wouldn't he approve food distribution? How could they prevent a famine without food? Freddy leaned hard on the table that creaked and tilted as he whacked his knife down in emphasis.

Rose Price did not listen. She was scowling, but not at Freddy's tirade. She was thinking of the Americans: she must be ready, she must wash, she must eat, she must rest, she really must, in twenty minutes she'd join Xavier to meet the Americans . . . She felt drained in anticipation.

The door again: Christa, looking strained, smiling thin greetings before passing the table, lying down, closing her aching eyes, breathing slowly and deliberately to calm herself after a stressful day in the field.

"Fuck it!" spat Freddy, in high gear now. "We're supposed to be heading off a disaster," he thundered, "making contingency preparations. We're supposed," he raged, waving the chopped pork on his fork, "to be saving lives, and what the fuck does everyone, and I mean fucking everyone, do? They get in the way, they stand in the fucking light, Government, Embassy, UNICEF, Security, Red Crescent, name me one bunch of plonkers who are actually assisting? Not a single one, they're watching their backs, scratching their arses."

He leaned across the table, calling:

"Rose, you tell those Yanks that we're ready and willing to dole out food, but they'd bloody better give us the clout to do the job or we are up shit . . ."

With a squeal of nails and a splintering of crappy joints, the table-top flipped onto Freddy's lap. Tin plates, tin cutlery, thick glassware, salt, tomatoes, perspiring Spam and clotted noodles slithered and crashed in unison onto the concrete floor. Exhausted, raw-tempered diners shouted and clambered out of the way while Freddy roared:

"Shit! Fucking thing! Bloody hell!"

His colleagues stood in a ragged ring peering down at the carnage that had been their dinner.

"Oh, what a pity," said a new voice.

A silhouette stood before the mesh door that clattered shut behind him. Then he stepped forward and they saw a small man, trim and neat though his checked shirt was very faded and his brown polyester trousers very shiny and too short. His hands were swathed in rags and from his shoulder hung a small red nylon rucksack, much repaired with thick black thread. His head was bald, his skin very black and his smile so broad that, even as he peered in sympathetic dismay at the disaster on the floor, he made you want to laugh.

"Can your dinner be saved?" he enquired.

"Don't bother," snapped Freddy, "it was inedible."

"I saw you," began Toby Kitchin, frowning. "Weren't you outside here . . ."

"His name is Mogga," whispered Christa through a migraine.

Rose Price sat up suddenly.

"You're here!" she said sharply. "Your hands must be scorched."

"They're rather sore," Mogga ruefully admitted.

Rose Price looked round the room.

"Lorna?" she called.

"Burns, eh?" returned the nurse, bustling forward.

Nyala Freddy was piqued.

"Hang about," he complained, "how come you all know this bloke except me?"

But Mogga was looking thoughtfully at the wreck of the table, bending to examine the ripped nails and the fractured joints.

"I'm a carpenter. I shall repair this for you," he said.

"If you can fix that, I want you in my team," said Freddy.

"Well, hold on," came an objecting voice, "Nyala's better off for staff than Um Keddada. We could use the help . . ."

"But excuse me," began Christa, still flat on her exhausted back, "do I not get assistance? I am short . . ."

"Oh, but wait a minute . . ." began Toby Kitchin.

"Please, please," cried Mogga, "I am only just appointed."

Mogga was hardly hired, and they were fighting over him.

*

"Allan Paronian, United States Office for Foreign Disaster Assistance."

Xavier thinks, *the man's family must be Armenian, with a name like that; he should know something about oppressed provinces.* Xavier sees a tall, slim figure with grey eyes behind thick round spectacles, a grey moustache and grey hair dragged over a tall, heavy skull, who supposedly answers direct to the US President.

Handshakes. Xavier is courtesy incarnate. Rose Price mutters curt greetings. Paronian indicates his sidekicks.

"Ellen Romotowski. Ellen's with Food For Peace in Washington."

Wavy blonde hair, big professional smile: *Hi, isn't this great!*

Xavier thinks: *Food For Peace? What peace? If someone had been better fed, might they have refrained from shooting Farah ibn Mashoud?*

"Jerry Nussbaum, our agronomist."

Mr Nut Tree, dark and curly and doubtless eager to teach the Fur to grow cashews.

"Peter Shapiro, air logistics."

A crophead: no-crap ex-military. He's in khaki; his trousers have large pockets on the thighs, as though he'll be running cockpit checks any moment. Shapiro is here to remind Xavier and Rose that, if they are caught short by a famine, then they'll be into airlifts with all their colossal expense and waste and inefficiency. The old aid worker's adage: when you see the C-130s flying, you know that someone's really fucked up – in this instance, Mr Xavier Hopkins.

"And Terri, who'll take minutes."

Terri is a beefy girl with a moustache almost as thick as Paronian's. Already she is lifting a laptop from its case, and an aerosol spray that she squirts up and down her solid legs.

They sit on the office verandah lit between two scalding petrol lamps, sipping warm pink *karkadeh* juice at which Ellen, Pete and Jerry peer suspiciously. Xavier wants to shout: It's only fucking hibiscus!

Terri would tap everything into her laptop: *Mr Hopkins: "It's only f****** hibiscus."*

Talk of infrastructure and intervention and supervision require-ments, transport aircraft and Title II Aid, whatever that may be. It begins as measured, polite discourse. Then it grows heated.

Jerry Nut Tree leans forward. He's so eager he wants to shake Xavier by the throat.

"Sir, (*Sir?*) from the satellite images, we expect 40% crop failure . . ."

Ellen takes Terri's spray, coats her own legs, smiles a piranha smile.

"We have 17,000 tons in-region right now, but if we delay . . ."

Peter raises an eyebrow and spits grit:

"If we act promptly, we could bring in C-130s, but leave this too long and we'd be reliant on leased Antonovs . . ."

You wouldn't want that, would you, Mr Hopkins? Then you'd have fucked up good and proper. You'd have played the part of a silly elf, and it'll be all over CNN.

"Mr Hopkins, what can you tell us about market prices for animals?"

Farah's bloodstained report is blowing about the desert. Xavier has no data! Nut Tree and friends see, and drive it home:

"We envisage a food shortfall of 12,000 tons a month . . ."

"If we don't have fuel in place . . ."

"With Global Acute Malnutrition already at 23% . . ."

Terri taps it all into the record: *Mr Hopkins was informed. Mr Hopkins has no excuse.*

Paronian watches as his henchmen strike and strike again until they're out of breath and sit staring in rhetorical incredulity. And now Paronian speaks, calmly.

"You don't look convinced, Mr Hopkins."

Xavier sighs. At which Nut Tree explodes.

"For chrissake how much evidence do you . . ."

"One moment, Jerry."

Paronian holds up a hand. He looks back to Xavier, cocking his head in silent interrogation: *Well, Mr Hopkins?*

"I agree that things are not good . . ."

"I'll say!" blurts out Nut Tree. He is blasted by a frosty look from Paronian.

"And yes," Xavier stumbles on, "there'll be a shortfall. But that's not a famine. We've been here before, in both senses. In 1985 we got it badly wrong."

"And people died," chips in Ellen.

My staff are dying now, thinks Xavier furiously, *shot on the road from Nyala . . .*

Rose Price intervenes at last.

"Far fewer died in '85 than we expected," she says, gruff-voiced. "Most survived surprisingly well. We're not sure how, or why. We'd worked out how much food there was in Darfur, we'd done our sums and it looked as though they must, necessarily, starve to death. But they didn't. It may be that they had hidden reserves, it may be that they managed to get by on things they wouldn't normally eat: wild grasses, berries. Things we hadn't taken into account."

"Are you recommending," enquires Paronian, his eyes upon Rose stony and unforgiving, "that we tell half a million people to go out and eat berries? I'm afraid the US Government doesn't work in that way. We give food."

Rose is furious, her eyes urging Xavier: *Don't let them do this!*

"We know," Xavier says, "that giving food at the wrong time causes more suffering than it solves. Even supposing the harvest is poor . . ."

"Supposing!?"

"Jerry, please."

"Even supposing," Xavier persists, "the harvest is terrible, the farmers still have to sell it. If you arrive with 50,000 tons of give-away grain, handed out for free, what chance do they have? In the short term, they eat. In the long term, they're bankrupt. That's what happened last time. Many people here are still destitute because we got it wrong."

Oh boy did we get it wrong. Xavier envisages something nasty under a blue tarp by the compound wall.

Then Paronian takes him completely off guard.

"Your father saw the Bengal famine of '43, I believe."

Xavier feels a cold shiver of panic: *What else does Paronian know about me? And how?* He sees Rose regard him in surprise.

"And how do you know that?" he parries Paronian, cool as he can.

"A conversation in Khartoum," the American replies mildly. He must have pumped the embassy; Xavier had told the trade attaché about Dad one woozy evening.

"That will have been an uncomfortable experience for your Pop," Paronian muses creamily. "You see, Mr Hopkins, I've made quite a study of famine. It comes down to preparedness, not blinding yourself to what's under your nose. In Calcutta in '43 you Brits just didn't see the people dying on the pavement, under your noses in every sense."

What a vulgar turn of phrase. Xavier is seething; Rose watches, puzzled and alarmed.

"We try," he retorts sarcastically, "to learn from mistakes."

Paronian gives the faintest malicious grin.

"Is that why you keep a boat out in the yard? Like, an aide-mémoire?"

Xavier cannot speak. Paronian sees that he is down. He says, silkily:

"Look, Xavier . . ."

Now, the victor's condescension!

"I'll be straight with you. We have some 42,000 tons of wheat and soya pre-positioned regionally."

He means, it's rotting in a warehouse and they want shot of it.

"I shall also make available a further 53,000 tons of Title II food currently in store in the US. I want to see that go direct to the hungry."

To clear the silos of Nebraska for more Government purchases to bolster their own farmers.

"I've put it to your ambassador that we don't propose to let that food go to waste, and he agrees."

There's the rub. The deal is already done, no matter what Xavier says, no matter what Farah had found.

Xavier hears his own voice, feeble and shaking, like a rabbit with a weasel's teeth in the nape of its neck.

"Some areas might benefit, perhaps," he whispers.

"Sure," Paronian agrees. "Preventive measures, a buffer. Meanwhile, we'll be preparing for the big one, OK?"

Terri taps it into her laptop. She's gloating.

Rose says, tight-lipped, "May we offer you more refreshment? Something a little different."

*

"Yes! Yes!" Nyala Freddy smacked his fist into his palm.

"At last," nodded Toby Kitchin, "We can *do* something."

"It is high time," agreed Christa, sitting up, "that we help the poor ones."

"I'm sure Xavier agrees really," offered someone else, and they all concurred: Xavier had just been holding out for the best terms. It was all for the best, the best possible, it was best to be *doing*.

So, yes, at the Resthouse the power had failed, the lights had failed, the fridge and the fans had stopped and the water was foul, and they cursed routinely as they felt obliged to. But at heart they were thrilled in an aggressive, pent-up way. Only Rose Price, who had brought the news, remained pensive. But that was just Rose.

Mr Mogga listened quietly. Rose noted that, now his poor hands were swaddled in clean white crêpe, he seemed calm, comfortable and happy. She felt her look drawn back to him often, and wondered why she'd taken so little note of him in the souk. He was not a striking man, far from it. He was not tall; he was readily dwarfed by any number of lofty Fur gentlemen. He was stocky, strong looking, but his expression was almost cherubic; his skin had a cool, silky quality. Rose wanted to run the back of her hand over Mogga's face.

When at last he spoke, his opinions seemed unfussed and positive. He was very well informed about the Emergency Programme: where had he learnt it all?

"It is wonderful what has been done," said Mogga.

"Hah!" scoffed Freddy, "tell me about that."

"Yes," Mogga obliged, "like the health posts. Some have had no medicines for two years, but now they have visits from our Nurse Lorna and our Doctor Maeve, and all the little ones are well and grow fat. So they rejoice."

Rose blinked; she never dared suppose that!

She went to the porch to light a cigarette. She looked across the sandpit of a yard to where the crone squatted scouring the noodle pan with grit and palm leaves. Behind Rose, the debate continued, and from among the voices that had grown sour with delay and aggravation, with being thwarted and opposed, there came again Mr Mogga politely dissenting and affirming, his words with an entirely different quality, a lightness, a spring, a nimbler step. Rose suddenly had an idea that, in a room full of irritation, one man was dancing.

At last they fell quiet in the gloom, some struggling to read by the light of warm, limp candles, two playing cards by a solar-charged lamp, others with their cassettes and their headphones and their music from home.

Mogga stood in the middle of the floor smiling in faintly bemused liking at everyone.

"Mogga!" called Rose Price brusquely, patting a bed in invitation. "Talk to me. There's nothing else to be done of an evening. Power fails every day. Might as well talk."

Mogga beamed at her and bustled up, perching on the bed's edge.

"You would like to discuss?"

"I'd like you to relax a minute," said the nutritionist, jutting her bony chin and blowing out smoke. Mogga smiled, accepting orders, as one must from a lady. He wriggled back across the bed until he rested against the blue-washed wall alongside Rose Price, his short legs jutting directly out in front of him and his hands upon his knees.

"Yes," he accepted, "sometimes we must relax. Then we can be more effective."

"Quite so," said Rose. "Leila, join us!"

They sat together: Rose Price, Mr Mogga, Leila Karim their agronomist.

"Tell us something," Rose demanded of Mogga. "Anything. Someone said you were a teacher."

"For seventeen years," he replied politely.

"Tell us about that. Tell us about your home. What's it like in the south? What about your parents?"

She blushed suddenly: there was a civil war, anything might have happened. But Mogga responded calmly.

"Miss Rose, why do you wish to know about my parents?"

Rose sucked hard on the cigarette so that it blazed and the ash fell.

"I don't mean to pry," she retracted hurriedly.

"You are not prying," responded Mogga kindly, "and I would like to tell you, if only to entertain you. But what?"

"I should like to know," interposed Leila, "what things made your father proud."

"Was he proud?" mused Mr Mogga.

PART TWO
Mogga and Leila

ONE

Long before Mogga's birth in the distant, tropical, southern province of Equatoria, his mother's spleen was already so large that it filled the left half of her abdomen. She had suffered from malaria so often that this organ, dedicated to the cleansing of broken cells from the blood, had become grossly distended. Like a civic landfill that cannot cope with the garbage, the spleen had, from infancy, swelled year by year in a despairing effort to sort good blood from bad. By adolescence it was already crowding her belly, displacing her viscera; when she became pregnant with little Mogga, there was scant room for the growing foetus. The village said later (when the boy's obliging nature became evident) that he'd stayed small so as not to cause his sickly mother grief – but she died nonetheless, shortly after the birth.

The baby dedicated himself to cheering his one remaining parent; he would roll and tumble before his father, Samuel, then look up to see the effect of these antics. Samuel Mogga was a beanpole of a man whose trousers did not reach his ankles, and whose limbs were jointed sticks that flapped and flopped like an articulated carpenter's rule. Samuel Mogga would stand peering at his progeny from nearly two metres overhead, blinking with paternal wonder – and little Mogga would recommence his farcical and unco acrobatics and his gurgling like a pretty stream in the spring rains, until, at last, Samuel Mogga smiled, bent his knee and put out an ineptly affectionate hand.

Little Mogga, ignorant coeval of Sudan's independence, passed his country's opening year in the care, first, of a village wet-nurse, then of the cook and the kitchen boy.

The two-room cement house that went with Samuel Mogga's headmastership of Iwenwe School stood in the upper corner of a gently sloping compound of ochre mud that turned greasy at the first touch of dew, and was drilled with the homes of a billion little creatures. Here, surrounded by a stoutly made head-high tangle of thorns, was safety. With the morning class assembled on logs before the blackboard under the shade tree, Samuel Mogga would turn to peer through his bottle-glass lenses and would see the naked child crawling on his small explorations across the gritty porch, piddling, fingering the warm lake, then wriggling onwards. Sometimes little Mogga would drop over the cement edge onto the dirt and set off towards the class as though to join in or entertain. Then the pupils would point and shriek with laughter, until the fat cook came waddling to bear the squirming boy back to the house.

Samuel Mogga took a bus south to Nimule for an 'upgrading'. Two weeks later, he returned. Little Mogga, squatting on the porch, saw the cook march across the compound to heave aside the old bed frame that served for a gate in the school's thorn fence. The toddler lurched to his feet to greet his father, and then sat down again, staring.

In his father's shadow, carrying a shopping bag made of woven blue plastic, stood a girl. She wore brown plastic slippers and a simple shift of cotton from which the red dye had been almost obliterated by sunlight. Her breasts were small and pert; her knees were scabby like an urchin's. She looked at Mogga with her chin jutted out in defiance, but her shoulders hunched in fear; her brow was furrowed in a stern frown, but her eyes were wide with apprehension. He sensed that she was appealing to him. So, from the first, little Mogga was predisposed to protect her.

She was a Ugandan. There was much coming and going across that border, but Mogga never learned why this teenager had thrown in her lot with his father. Had her own people rejected her? Had Samuel Mogga bought her? Had she offered herself? There was, in her pert manner, the hint of a losing gamble. When, in later life, he remembered her, it was for her loneliness.

Her people were Acholi: no Acholi had ever lived in Iwenwe. On one side of the slow brown river, in the thatched mud cones strung out along the road, everyone was of the Bari tribe. On the far bank skulked a handful of Azande families; Camp Azande, their place was called. Nobody welcomed an Acholi coming to Iwenwe, except Samuel Mogga and little Mogga. Samuel peered down at her, myopic and resolutely dutiful. In the house and compound, New Mother drew herself up and put her shoulders back. But, in public, she went shrinkingly.

She said very little at first. In the early morning, emerging from behind the curtain where she slept with Samuel Mogga, the girl went to the porch and, in silence, peeled yams at the cook's bidding. She went to the washhouse and soaped Samuel's thin grey trousers. Thinking herself alone, she sang in a whisper:

> *Baby, baby, baby,*
> *Where's your mama gone?*
> *She's gone to the well*
> *With a bucket and rope.*

Little Mogga did not understand a word of the Acholi rhyme, but the sweet melody pierced him. Cook did not sing; his father Samuel certainly did not sing. New Mother caught sight of little Mogga gazing at her, naked and potbellied, sucking a piece of roast yam. She fell silent, as though she feared a beating from the toddler, and she continued to knead the wet trousers in the white enamel basin with a green rim. Then she glanced up, smiled hesitantly and sang again, just loud enough for the child to hear.

> *Baby, baby, baby,*
> *Where's your mama gone?*

Still Mogga stared at her. He sucked his yam, rubbed one filthy grey-brown ankle with another, leaned his squashy little buttocks against the corner of the house and grinned back at her. At which, a touch of spirit came into her voice:

> *Baby, baby, baby,*
> *Your mama's gone for water.*
> *What has she found, baby?*
> *Your arse is full of flies!*

61

They beamed at each other. She sang it again, and Mogga giggled, sensing that he had played some part in her cheering up.

From then on, she sang to him every day. When at dusk he laid his head on her lap, she trilled happily:

> *The pretty girl's buttocks*
> *wiggle as she walks*
> *down the Nimule road.*

But when the village weeding gangs gathered in the fields, then no one came to help an Acholi girl in the school maize garden. On such evenings, she sang differently:

> *One day the slavers came for us -*
> *My brother fought them alone.*
> *No warrior stood by him.*
> *I saw him fall.*

Her eyes sank and her shoulders sagged. Little Mogga would sulk and scratch with a twig at the lines of ants marching across the kitchen yard, so as to share out the sadness.

He must do something to save her from her misery. He was senior here, for he had arrived before her, so it was his job to protect her and make her happy.

So he danced for her. He stamped his foot on the ground till she took notice. Then he began to gyrate, spinning unsteadily with his arms spread out like wings till he grew dizzy, and the girl stared in astonishment. He stopped, he teetered, demanding that she surrender to his merriment. He stamped again, he spun about – and looked at her. The girl patted her knee, uncertain, doubtful. Mogga beamed in triumph and the girl put down her knife and patted the rhythm with both hands on the old red dress over her thigh.

Such was always the end of the singing; whenever her grief took hold, Mogga would dance it out of her, capering on his chubby legs till she clapped with delight.

At dusk, Samuel Mogga would turn on the transistor radio, a tiny thing with a case of cream-coloured plastic, cracked across the corner, and the word *Realistic* in gilt italics on the front. Batteries were costly; the Eveready cells were warmed in the sun to extract last quivers of energy. Samuel eased the tuner till he grunted in satisfaction, cocked his head towards the *Realistic* and began muttering a dark commentary on the news. Sometimes there would be a man's voice wailing repetitively and echoing strangely; for Mogga, the acoustic of a mosque was quite alien. As Samuel listened to the Arabic a moment, frowning, Mogga would watch him, seeing his father's incomprehension tinged with unease, even fear. The boy longed to understand the sounds, so that he could offer comfort.

Five years later, little had changed at Iwenwe School except that Cook had left them and Samuel Mogga's sight had almost gone too, so he stopped teaching long division because it never came out right. The household was a small and quiet one.

Each morning, Mogga crossed the compound to the class logs. He was still a merry child, and he was clever with his head and his hands. Having learned to read, Mogga picked up the single mouldering arithmetic book; before Samuel knew it, Mogga had taught himself sums, with a little piping of pleasure when he got them right.

Mogga's ebullience and gleeful consumption of learning saved his father from utter despondency, but the years and the poverty wore away Samuel's spirit as surely as the rain eroded the mud-brick houses. The school's small flock of milking goats ran away, the white ants rendered the latrine unsafe, and devoured a boxful of new exercise books that he'd stored under his bed. When he carried this box to the excited, expectant class, he was mortified to find, under a crust of blue card, nothing but dust. Day by day, the shrinking resources, the faltering achievement, the dwindling classes cut away his soul. Had it not been for the unquenchable enthusiasm of his son, Samuel would simply have given up.

New Mother withdrew into herself. She bore no children of her own, and in her first decade at Iwenwe she made not a single friend except young Mogga. At the traders' tinsheds, she obtained goods but no response. In ceremonies, there was no place for her.

The women looked straight through the Acholi girl, as through mist. They paid more attention to the village ghosts.

At night, when Samuel took her to the bed behind the screen of grass matting, New Mother always glanced back to the child on his blankets on the far side of the room. It was a look of timid, embarrassed hope as though she asked the boy's protection.

Which Mogga gave her. If he saw a centipede or scorpion making for that secluded corner, he would fetch a stick and scrape it away. One night when his father was absent, he saw, from his own position low on the floor, a moonlit hunting spider – that spins no webs but rushes after its prey – now gyrating towards the girl's bed. Mogga leapt up, seized his stick and thrashed at the dark floor.

A moment later, New Mother was calling: "Eh, what is it? What is happening, what you doing?!"

She was out of bed, peering in alarm at the boy whacking with his stick – until she screamed, howling and hopping, falling back onto the bed, sobbing with pain from the spider's bite.

She lay in bed all the following day, moaning, while Mogga, dismayed, went again and again to the river for cold water, to put compresses on her foot.

Mogga brooded about this event and never forgot it. It contained, he sensed, a profound injustice both towards those he tried to protect, and towards him.

It was some days before New Mother sang again. Mogga feared that the spider's bite had silenced her. But it recommenced at last, the distracted crooning:

> *My brother lies in his grave*
> *and cries to me in my dreams.*
> *I hear that song at night*
> *And shiver, worse than cold.*

Sometimes she would look up, staring eagerly towards the fence as though a chattering procession of Acholi were passing there. But then he'd see her eyes drop slowly, till she took a breath and picked up the soap.

Samuel Mogga would watch her as she worked. The teacher would stand, spindly in the sunlight, his ankles bony grey between the broken shoes and the thin synthetic trousers, peering myopically as though waiting for an acknowledgement or a rebuke, but receiving neither.

*

One day in 1969, at the age of thirteen, Mogga was teaching the numbers to the younger children of Iwenwe. He had a talent for it; he made them laugh, he clowned, he drew faces in the numerals. As Samuel sat watching from the porch, an acquaintance came to call, an elderly gentleman carrying a black umbrella. He asked Samuel what the news portended for Iwenwe, what position they should now be adopting.

"Which news is that?" enquired the schoolmaster. (The *Realistic* had long since expired.)

The visitor, who had only come in order to be the first with the report, raised his eyebrows in rhetorical surprise. Thus it was that Samuel and his boy learned of the coup d'état of Colonel Jaafar Nimeiri.

Samuel Mogga resolved that, in such an uncertain world, the family should not keep all their eggs in one basket. He announced that his son would attend the Vocational Training School at Mateki. Mogga thought sadly of leaving New Mother with her songs unheard.

But she pre-empted him. There was unrest in Uganda, and people washed back and forth across Sudan's border. Many of these were Acholi, and word of their passage reached Iwenwe. One day, Samuel Mogga's wife vanished. Samuel asked everyone where she had gone: someone said that she'd been seen walking south. But no one wanted her back, and Samuel Mogga was too worn away to go after her. Indeed, he said very little about her disappearance.

It was young Mogga who felt it most, for he had, so long before, set himself to protect her. For some days he could be seen beyond the compound gate gazing down the red mud track that led away into the forest. His expression was sorrowful, but even more it was bewildered. He did not understand. Either his protection had failed, or she didn't want it.

*

Three years of his father's pleading and scheming brought Mogga to Mateki Vocational School, aged sixteen. From the outset, he was delighted. There was a carpentry shop with treadle-lathes from a Norwegian church fund and hand tools from a French charity, whose handles were massive chunks of transparent yellow plastic, which so fascinated the students that they bit at them repeatedly. Here, to their own astonishment, barefoot village girls in skimpy school shifts proved adept at turning bowls, while boys cut and knocked together joint stools, occasionally even selling a set of creaking chairs to some sweat-drenched political on tour who'd carry them away on his pickup. There was a tin-roofed shed with forges built out of a *Cottage Industries Manual for Hot Countries* printed in London. The forge fires were puffed by pedal power; one person could make a ploughshare unaided. To haul those ploughs there were two oxen (bought with Dutch money), massive animals brindled black on brown, with huge heads that seemed too heavy for their necks. They were the Principal's pride, the students' delight, the treasure of Mateki Vocational School, warm slow flagships that sailed majestically over the fields, trailing a heaving wake of pepper-scented loam. They were known in local cow-speak as 'the Ruddy-flanked One' and 'the Cold-lipped One'. Mogga smiled happily at the names as any Equatorian would, but the Principal worried what the French, Norwegians and Dutch would think; he declared that 'Victory' and 'Prosperity' were more suitable, and had these painted on a wooden signboard nailed to the corral gate. The students humoured him, and ignored him. Mogga, however, kept a prudent distance from the lumbering, stamping oxen, having no talent for cows.

Every evening, Mogga walked the boundary, skirting the fields till he came to a splendid old baobab tree that stood on a rise above Mateki township. From there he looked back and saw the simple mud-and-tin classrooms in the well-swept compound, poverty made neat. He saw the new farm sheds, where the girls had gathered and trimmed the thatch while the shouting boys had swarmed over the skeleton structure of crooks and boughs, tying down the thick bundles as the dust streamed in the sunbeams. He saw the netball courts they'd made, and heard his friends' laughter. He admired the kiln like a tall hat of dusky red that they'd built from the *Cottage Industries Manual* and which they fuelled with their own charcoal.

He thrilled to see plans on the printed page take on reality in the schoolyard. Though there was decay and disturbance everywhere in the country, what a future they could build, if only they could get the plans!

He studied for a year, at the end of which the Principal begged him to stay on, teaching. He was seventeen years old.

He was entirely junior: there were nine staff at the school. But whether through his charm and talent, or through creeping accidie, his elder colleagues were ever more ready to leave things in his hands. They were erratically paid, and had little time for their jobs; they had enough to do keeping their families fed, tilling their own small plots and chasing petty trade. The worse the condition of the country grew, the more people about him leaned on young Mogga's unusual energy and optimism. Week by week, the rural economy of Equatoria imploded, and the Principal of Mateki Vocational School found ever more compelling reasons to be absent. He'd say:

"Mogga will hold the fort!"

At first Mogga would grin shyly, his round and soon balding head bobbing deferentially on his small, stocky person. But the senior staff never made the least objection – for what benefit was there in work that paid neither salary nor status? They murmured that young Mogga had administrative talents. Soon it became an accepted thing: Mogga held the fort, while his colleagues followed their Principal's example, leaving their lesson plans with Mogga. You might have found them in the cross-border markets of Yei and Nimule or the back streets of Juba, where Sudan pounds and

Uganda shillings in gritty bundles reeking of goat still bought a man some *arigi* and pleasure.

Their absence presented Mogga with few problems; he showed undoubted flair for organisation. The more tricky the calculation – perhaps to get five classes in different skills under way with only two teachers between them – the more excited Mogga seemed. The more outrageous his colleagues' 'sick days' and 'paternity leave', the more enthusiastically Mogga would thumb through the 'Cottage Industries Manual'. Then he'd gather the Vocational students about him in a bright twitter of cheerfulness.

"Today is Design Day!" he would declare, setting them to turn a heap of bamboos into a wind-powered bird scarer. He took delight in their wildest notions:

"Yes, yes! The pigeons shall see this and drop dead of laughter."

The next morning he would announce:

"Today is Communications Day!"

By the evening they would have devised a burlesque to be played in Mateki market, propounding the merits of mechanical crop-minders to free the village children for school.

There was, in his merry face, in his quick eyes and humour, an absurd but contagious courage. The school workshops were soon littered with bamboo devices whose function one might spend weeks in deciphering. If the crop-eating pigeons of Mateki curiously failed to take fright and depart, still Mogga was content that innovation was flourishing.

Under Mogga's guidance, the Vocational students wove brilliant cloths in rather odd lengths, threw pots of indeterminate function, and spun, beat, planed, drilled, spoke-shaved and transplanted in every corner of the school. Some even became – with those gleaming yellow chisels and plentiful practice – quite presentable craftsmen. They were (the Principal would say grandiloquently on his surprise visits) the seed corn of Equatoria's bright future harvest.

But, year on year, that harvest was stunted. In Khartoum far to the north, Sudan's élite looked away, and the Arab ministers washed their hands of the dismal southern tribes. The impoverished Bari and Azande, the struggling Shilluk and the Banda with their tiny sorghum fields, they could pay no taxes, and Khartoum was in no mind to waste scarce funds bailing out simple woodlanders. When the Dinka cattle fell sick, with their eyes pouring infected tears, their tongues raw with ulcers and their breath foul, there was plenty of rinderpest vaccine in the Ministry refrigerators – but the refrigerators had been turned off for lack of fuel a year before. No one was spraying tsetse flies, no one was inoculating children; the Immunisation Department's last car had its rear axle up on bricks, and the staff had gone to their own villages to salvage the millet crop. Things fell apart.

"Take the reins, Mogga!" the Principal of Mateki School beseeched him once again, clapping Mogga on the shoulder. The Principal, who had not been paid for eleven months, vanished entirely. Now aged twenty-four, Mogga's head gleamed with a shiny baldness that bespoke determination – while being rather charmingly offset by the black curly tufts over either ear. In 1983, the year that his de facto direction of the school became official, there was a mutiny at the peculiarly nasty, rat-infested barracks of Bor. A civil war began.

*

And yet, even as the country's divide hardened, Mogga made a friend of an Arab, the loneliest man in Equatoria. He was a Government forestry officer, one of the sprinkling of northerners that Khartoum posted to the south, a token of National Unity. But he was powerless. The people of Mateki cut what they liked from the forests, where and when they liked: the young man had no way of stopping them. His salary too was months in arrears, there was no word from the Khartoum Ministry, and his repeated petitions to return home all met with stony refusal.

And so, unofficially, he had become a shopkeeper. He had borrowed money from his uncle, a fatter, wealthier man who traded from the railhead town of Wau. But the nephew's efforts to set up in business and acquire substance had gone badly wrong; an investment had backfired or a consignment had gone astray – who really knew? Mogga heard that Tariq the young Arab had made a glorious fool of himself. The boy had appealed to his uncle: that corpulent, soft-bellied but hardheaded man had bailed him out, but at a terrible price. Tariq was stuck, flogging cans of cooking oil, plastic utensils, tin buckets and hoes delivered by truck to Mateki, a town where he was detested by everyone. He never earned enough either to resign his Government post or to pay off his debt.

Mogga was idling in a back lane one day when he heard a sound that startled and stopped him. The sound was plastic, almost *Realistic*, a wailing in a huge walled space. He stood quite still and listened.

He saw Tariq, radio in hand, crossing the marketplace, marked out by his skinny Arab look, his glancing over his shoulder, his helplessness. Instantly, Mogga felt an urge to protect, to shield. Mogga followed the young man to his house; Tariq thought he had come to curse or assault him. But Mogga beamed cheerily and came away with an arrangement for Tariq to sell at his shop the wooden bowls from the school lathes, the stools and pots they made. It was all most satisfactory, but for Tariq it mattered far more that Mogga sat with him and listened to the radio, and listened to Tariq's desperate, yearning talk.

In return, Mogga quenched a burning curiosity: he asked Tariq to teach him Arabic. At the request, the young man's eyes had grown moist with excitement, with gratitude, with enthusiasm. The lessons, and then the conversations, continued for seven years.

*

Raids began, in themselves nothing new. For centuries the cattle nomads of the northwest, the tribes of Rizeigat and Misiriya Zurug, the Malwal, Ngok and Rufaa had poached and preyed. The thefts, rustlings and vengeful forays had suited central Government nicely: a neat mechanism by which the unruly tribes exhausted each other. Now, when the raiders came south into Bahr al-Ghazal and stole the Dinka herds, the Government (in whose eyes all Dinka were rebels) took no notice. They ignored the reported nature of the Dinkas' gunshot wounds: vicious, from long-range bullets exploding on exit from the body and tearing out large masses of tissue; the work of modern high velocity rifles. They referred to the northern boys as 'militia'. The people called them *fursan*, the 'cavalry'. They rode horses and strong, fast mules.

It was rumoured that bands of *fursan*, with their mounts, were transported in government trains to strike where least expected. They appeared in the Dinka villages at dawn; the people were shot as they ran, or were herded into barns and byres that were then ignited with rocket-grenades. Millet fields were torched or trampled by laughing riders; fruit trees were hacked and broken; herds and humans were hauled away and sold. Across the south, trade took fright, all balance and all tranquillity ended.

*

A timid tap on the door, like the tip of a branch on a window-pane, so quiet that at first Mogga does not notice. He is sitting in his spartan, blue-painted office, laboriously composing a report for the Norwegian sponsors, absent-mindedly scratching his scalp with the blunt end of his pencil. The tapping comes again, and he looks up as the door edges open.

"Oh, Marcello! Welcome, come in!"

A very tall young man enters. He has a high forehead and his skull seems overlarge, like a swollen balloon above his eyes. A star graduate, the best carpenter of his year. He shuffles awkwardly into the room, murmuring obsequious greetings. Mogga peers up at him in sudden unease. The young man Marcello says nothing, though his head nods and bobs like a bird's. To fill the silence, Mogga says:

"So, you are come to see us?"

"Sir . . ."

"And are they pleased with you at Lawila? Have you been building for them? What have you done?"

Marcello offers, with both hands, a shred of grimy paper; Mogga spreads it on his desk, slowly, so as not to tear the rubbed folds. It is a letter from the elders of the Church of Our Lady of Perpetual Succour, Lawila.

"We give thanks that Master Marcello has learned the trade of joinery so well. Now he can mend the roof of our health post and make the beds that we are needing urgently. But we are sad that our situation is dangerous now. Also for young persons it is dangerous, for reason of *fursan*. So he cannot be safe here now. So we tell Master Marcello to return to you and ask that he receive more schooling for now."

Mogga stares at this letter. He can think of nothing to say but, "So, you are come back."

In succeeding days and months, Marcello is followed by a steady trickle of Mateki graduates, the 'seed corn of Equatoria' who are hunted now on account of their education. What can Mogga do? He cannot drive them away to their deaths. He tries to devise work for them, he writes to Norway, maybe they can sell their produce . . .

By 1990, Mateki Vocational School has become a camp, a refuge, groaning under a weight of accumulating expertise, with two score redundant young artisans milling in the compound watched from the office by Mogga, their protector.

*

Word came that his father was ailing. When Mogga reached Iwenwe, Samuel was already buried at the forest's edge where the graves were marked by no more than a heap of stones to keep the wild pigs from devouring the corpses. Mogga stood alone, examining the stones and the heavy, red soil: raw as flesh, thought Mogga, who considered the small space now occupied by his father's long limbs: the knees must be drawn up to the belly.

In the school compound, the grass was advancing from the perimeter. Mogga looked at the decaying logs on which Iwenwe's children had sat in rows, where he himself had sat. He surveyed the open ground pounded by his dancing for New Mother. That ground was as smooth as skin, watertight and impenetrable – until it was split open by the grass.

The schoolhouse was closed with a small Chinese padlock.

"The police came," said the neighbour. "They locked the house because it is Government property."

Mr Mogga was lodging in the man's store hut, bedding upon a pile of hessian. The neighbour handed Mogga a fibre suitcase split down one corner: his father's moveable goods. Of his mother with her distended spleen, no trace. Of the Acholi girl that his father had brought home, of her dusty, lonely eyes, her strange tongue and her songs – no trace, except in Mogga's head.

He set off walking the three days back to Mateki, carrying his father's suitcase.

He approached the township through the pale green millet shambas, the crop standing high enough to screen the paths, especially if you were a stocky figure like Mr Mogga. Here and there he must jump the little irrigation ditches, which in these hot days were stagnant, green and foaming. As he approached the first houses he caught a taint in the air that disturbed him: smoke, but not of cooking fires; more acrid. Then he noted the silence: no dogs, no cockerels, no mother calling or child squealing. No pounding or hammering, no talk. He stopped, tipping his head, his skin beginning to prickle.

He caught a sudden sound of bare feet running, slapping on mud, and a single shot that trembled the millet stalks. Then a tearing of brush as a fence gave way, and an old woman's screech of outrage, cut short. Silence again. On the narrow dyke between the millet and the ditch, Mogga stood motionless, peering into the algae, straining to hear. Somewhere there began a heavy, desolate moaning. Distantly, a child started screaming at the top of its lungs, over and over. Something collapsed with a crackle and whoosh of fire, and a creaking clatter that he knew was a tin roof falling. He raised his eyes and saw a cloud of black flecks twizzling up over the crop. He moved a few yards along the path, nearing a corner.

Then he saw a foot, protruding from among the densely planted millet. A man's leg, twisted at an awkward angle. He saw the buttocks in tight red football shorts, and a mud-smeared blue T-shirt. He could not see the face. Mogga began to tremble unstoppably, hurrying to step round the foot that jutted across the path. He was about to rush past, into the village, when he glanced back. Now he could see the face that appeared to strain with effort, the mouth agape and the eyes staring into the millet crop. The man had fallen and rolled or had been kicked, for his cheek was covered in earth that clung also to the lashes of his right eye.

It was Marcello, his prize carpenter.

Mogga entered Mateki and found the women and children, keening or drifting in shock. There were no men anywhere. At the far end, Tariq's shop was ablaze and Tariq was behind the counter.

*

"Sir," said his neighbour, "These are dirty Dinka people. Have a care for your personal effects."

Mogga's effects amounted to nothing but his little red nylon rucksack, containing his other pair of underpants and a *Readers Digest* of his father's. He considered the Dinka, who swarmed over the train like cockroaches on a dog's carcass. They sat on the roof of the long wooden boxcars, they squatted on the couplings. Some had forced open the stiff wagon doors and hauled their relations inside, though the interiors were sweltering. By the tawny water below the bridge, the last families were stuffing their goods into plastic fertilizer sacks or straw baskets, before swarming up past the grumbling diesel to find a perch, grazing their shins and cutting their feet on rough slats and dirty bolts. From every wagon, helping hands stretched down, accompanied by a tremulous half-throttle chatter of frightened, hungry people whose diaphragms were too fluttery for shouting.

"Let us take our place, Sir, let us not be left behind. Here it is every man for himself."

The man was appealing to him. Mogga did not see why he, out of all these hundreds, should be appealed to. Then he understood that the young man was seeking an ally. He was Indian, slightly made and, among the ragged Dinka, his clothes stood out by their neatness. Perhaps he believed the Dinka would stamp on his hands and push him off the train. Mogga thought the fellow was another small shopkeeper. The Indian scattered about him the anxious and aggrieved glances of someone subjected to petty pilfering from his store.

The Dinka did not look menacing, just nervous. They did not look like the rebels the Government called them; they looked lost. Once they had been warriors, cattlemen of the savannah whose conical brushwood houses had no compound fences because the inhabitants were so ferocious and their possessions stripped to essentials. Their scant goods were now pathetic; their clothes – unaccustomed shorts and blouses scrounged for the journey to the city – hung about them in tatters. Their villages were burned, their cattle shot; they had nowhere to go except away. Yesterday they had been a proud community; today they squabbled over that little dish of meal, that dried-up cake of maize, that precarious foothold on the wagon.

But their numbers gave some strength, for they had blocked the line at Jaula Bridge by sitting on it, knowing that the train must slow there for the crossing.

"You appreciate, Sir, that we must take care. Society has broken down here."

"Not so," cried Mogga, suddenly breaking his silence. "There is a deal being done, look."

He was watching the front of the train. Those who blocked the line were as anxious as any to gain a good position on the wagons, yet the moment they stood up from the rails, the bridge would be clear and the train might pull away. But the engineer did not open his throttle when the crowd got to its feet; he waited resignedly, seeing that matters were beyond his control. Besides, the train had survived its journey through rebel territory to Wau and was returning empty, so why not give them a ride? The last Dinka got off the rails and squeezed onto the roof.

Mogga observed this carefully. Then he heard *Sir! Sir!* being called, and looked up. The young Indian shopkeeper had secured a patch on the rear wagon, was gesturing Mogga to follow up the black ladder. Mogga contemplated the huge greasy coupling. He was afraid that the train might jolt, might toss him under those enormous wheels with their great flanges polished by thousands of kilometres of slow, hot grinding. He imagined his body crushed, he visualised his abdomen bisected and the halves dropping either side of the rail – and he tweaked up the shoulder straps of the red nylon knapsack and climbed quickly. Oddly, it was the first time in all Mogga's thirty-one years that he had climbed a ladder. It was narrow and vertical; one could not rest there, only hang. He did not enjoy the novelty.

He saw a small space on the convex roof and the Indian beckoning urgently, pushing aside the poor belongings of the Dinka. Mogga stepped over sacks and limbs to reach it. He was about to fold his own legs under him when the engine moved. A slow-motion rattle ran through the train of eighteen wagons. He heard it coming, coupling to coupling, but still the jolt knocked him off his feet and he fell across a thin woman who cried out in alarm. As he attempted to regain his place, he tumbled over her a second time, and she cursed him.

The diesel smoked and roared and they moved onto the bridge, creeping above the river, over the enormous girders. They moved so slowly that Mogga could read, embossed on the steel: *Donaldson, Falkirk*. The red oxide paint had almost all been scoured away by sand in the wind. Mogga shuddered at the thought of scratching his fingernails over that surface. The train slowed, almost stopping halfway across the water. Along its length, a few Dinka stood up on the roof to see.

With a flatulent growl from the distant engine, the couplings banged with another violent jerk. Mogga heard it coming, was ready for it – but from halfway along the train came cries and screams. He glimpsed a tottering black shape that struck the high girders, smacked onto the timber baulks beside the line, flailed through the air and twizzled into the water, splashing, disappearing. The Dinka shrieked and pointed – but there was nothing to be seen, and the train rolled on without compassion.

"If these Dinka will not sit still . . . !" expostulated the young

Indian, reducing the death to a nuisance, an irritation. "These people have no sense."

Mogga looked at him, and it seemed suddenly to occur to the shopkeeper that he was perched on a wagon roof with several score of those senseless primitives who might casually topple him into the river also. But no one bothered to reprimand or murder him. The Indian fingered a tear in the side of his shirt.

"This has happened as I have climbed the ladder," he lamented in a low voice. "A good shirt, but I do not have a needle." He appealed to Mogga. "This shirt is imported, you know. It is no cheap African thing."

In his mind's eye, Mogga saw his father's trousers, always too short on that human beanpole, the grey-brown ankles always showing. Mogga tried to keep his image of Samuel upright, at the blackboard perhaps. But the figure persisted in lying down, clammy, shaking the iron bed with malarial rigors.

He felt his scalp growing tender in the strong sun, and from the knapsack took his one handkerchief, knotted it and placed it over his baldness. On all sides, the depopulated savannah stretched, termite mounds its only mountains. It was so flat, thought Mogga, that it seemed the horizon itself was out of sight, that you'd have needed to climb a ladder just to see that.

Along the decrepit track, the goods train with its top dressing of Dinka crept as gingerly as five hundred tonnes can creep. Mogga had heard that derailments were common: beneath the wagons, the rails flexed and sagged into the untended ballast. He wondered if, 100 kilometres ahead of them, there might not be another train rumbling equally slowly southward down this single line. Was there anywhere to pass? How would either driver know to wait? Mogga's mind filled with pointless worries. The Dinka on the wagon tops fell silent also, and contemplated a future in the shanties of Khartoum.

"They do not talk, Sir," said the young shopkeeper, "because they do not know where they are going. These Dinka know nothing of Khartoum except the name and that people go there when there is nowhere else."

People who understood only conical huts and green millet on a red soil; whose landmarks were fat baobab trees; whose daily clothing was a powdering of dust on back, breast and genitals; whose every second thought was of cattle. Mogga imagined the train shuddering to a halt in the Khartoum railyards and the Dinka clambering down. What would they do with themselves? What would he do himself?

"Of course," said Mogga, "A desperate thing it must be always, to leave home."

"No, Sir!" said the shopkeeper. "My people do not think so, you see? We have left India to seek our fortune in Mombasa. When it was crowded in Mombasa, we came to Nairobi. When there was competition in Nairobi, we came to Uganda. When Mr Amin has thrown us out of Uganda, we have come to this Sudan; it is not so hard to move on when need be. Never too attached, Sir! Never waste your effort on a useless place. Move on!"

Which was why the fellow was so sadly in need of friends, thought Mogga. Just like New Mother.

The Indian seemed consoled by his own little lecture; he reclined, stretching out down the roof's curve. Mogga remained cross-legged, considering this terribly certain young man. Mogga had seldom felt certain about anything, except his duty to protect New Mother, and Mateki School, and Marcello and Tariq.

Mogga shuffled his buttocks round so that he was facing forward. There at the peak of the wagon's roof he sat, with a hand-kerchief over his skull, face into the breeze, which, at this slow rate of progress, cooled him pleasantly. Like a comical black tufted Buddha, his hands in his lap and a child's red nylon knapsack on his back, he rode among the Dinka into the hot tracts of central Sudan.

For two days the ponderous train heaved northward. They rumbled across the wide yellow shallows of the Bahr al-Arab, and on. Beside the track, the soil turned drier, dustier, sandier. The trees changed shape, their crowns losing their rounded fullness, flattened by the pounding sun. The thorns grew longer and harder.

In the distance, a dun-coloured haze blurred the horizon.

"You see that?" said the shopkeeper sprawled to Mogga's left, propped up on an elbow. "It is the sort of storm they have, Sir: dust only!"

He regarded it with a gloomy frown.

"A hard, hot country," he mused.

In front of Mogga on the roof clustered the remnants of a family: the thin, worn woman over whom Mogga had tumbled, and two skinny little girls. One of them was scared of him and tucked herself behind her mother's arm. The other now met his gaze. Mogga put out his two hands in front of his crossed legs, two fingers of each hand held downwards like the long limbs of two dancers. He made those two little figures dance together for the watching child, kicking out straight or lifting the knuckle 'knees', skipping side by side or turning and dancing face to face as Mogga sang to her in Acholi:

> *The pretty girl's buttocks*
> *wiggle as she walks,*
> *down the Nimule road.*

The Dinka child peeped at him, edged closer to her mother, and watched some more. Mogga thought he'd drawn a blank but she suddenly gave him a toothy grin. She's smiling, thought Mogga, she's smiling, and she's going to the shanty camps!

So the long train with its glaze of people rumbled northward, while the air about them desiccated.

*

At a junction on the edge of Kordofan, the line forked: west for 350 kilometres to Nyala in Darfur, or 600 kilometres northwest to the White Nile, another 100 kilometres across to Sennar on the Blue Nile, and a final 250 kilometres north to Khartoum – many days at a hot painful creep all the way. The very thought made the engine judder and overheat and belch blackly. They stopped to rest both driver and diesel.

Two hundred yards away in a siding there was another train stopped. Mogga saw horses and mules tied to fences or to the ironwork of the wagons. There were knots of men also, but they showed little interest in the new train arriving. Mr Mogga remembered horses that travel by train.

The flock of Dinka on the roof climbed down, frantic for water. There was a deep borehole, and two big galvanised tanks into which the water might gush to quench the thirst of goats and camels. But there was little hope that the pump would be started for a few hundred Dinka. There was, though, a well nearby, a simple pit edged with timbers deeply slotted by cords that looked like a mouth with cracked lips. There stood a man hoping to hire out his rope and leather bucket, one pound a dip, but the Dinka spread like oil through the rail yard and were soon shouldering him aside, swinging old tins on lengths of wire and rough cord down the dark, splashy orifice.

"See how they fight over water, Sir!"

The Indian frowned, his hand gestures decaying from elegant exposition to an angry flap.

"Ah, no," retorted Mogga, "they cooperate, look! That waterman has been made to stand aside, and the Dinka share their wire and tin. Everyone is drinking."

"Oh dear, Sir," sighed the shopkeeper, fearful that Mogga was lost to reason. "Indeed, Sir, I would like to suggest to you . . ."

Mogga was cautiously lowering himself over the end of the wagon onto that awkward narrow ladder. He too needed to drink and ease his cramped legs. The Indian continued talking to the sinking pate, his voice rising as Mogga dropped downwards.

". . . I have some small funds. Do you have funds? I see *dukas* by the station where beans and bread . . ."

Mogga stepped gingerly off the ladder, slipping down to the sleepers, knocking his elbow on the wagon's buffer. He walked across the dirt to the shade of the office, resting momentarily against an overturned barrow. A straggle of brushwood stalls lined a road leading into the small town whose secluded brick compounds were so unlike the thorn villages of Equatoria. He wondered if lonely women sang strange foreign songs in these compounds.

The Dinka flocked around the well; extracting water with tins and wire was slow work. Some had found scrap wood and had lit fires between three or four rocks to boil the handfuls of meal that they carried in knots of cloth. Always, the Dinka looked about them, watchful. Near the borehole, a herd of camels stood patiently. Mogga knew nothing about camels, but he thought them weird-looking and seemingly in poor condition. There was a droop in their necks and their coats were drab, with patchy mange on their flanks where the ribs showed. Around them, tall men in long cotton shifts stood minding the herd, eyeing the Dinka.

Mogga wondered who constituted authority in the junction town. One man in a frayed grey-green uniform was drinking in the shade of a tea stall near the station. The three train-crew were there also, seated on low stools with bowls of gristly stew that they gobbled urgently. From every stall, the ragged uncouth Dinka from the south were scrutinised by men who considered themselves to be proud Arabs. There was stillness, a mid-afternoon tiredness. Mogga debated spending a little of his reserves on a cigarette.

He saw the Indian shopkeeper seeking him out, approaching the shadows where Mogga stood. Mogga's heart sank a little, and he felt an impulse to slip behind the building. Too late; the man saw him, grinned sheepishly, and turned his way. But as the Indian came near, he stopped short, and everyone's attention switched to the front of the train.

Over the line and around the engine came a pack of men with swirling grubby robes and bandoliers over their breasts. Their voices were raised; they carried rifles; a few rode strong mules or ponies at a quick trot along the train. They were yelling in Arabic and the Dinka recoiled, gathering up their children and their pans and retreating hurriedly to their wagons. Some crept underneath, to hide behind the massive wheels. But the rifleman screamed and poked with their guns until the Dinka came out and stood in terrified perplexity, looking round for their village neighbours. A few scrambled quickly up to the roof, but the gunmen clubbed at any more who tried to climb, pointing their rifles at those who now crouched exposed on the rooftops till they came down again.

"Rizeigat!" said the shopkeeper, now at Mogga's side, in a staccato chatter, "militia of the Rizeigat people. They have come by train, Sir, taking Dinka cattle, taking slaves. These are very irregular troops, Sir."

Mogga frowned at the guns: none of the usual rusty Enfields and old muskets of the back country arsenal. These were all of a type, modern, with grey plastic stocks. Issued by someone exploiting the habitual hatreds of the tribes? The shouting redoubled as the Rizeigat whipped up their own strutting bravado. The Dinka clustered nervously in front of the wagons, pulling their children to their sides. They clutched their scruffy bags of belongings, waiting.

The Rizeigat gestured toward the wagons, commanding these southern animals to open the sweltering wooden boxes. When the Dinka didn't move, the blows came, rifle butts smacking into their faces until blood glistened on black skin. Then they obeyed. Down the long train, the trundling and clattering of roller doors revealed the dark, baking interiors. The Rizeigat shouted again, calling the Dinka filthy rebels; the Dinka began to climb into the wagons. Children were lifted up bawling, parents scrambled after, and the rifle butts came again if they were slow, thudding into flanks and spines, bruising and wounding.

"They cannot be shut in there," said Mogga. "Without water, they cannot bear that for long."

The train driver, an Omdurman Arab, dithered uncertainly fifty yards off. Some of the Rizeigat spotted him and shouted furiously, though whether to come to his cab or to stay clear was unclear, for the man didn't move.

"Sir, maybe these Rizeigat only want the Dinka out of their sight. They will send them in the wagons a few miles only and they can come out again. Sir, how shall *we* travel? This is a question that is now concerning me."

Mogga stared at the tumult. Arguments had begun, some of the previously cowed Dinka now beginning to protest. The men and women were in front of their families, trying to stand their ground before the militiamen. They earned only more blows and fell with broken heads, bleeding copiously into the dirty sand by the railway track.

"Oh, look at this now!" cried Mogga. His legs trembled, he felt sick. He winced as an argumentative Dinka man just thirty yards off received a rifle butt in his teeth and staggered back against his womenfolk. They collapsed against the iron wheels in a shrieking cluster, the Rizeigat towering above them.

"We must do something here!" cried Mogga. He stepped out of the shadow of the station building.

"Sir!" shrieked the shopkeeper, "Sir, do not even think . . ."

Mogga walked forward, gathering speed with his determination.

"Sir, I beg of you!" Weeping with anxiety, the young man lurched out of the concealing shadow in Mogga's wake. Mogga raised one hand like a bishop and bellowed at the militiamen:

"I protest! I protest at . . ."

The nearest Rizeigat turned and saw him. As Mogga opened his mouth again, a man jabbed the barrel of his rifle into Mogga's stomach. Winded, he fell to his knees and retched. The Rizeigat seized his arms to haul him to the wagons.

"This man is not your Dinka! This man is not your Dinka!" the Indian trilled. "This man is not your Dinka!"

Mogga felt himself falling against a solid wall of noise. The flesh of his stomach was deeply bruised by the gun barrel and the pain made his head spin. He heard the Rizeigat bawl: *Stand up! Stand up!* He felt their fingers on his upper arms, gripping so hard he feared they'd strip the muscles off the bone. He half-rose, then fell again and near-toppled his captors. He dimly heard the shopkeeper begin an insistent refrain: "This man is a Government officer. This man is in the employ of the Government. This is an official person!"

As Mogga tried once more to stand, he heard a dissenting voice among them, felt their hold on his arm slacken. There came a new sound that made him tremble, then vomit: first one, then a hot splattering of shots, very loud, very close.

The fingers tearing into his muscles loosed him and Mogga tumbled forward onto the dirt. In that instant, the Rizeigat lost interest in Mogga. The shopkeeper cried again, "Get up, Sir, come away, Sir, come away, please!" The shooting came again and Mogga looked up towards the train.

Almost all the Dinka were now inside the open wagons, some at the doorways, some out of sight, cowering. By the engine, Rizeigat were gathered in a tight knot, jabbering together. They ran along the train, and in their arms they carried bundles of fodder seized from the camel yard, soaked in gleaming diesel oil. There was smoke, and the flaming bundles were being tossed into the wooden wagons, and flame and filthy black smoke were belching from the doorways. From within came shouts of rage and disbelief. The Rizeigat waited, facing the blazing wagons, watching the dark doorways. The first scorched figures appeared, leaping, throwing themselves into the air, men flinging themselves into the sunshine, a gaunt mother shrieking pleas for her two daughters – and the riflemen shouted and howled with laughter, the bullets smacking into the Dinka as they jumped one by one, lurching in mid-air with limbs thrown outwards, tumbling.

"Oh, Sir, *please!*"

The young shopkeeper hauled at Mogga's bruised arms until they fell into the shade of the station building. Sobbing, Mogga slumped on the concrete, unable to look back at the train. It was, in any case, disappearing in a welter of black smoke out of which came a crackling that was wood burning, and bones snapping, and assault rifles at their work.

*

It was days before Mogga spoke again. The young shopkeeper had vanished. Clutching the little red nylon knapsack, Mogga rode out of town on the first lorry that the Rizeigat allowed to leave the transport souk. As it happened, the lorry was travelling not north-east to Khartoum but westward through the desert to Nyala in Darfur. Mogga had merely proffered money, had not enquired as to its destination. Thus it was that he came to Darfur, the west of Sudan and the very centre of Africa, where he learned that a famine was expected daily and that a team of foreigners were seeking to employ competent persons. So he took a job at an office where they said they'd recently lost a very decent young man in an ambush on the road from Nyala, and which had in its compound, for reasons Mogga could not imagine, a boat propped on its side against the wall.

TWO

When he'd been only a week in the Agency's employ, Mogga returned Fauzi's piano. He came to Fauzi's gate, early evening, holding it out. Fauzi blinked in astonishment.

"I was out in the villages beyond Tawila," smiled Mogga, "where Miss Christa sent me, and look what I have found."

Fauzi almost burst into tears. He took the piano to him like a child taking a favourite soft toy back to his bosom.

A few days later, Dr Maeve lost a tyre.

It went from right outside the Resthouse. The theft occurred during an evening meeting of the entire team, who had all driven in from desert outposts for a weekend of bickering that gave Xavier a sore head. Six white Land Rovers were drawn up in the sand outside the perimeter wall. The back street was unlit; deep dust muffled footfalls. The staff drivers had unloaded the roof racks, the sand-ladders, the jerrycans of diesel and water, the tarps and tools, had locked it all inside the vehicles and then drifted off to the souk for a meal. So the thieves had slunk up in the shadows to Dr Maeve's Land Rover at the back of the line. With a knife they'd hacked through the rubber mount of a small rear window, opened the back door and removed a brand new spare tyre – one of the rarest, most precious commodities in all Darfur.

The drivers, full of rice and fried egg, discovered this two hours later. They came sheepishly tapping at the Resthouse door, calling softly to the old watchman by his little charcoal brazier. They hovered by the latrine, coughing and murmuring.

Eight Europeans and two Sudanese sat in the cool yard, around a low table messy with snacks and green sodas. Xavier, with a vein throbbing visibly on his high forehead, urged his young team to be constructive, but they were fighting their corners. They had their individual patches of the province, and each thumped the table: "No one starves in my territory, not on my watch!"

So they bickered, demanding a greater share of the roadworthy vehicles, of the scant fuel, the coming food, or more than their share, producing reasons and rhetoric why 'their' villages were most at risk.

It was doing Xavier's head in.

"For pity's sake," he exploded after an hour of argument, "this is a disaster relief team, not a competition! If there has to be a food distribution at all, which I would much rather there wasn't, then we are going to monitor it in a professional manner. And I can tell you now, if I think the distribution is not working out, I shall insist on Khartoum calling a halt."

Taken aback, they bit their tongues and deferred to his authority, but just for a while. They had heard his doubts and they sensed that his position was weak; the food *was* coming, and if Xavier Hopkins didn't like that . . .

Thus, most of the team were too excited to observe that Mogga, the new man from the south, had stood up, had gone to ask the drivers what was wrong. Rose Price noticed, and twisted round in her gaunt, skinny way to look, and Toby Kitchin called:

"What's up, Mogga?"

Then everyone was in the street shining torches at the slashed rubber of the window, consoling Maeve, cursing the drivers, and threatening to sack them all. (Recruitment of competent men had been hideous with labour law and traffic regulations – in the dunes of western Sudan! – and expensive in pay-offs, so the drivers felt safe in their jobs. Still: a nasty moment.)

The police would not move until morning. That night, each driver and turnboy slept uneasily in their vehicle.

In the dawn chill, young Musa stepped down from the third Land Rover in line. Wrapped in a thin blanket, yawning and shivering, he urinated against the wall, stared at the ground a moment, and then rushed to wake the driver of the violated car. A moment later, they were hurrying down the street. The stolen tyre had been rolled away; the zigzag print of the tread was still sharp in the dewy sand. They followed around corners and down a narrow lane, to where the track vanished under the steel gate of a compound not 300 yards distant.

They went straight to police headquarters near the banks of the dry town *fula*, not bothering to wake the team. By the time the Europeans had woken, lit the charcoal stoves and smeared leathery bread with lurid red jam, the drivers were back, on a jeep top-heavy with armed men. Before tea was brewed, the thieves were under arrest.

"Oh dear," said Mogga.

"Marvellous!" said Xavier, deciding on a cash reward for the turnboy Musa. "We'll have the tyre back by lunchtime. What's the problem?"

"I'm not sure," murmured Mogga unhappily. Mid-morning, Xavier was summoned. He looked around for someone to accompany him and interpret.

"If you wish," offered Mr Mogga, "I can assist you."

Xavier peered at him. He realised that, when he'd hired Mogga, he'd not seriously credited the man's claim to speak Arabic.

"Let me do this," said Mogga.

"Oh, right," said Xavier hesitantly.

He might have asked, how is it possible? It was no more likely that a southern Sudanese should speak good Arabic than that a Cockney should be fluent in Gaelic. But Xavier needed help and Mogga was smiling quietly, confidently.

They drove past the cracked expanse of the *fula* and walked into the police station side by side: Xavier Hopkins, taller than any policeman, his pale and bony face bearing a robust conk and fringed by thin, straw-coloured hair; Mogga, five-foot-three, stocky and strong with twinkling eyes and a gleaming head.

They were kept waiting in a lean-to passageway enclosed by chicken wire. Smirking constables in black boots and khaki strolled past with carbons of depositions. Then they were taken to the duty officer. In the corner, a young policeman clacked reports into a flimsy portable typewriter. Mogga and Xavier sat on wooden chairs in front of the desk, Musa standing behind them, terrified.

"We have taken prompt action, you see," said the officer, feeling for a proper balance of courteous efficiency and manly disdain.

"May we take back our tyre?" asked Xavier, who was aiming for dignity without tactless self-confidence.

"No," replied the officer, "it is evidence."

Xavier looked questioningly at Mogga. Curious, he thought; I hardly know the chap, and I'm looking to him for guidance . . .

"You must make a denunciation," said the officer.

"Certainly," Xavier murmured glumly; they'd be here for hours.

The junior clicked out the curls and serifs on the Arabic typewriter, and then offered it for signature. Young Musa, fingers creeping from word to word, read the document to Mogga who translated for Xavier. Then they were dismissed – but the officer signalled to Mogga and mumbled something at him.

"What did he say?" enquired Xavier, not liking Mogga's frown.

"You see," said Mogga, "we have *sharia* law now."

"Yes?" nodded Xavier impatiently.

"These young men who have taken our tyre are thieves," Mogga continued. Xavier raised an eyebrow. Mogga added, "Which means amputation."

"Ah," groaned Xavier.

"Actually, cross amputation," Mogga went on, "left foot, right hand. A Muslim eats with his right hand. After shitting, he wipes his bottom with his left. He cannot touch food with his left hand, so amputation of the right can make him very hungry."

"Oh Lord," said Xavier.

The Programme team didn't like it either.

"Our business is to prevent famine," averred Toby Kitchin, pompous and earnest, "not to have people starve with their hands chopped off."

"*We're* not chopping anything," said Nurse Lorna, wringing her hands as though to check their fixing. "The law's the law."

"But Toby's right," Rose Price breathed through her cigarette. "Never mind the logic, it's how it will look."

89

"It won't make us any friends, will it?" roared Nyala Freddy, who always roared. "Sudanese mutilated for our sake!"

"But they're criminals."

"They're poor," shrugged Toby.

Christa spoke: "It must not be that someone can steal from our Programme, which is to benefit the hungry ones. These are shit bastards."

"What if they're destitute?" asked Rose.

Xavier looked at Mogga.

"Do they always amputate?"

"Oh no," responded Mogga.

"Well, then . . ." began Dr Maeve cheerily, wanting her tyre back.

Mogga continued: "It may be a very large fine. These boys cannot afford that fine. No one who needs to steal a tyre could afford the fine for stealing a tyre."

"Bloody farce!" Freddy swore.

"The family," explained Mogga, "would pay because of the disgrace."

"A family already on its uppers," Rose said. "That'll go down a treat in the press back home: *Aid team demands limbs or blood money.*"

Xavier decided that, far from getting a reward, Musa should be garrotted.

"We must," he ordered, "continue the business of our meeting. We've a famine to forestall."

Mid-afternoon, they took time out. Xavier's head was pounding, the vein on his forehead bulged. He went to his office, sat at the former headmaster's desk, lifted the tin dust cover off his glass of warm water and stared into it vacantly.

"Got a moment?" said a sharp, nervy voice. Nyala Freddy, his spectacles fogged with intensity. *He's followed me here*, Xavier realised, *he's driven after me.*

"Yes, Freddy?"

"I have to say that it's not on, it's really not."

"What isn't on, Freddy?"

"Amputation. I want no part of any organisation that has Africans amputated."

"It's out of my hands," replied Xavier.

"Withdraw the charge!" Freddy boomed at him.

Xavier studied the young man jigging about in front of the desk, and wanted to slap his face.

"What I must do is consider all arguments," Xavier said flatly.

"Right!" said young Freddy, prancing excitedly, "because everyone agrees . . ."

"No, I don't!" came another voice. It was the nurse. She'd pursued him also. "You've no right, Freddy. I don't want to be robbed."

"You won't be."

"One minute . . ." Xavier began, standing.

"Or raped!"

"Who'd rape you?"

"What do you mean by . . ."

"Hold it, you two."

"Withdraw charges and we'll be sitting ducks."

The Director finally lost patience.

"Be quiet, both of you!"

They fell silent, staring at the floor, sulky children caught scrapping.

"I hear what you're saying," snapped Xavier, towering over them. "I value your opinions, but finally it's my call, is that clear? I have to keep this Programme on the road. There's a crisis on, you know."

He realised that he'd almost said, 'There's a war on,' and that he had to 'run a tight ship'.

"Fine, say no more," peeped Freddy, flouncing out petulantly, Lorna following. Xavier felt something moist hit his lip: a drop of sweat flung off Freddy's hair.

Wearily, Xavier drove home. Passing by the police station, he saw a kerfuffle in the street and two young men – teenagers – dragged in handcuffs to a waiting jeep. One of the youths had a black eye, the other limped painfully. The disturbance was caused by two women wailing, beseeching and clawing at the policemen who pushed them off roughly.

Xavier often wanted to get on the first plane back to Khartoum, to resign. But there was a famine coming, supposedly.

*

That evening, Xavier had meant to write to his parents in Dorset. But he couldn't write. His head seethed with unkind thoughts about thieves, but more about his team and their petulant immaturity. They needed smacking. Xavier loathed such feelings, and that made him angrier still. Exhausted, he fell asleep on a cane recliner out in the courtyard.

He was woken by the slight judder of a chair dragged a few inches on the concrete.

"Forgive me," said a quiet voice. Mogga was looking down at him. "I disturb your rest . . ."

"No matter," breathed Xavier. He reached for some lukewarm tea, realising with some surprise that Mogga was almost the only team member not guaranteed to aggravate him. He sipped the tea. "I daresay you saved me from a nightmare about amputations."

Mogga stood awkwardly, his head to one side as though he were considering a beetle in the corner.

"I have heard the opinion of Freddy and the others, Sir. There is much discussion."

"What do you think, Mogga? If I withdraw the charge, we lose the tyre and more stealing follows."

"Oh, yes. And to claim it back we must make a denunciation."

"But it's inhuman to have two young men mutilated for the sake of a wheel."

Mogga did not reply for a moment, but gazed abstractedly up into the trees. Xavier waited.

"To withdraw is to make the judgement ourselves," said Mogga at last. "That is not our place."

Xavier peered at him; this was not what he'd expected.

"You surprise me," he said.

"They have so little law here, you see," Mogga murmured, as if he were speaking of food.

*

Early next morning, Xavier had a rude awakening. Something hard and damp bounced off his pillow, glancing off his mosquito net and grazing his face before falling onto the dirt below. Startled, he sat up. A large animal knuckle, covered in bloody shreds of muscle and grit, rolled on the ground. It must have weighed over a kilo, and had been stolen in an air raid on the butcher's souk. Overhead, a bad-tempered red kite wheeled and shrieked before settling noisily into the tree above his bed.

Xavier sat up, his bare calves furred with ginger hair pricking in the morning cool. There was blood on his pillow.

Early at the office, he found only Mogga who was studying the radio manual with a resolution that seemed comical, even faintly pathetic, until one realised that Mogga had the persistence to work it all out.

"I have to go back to the police," said Xavier.

"Yes," agreed Mogga, and Xavier realised that Mogga was waiting to accompany him.

But the sergeant would not let them past the duty desk. Xavier asked again, wondering if his own near-two-metres height was imposing or merely irritated the Sudanese. He saw the lieutenant busying himself at the far end of the corridor, speaking to someone who Xavier vaguely recognised as Colonel Hassan al-Bedawi of State Security. The two men glanced at Xavier and Mogga but did not acknowledge them.

The sergeant came back, grinning: "You may go now."

"But about the tyre . . ."

"It is returned. You can go." The man moved smartly out of range.

"Something has taken place," observed Mogga.

They left quickly, the vein on Xavier's scalp bulging and beating. It had happened: amputation, mutilation. He heard again a bloody beef knuckle hitting the ground. The Land Rover wallowed along the sandy street and he felt sick.

A reek of thin Libyan coffee drifted through the Resthouse verandah. The team was milling about, some with towels round their waists. A chilly splashing came from the bathhouse. They were avoiding his eye. They muttered greetings, then slipped past him. Xavier was bewildered.

Then he saw the spare tyre in a corner of the dining room.

"Someone," he said loudly, feeling anger rising, "one of you has paid the fine, correct? For our own goddam tyre!"

"No," said Freddy.

"Not one of us," said Lorna, perched on a string bed and painting her rather large toenails. "Not one of us at all."

"They're colluding," he thought. Suddenly he lost his temper. He was utterly furious, helpless in this country that would not be helped, and undermined by his own staff, a bunch of impetuous, *stupid* . . .

"We've all paid it," continued the nurse brightly, "and the boys have been released. They're very grateful, so there's an end of the matter."

They'd talked each other round: extraordinary! Xavier surveyed the verandah; they'd all appeared from somewhere, were perched on the cots, sipping disgusting coffee and pleased as hell with themselves.

"OK," he said, "we have to talk about this. Did you pay, Mogga?"

"They did not ask me," replied the black simply.

*

He knew why they'd done it. It was a signal, a collective message from the team to Xavier: they were telling him that they saw how vulnerable was his authority.

Had Rose Price contributed to the payment of the fine? Xavier didn't know, and didn't want to ask Mogga. Xavier wanted to keep Mogga as his personal assistant, but that was a weakness too, wasn't it? Gathering your little faction about you . . . It would appear far stronger to show that there were others who needed support more urgently, now that the floodgates of expectation were open, now that, against all his best judgement, there would be food trucks wallowing across the sands towards Darfur. Tempers would be sure to rise. Xavier allocated Mogga to Toby Kitchin, who was hard-working but a worrier and needed a steadying hand.

But then, when Leila Karim came saying that her Land Rover was broken and that she needed an escort urgently, Xavier told Toby that he'd have to do without Mogga for a few days. No one could have Mogga to themselves, and now it was Leila's turn.

THREE

In her grandeur as Lecturer in Agronomy, in the days before her move to the crisis team in Darfur, Leila had her own desk in an office at the University of Khartoum. Behind the desk stood a modest steel bookcase where, among the monolithic foreign texts, stood a colour book of school geography. Her colleagues had no idea why it was there. Leila was an enigma, tall and proud, her face hawkish but handsome, her eyes dark and inclined to fix upon you uncomfortably. She was skilled, they felt sure, but she was so reserved that few felt they knew her. Was she truly married? Surely – but no one had ever met a husband who, if he existed, must have been a remarkably tolerant or foolhardy man for he seemingly raised no objection to her continuing to work after marriage, though it meant an office shared with several men. They wondered, was her reserve the price she paid, or was it the reason he trusted her? With few close friends and a reputation for stubbornness, Leila's colleagues admired and went a little in awe of her. They speculated quietly about her home life and smiled at the colour book of school geography.

Had they dared ask, she would have told them that the book came from her father's house. It was his own, from his schooldays.

The house, the family home, was a cement box in the dusty Khartoum suburb of El-Shábiya, a dormitory for poorly paid public servants. Leila had first tugged the schoolbook from the shelf when she was just five years old. Inside the book, the little girl found a speckly picture of a white mass crashing into water of a peculiarly intense azure. The colour was crude and the illustration bewildered Leila. Every day she saw the Nile, but this looked nothing like it. The Nile's banks were low and dun and did not fall, did not swamp the little skiffs or barges or menace them at all. In the photograph, there was a sleek red boat (quite unlike the oily Nile ferries), and this boat must be huge for there were ant-like figures gathered on the deck, and the blue-white wall, mightily tall above it, was teetering and toppling.

"That is a glacier," her father had said, leaning over the child perched on the black ottoman, "made all of ice such as we have in our kitchen. That is a ship, and this is the Antarctic Ocean which is a water wider than the desert but utterly cold, Leila."

This, at five, was the limit of Leila's notion of the world beyond Sudan. Later, she took an ice cube from the kitchen and, with it in her mouth making her palate ache, she sat with the book on her lap gazing at the picture: a blue desert onto which the frigid mountains fell.

Mahmoud Abd al-Haq was completely delighted with his daughter's curiosity. Not long after, he came home from work carrying a battered cardboard box and called to the whole house that he had a gift for his girls. The box was heavy; Leila and Khamisa shuffled in silent speculation. Mahmoud placed the load on the dining table and they closed in on it.

"Wait!" he commanded, and went again to the car. He returned with a second box.

"Now you may open one box each," he said.

Khamisa, older and stronger, heaved out a large book bound in green plastic. She put it down at once, peering into Leila's box to see what else there was. Both cartons were filled with books: sixteen of them in a uniform binding.

"What is this?" the girls' mother wanted to know. Enormously pleased with himself, her husband stood the books in line between the two boxes.

It was an encyclopaedia. Mrs Abd al-Haq picked up *Quebec – Steel* at random. Inside the front cover was a stamp which (had she been able to read) would have told her:

UNITED STATES INFORMATION SERVICE LIBRARY – WITHDRAWN

Although the books showed only modest signs of wear, the edition was some thirty years old.

"So what is the use of it?" demanded Mrs Abd al-Haq. Her husband, predicting this complaint, had already prepared a defence.

"Our nation," he parried glibly, "is, at the very least, a century behind the latest developments in America. A few years leeway will not be a great handicap."

"I do not understand what you are saying," said Mrs Abd al-Haq. "I merely wish to know what you think our girls will be doing with such books? They don't know English, they have yet to read Arabic."

Khamisa slipped away from the table and switched on the television. Leila continued to turn the pages, dazzled by a thousand pictures of things whose name and nature she could hardly guess at. Her father beamed indulgently at his daughters.

"You shall see," he purred, "you shall see. This shall be a tool for their futures."

"I hope they do not waste their futures as readily as you waste our money," said his wife, heading for the kitchen to berate the servant for indolence. Hours ago, she'd ordered *halawa*, boiled lime and sugar for the stripping of body hair.

*

Corporeally and metaphorically, Mahmoud towered above his daughters. At least, that was his notion. He thought of himself as a lighthouse, tall, stern and bright. But he indulged Leila and Khamisa endlessly, playing, chattering, reading with them while other Omdurman fathers smoked away their evenings in cafés. Mahmoud's girls knew themselves to be the centre of his world.

Mahmoud Abd al-Haq (so he told everyone at the National Bank) was an ardent progressive. When she was older, this puzzled Leila. She knew that the vast majority of her opinions were inherited wholesale from him; she had been born with liberal notions in her blood. Indeed, when she examined the broad spectrum of her convictions, she knew that the more reasoned an opinion seemed, the more certainly she had taken it on trust from her father.

So how (she asked herself) had her father come by his own views – given that *his* father had been a minor tribal chief of the most crusty conservatism?

Once, when they were small, Mahmoud took his girls to see the Omdurman camel market. His tribe was the Bani Amer; he intended Khamisa and Leila to taste that particular glory and to compare the wild Kababish of Kordofan and the lineages of the north. But it was a year of drought; the grasslands had shrivelled instead of flowering. When they came to the market field, there was a dreary pall of yellow dust from the hooves of an astonishing throng, hundreds on hundreds of camels. There were huge stud bulls and light racing camels, brood mares and their young, all the treasure and pride of the tribes. And all were up for sale. The nobility of the sands were destitute and were asking a pittance for their entire herds. But the animals were ragged and diseased, staggering hulks of bone and mange. No one was buying.

Profoundly shocked, Mahmoud held his daughters by the hand and stared at the rout of tradition. Leila felt his grip tighten uncomfortably on her own. Anxious, she looked up at him and saw his gaze turn to the road nearby where the trucks and cars flocked, every one of them Japanese.

"We can do nothing here," he said in a whisper.

Then there was the day when the girls and their mother were sunk into the black leatherette settee before the television watching an Egyptian soap opera. Mahmoud in passing had scornfully told them to switch to a Sudanese series – only to be told that there was no such thing.

And there was the day he came home from work incandescent with anger and humiliation, having discovered that every one of the foreign banks in Khartoum could transfer money out of the country within twenty-four hours, whereas the antique systems of the National Bank could not move funds between two departments in much less than a week.

He winced and shrank at these experiences, again and again. His conviction and determination grew that the family Abd al-Haq would put their best efforts into redressing the country's shame.

*

Though he yearned for a son, Mahmoud Abd al-Haq never blamed his wife, nor took another, nor divorced her as his friends advised. He declared that his girls were as good as anybody's boy; several of his acquaintance privately thought this claim offensive. Mahmoud called his daughters the vanguard of a new Sudan. He would not hear of having them circumcised, and it was axiomatic in the house that the children would proceed to university and thence to professional careers.

So he would linger with Khamisa and Leila, enthusiasm writ broad upon his face like some artist's impression of a model father in his modern house with his go-ahead little girls.

"What will you be, Khamisa?" he said, having gathered them on the sweaty black settee with the elderly encyclopaedia's pictures of the Seven Wonders of the Ancient World. A crude air-cooler, Khartoum-made, dripped onto the terrazzo floor. The machine was stuffed with watered straw and sat on a trestle in the yard outside, roaring through a hole in the wall.

"A doctor? Leila, shall your sister be a doctor?"

Khamisa was frowning at a pen rendition of Babylon's Hanging Gardens. Leila was in awe of her prim big sister who, even from primary school, their father intended for the sciences. Khamisa ruffled the pages, pausing at a red-and-black cross-section of the heart. Mahmoud crowed.

"You see? You see this?" he shrilled to his wife as she laid his coffee tray on the glass table. "Look what she picks out! The heart, look, instinctively she goes for that! She will be the foremost heart surgeon in Sudan."

Their mother gave a sour little smile. She had some thoughts on surgery herself. Leila was five, Khamisa seven.

Mahmoud turned on through the volumes, and found that colour diagrams accompanying the article on reproduction had been excised. But, of course, the encyclopaedia was second-hand

and from a library. Anyone could have done it. He cursed vehemently the narrowness of Sudanese minds and Khartoum education. He repeated these thoughts rather loudly at the bank and in the fragrant cafés of the souk. Some of his friends wished he would learn a little moderation.

*

That Friday morning – their father was at the mosque – Leila found her mother putting Khamisa into the prettiest of new clothes. She was hurrying, tugging roughly at the zips and ties, while Khamisa stood curiously pale and quiet, clinging to a new bangle in pink metallic plastic. Leila watched from the doorway, scratching her right ankle with her left big toe.

"Why is Khamisa having new things?" she murmured, unhappy at her sister's expression. She was jealous of that full red dress embroidered with little black camels about its hem, but felt no desire to wear it just now. Her mother, sewing on a hook, was flustered and did not look up.

"Another day for you, my precious," she said to Leila. Then, taking on her arm a yellow plastic basket in which fresh underclothes of Khamisa's lay folded, she led the two girls out into the sandy street to a house ten minutes' walk away.

For much of that morning, Leila crept from corner to corner contriving to be forgotten. There were four of Khamisa's school friends, a crowd of women and a reek of cloying perfumes that made Leila want to gag. There was singing that had nothing to do with joy, everything to do with blotting out cries. There was a feast spread out, *marara* of raw chopped liver with onion, lime and blistering pepper, but Leila felt no hunger, only a nausea of apprehension.

The little girls were given fizzy drinks and coconut sweets and were seated on a couch in their new dresses, but Leila did not see them smile. The women fussed about them and shrilled, "This is your wonderful day!" but Leila saw terror in her sister's face. Khamisa clung to the blue glass of juice but did not sip, did not move. She was petrified, she would speak to no one.

There was a back room to which the children were led one by one with shouts: *Bring the little bride!* When Khamisa was taken, Leila slipped round through the kitchen and looked in through the grimy louvres. She saw her sister stretched out on a rush mat like a newly slaughtered animal about to be paunched. The flock of women knelt about Khamisa grasping her wrists and heaving her skinny legs apart. The pretty red dress with camels was hauled up round her waist, her panties discarded. Leila saw her sister's torso squirm and twist in protest. She saw a lady in dark green robes crouch between the convulsing legs. Then the knees were suddenly rigid, there was blood and Khamisa screaming, and someone led Leila away from the window.

*

Mahmoud's rage knew no bounds – but the thing was done. For all his cursing and threats, for all he slapped his wife's face terribly, he could not replace the flesh sliced off his daughter. He shouted that he would send the culprit to jail – but no one would give him a name. Khamisa spent two weeks in the bedroom with her legs bound together, the wounds closed with cigarette papers. Her pudenda were smothered in egg white that became crisp and flaky, and was stained and streaked dark red. She took a high fever and the doctor came to inject her, muttering darkly about unsterile procedures. The girl lay mute; her hair clung in black sweaty snakes to her cheek and neck. A sour reek that Leila never forgot came from the room.

One evening, Leila heard her father speak words to her mother that were clear and simple and yet she could not understand. He said, "Do that to my Leila, and I shall kill you."

What could he possibly mean? Leila appreciated that one killed chickens before eating them, but could not readily apply this idea to her mother. If Mother understood, there was no audible reply. For several days Mrs Abd al-Haq went about tight-lipped, smiling down at the floor like a woman who knows that she has done her duty in the face of dull ignorance.

*

102

Mahmoud redoubled his educational efforts. He took the girls to every part of the Three Towns at the meeting of the two Niles. He showed them the palace steps where General Gordon in white dress uniform fell with a spear through his ribs; they saw the swirling dance of the *darawish* in the shadow of the silver dome of the Mahdi's tomb; they witnessed the strut and swagger of all-comers Nubian wrestling on the dirt in front of the Khalifa's house.

He purchased more books – some of them new – to an extent that Mrs Abd al-Haq wept, pleading with him to remember his paltry salary. He took Leila and Khamisa to the museums and the university, and to the zoo where sad gazelles nosed at limp fodder and there was a dead fox in a corner that made Leila sad and her father shout at a keeper: *Shame!* They went on the greasy black ferry to the groves of Tuti Island, and to the dusty botanical gardens. They went downriver on the steamer to inspect the vast cotton scheme of the Gezira.

Mahmoud declared they'd make a family picnic of this and his wife complied, bringing *kisra* bread of fermented millet, thin and sour, with stews of mutton and okra, oiled beans, omelettes and halva. They ate under a tree on the riverbank, after which Mahmoud with a resolute expression took the girls to clamber onto a concrete sluice among the grand irrigation works.

"What can he be thinking of?" their mother yawned. Mahmoud remained there with his girls in obedient silence beside him, Leila puzzled and watchful, Khamisa bored. He gestured to left and right, indicating the docile water that flowed in its channels and the cotton plants in regiments. Perhaps he was hoping that Khamisa (who'd become a little cool about medicine) might take inspiration here and become a leading agronomist one day. Perhaps Leila might study hydrology. In some important arena, surely, his daughters would be effectual as he had never been, never *would* be in his fatuous bank labours.

He spoke later (though it never came about) of a trip by bus to Port Sudan, to view the Red Sea:

"It is neither Red nor Blue, Leila, but it is truly something, you shall see!"

Bizarrely, he proposed taking them to the railyards where the broken locomotives stood. For once, Khamisa abandoned her sullen boredom for open rebellion. She'd grown headstrong, taut with teenage willpower, and used cruel words. She told her father that he was weird, that inspecting irrigation technology was dull but at least comprehensible, whereas inspecting *broken* railway engines was eccentric, was perverse, was *laughable*! She hinted that all Khartoum said so – and Mahmoud lost his nerve and did not insist.

"It is up to you, absolutely," he declared. "My girls have their futures in their own hands. This is, of course, the most important lesson."

But Leila went with him uncomplaining, for love, and it became accepted that these curious tours were for Mahmoud and Leila only. People smiled secretly, perhaps even pityingly, to see the bank clerk and his daughter trailing across town. Leila never quite knew, though the visits continued year by year, what she was supposed to think of her country but she thought his point was this: that she *could* be (if she so wished), she *might* be (nothing should stop her; he'd see to it!) that very chief technician who would restart her nation's trains. Mahmoud would stand beside his girl, staring despondently at some spectacle of backwardness with his hand rising a little from his side as though he longed to enthuse, to speak proudly, but felt his wrist weighed down with the decay of everything.

"Look," her father said, wherever they were, said over and again, "*Look!*" as though just in the looking she would find the vocation to be everything necessary, everything so glaringly needful in Sudan.

These trips lasted until Leila was twelve. Though he could by no means forget the mutilation of his firstborn, perhaps Mahmoud now thought Leila safe.

*

They went away, mother and daughters, on a holiday. They went to Sennar, 300 kilometres in a bus southward between the Blue Nile and the railway that was not working. They went for three weeks to stay with an aunt, while Mahmoud Abd al-Haq attended his office. There he sat doggedly, day after day, penning summaries of last year's reports, for whose benefit he never knew. Around him, clerks in neat khaki uniforms and old leather slippers totted columns on sheets of cheap grey foolscap, while lady secretaries in blue and amber chiffon robes pressed the keys of massive type-writers that clacked so slowly, lashing into the carbons like a military policeman's whip. Cowed messenger women, silent and creeping, brought coffee and memos to the Chiefs of Department, who would look at the latter next week. There were three printer-calculators in the room, but only one functioned. The standard fan juddered, oscillating jerkily, like an awkward question that always came back to him. Mahmoud could think of no answer other than patience.

Of an evening, while his women were away, he went to the cafés and listened to the talk. He needed company, of course, and these were decent men. But in his heart he knew that they had little to say to the future. That was reserved for his daughters.

The bus brought the family back and Mahmoud embraced the girls fondly. Khamisa shuffled into the lounge and lay on the black settee complaining of a headache from the bus. Leila was very quiet and still. When Mahmoud kissed her on the cheek, she leaned towards him almost imperceptibly. Puzzled, Mahmoud watched her walk slowly towards the bedroom. She looked pale and moved stiffly, as though all her joints were inflamed. Her mother watched Leila also, then observed tartly that they'd been on a bus all day so he wasn't going to expect song and dance, was he?

Khamisa returned to school the next day, but Leila did not get up at all. Her mother dismissed enquiries, saying that she was just like a teenager and they were all the same: let her rest, please, and don't fuss. But when Mahmoud came home in the afternoon, he found Leila with her face buried in the pillow and the pillow soaked with sweat.

"What is wrong with her?" he demanded of his wife. "Have you called the doctor?"

His wife mumbled something and sidled out of the bedroom. Surprised, Mahmoud pursued her.

"Have you called the doctor? And why not? Leila is unwell, can't you see?"

Still the girl's mother mumbled. Mahmoud bellowed at her:

"Send that servant girl at once. Heavens, what is it with you, woman? If you are not talking today, I shall send her myself. Our girl is sick, let us have some action in this house!"

The physician came, a personal friend. Mahmoud, fearing malaria, typhoid or meningitis even, searched his desk for some cash because the drugs would be expensive. But then he heard the doctor ask for boiling water and clean towels. His wife emerged from Leila's room and shut the door firmly, trying to slip past him. Mahmoud caught the pallor of panic in her face. He grabbed at her shoulder, roughly turning her towards him. She would not look him in the eye.

"What is it?" Mahmoud hissed at her. Something dreadful was congealing at the back of his mind. He studied his wife with loathing. She fended off his hands and moved into the kitchen, saying, "The doctor has told me to light the stove."

Mahmoud sat on the black leatherette ottoman, motionless, listening to the low voices that came from the bedroom. From time to time there was a girlish whimpering. Mahmoud's heart froze – and cracked.

When the doctor re-emerged from the bedroom, when he had done scribbling chits and prescriptions, he snapped his attaché case shut and looked at Mahmoud quizzically.

"I thought you had decided against all that?"

"All what?" asked Leila's father, his voice defiantly flat.

His wife came out, carrying a pan of stained water. The doctor let his glance follow Mrs Abd al-Haq a moment, and then studied the father hunched on the ottoman. Mahmoud's face seemed to have lost all tone and all expression.

The doctor placed the prescriptions on the glass-topped table.

"Don't delay. It was total, Pharaonic, and badly done. There is a lot of infection. I'll be back tomorrow."

*

Mrs Abd al-Haq wondered if her husband would kill her. But not only did he not raise a hand against her; he barely spoke at all. Leila kept her room for a week, and in the first four days Mahmoud did not talk with her, did not even go in. At last he sat on her bed and held her hand a minute, but looked out of the window.

His wife was not sure whether he was accepting defeat, or was brewing up to some cataclysmic rage in which she would be divorced or slaughtered. She was glad of the support of her friends who assured her that she had saved Leila from uncleanness and spinsterhood. In the meantime, if Mrs Abd al-Haq were to need refuge . . .

At this, tears sprang into her eyes. How could she have landed the one husband in all Sudan who didn't care about his daughters' future? Who had no thought for the ignominy of the uncircumcised? For the misery of the unmarriageable? Didn't he love their girls?

The friends hushed and consoled her. Leila would soon be married, surely, and if her father had a scrap of decency he would come to understand that Mrs Abd al-Haq had acted properly.

But still Mahmoud said nothing. The mutilation could never be reversed. Protest and recrimination would merely dignify the atrocity, lifting it to a plane of rational debate where his wife could come out with travesties of justification. He did not want to listen to that, to hear *reasons* why his daughter should have her genitalia cut away. There was nothing left but sorrow. And, since his wife was so out of sympathy, she would be excluded. This was his revenge.

So Leila came from her room, weakened, cured but not healed. Between her and her father, few words passed. But, a few days later, he took her to the airport. They went – just the two of them – to look at the jets: Boeings, Fokkers, Antonovs, 200, 300 tonnes apiece. Father and daughter gazed at these astonishing vessels that rose from the squashy tarmac and spread across the sky, across the modern world. Then they took a soft drink together and came home. As they re-entered the house, Leila saw her mother glare at her father and realised that the trip had been a riposte, even a small victory.

*

Mahmoud still placed confidence in Khamisa who grew into a young lady of quick intelligence and caustic wit. She won a place at the University Languages Faculty and suddenly there was ambitious talk in the house: of the senior Civil or Diplomatic Service, of posts abroad, a scholarship perhaps. Mrs Abd al-Haq made little contribution to these discussions. Mahmoud did the speculating, Khamisa enjoyed the limelight and Leila watched, secretly perturbed by the sudden flux of her father's hopes.

When Khamisa became engaged to marry, announcing this within just two months of starting at the Languages Faculty, Mahmoud shrank from her in dread. A week later, Khamisa stopped attending the university. When her father asked why, she replied that it was her fiancé's wish. The young man was going to Bahrain for a year; he preferred Khamisa to remain at home and she would certainly obey. Mahmoud stared, mesmerized by a snake he thought he'd at least scotched. When he came to his senses, he began to protest – but Khamisa coldly reminded him of his own teachings: that their life decisions were in their own hands, no one else's. Their mother gloried in every detail of the wedding plans from the day the engagement was announced, but Leila thought her father's spirit would never recover.

At sixteen, she was conscious that all those tremendous hopes now focused on her alone, and were a great burden.

Still they went about together. The girl was tall now, was outgrowing her father. Walking in the street with Mahmoud one day, a group of young men came towards them and Leila lowered her eyes. As soon as the men had passed, her father stopped, turned her by the shoulder and slapped her face.

As she gazed at him in mute astonishment, he snapped:

"You looked down! Why did you look down? Are they better than you? Are they worthier, are they kings or presidents that my daughter must lower her eyes?"

She saw that he was trembling.

She became afraid; the more he believed that there was nothing he could do of worth in this world, the more he placed that duty upon his Leila. If she had known some terms in which she could have remonstrated without wounding him still further, she'd have spoken. But her father was shrinking day by day. His health, his courage and his authority were failing, and it broke her heart to see. Three months after delivering that slap, Mahmoud's heart failed also.

Mrs Abd al-Haq was principally distressed for her own financial position as a widow, but Leila's silent grief knew no end. Though she did at last marry, she kept Mahmoud's colour book of geography all her professional life.

*

Her husband was called Othman. In El Fasher, Colonel Hassan al-Bedawi of State Security came to know a lot about Othman, and in due course would arrest him.

Dr Othman Abd al-Karim was Senior Lecturer in Sociology when Leila first arrived at Khartoum University. He was known as a deep scholar, a conscientious and thorough man and, even better for the university's repute, he had studied in Paris. Furthermore he was a noted modern Muslim, honoured for his compassion and his charity. His study was the social organisation of poor village farmers.

He had turned his attention to the Rahad Scheme, a vast complex of canals to the east of the Blue Nile above Khartoum, where the corporation charged with making the desert bloom had found difficulty in recruiting gardeners. Sixteen thousand tenancies needed fifty-seven thousand seasonal labourers to gather the crops – but, though the scheme included forty-six model villages for these labouring families, still there were awkward shortages. Some people there were, but perversely many of these had refused to go into the fields. In one particularly dismal year, the Rahad Corporation had had to call upon the Army to help with the harvest.

Dr Othman Abd al-Karim's proposal – to investigate the

peasants' strange reluctance – had been warmly welcomed by the authorities. It was murmured that his recommendations would take the Rahad Scheme forward to prosperity, and that Dr Abd al-Karim could expect considerable career rewards when he delivered.

But, as Othman began work, he found himself rather liking the obstinate villagers. In the Khartoum ministries they were regarded as ignorant, primitive and reactionary, but Othman saw them differently. They were, certainly, of conservative tribal stock, of the Arakien, Shukriya and Kawahla tribes; traditionalists all. The women would not work the land, but followed the injunction of the Prophet: "Wives, keep to your houses." They would be ashamed to be seen hoeing in gangs in the sight of men. Besides, they were too busy minding flocks of babies, being themselves splendidly fertile. They were illiterate and they married very young, and now there were some 25,000 children (and just five elementary schools, starved of books and teachers). The growing families needed cash; in search of jobs that paid, the men headed for the city. Even that was difficult, for the roads were unpaved and soon collapsed into potholes full of mud; bus and taxi drivers avoided going there.

The more Dr Abd al-Karim delved, the more he sympathised. But the Government wanted solutions, they wanted to hear that the rustics only needed patriotic exhortation; they did not want to be told to build another fifty schools, or to pave the roads, or that one doctor for 60,000 people wasn't acceptable in an area known for malaria and dysentery. They wanted to hear that the peasants were grateful but misguided, and that leaflets and public meetings hectored through microphones by dignitaries from Khartoum would solve everything. They did not want to hear that the peasants understood very well what was (or was not) happening and disliked it.

Dr Othman Abd al-Karim's investigations were luring him into perilous waters. When he spoke with colleagues at the university, he saw the smiles stiffen. He began to watch his tongue.

The one person with whom Othman could speak freely (albeit in a low voice) was Yusuf Mohammed Modawi, a botanist who was compiling a survey of every species of tree and shrub in Sudan. The epic dimensions of this, the hardships, the travels it entailed in a land where travel is very hard, left Othman breathless – as did one of Yusuf's assistants, a startlingly beautiful if somewhat haughty graduate student called Leila Abd al-Haq. The girl returned Othman's interest. When the three of them spoke together, Othman's clear thinking and his honesty struck a deep chord with Leila, even more so his reluctance to tell the women of Rahad what to do.

With Leila in the midst of her own doctoral thesis – on the survival of shrubs in spreading desert – she and Othman were married quietly in Omdurman. She had wondered often, watching Othman when he was abstracted; have I correctly understood this man? Might he prove as oafishly reactionary as others, and dismiss my notions of working on? In the great sorority of Sudanese women, it was expected that she would set aside her career and follow his. But Leila – now Leila Karim – felt sure of Othman, and worked on to finish her study.

Only one thing interfered: month followed month, and no children came. When a year had passed, there were moments of reserve between them when something should have been said – something reassuring – but was not.

And then Yusuf Modawi the botanist died of untreated typhoid while gathering specimens in the Red Sea Hills. He had driven alone from the coast up into the remote valleys and villages of the Beja people. When he fell sick, there was no one to drive him back in time.

His death left Othman feeling isolated. He continued taking his questionnaires to the Rahad villagers and collating their unpalatable replies. When his professor and the Ministry men cornered him, he gave them to understand that answers would be forthcoming, that he would shortly present his proposals. In truth, Othman was staving off the day when he would have to say things for which no one (except Leila and the Rahad tribes) would thank him.

But he was forestalled. The rector of the University College of

El Fasher, Darfur Province, died of meningitis, an infection that killed many in those remote western parts, especially when the vaccine had been left out in the sun. The post needed filling promptly because the Saudi Development Agency, which had built the college, was watching. One morning, a puzzled and apprehensive Dr Othman Abd al-Karim was summoned to the Ministry of Higher Education in Khartoum – and walked out as El Fasher's Rector-Designate.

Leaving Leila to prepare for the viva voce examination of her thesis on desert shrubs, Othman went on ahead, 800 kilometres and three days by Land Rover across arid Kordofan to find them a home in Darfur, his research on the Rahad Scheme complete but his dangerous conclusions not yet submitted.

The house he rented in El Fasher was, in the traditions of that town, capacious and uncomfortable. The rooms were close and hot under a hardboard ceiling where colossal spiders marched, with a tin roof above that clicked and creaked in the sun. There was a bathroom, but the pale blue-tiled tub held small drifts of sand, not water, for there was none in any tap. The floors were always gritty however much you swept; several of the windows had brown paper over the lower half of their opening, but still the dust blew in from the yard. On the wall outside the garden door there was a porcelain washbasin that looked as though someone had forgotten to build a bathroom around it, but the pipes were not even connected. There were three circular flowerbeds edged with brick and filled with a dust that might have been fertile if you'd watered four times a day. But there was no water. All day long the housekeeper had one ear tuned to the street, to the slow *tock tock* of a stick on a plastic drum that meant a water-boy was going by, dragging a donkey that staggered under bulging skins, black and dripping.

Sadia, the young servant he'd hired, sat outside the kitchen shed with its chickenwire windows. There was nothing in there but one wooden cupboard that contained little but greasy candle stubs, a can opener and scorpions. A half sack of charcoal leaked black dust over the floor. Two charcoal stoves, rusting steel trays on four legs, sat on the concrete outside where her two fat brown toddlers crawled, their hair red with henna and charms in leather wallets about their necks. Such were the only charms of the house when Othman moved in – and though Sadia's children were sweetness itself, he could not look at them without a shadow passing over his face.

He bought some plants from a Government nursery project on the edge of town and dug them into the circular brick beds, but Sadia ignored them and they failed to thrive. He bought water-pots from the souk, which had been decorated with simple patterns of sunflower seeds painted silver. When the weather turned cooler and the air damp, these seeds glued to the pots' flanks began to sprout absurd white roots. He was no homemaker, Othman, but Leila knew him for a good, undaunted man.

When her doctorate was confirmed – and when at last SudanAir found some kerosene – Leila Karim hurried to join Othman in El Fasher, flying in the fat Boeing that looked so incongruous on the dirt airstrip outside town. She took the house in hand, urging Sadia to flick away cobwebs and Mustafa the bemused half-witted watchman to whitewash the latrines. But she remembered her father, and she remembered Yusuf's magnificent but incomplete survey of the Shrubs and Trees of Sudan. She put her domesticity on hold and considered what to do.

Another month, and another . . . Still no child came.

She ate the early evening meal with Othman, out in the garden, from a broad aluminium platter that Sadia arrayed with fragrant foods (the girl thus ensuring a plentiful supply for herself and her little ones later). The platter rested on a low, sturdy wooden support, and they sat on either side of this leaning towards each other, extending their right arms with elegant curls of the wrist to tug and twist apart the thin *kisra* bread. They ate well, *aish* the gruel of millet, with stews of tomato and onion thickened with ground bone, accompanied by wheat cakes with honey. They ate camel liver on special days and pancakes stuffed with halva. They sat quiet and undisturbed for an hour, listening to the *tock tock* of the waterboys.

Leila said:

"It is time that I found a way to start work here."

Othman glanced up at her from his food, then continued eating.

"I have an idea," pursued Leila. "The nursery project, which is funded by the World Bank. They are trying to find trees that can be grown commercially in this Darfur sand. They could certainly use me. And think, Othman: I could complete Yusuf's survey."

Othman remained silent. She studied him carefully, hoping he would speak or return her look, at least engage her with his eyes. But he did not. She felt a noiseless cry rising within her, a silent rage. She wanted to pound her fist on the aluminium platter in front of them, to screech something about the mutilating and re-making of a woman – and then to pour out to her good Othman many, many hopeful and loving things about joint effort and firm purpose and mutual support and achievement . . .

But none of these would have been an answer to Othman's melancholy silence. Nothing more was said, or given or taken. The less movement there was between them, the cooler they became.

*

Six months later, Othman's Rahad study was published in Khartoum – and a chill gust of disapproval swept from the capital to the western desert.

Even in Sudan, it could be awkward sacking a university rector for highlighting a need for schools. Othman's life, however, and that of his Darfur staff, could be made exceedingly difficult. Funds were delayed, so his lecturers grew resentful and restless. The Saudi-built complex in El Fasher had its own generator (bypassing the feeble town supply), but no diesel was delivered; without air-conditioning, the thin-walled prefabricated buildings were hotter than any mud hut. Textbooks and equipment never came, so the faculty had to work late and hard improvising classes. Academic colleagues in Khartoum ignored their work, even their existence. Permits for research were 'lost'. Day by day the pressure mounted, though Khartoum was piqued to find that Dr Abd al-Karim had rapidly inspired loyalty in his team. The new Rector wrote to the press; occasionally his letters were printed. He wrote of academics' right to teach something meaningful, and the right of the Fur to study.

Othman wondered at himself, since he had grown up with as many engrained prejudices about the Fur as anyone in Khartoum, and here he was championing them. But when he told his young wife of what he was doing, he saw a glow of pride in her and knew that he would continue. Then he learned that he was being spied on, that his mail was being opened, that certain colleagues were in the pay of State Security.

One of his young lecturers, a mathematician, tipped him off, coming to Othman's office afire with indignation. The young man announced bluntly that he had seen the lecturer in chemistry emerging from the headquarters of Colonel Hassan al-Bedawi.

"Who is he?" asked Dr Othman.

"*Who . . .?*" exclaimed the mathematician. "He is State Security here, Steel Fist's right-hand man!"

But Othman would not be drawn. For all he knew, Security might be subsidising mathematics also.

"Well," he responded carefully, "I am happy to know that we are all in such competent hands."

He looked the young mathematician straight in the eye. The look said, *I understand entirely what you are telling me.*

This same evening a note came to Othman and Leila's home, passed in to them by the watchman. It was from a young man lodging next door, and it was written in English:

> In the name of Allah, the most gracious, the merciful. Good evening. I am 26 years of age. I have a BSc from the University of Khartoum. I have been joining the Islamic Bank of W.Sudan at its local branch in El Fasher. Unfortunately bank does not satisfy my needs for the following reason:
>
> 1. The administrative corruption and this affect the decision making process of the whole bank.
> 2. The unequality between salaries and market prices.
>   For the above I decide to leave this institution but when

I find an alternative. I thought it best to write to your goodself. My certificates are on my hand on request.

Kindly accept my deepest regards.

"He writes to us in English," Othman remarked to Leila, "so that others may not read this."

"Or because he regards us as foreigners," replied Leila.

They fell quiet, thoughtful.

"Othman," said Leila, "Be careful."

Three days later, Dr Othman Abd al-Karim was arrested from his home.

Leila did not witness it. She had driven herself out past the city wells to speak with the Director of the tree nursery, at which the startled and delighted man had asked her to start at once. He had shown her round the high-fenced compound in which were thousands of seedlings in little black plastic bags, shaded from the sun by *rakubas* of brushwood and watered by a pipeline direct from the city pumps 200 yards distant. These were hardly the conditions faced by the average Darfur tree. But Leila held her tongue, for without doubt the desert was creeping across Darfur.

"To put it bluntly," the Director had said, "anything is worth a try."

But when she reached home, she found Othman gone and their cook in hysterics. Sadia was pleading with Mustafa the watchman to let her leave at once with her roly-poly babies for surely State Security would be back, having arrested Dr Othman they'd be back to ransack the house and drag anyone found there to prison. But Mustafa had planted himself firmly at the gates.

"Shame," he muttered, shaking his head at Sadia. "Shame."

Plead as she might, stamp her bare feet on the cement as she might, he would not let her go. They had been facing off in this manner for an hour when Leila returned.

Her voice thin with shock, Leila told Mustafa to let Sadia depart. The girl swept up her fat brown offspring, one under each arm, and was out of the gate the moment Mustafa opened it.

Leila stood in the hot sun of the yard, in the uncanny silence.

"What happened, Mustafa?" she begged the old fool in his rags, "What did they say?"

Mustafa gave her a smile of pity and a little sigh, and wordlessly swept his hand about to indicate the emptiness of the house, the absence of Dr Othman Abd al-Karim.

In the days that followed, sitting in the antechambers of Colonel Hassan al-Bedawi, Chief of Security (Darfur), gleaning scraps about a supposed coup in Khartoum that Othman had supposedly been connected to, Leila Karim felt the full meaning of powerlessness. She could do nothing; she could know nothing that Colonel al-Bedawi did not want her to know. The 'coup' had been a mere sweeping, a tidying-away of disaffected ministers and disenchanted generals whose grumpy looks had needled the paranoiacs at the top. Othman was by no means implicated, but the affair was a glorious opportunity for certain senior planners, men whose expansive claims for the Rahad Scheme had been embarrassed by its failures, whose creaming off of construction funds had been exposed in a very bleak light by Othman's comments on the curious lack of schools and clinics. A chance, too, for certain top academics, whose own servile 'researches' had so nicely fluffed up the Government's self-esteem, and whose results Othman had questioned with exasperating clarity and simple figures. And for those guiding fathers of the National Islamic Front whose wisdom had not been fully appreciated by the Rahad peasantry Othman had interviewed, and whose benign paternal hands looked sweaty in Othman's reports. Too many people thought Othman a thorough nuisance. A coup was just what they needed.

Leila saw this in the faces of the Security Chief's juniors. For hour after hour, on a bench in the courtyard of the Security building near the airport, Leila sat upright and straight-backed, the epitome of dignified Khartoum womanhood with a pale blue *tobe* drawn over her head, her hands resting very still in her lap, the dark of her left wrist adorned by the thin leather band of her watch. As Security staff passed by, though she did not turn her head, they felt her unflinching dark eyes upon them. And these men – less educated, less intelligent by a mile, lesser in everything but power – were piqued by her, and were thrilled to have their terrible grip upon her and Othman.

She was left to stew and grow weary, to let her fears grow wings in the empty courtyard. As time passed, she grew familiar with every stone and gutter. She noted that just one window looking in on the yard had slatted blinds, and from time to time she was aware of a shadow moving behind these blinds. But she could not make out Colonel Hassan al-Bedawi observing her, nor would she have recognised him.

After four days of prevarication and denial she was granted an interview. A young policeman brought her to stand exhausted in front of a small desk, behind which sat a junior officer whose face wore the viciousness of a man hoping to impress his masters. He did not offer Leila a chair. The door to the inner office stood open nearby, and someone moved quietly in that room.

"Yes?" said the junior before her. Leila was bemused; he had summoned her, after all. She said that she was the wife of Dr Othman Abd al-Karim.

"What of it?" demanded the man whose uniform armpits were dark with sweat. Leila fought to keep the contempt out of her eyes.

"I wish to know where he is," she said. Her voice was low and smooth, quite full, almost mannish her husband had once said.

"He is in jail, of course. The new jail south of town."

The high security jail, home to many a malcontent.

"With what is he charged?" she tried.

"Nothing," said the man, "until we see fit. In treason, special rules apply – many special rules."

He would tell her nothing more. Leila had an unsettling sense of a presence behind that open door, listening.

There followed a curious interlude of some months in which she was seemingly married to a ghost. She would drive out to the jail behind its high wall of mud brick topped with razor wire. No one would answer questions, nor was there any message from Othman. Without a word they took her offerings of food and clothing, but for her husband's presence there she had only State

Security's word. Othman's family engaged a Khartoum lawyer, and the man would have flown to El Fasher on the Boeing – but SudanAir announced that Darfur services had been suspended (they had run out of kerosene again), and the lawyer was not willing to travel 800 kilometres overland across the desert. Anyway, he opined (feeling much safer staying where he was), what could he do there? Dr Abd al-Karim was under arrest; they could as readily begin proceedings in Khartoum. Mrs Karim would do well to return to Khartoum herself, after all there was a famine coming, didn't she know.

Leila would not flee; not for anything would she abandon Othman. She would as soon have abandoned her father's belief that this could, one day, be a civilised country. Indeed, these two causes became as one for her: Othman, and her father's ideals. But, if nothing else, she would soon run out of money. She went back to the Government tree nursery but the Director had heard rumour; he was so sorry, genuinely, but no . . .

It was then that she learned of the foreign agency that, in the name of the Rest of the World, had taken on the extraordinary burden of keeping famine at bay.

She made an appointment, hoping she would not have to reveal anything to Mr Xavier Hopkins, the Englishman with pale, wispy hair, taller even than herself. But Xavier's local managers had told him all about the arrest.

"I hear that your husband has some difficulties," said Xavier calmly, "with Colonel al-Bedawi."

Leila looked down a moment – until the memory of a stinging slap in the street stung her anew, and she looked up proudly.

"As a foreign agency," continued Xavier, "we try to avoid getting embroiled in politics. Your husband's affairs are no business of ours, and I urgently need advice on the state of the harvest. Also, I've got goat projects that are foundering, and the Pest Control people are clamouring for help. I should be very glad of your assistance."

He gave her a kind smile, and she decided of a sudden that this was a good man, honest and brave.

"Tell me," Xavier added, "are you needing a housekeeper by any chance? There's a young widow I should like to help."

*

So the widow Farida came to look after Leila; two women minus their husbands. They did not discuss the matter, but perhaps the fortitude of each was kept up to the mark by the example of the other.

And Leila also was working again, but before long her courage was taking a battering. She laboured to support her jailed husband, to cherish the legacy of Yusuf Mohammed Modawi, and to honour the ideals of her father. None of these was going well. She drove every second day to the jail with food, clean clothes and a letter, but she received no reply, and had no idea if anything reached Othman. When she was out in the field and had a scrap of spare energy, she made notes towards filling the final gaps in Yusuf's survey, but the task suddenly seemed greater than she. With information and cash and supplies, Leila worked to keep the Agency's small projects alive, though these were feeble little shoots. And she employed every ounce of her tact, knowledge and authority to persuade Government officials to part with data concerning crop forecasts, until she at last realised that they had none; they hadn't a clue how hungry Darfur might be this year. She realised that Xavier Hopkins wanted her, somehow, to work it out herself.

Day after day she came to the school compound that was the team's headquarters. The expatriates were always furiously busy – though, with information so scarce, what could they be doing? Some would nod a *Good morning* to her; some scarcely noticed her. Of the Sudanese staff, the monitors and drivers regarded her with curiosity, but others looked straight through her, like Fauzi the storekeeper, always hovering near the expatriates. The secretaries viewed her with suspicion: a woman of accomplishment, a woman who aspired to roles far beyond anything they dreamed of. They would bob their heads and hurry past.

Certain people were unfailing in their courtesy and welcome: Rose Price, the strange, gawky Englishwoman who would stride across the sandy yard towards Leila, taking the cigarette from her mouth and greeting the Sudani with a weirdly un-beautiful smile, giving sharp little nods of approval like some long-legged wading bird. Toby Kitchin, an English half-caste and very young; he was a sweet-natured worrier, anxious and keen. And Mr Mogga, the little black man from the far south. He was the only other person who ever got a smile from Rose Price; he would come out of his way to enquire if Leila was well, to be so interested in her programme that she was tempted to invent urgent business that did not exist. These three might be seen together each morning, the heads of Miss Price and Mr Mogga bobbing up and down with enthusiasm in front of Leila Karim.

But afterwards, in the hot cement room allocated to her for an office, she contemplated failure. It was not something her father had ever imagined for her. But though her projects all continued in their way, yet they had failed through smallness, through insufficiency. A handful of poor women – half a dozen in that village, some more beyond those hills – had planted vegetable gardens, harvesting some onions or calabashes whose sale had not excited the village souk, let alone liberated the sisters from penury. A cluster of families now raised goats of a brindled white-and-tan Egyptian breed, sturdier and more milkable than the Darfur stock that had been decimated by pneumonias and blinded by fly-born parasites. The Egyptian animals shrugged off diseases, yet there were so few of them, and those few a draw for bandits. The villagers could not afford to risk experiment. Had someone indemnified them against disaster, they might have been talked round, but Leila could offer no insurance. So the soft desert sapped every effort; you only had to drive across the dunes to feel weary.

The functionaries in the Government offices of El Fasher whose gracious permission she must seek for every trifling proposal, these men scorned her womanhood and resented her vastly superior education. They gave her scant courtesy when she came to their doors, and they ignored her letters. They knew that she must fail as they themselves must, and they relished that certainty.

Leila held herself tall and proud as ever, but something in her was cowed, her spirit looked down. Her father would have slapped her face to see it.

But just now there was a man studying her from the doorway.

"You are to go to Seraf Umra?" enquired Mr Mogga.

"I have deliveries to make," replied Leila, lifting her look from the school desk. "Antibiotics for the small stock, pumpkin seed for the gardens. I am the farm wife's postman."

Her voice was calm and level; not a hint of wavering or shrillness. Mogga studied her closely a moment, his head on one side. Then he straightened and beamed at her.

"I shall be taking you," Mogga announced. "To Kebkabiya and Seraf Umra."

Leila closed the file on her desk.

"You have been ordered?" she asked.

"I was volunteered," Mogga grinned. "It's a long trip."

"You are kind as ever."

"It is my delight," Mogga riposted. "We shall be together some days."

"And who will travel with us?"

"Adam Zachariah shall drive. Fauzi is sent to make some inventories, so he shall accompany us."

"On the piano?" she enquired with a furtive smile.

"Oh, the music we shall have!" Mogga laughed aloud. "But I hear that the piano is broken. God is merciful, and I shall sing to you instead. Be ready tomorrow!"

And he vanished in a busy whirl, leaving Leila with a vexing notion that he had seen her downcastness.

She dressed next morning in a lemon yellow *tobe*, determinedly holding herself well. By the steel gates the watchman guarded a small fibre suitcase, and Farida packed a cardboard box of food, which she tied with string. Leila had sent her own driver trudging to the jail with a note: she would be away some days.

With the turbocharger whistling, Mogga's Land Rover rushed away through the sands. They drove due west from El Fasher out of Wadi al-Ku, turning onto the grand west road that the Italians had built, over ground that seemed to swell in the heat into a dome that they were forever climbing. Here, where the road was 'good', Adam Zachariah drove fast over the corrugations and the Land Rover shook, the seats rattled and the two spare tyres, the drum of diesel and the white jerrycans of water strained, squeaked and squealed in their strappings. In the rear sat Fauzi who, with no piano to cuddle, strove to sit upright and be dignified. Mogga leaned forward between Adam and Leila, excitedly chattering his notions over the road noise, while Leila smiled slyly, wondering with which of so many opinions she should concur.

She tugged the corner of her yellow *tobe* about her throat and fingered the winder for the door window. Immediately there came both a cooling draught and a swirl of dust.

"The dashboard vent, Miss Leila! Open the dashboard vent, for comfort with less dust."

Mogga would have leaned right across her to assist, had it not been so uncouth.

"Thank you for that advice," returned Leila, opening the stiff little steel lever of the vent.

On they rushed and rattled, past broad stony fields of millet that were grey-brown in the hazy sun. The plants were stubby and crisp, none more than a few inches high, and gasping. Leila gazed at them.

"What do you think, Miss Leila?"

"I wish I could go with a little tin can of water for each stalk," she said abstractedly.

In the middle distance, she saw a man. He was tall, very black against the tawny ground, with a white cloth tied about his middle. He hacked at the baked earth with a hoe in a way that seemed to Leila utterly courageous and ageless, a labour as limitless as the land about him. She looked for trees, but saw only the ominous, spiny *acacia nubica* shrubs that signalled overworked land and whose branches gave out a startling putrid smell when broken.

Half an hour later, Adam Zachariah became restless at the wheel, slowing the car and peering about the landscape.

"My family's place," said Adam. "May I? Just a minute, just to ask . . ."

He ran down the bank of the road into a field of sorghum, a stocky young man but tall amongst the thirsty plants.

"It looks small," said Fauzi abruptly, voicing the common fear.

"Maybe not so bad," Leila murmured, studying the field.

Fauzi would not be cheerful.

"It looks dry," he insisted. "They are poor people."

But Adam Zachariah was climbing back up the bank, pulling open the Land Rover door. He was grinning, holding out a handful of stalks: short, but the grain was swollen.

"It's all right!" panted Adam.

"They will have a harvest, Miss Leila," Mogga joined in, so enthusiastically you might have thought it was her achievement.

Leila smiled again.

Now Adam Zachariah became a fount of stories, laughing and pointing as they scudded westward.

"You see this bend? I was driving a Nissan truck from the souk and the drive shaft snapped, yah, we rolled down the bank! I was cut bad across the leg and I stopped the blood with battery acid. Don't you worry, Miss Leila, Allah is with us!"

He tapped the charms in leather cases bobbing from the mirror.

"Over there, the Red Cross driver Mohammed Harun and Abdella from the Salvation Committee, they saw two bandits in white *jellabiyas* aiming at them from the hillside. 'Bandits!' yells Mohammed Harun, 'Get us out of here!' So they screech about into Tawila and come back with the police and many guns to where the bandits are still waiting on the hillside – look now, you can see it – only they are just two big white rocks!"

They all laughed, though briefly. It had not been white rocks by the road from Nyala to El Fasher, when Farah had passed that way.

Leila at last began to relax.

They rushed onwards. After Umm Bulli they began to climb, skirting the northern slopes of Jebel Marra.

"The mountain at the centre of Africa," announced Fauzi, who would have liked to play a grand flourish on his piano.

In the cooler air, the silken clay of the road became greasy, with a sticky tearing sound as the tyres pulled at the surface. They rose twisting among boulders and gullies. Grasses, trees and shrubs were green and, in the late afternoon, there were wisps of cloud. They passed a group of barefoot woodcutters, thin blankets over their shoulders and long, black-handled knives in their belts. Their faces wore a satiny sheen of sweat and mist.

At Kaura, still climbing, they met a stream that ran clear and bright from a gorge. They stopped for tea at a roadside stall where the hushed mountain people came out of the clouds to sell their charcoal.

"The Italians had their road camp here," said Adam Zachariah. "You see that hilltop? One man took a bet, he drove a little Suzuki jeep up there through the rocks, and he got right up, only on the way down he turned over and the roof was broken, but still he drove down!"

Leila was gazing to the south, to the cool green slopes and the ancient, rough terraced gardens.

"What do you see, Miss Leila?" asked Mogga.

"I see bananas growing," she smiled.

"We had good bananas at my home," Mogga remembered.

Leila indicated with her elegant fingers.

"I see *terminalia laxiflora*, those broad trees on the open slopes, which here has yellow fruits but Yusuf Mohammed Modawi found red fruits in south Darfur. There is the candelabra *euphorbia*, and above there is *euphorbia abyssinica*, a noble tree, spiny and strong. It has thick milky sap and big green and crimson fruits."

"Ah!" breathed Mogga, profoundly impressed, "You know so well."

Adam and Fauzi regarded her too, and Leila spoke again:

"By the river, those tall trees are *syzygium guineense*, evergreen, like almost nothing else in Darfur."

"Oh," nodded Adam and Fauzi together, subdued by her.

"In the valley there, I see *melanoxylon*, the ebony tree."

"We call it *Babanus*!" cried Adam Zachariah, "I know it!"

Mogga frowned.

"Hush, Adam."

"But, it is *babanus*. And over there, the black one, is the *jokhan* tree . . ."

"*Diospyros mespiliformis*."

"*Jokhan* is the wood for making saddles. And that one, you see? That is our *ginkhir* tree, of which the honey is lovely."

Leila studied Adam Zachariah in surprise.

"Let us drive on," she said.

*

At Kebkabiya, down the mountain's western slope, there is a peaceful town in a grove. Here at the Agency house the Land Rover halts and, very promptly, Mr Mogga is out of the vehicle and opening the door for Leila. Elegantly, she steps down, straightening her *tobe* with a deft little tug left and right.

"Thank you, Mogga," she acknowledges, inclining her head.

Leila has a gift for Hamid the Plant Protection Officer. She walks without hurry to the rear of the vehicle, her boys in a swarm after her: Hamid, Mogga, Fauzi and Adam Zachariah. She waves her long fingers in a backhanded curl and they rush to open up, Adam and Mogga colliding and giggling. There in the back, wedged in beside the spare tyres, are five gallons of death-to-locusts.

"Ah!" sighs Hamid happily, nodding his head in vigorous thanks to Leila, "I shall slaughter them as they fly across from Chad. They shall meet destruction in Darfur!"

"How?" asks Mr Mogga. "How shall you destroy them?"

"I have a jeep," he replies, "with a spray mounted on the roof, one jeep for this whole province, you shall see how we shall fly about after those locusts!"

With bright eyes young Hamid takes the cans from the Land Rover, while neighbours in the tree-lined street clap him on the shoulder. This is news that all the town will share and cheer, the boys tugging at donkeys, urchins with fingers in their noses, teenage boys on errands in the souk, and an old woman in a rickety wheelchair with twisted wheels pushed by two teenage granddaughters, she beams also.

*

On a bluff over the dry wadi stands the Agency office and dormitory. Leila sleeps behind a brushwood screen in the back yard. In the morning, Mogga finds her gazing into nothing across the wadi.

"What are you looking at?" asks Mogga.

"The riverbed," she pulls herself together and lies courteously.

Adam Zachariah joins them saying:

"When the rains fall on the high Jebel Marra, the water flows in these wadis but under the surface of the sand. You cannot see it, but you can dig a hole in the sand and water comes which will fill with fish."

"Oh!" laughs Mogga. "Adam knows everything."

He wants to clap his hands at the teeming world. He catches Leila's eye, looking for that same delight in her – and she can't help but smile.

In the cool, and before the diesels cough and the town clamour begins, they go companionably to the souk. Mogga observes how Leila walks among the Agency staff and how they escort her protectively to left and right. For they sense her defensiveness, as though even here she is watched by mocking Government functionaries. But they see pride in her also, and they wonder where such pride comes from. Leila says little this morning, absorbed in her thoughts.

They consume sour *kisra* bread and bowls of coffee scented with cardamom and canella bark, seated on narrow wooden benches under a tamarind tree where the sunlight dapples down.

Then they drive away toward Seraf Umra.

Mogga has bought guavas in the souk; he passes them round and the hot Land Rover fills with their thick, sweet scent, the hard black pips unbreakable between the teeth. The track winds between scruffy *mukheit* bushes with bitter indigo berries, where the larks are stabbing at the ground for sand-lion grubs. They cross dry wadis, then turn through copses of thorn trees where stubby falcons rest from the heat and the carmine bee-eaters sail gracefully across the trail, swallowing wasps and hornets. The banging of the vehicle sends up flocks of black-headed finches that flitter away like leaves in a storm to settle seventy metres off and start pecking again. Leila and Mogga exchange a smile of pleasure.

"Look!" cries Fauzi, and Adam stops the car smartly.

There are nomads leading two dozen camels between the thorn trees and across the road in front of the Land Rover. The animals are draped with richly coloured mats and bags. The women ride under wicker awnings hung with red-striped cloth, swaying but secure, shadowed and unsmiling. The robed men, walking, pull the lead reins and bow very slightly to the Land Rover, a bow so delicate that it makes aristocrats of both giver and recipient.

The nomads pass over the dry riverbed, the camels lurching up the far bluff to start away south.

"They do not need a road," observes Fauzi solemnly, "because this is their country."

Mogga looks at Leila and sees that she is watching the nomads wistfully.

"What are you thinking, Miss Leila?" he enquires politely. She is startled; once again he has noticed her lowered defences.

"I was remembering a camel fair that my father once took me to," she replies, her voice flat and distant, "when I was small."

Farther on, there is a broad tree by the roadside and a boulder the size of an elephant, and in this shade is a cluster of four women, winnowing. They wear brass rings through one nostril and bracelets of brightly coloured plastic, with *tobes* of thin cotton that they have dragged up between their thighs for work, baring their knees. Seeing the Land Rover halt and a little black bustling towards them, they hoik their wraps primly up over their heads.

"Look at this," calls Mogga. "Tell me about this."

There is a heap of cut grass in the shadow of the rock, and a tawny mat with curling corners where the women thresh with long sticks. They pick up the grass in handfuls and shake it, peering closely at the scant seed that falls, then sweep the product with broad, soft brushes into a heap.

Mogga peers too, at the small mound of red-grey, gritty powder. He turns to Leila.

"You see it?" he demands.

"It is grass," observes Leila, struggling to recall its name.

"Grass!" cries Mogga. "They are threshing wild grass."

"It is *adar*," replies Adam Zachariah, "it can be eaten in hard times."

I did not know that, thought Leila.

"It is like dust," exclaims Mogga. He turns back to the women. "How long have you been doing this?"

Fifteen days.

"Oh!" exclaims Mogga, skipping from foot to foot in excitement. "These are the people to assist, Miss Leila."

She gives the women ten shillings.

They drive on, twisting to look back at the threshers.

"My father," says Leila, "wanted to bring science to Sudan, machines and techniques of every advanced sort. Can such things co-exist with people threshing wild grass seed?"

"That is their science," Mogga replies.

Broad spreading trees mark the sandy centre of Seraf Umra, the foliage so thin and feathery that the birds' nests cast more shade. Here are the tin booths of the merchants, their corrugated fronts up on wooden posts, while the best restaurants are secluded with brushwood and matting. The population squats and lolls in the shadow; the townsmen in white robes and neat white skull-caps gather to chatter and gossip. A little apart crouch the country women, their filthy drapes looped across their haunches and their heads, the ragged ends trailing in the grit by them. They squat with their elbows on their knees, their forearms held up in front of them displaying their only wealth, a copper bracelet on each wrist. The long black fingers, strangely unharmed by hard labour, waggle elegantly before their faces in the evening light, so expressive you might say they have an extra joint.

"Here," Mogga cries, "right here, stop your motor."

He bustles to the nearest café, a little compound enclosed by rough screens of hessian. A moment later he reappears.

"Milk!" exclaims Mogga. "Sugared milk. Come along now."

He bangs on the car door with the palm of his hand until Leila opens it.

"Mogga, good heavens," she reproves him, "how commanding you are today."

"Miss Leila, we must have you strong, for you are here to do a good deal of important work."

Is he mocking her?

"Please," he says, and he holds out a hand to assist her down from the cab.

Once again, like a queen, Leila descends from the Land Rover. It is becoming habitual with them.

Mogga chivvies her into the café enclosure behind the hessian. At once, men are whisking up a chair from which they flick the dust. They bring her a square steel table that is rubbed and polished in her honour.

"Are you comfortable?" Mogga wants to know. She thinks he is about to call her Madam. They are all watching intently: Mogga, Fauzi, Adam Zachariah, and half a dozen locals.

Now here is the proprietor gliding forward, bearing a bowl of green enamel with a black rim, half-full of fresh goats' milk. He places this upon the steel table and shouts impatiently at a boy who rushes up with a red biscuit tin from which the boss shovels sugar – four huge spoonfuls – into the bowl. When he stirs it, they hear the sugar swirl and scratch like sand.

They circle around Leila, her circle of men, and flap their hands eagerly at the milk.

"Drink," they cry together, "Madam!"

So Leila raises the green enamelled dish and nods across the chipped black rim at Mogga. Of a sudden, unaccustomedly, she feels greatly valued.

"I thank you," she smiles, "and I thank God. *Bismillah*."

"*Bismillah!*" they beam at her happily.

Afterwards, she walks with Adam Zachariah past the sellers of pomade and vests and string beds until she comes to a group of silent countrywomen squatting with palm-fibre mats in front of them. On the mats are small heaps of a dark green weed.

Leila stares at the limp plant. She does not recognise it – but Adam does.

"*Kawal*," he enthuses. "You know *kawal*? In bad times it is as good as meat. This lady can sell you *kawal* that she has made, or we can buy the weed and make it ourselves. I have done this, with my mother. We find this growing in shady places. We beat this until it is pasty, then we pack it in a big clay pot. We put green leaves on top and seal it up with mud and we bury it – you smell it rotting! Two weeks, then we make these balls and dry it in the sun."

He is delighted to tell her.

"And this?" demands Leila, swallowing her pride.

Three country girls sit with their knees drawn up. They have brass rings on their wrists, with pale fingernails and glistening black foreheads, smooth and rounded. Before them on the ground are pans filled with a tawny powder.

"Miss Leila, that is *haskaneet* seed. We can eat this when there is no rain, for *haskaneet* does not mind. But it is hard work for these ladies because it is a thistle and you must rub it between leather."

It looks, thinks Leila, no different from the dust of the souk.

"What have you brought to Seraf Umra?" demand the policemen in the tin-roofed oven of a police post.

"Medicines for goats, seeds for some ladies' gardens," she replies. Leila wishes Mogga were with her. The policemen are eyeing her curiously, wondering whether to jeer, to extort, or to be gentlemen. They glance at their officer for a lead. It could go anyhow.

Ah, dear God, Leila thinks, must I be humiliated?

But now, a small commotion: Mogga appears. He has found the local Agricultural Department, a paunchy fellow with a pockmarked face. Suddenly the little office is full of deference. The policemen are offering chairs, are holding forth on goat breeds and disease resistance.

Moments later there's a shrill of children's laughter. The officer barges outside but his bluster is forestalled, for there is Mogga cross-legged in the dust, playing knucklebones with the street urchins who howl with protest; Mogga has deftly tossed the marker to lodge in the hair over his left ear! He is calmly gathering every bone from the ground.

"I shall win everything they have!" he cries merrily, till a shrieking girl grabs the pebble off his head and they shout and dispute.

A woman in tawny rags edges forward, a miserable cowed presence. She holds out a scrap of black plastic containing a few small banknotes, she whines and mumbles.

Mogga leaps to his feet. He takes coins from his pocket and drops them into the grimy plastic. The Agricultural man hurries to match him, and the police too are digging into their uniforms.

The police! That is something. Leila regards Mogga with awe.

*

At dusk, in the compound of the official Resthouse, they make camp. Adam Zachariah has parked the Land Rover well away from the reeking pit latrines (no one would want to sleep inside the cockroach-infested brick blockhouse anyway). Leila looks about her dismayed, thinking that even the privations of El Fasher have something to be said for them. But Mogga and the men are in a huddle of discussion.

"Miss Leila," he calls, "we have it decided. Tonight you shall sleep like a princess."

Where are his ridiculous notions taking her now? What can she do but trust him? At Mogga's prompting, Adam Zachariah swarms up onto the roof of the Land Rover and heaves the spare tyres down to Fauzi. They roll away and Fauzi must chase them, miffed for his dignity. The black foam seats are taken from the vehicle and laid out on the roof rack. Now Mogga has taken four chairs and is lashing them upright at the corners of the rack with electrical cord. Fauzi passes up one of the big box-shaped mosquito nets and, before Leila's admiring eyes, a gauzy palace takes shape on the Land Rover's roof.

"For you," laughs Mogga. "You shall sleep cool and safe, high above us all."

"I thank you again," she says, with a bow of the head.

When night falls, when their meal of bread and tinned fish is eaten, they lie down in their places about the Land Rover. Adam

Zachariah will be inside on the floor. Mogga and Fauzi have only a plastic sheet under the second mosquito net, draped over the sand down from the car's flank. Leila lies above them all in regal comfort thinking about country people, and country plants.

Adam Zachariah sets off for the latrine, carrying the lamp across the compound in a pool of white light. Two minutes later he is back.

"There's a snake in there," he grumbles unhappily. "I heard it hiss."

"Adam, it was the lamp hissing," smiles Mogga from his bed on the ground. Fauzi sits up, staring towards the latrine.

"Just pray it stays in the latrine," replies Adam, turning off the lamp.

Mogga begins to say, "Good night to you, Miss . . ."

But there's a shriek from his side. Fauzi leaps to his feet, waving at something black that curls and writhes on the sand at his feet.

"Get away, snake! Get away!" he shouts, stumbling and kicking frantically at it in the dark.

"Fauzi!" cries Mogga in horror, scrambling up also. Leila cries out from the roof, Adam is grabbing for a torch and a stick, but Fauzi's arm snags the mosquito net and drags it down over them like a bird trap but with the snake inside, poised to strike at their toes.

The snake doesn't move. There is a moment of incredulous, fate-struck silence as they gaze at it and await death helpless in the fine entrammelling mesh. Still the creature doesn't move. Until Mr Mogga, swathed in white netting like some cobwebbed ghost, leans forward and peers more closely.

"No!" shouts Fauzi in horror, for Mogga has crouched and picked up the snake, holding it out to him.

"It's your belt, Fauzi," says Mr Mogga, jingling the buckle. "It's the belt from your trousers, that was on the sand there."

Fauzi takes it in his clammy hand as though the belt might deliver a death-bite still.

The first laugh comes from a silhouetted figure crouched above them. Leila, kneeling on the roof and peering down, is giggling.

Then Adam Zachariah is laughing aloud and Mogga is snorting with joy:

"Oh Fauzi, your belt! We nearly died of a belt. Miss Leila, look what has killed us!"

They are weeping with laughter, all around poor Fauzi in his netting – till he too begins to shake, to grin, to bellow with them.

PART THREE
Our Mogga

ONE

Often, in his anxious, sleepless nights, Xavier Hopkins shared his string cot in the garden with General William Hicks Pasha. They were comfortable together. William Hicks, thought Xavier, would have understood. Hicks, that woeful out-of-his-depth leader of the Egyptians in Sudan, whose spade beard waggled ever more trim as his army fell apart. Hicks, honourable commander of the doomed, struggling with indolent colleagues and hopeless troops. Hicks, naïve mercenary of foreign powers eager to control Africa from a distance. Hicks, patted on the back by every perspiring frock coat in Cairo and told what a stout fellow he was, before being despatched. They must have known, in 1883 they *must* have known that between the turbulent tribes and the incompetent Egyptians and the waterless scrub of Kordofan would be an end of Hicks. Yet they sent him off from Cairo to Suakin on the Red Sea, to march over the desert to Khartoum, there to exhaust himself in an administrative farce before trailing off to his death in the western scrub.

All pretty much like us, thought Xavier sardonically as he gazed up through the mosquito net at the sleeping kites silhouetted in the tree over his bed. Naïve, mercenary, in the pay of foreigners and lost in the *goz*. Ah, yes; Xavier liked to confide in this ghost who shared his string cot, for Hicks would have recognised his predicament.

Hicks would, for instance, have nodded in glum recognition at the four radio messages from Khartoum, placed at intervals this morning on Xavier's desk, *viz* –

09.40 hrs. EXPECT DELIVERY 10,000 TONS HIGH
ENERGY BISCUITS FOR CHILDREN'S
SUPPLEMENTARY FEEDING.

Then –

10.20 hrs. CORRECTION: EXPECT DELIVERY 10,000
TINS OF HIGH ENERGY BISCUITS.

After which –

11.25 hrs. CORRECTION: EXPECT 10,000 BISCUITS.

And finally –

12.20 hrs. BISCUITS UNAVAILABLE.

Ah yes, Hicks would have known, would have courteously torn Xavier's hair out for him.

And Hicks would have sympathised with Xavier's dire unease at his stupendous task: a dozen foreigners to prevent a famine in a province the size of France. Hicks, who had written to his wife:

> If I only rise to the occasion as I hope I shall and make a good business of the unpromising material I have, the upshot may be very great, but the responsibilities and anxieties are rather overpowering at first.

Hicks, who had known that the great men watching from the Imperial wings would cheer loudly as long as he did well, but would be nowhere to be found when it went sour. Hicks, who had begun to suspect from their blandishments that he was being set up:

> They congratulated me on having such an opportunity to distinguish myself.

Hicks, who had felt the awful burden of expectation:

> All here recognise the difficulties I have to overcome. The retention or loss of the Soudan depends upon it.

Perhaps it still does, thought Xavier Hopkins, pulling the light blanket closer about him. For now we have said that we shall feed Darfur though we have not yet found a famine, and the flood-gates of expectation are open once again.

At times the folly and anxiety had so pressed upon Xavier that peculiar sensations had tormented him: a racing of the heart, a tightness of breath, a weakness in the arms with tinglings in his wrists and hands that bewildered him until he remembered something he had heard about panic attacks. Yes, he was on the verge of panic, although only one corner of the food programme had as yet begun. But Xavier was nothing if not a decent man, and his decency lent him courage. He had a young team, many of them inexperienced, and he must lead them. They were his charges; if he were to send them out into bandit-infested countryside then it would be for a damn good reason, and properly planned. For a brief instant, Xavier thought of Farah ibn Mashoud, shot with a high-velocity rifle on the road . . . But he suppressed the thought ruthlessly. If Xavier felt panic wash through him, he would not let it show.

Had Hicks ever panicked? Surely, secretly at least, when he was lost in the scrub. And Xavier knew what that felt like.

Every day, Field Director Hopkins felt himself to be lost, in some sense of that word. It was a game he played with himself, asking: "In what sense am I lost today?" It might happen as he was driving through the streets – sand pits, really – between endless blank-walled compounds without names, numbers or signs. Then he could easily be quite lost. Sometimes, he would be enveloped in mists of confused policy, a fog of impossible logistics, a blizzard of reproach and a deluge of conflicting interests, and he would think, "I am lost, I can see no way forward!" At other times the operation appeared quite hopeless, even in prospect. Just so, Hicks, in September 1883, even before they had all marched out of Khartoum to their deaths, must have surveyed his medieval, chain-mailed troops and said to himself, "We are lost before we start." Xavier remembered the despairing letters Hicks sent back to the capital after his native guides had deliberately wandered off track in Kordofan: "I am lost." And finally, as 50,000 warriors threw themselves on his demoralised men in a dry forest, how brave, lonely William Hicks must have cried: "Lost! All lost!"

Xavier recognised the feeling. But, always, he would pull himself together, issuing stern directives to his Agency team that restored, for a while, the illusion of control.

As to being geographically lost, Xavier had every sort of map that Stanford's of Longacre could provide. He had Bartholomew's *East Africa*, fifty kilometres to the centimetre, on which fine red lines spidered like broken veins indicating roads some of which were all too real (the road from Nyala to El Fasher, for instance), but more that Xavier knew from bitter experience did not exist. He had maps which his computer had 'generated', a term evocative of the fiction Xavier felt that he was living through. There was also the cumbersome 'air operations chart', covered in grids, target circles and reference numbers as though the country was aligned for destruction by the bombardier of some battle-satellite. In spite of the chart's size (a metre across) and its large scale (ten kilometres to the centimetre), it was strangely uninformative, with details that a pilot would supposedly notice from the air, but which belonged in other times. There was, for instance, a black mark: 'mission'. What, Xavier wondered, does a mission look like from the air? Any Christians in Darfur now would duck under camouflage netting if they thought you could see them. A tiny rectangle in square *PQ* was labelled 'winter quarters': of whom, of what, out there in the scorched Kordofan desert? In square *PN* was marked a 'tower': who kept watch – some melancholy Nilotic Montaigne? Who was preparing to sell their life dear in that 'fort' in square *QM*, on a waterless hilltop far from any road – some last descendant of Hicks Pasha and his force?

To the west, across the border into Chad, at the conjunction of several squares, the colour of the mapping changed from a light to a darker green, and here the cartographers had printed: 'Vegetation irreconcilable'. Hah, mused Xavier donnishly, the stern dry thorns of the north have turned their backs on the soft corrupted mangoes of the south. In a few, far northern squares he saw the phrase, 'Dark area'. That, Xavier decided, must refer to the region's morals.

The maps did not agree, and in quite inexplicable ways. What could explain the disparity between the Microsoft computer maps and the sketches made for him by the Agency's own monitoring teams? The locals and the Americans had recorded hardly a single town or village in common. To the west, the local men knew all about Seraf Umra and Segrin, Girab and Bellafarash, and had carefully inked them in, but the Americans had never heard of them, nor of the tracks that went there. In that same district, Microsoft seemed well informed about Girgo and Nuqdaiyah, Tombasi and Tinniyat, but these important settlements apparently rang no bells with the people on the ground; did they exist at all? Had some 'guide' been pulling the Americans' legs, as they had the miserable Hicks'? Xavier compared the two dozen names on rival sheets, and found just three in common.

Maps, which anywhere else gave him such pleasure, here gave him a hard time. It's the same with every aspect of this operation, thought Xavier sadly. We all have our versions of Darfur, and no one else's tallies with our own.

Little wonder that the Health Ministry had no idea where its own clinics were. Little wonder that bandits evaded the army with such contemptuous ease. It was almost reassuring: need one be surprised if no food was ever delivered, when nobody was sure where the recipients lived? Or if the trucking companies refused to waste their diesel searching the sands? Perfectly reasonable. Probably the desert settlements calling for food were fictions; none of them appeared on any map. The whole food crisis was a con, a red herring, a fraud, a joke.

Xavier even managed a grim smile, as he drifted off to sleep on his string cot.

But the next day came news that threw them all off balance. Out of the filthy static jumble of the radio came a major policy decision, taken in Khartoum, unexplained and without any reference to him at all: World Food Programme grain deliveries would commence forthwith – but only to El Fasher town and its immediate environs.

Xavier swallowed his outrage and considered the matter. As a policy, it was bizarre; it would be divisive, it must create terrible tensions; surely Khartoum could understand that? He would radio, he would write, but he knew that no one in the capital was listening. He needed allies, people with clout, on both sides of the desert, but Xavier could not see that he had any.

In the meantime, the new policy meant that Toby waiting in Kutum, Nyala Freddy, Lorna stuck 300 kilometres away at Geneina, and all the other far-flung and expectant districts got nothing. And it meant that supervision would be the responsibility of one person only: Christa.

She could do it, thought Xavier, as long as she kept her head. He made a swift decision and gave Christa the best help he could think of: he allocated Mr Mogga to her staff.

*

When she first came to Darfur, Christa slept in the air all the way from Khartoum over the deserts of Kordofan to Darfur.

"It's all the same," said the pilot. "You'll be sick of the view soon enough."

The aircraft, an ancient Islander, was slow. "An airborne donkey-cart," the pilot grinned. So she dozed off, seeing nothing, her head against the vibrating window.

Below them lay a broad swath of tyre tracks in the sand where ten-wheel freighters had dragged their spoor. Then the desert dust rose up towards the plane. The crags and scarps blurred as though painted on cream cartridge, a watercolour of a place without water. Ancient rains had left wide dry wadis that were visible not by their contours but by their colours only: deepening grey and olive in steps, like sub-sea levels on a map. Trucks would stick there in the soft alluvium. If the rain ever came again, sorghum might grow.

Farther west, mountains of split rock, crumbling more each century. Then mile on empty mile with nothing but a ringworm of grey thorn around abandoned villages. Beautiful and terrible scenery. Had she studied it, Christa might have been more guarded, more wary in her enthusiasm for the task ahead. But she slept soundly, and only as they landed at El Fasher did she wake, full of spirit.

*

She came from Aachen. Her full name was Christa Lerche, meaning Christa the Lark; her singing was a weak, embarrassed little piping, but she had the neat, quick movements of a bird. She was thirty-two, small and orderly. Her fair hair drifted about her face. She stood with her feet close together, a leather bag on her shoulder and a large red daybook under her arm. The office cat ran to her when she crouched and called, "*Kätzchen!*"

She was appointed Food Emergency Officer for El Fasher District, and her first job was to help Xavier Hopkins to establish if there was a food emergency at all. After weeks of fruitlessly importuning Colonel Hassan al-Bedawi of State Security, the latter changed his mind; she could take a team into the villages to estimate food stocks. Christa was, on the one hand, faced with every obfuscation that a wily people could contrive in the cause of freeloading, and on the other hand was lumbered with dimmocks like Fauzi and his piano. She disposed of the latter, at least.

With the decision to feed El Fasher District, it became Christa's responsibility to administer grain deliveries to 120,000 people. Xavier Hopkins had feared she might not be up to it, this one small woman. He heard that she was drinking *arigi* regularly, every evening. But then, he had never seen her drunk or hung over. Of an evening she loosened up, but she never lost control.

She told Xavier how she was relishing the coming task. She had a gleam in her eye; he realised that he had no one tougher. He told Christa that he was assigning Mr Mogga as her interpreter and assistant. Her face lit up with pleasure and they became a feared team.

"The poor ones in the villages have nothing," she said, "and I am here to deal with that." She looked about eagerly for obstacles to surmount.

At last, a sputtering and intermittent flow of relief grain began, despatched across the sands to Darfur by harassed Agency staff in

Khartoum, whose maps were no better than Xavier's and who knew nothing of the Fur villages beyond a list of names. The dispatchers would give one such name to a driver who would frown and declare that he had never heard of it, or that he knew for a fact that the place had moved, or had ceased to exist, or was twice the size, until the despatchers swore and shouted, "Go! Just go!"

On the far side of the Kordofan desert, each truck entered Darfur seeking a settlement of brushwood huts, one of thousands. As if the risk of bandits were not enough, each load of grain was accompanied by no more than a flimsy pink waybill so easily misread by store man or driver, or by the elders of some other predatory clan. Each truck had a crew to dig, jack and repair, to roll the greasy diesel drums, and to ease a percentage out through the sacks' loose stitching. At every stage, the dishonest preyed on the disorganised.

Christa declared that 'leakages' must stop – and soon a truck driver was found skimming the loads. Then Mr Mogga reported jail officers selling the prisoners' rations in the souk. Next, Christa exposed a shipper whose wheat had been spoiled by rain, and who had mixed this grey, tainted, musty mess throughout the good stock, to keep up weight. Soon, the little woman and Mogga her black, her *zurqa*, were respected in town. She smiled and said, "Mogga and I shall work night and day. I have a nice feeling here."

It was a crusade fought with lists, tallies and inspections. "Trust is good, checking is better!" she laughed, ordering her staff into the souk to trap grain racketeers. Xavier Hopkins saw that she was utterly determined.

A delegation of villagers crowded into Christa's office to denounce Mohammed Shattah, a Government officer, for hoarding and profiteering. So Mogga took himself quietly down to the souk one evening. Small, shuffling and unregarded, Mogga observed sacks being hustled from the rear door of a Government store and piled high on a pickup. An hour later, Christa and Mogga arrived unannounced at a warehouse owned by Shattah's brother on the far side of town – and there were the sacks, bulging with Australian wheat. Astonished by the little firecat woman and her

144

stocky black sidekick, Shattah – a towering, muscular, sweaty man – offered 'an arrangement', but Christa wanted a public example made.

"Whatever you do," urged Xavier, "don't actually accuse him, not in public."

"Oh, but I have!" sang Christa happily. "I have called Shattah a big thief and we are taking the matter to the Governor and this one shit bastard will go to jail."

She tucked her red daybook under her arm and sailed out across the yard, fussing with the cat as she passed: *O, Kätzchen, komm, komm* . . .

Her office was a cool house, with a shade tree in the compound and a blind watchman. Christa nailed the Programme sign to the street wall, bought a goat and held a roast for her staff with bottles of pop, unleavened bread and Mogga basting the meat.

"I am teaching them the German national anthem," grinned Christa, "and we shall work as I do in Germany, *zack! zack!*" She chopped the air with her hands, karate style. Mogga and her team did all that she asked of them.

She lived in the Programme Resthouse. Some of the team had found other houses around town and had moved out, but Christa stayed on with the rump."I *like* this team," she reiterated, "I have a warm feeling now."

In the evening, Christa liked to read their cards and their palms, over a drink. Only Mogga's hands she could not interpret, because of the burns that had scarred them.

Xavier found her one afternoon at the Garsila truck stop, a strip of dirty sand lined with brushwood shelters, where tired drivers hunkered on rickety stools with Libyan 'Marlboro' and the cooks served gristle in thin gravy. Christa stood in the shade of a ten-wheeler, hemmed in by complaining elders. Mogga, dwarfed by these men, stood protectively by her side, interpreting and watchful.

Christa said to Mogga, "Please, you will ask them, how was the grain, how was the quality, were they pleased? And where are the waybills?"

She popped the pink slips into her daybook, while the locals clamoured at Mogga: "Why has this woman sent food for one week only?"

Xavier noticed that they did not look at Christa, but at Mogga. Their entire wrath was focused on the little southerner who absorbed it like a protective filter; the foreign woman was largely ignored, so that she had to wave her hand to make a point.

"They must understand," she cried, "that it comes not just from Khartoum but from Port Sudan. That is nearly 2,000 kilometres of desert, which is very expensive!"

"*Kalam kwais*, very true," said the men, "But what are we to eat next week?"

"You have my word: more is coming," she insisted. She took Mogga by the arm and led him away to begin interrogating the transport crews.

"Can you believe those truck men?" she told Xavier. "One says he will not risk his axles. He put the food down six miles from Keila and has told these poor people they must walk and fetch it. That is a real shit bastard, no? Another shit bastard Mogga has caught asking 300 Sudanese pounds for unloading, threatening to take the food elsewhere. I shall report him."

She perched on a shaded bench cradling sweet-scented tea. Nearby, the Garsila women milled around the well, sniffed unhappily at the foul water in their buckets and peered into the depths. Three girls squatted by small bundles of fodder gleaned from the desert: the only thing left to sell. Garsila's thin donkeys watched silently. No one bought the grass. No one had cash.

Christa's eyes were dust-reddened, her team exhausted. To visit twenty-two villages, she'd allowed a day and a half.

"Don't check *every* delivery," said Xavier. "You'll burn yourselves out. Sampling checks will do, get the broad picture."

She listened politely, and said that best of all would be the complete picture. She still had twelve villages to see, and tomorrow was Friday, the Sabbath.

"Don't strain your staff too soon," he persisted. "That's my advice. Things are likely to get tougher, you know."

She replied, "We can do two villages this evening, six before breakfast, and the last four on the way home to Fasher. What do you say, Mogga?"

Mr Mogga was peering at the pink burn scars on the palms of his hands, scratching thoughtfully at them. He lifted his gaze to study her a second, smiled and chimed in: "We must follow every sack!"

*

But soon there were few sacks to follow. A fraction of the promised food arrived across the desert, though rumour spoke of bulging warehouses at Port Sudan. Xavier shouted into the radio on Christa's behalf, demanding that the despatchers in Khartoum do some despatching, and those poor harassed souls shouted back through the static of this problem and the other, that they were doing their best. The promises rang hollow; for Christa's team, there was nothing for it but to explain, beg patience and bear the scorn. The Resthouse reeked of anxiety and impotence. After work, feverish and dehydrated, Christa lay with cool flannels on her fore-head. Her thin and fragile hair went limp.

"Now it will fall out," she said.

She brooded, her temper short and her tongue loosened. If her computer battery ran flat, she cursed Sudan. If there was no water, she castigated the Programme. If there was no Land Rover, no diesel, no money, or her calls to Khartoum went unanswered, she stamped her foot.

"This is not acceptable. When I am better, these things will be properly done, *zack!*" (her little chopping gesture in the air), "*zack! zack!*"

She then regretted such extravagant movement: "I cannot believe how I am sweating."

Meanwhile, Mohammed Shattah the grain hoarder went untouched: no proceedings, no disgrace. He had written to the Governor complaining that Christa had insulted him. Xavier sweated to repair the breach, and curtly told Christa to drop the matter. That evening, she took one look at the cold kidney beans and gritty bread at dinner, lay down on her bed and raged:

"Today I have wasted two hours looking for one incompetent fuel store man before I can go to the villages. Then we are exhausted and late and we can do nothing. We should have fired this man. It is not acceptable! Every day I must send Mogga to villages to apologise because this stupid Aid Programme cannot deliver food. I have to be polite to this Shattah because we have no courage to accuse him. Now I shall get sick. Shit water, shit staff, shit work, shit meals all covered in oil: how can I work if I can't eat?"

"Christa," someone began, "we're all feeling the strain . . ."

She exploded.

"*Strain?* This is not strain, it is incompetence. I expose a thief and nothing happens! If Mohammed Shattah is not a shit bastard, *who* is a shit bastard? He is an enemy of the poor ones and of our Programme."

She subsided, a cassette of Mahler songs in her earphones, muttering, "No, not acceptable, this shit."

From across the room, Mr Mogga watched her, thoughtful.

It was the same each day: no food trucks, or a radio message that they had left Khartoum, but no sightings since; or one truck instead of ten, so that bitter disputes broke out, village against village. Every morning, delegations of men in *jellabiyas* marched to Christa's office saying that their children and donkeys were dying. Mr Mogga, always by her side, sifted out of his translation the patronising tones, the subtle and unsubtle insults in the complaints, while Christa reiterated excuses, reasons, requests for patience.

But her despondency deepened; she lay morosely on her string bed, muttering.

"Who is the enemy, where is the problem? I work and work, and *still* no food comes. What to do? *Who* to fight?"

Her eyes were dry and sore; she rubbed them redder. Xavier thought of sending her to Kenya to rest. But then came a coup that revived her spirit: she caught Mohammed Shattah red-handed.

A little sorghum seed had arrived; Mogga learned that the

Governor had set Shattah to organise distribution, and Christa came to investigate.

"It is my concern only," said Mohammed Shattah. The man's peculiarly rancid odour filled the room.

"Excuse me, no," said Christa through Mogga, "My organisation is monitoring this programme, and where the seed goes is indeed my concern."

"Oh?" smiled Shattah sarcastically, "Well, nonetheless, it is my job, and on the Governor's orders. You know what this is?" He waved at Christa a piece of paper covered in Arabic handwriting. "No? I'll tell you. It's a distribution list." Now he eyed Mogga, "Do you happen to read Arabic also?"

Mogga looked awkward. "No, I cannot read it."

Mohammed Shattah grinned and slapped it onto the desk.

"Well, be thankful that some of us can. I drew it up. *I* decide who gets the seed."

But Christa was peering closely at the list.

"These are the names?" she asked.

"Just so," replied Shattah.

"I see," said Christa. "Thank you."

Before he could stop her, she had folded the list, tucked it into her daybook, walked out of his office and gone back to her own, calling for young Osman the turnboy to come and read it to them.

"Mogga!" she crowed, while Osman read out the list, running his finger down the paper. "It is just his cronies and mistresses! *To Ahmed Saif, two sacks.* Who is this Ahmed Saif, could he be the same as here: *Saif, Ahmed – three sacks?* And here: *To four poor women – two sacks.* Can't he name his women even? And my God, listen, this man is mad! *To Mohammed Shattah and his brothers – four sacks!*"

Shattah came to her office. He stood massively before her, patches of reeking sweat darkening his *jellabiya*, deferential, nervous, asking for his list back. Christa smiled sweetly, saying that she'd sent it to the Governor. For once, even the Governor was outraged.

"She's making powerful enemies," Xavier said.

Rose Price replied, "Yes, of course, that's what keeps Christa going."

"But it's a hiding to nothing," he groaned. "We can't prosecute Shattah and the Governor certainly won't, not at our request."

And indeed, the next time Christa went to Government House, there was Mohammed Shattah at his desk, regarding her with a nasty leer. He'd been reprimanded, he was on probation – but he was still there.

Stunned, her despondency returned. As the heat became more humid, Christa became wan and fragile. At each day's end she would sink onto her cot, picking weakly at her cotton dress: "I am just sweating. I cannot believe this sweating."

They sent from Wadaa, saying that the babies were all dead now and why was there no food and would she come today, please? Christa pushed herself up wearily, though her colleagues protested, "Christa, for God's sake, rest. It's a scare story, it'll keep a day."

"No, I must go," she mumbled, "those poor ones have nothing."

"It's nonsense!" they cried.

But just then Mogga arrived with Daud and the Land Rover. Mogga studied her for seconds only, before saying firmly:

"We are ready, Miss Christa. I have brought fresh water, some bread, eggs and fruit for our lunch. Shall we go?"

Christa got to her feet, a trifle unsteady. She looked at Mogga and Daud with undisguised pride and walked out to the vehicle with them.

Dr Maeve went to Xavier demanding that he arrange two weeks' Kenya leave for Christa, that he order her to go. Christa did not protest. She had her team well drilled; there was little that Mogga, aided by Magda, Daud and Mahmoud, could not manage for a fortnight. The Islander was to bring two new nurses to Darfur, and to collect Christa and others needing respite. She packed a swimming costume into a small bag and began to talk of the beach at Malindi, her tone merry but brittle.

Two days before her departure, she was called to a village

southwest of town. "We are starving," the delegation entreated, "Six people in Radam Central have died this week."

"Radam Central?" she wondered, "It is the only area where anything has grown this year. They are all right, I think – but we have to see. Come, Mogga."

Over the sands, the village children scampered calling, *Khowajiyah! Khowajiyah! Foreigner!* Slime hung from their noses, the flies walked on their potbellies. They scuttled tittering into the dry stick compounds, while a knot of men stood picking at their clothes by the shade tree, murmuring.

"So, just who was it that died this week?" began Mogga to the headman who seemed flustered and said aloud, "No one."

"Then why did you send word of deaths?" persisted Mogga.

"We knew you would have to come," another man spoke up defiantly. "We need you to get our food back from Radam al-Souk. It was sent there by mistake, and it's ours."

"Explain, please," demanded Christa.

Radam al-Souk was a separate market village two kilometres away, beyond a dry wadi. A truck crew, weary of searching the desert, had dumped relief food for both communities at the souk, whereupon the market traders had distributed it amongst their families.

"I can believe anything of Radam al-Souk," said Christa, staring over the wadi with eyes unusually dark. "It's Mohammed Shattah's village."

They crossed the wadi. The lock-ups of Radam al-Souk stood in two rows, the ground speckled black with goat droppings. From a brick building nearby came the *tug-tug* of a diesel mill grinding down the evidence.

"Tell them the food was for Radam Central," said Christa to Mogga, holding her red daybook in front of her breast like a shield. "They know that they cannot keep this."

Tall, unforgiving men faced Mogga, the wind pulling the white *jellabiyas* back between their knees. Behind them, a crowd swelled for the fight.

"The wheat was given to us," said the men.

"But by mistake," said Christa. "I am sorry for that, but you know that it belongs to your neighbours, and your neighbours are hungry."

"They don't look hungry!" shouted a youth. The crowd shrieked with bitter laughter.

"Anyway, it is too late," said an elder. "We have distributed it."

Christa's small feet were tight together in the goat droppings. On the red daybook, her fingernails were pressed bloodless.

"Then collect it," she said, not raising her voice.

"We can't, we've eaten it," someone retorted, and they cackled at her.

"Twelve kilos each?" demanded Mogga, "in two days?"

But they would not collect it. Christa changed tack, and spoke icily of the need for neighbourliness.

"*Kalama jemilla*," said the old men, "Fine words," but they did nothing, while the young men pressing up behind called, "We have stomachs also; do not tell us about your mistakes, but send more!"

Christa flushed with anger. She said she would radio Khartoum; deliveries to Radam al-Souk would be suspended. A murmur went through the crowd. The villagers regarded her with loathing, while barely refraining from spitting in the face of the black man at her side. Then they turned their backs.

In town, Christa went directly to the radio hut. She gestured the operator from his chair. Her lips pursed, she sent her demands through electrical storms to Khartoum. Her voice was glacial and her message punitive, and through the hiss and hum came confirmation: Mohammed Shattah's kin would be starved into submission. She was satisfied.

But, when she put the microphone down, a shiver went through her slight frame. She was staring into a snake pit.

Mr Mogga was watching her from the doorway.

She said, "Why do you look like that? Do you think I can let this go?"

Mogga said, "My concern is for your health. You must have a nice holiday."

Thursday morning, early, Mogga and Magda came to her office for last instructions. They shook Christa's hand as though she were retiring, with emotion in their faces. Xavier drove her to the airfield.

A row of grimy jeeps waited by the fence. The windsock hung still. Through the open window of the tower came a radio crackle; a controller leaned out and called, "Islander!" An electric brilliance appeared in the hazy sky, like a star held over from dawn, which slowly descended and grew until the high-winged Islander lowered itself gingerly onto the pink gravel. Christa picked up her bag, glanced back at the ragged white margins of town – and saw a vehicle, pluming dirt.

It was Daud and Mogga, scrunching to a stop by the fence; Christa hurried to them

"Christa, come!" Xavier called to her from the wing's shade. "Pilot needs to go at once, there's dust threatening."

She shouted back, "No, I cannot."

"Two minutes!" Xavier yelled again, but she walked towards him, calling:

"I do not go today."

"What?"

"A truck has passed El Obeid with 200 sacks for Radam al-Souk. I have to stop this."

He stared at her, incredulous.

"We'll sort that out. Mogga can deal with rumours. The plane's going."

"It's not rumour, it is news. I will not go, I must prevent any truck from reaching that shit bastard village. It cannot be allowed."

"Christa . . ." he began, but she screeched, "No! I do not go to Kenya today! Mogga, *you* understand this?"

Mr Mogga nodded. Two minutes later, the Islander taxied away without her.

She tried the radio, but the weather in the east was bad, the clouds seething with static. She went with Mogga to the police, demanding that any truck with a waybill for Radam al-Souk should be intercepted and sent to her.

The truck driver, however, was a Darfur man. He didn't bother to stop at the transport park for a guide, but headed directly across the *goz* to the villages. His ten-wheel vehicle and its banner of dust were seen on the edge of town, lurching towards Radam al-Souk.

"I prayed that we could stop them," sighed Christa, exhausted and afraid. "Now I must go to that village again. Why do you look at me so, Mogga?"

He replied, "Again, I am concerned for you."

"You think they will crush me?" she whispered. "I think so, I think it is too much for me, I cannot stand against them."

She was trembling with incipient hysteria, which at any moment would engulf the little woman. A flicker began in her lips and her eyelids; she was teetering . . .

"Where there's a will, there's a way," said Mogga calmly. It had been the favourite saying of the Principal of Mateki school.

Christa peered at him anxiously, her eyes wide.

He continued, "They are poor oafs. When you thwart them, I shall be there to see."

His gaze stayed on her, smiling gently, unfussed, faintly humorous – and the terror passed, draining from her. Of a sudden, determination surged back.

"Mogga," she said, "we can never allow this food to be misdirected. We are dealing with a crisis here. They will see that my justice is quick, *zack! zack!*"

They left in pursuit, the turbocharger whistling, Daud's excited fingers tapping on the steering wheel. Leaving town, they paused at Government House. Christa demanded an escort from the Darfur Salvation Committee and (she absolutely insisted) Mohammed Shattah also. He came out to the vehicle, puzzled. Only once they were beyond the airfield, driving hard over the *goz*, did she name the village in trouble. Shattah scowled – and said hardly a word all that day.

They were too late. They met the red truck empty, swaying lightly back across the dunes. Everything had been delivered as specified to Radam al-Souk. Christa and Mogga asked the truck driver to return to the village with them. Nonsense, he said, he was going home. The Salvation officer ordered him to turn around, but he retorted that he took his orders from Khartoum. They beseeched him, "You *must* come with us and collect these sacks!" The man looked bewildered, saying, "I have brought food a thousand kilometres for my starving countrymen and you ask me to take it *back?*"

For long minutes they argued and appealed; Mohammed Shattah walked ten yards apart and stared discomforted at a *mukheit* bush. At last the trucker climbed into his cab, the diesel snorted and both truck and Land Rover heaved about, back to Radam al-Souk.

The people saw, and gathered on the wadi's crumbling edge.

"Ah, it's the young lady who said we were to have no more food. What, you've sent us *another* truck by mistake? Is it that you think feeding people is a mistake altogether, or is it just that you are not so good at your work? When Sudanis trade, we see to it that the right person receives the goods. Hey, Mohammed! What do you say? Won't you explain a few things here? Brother, are you listening?"

Mohammed Shattah stood aside, stirring the goat droppings with his mucky leather slippers, peering intently at driftwood and flotsam strewn across the wadi. Incredulous at his silence, Shattah's relations waited for their mighty town cousin to chastise these tormentors, while the Salvation official eyed him curiously. But Shattah said nothing.

"At one moment," Christa told Xavier that evening, perched on a bed in the Resthouse yard, "I thought they would attack us. Mogga was worried. He kept looking at me, he knew that I was scared – but it was not me they would have struck, it was Mogga. It took just hours! One time I walked towards the shed where the sacks were but they stood in front of me and would not let me pass. Then the Salvation man proposed a compromise, fifty-fifty, and for a moment I am going to give in, I think, this is all we can do, but Mogga understands that there can be no compromise. Mogga says to the Salvation man, 'Will you betray Miss Christa now?' The man doesn't like Mogga for he is just a southern *zurqa* and this is an awful moment like civil war among us. I see the villagers begin to smile. So I say, 'No! This food they are not entitled to, I have authority to take it back,' and Mogga shouts it loud and clear. That Mohammed Shattah, he truly hates Mogga, he doesn't know what to say. If he argues for his own village this Salvation official will tell the Governor, and if he helps me take the food away his people will tear him. And I think, good, so I am sweating and you are sweating too."

She paused in her story. The yard was cool and pleasant now. She sipped at her water flask; a dribble ran from her mouth. Her face sagged with exhaustion.

"At last, we are so tired. I agree that I will take 175 sacks and leave sixty and these people say, OK, take your sacks. They stand and look at me and these sacks weigh sixty kilos each. There is the empty truck and what to do? I offer to pay them to reload the lorry, two-fifty Sudani pounds each sack, and they laugh loud. Then some want this work because at least they get money, but others shout, no, let the woman and her *zurqa* load their own truck!"

Christa attempted to peel an orange, but her hands shook and she dropped it in the sand. She picked it up and poured over cool water from the stoneware jar.

"I walked up to the man who was holding the big key for the store and I just took this from his hand. I said, I shall cross the wadi to Radam Central, I will return with men from there and I will pay those men three pounds per sack to reload that truck. At this, Shattah says, 'Please . . .' I see he panics. I say to this fat bastard, 'Oh, Mohammed? *You* will help me load all these sacks now? You and I?' Well, you know, I did not finish what I am saying because Mohammed's brothers and uncles think Radam Central will get money *and* food and they will get nothing. And you know, they reloaded the truck. We have taken the food to Radam Central."

She was quiet for a moment, as the night gathered and the town dogs woke and scrapped. Something moved in the heap of palm debris by the wall.

Christa said, "Today I thought would be my day off. I have worked seven hours in the desert, and there is a possibility of another truck tomorrow. Just now I must find Mogga and we must visit the police. Then I believe I shall have earned my holiday, when the plane comes back."

*

Next evening, the team went out to Jebel Sarjein, a stony hill with a long double peak to the north of town. They passed through thin plantings of shrivelled millet that had germinated and tried to grow, but which would never flower. Some they crushed with the tyres, driving to the hill's foot.

It was a place for taking breath, bare and uncluttered, good to scramble up in the cool. There they could watch the light fade, and observe the farmers going home, walking their donkeys over the undulating *goz*. They could see the distant mountains and, as dusk fell, thin grey plumes rising from the far settlements. Kites and ibises and geese moved in the sky. But on the hilltop, no sound, just light pattings of a warm, dry wind.

"You feel this wind?" said Daud the driver, "It is the *gharwa haboob*, the end of the rains, but the rains have not come. What is the wind doing here now?"

Christa poured hot water from her flask, fished in her bag for a chamomile sachet and jiggled it in the tall glass she'd brought. It would be another fortnight before the Islander could fetch her out to Kenya. But her spirits were back.

"Mohammed Shattah came to my office today," she laughed to Xavier, "to be my friend! He is scared of me. I tell you, that one shit bastard is going to jail."

Daud chuckled; on their return from battle, he had been unable to find words for Christa's courage. Mogga was peering into the palms of his hands; Xavier thought he saw a flicker of pain cross Mogga's face – but perhaps it was simple weariness. Xavier felt suddenly, desperately relieved that nothing had happened to Mogga. Who else could have kept Christa going?

Christa gave Mogga the glass.

"Here, my good friend, this *Kamille* is made in Aachen, it is the best. Thank God for this wind; now I am not sweating so much."

TWO

Time for a party, thought Xavier; teams cannot live by bread alone, they need circuses. There were birthdays coming up, Nyala Freddy and dumpy Lorna at Geneina. Xavier would call everyone in; he'd hold a fine bash in the yard of his house, pretty with its trees and hints of gardening past. He'd invite everyone, all the drivers and storemen and their families, the Sudan Red Crescent too. He'd roast another goat with noodles, scabby souk tomatoes and Libyan tinned tuna. Xavier ordered: buy ice if the factory is operating, and *arigi*, but only through Mogga and Fauzi and keep damn quiet about it.

What to do for beer? Mogga brewed a sour cloudy soup that mashed in a plastic bucket for two days, topped with froth. What to do for a barbecue? Xavier would have one welded up right now, today, in the souk. He'd summon the useful Farida to supervise the cooking. What to do for crockery? Paper plates from the souk, as at any smart Fur wedding. And fairy lights? Suleiman the Egyptian workshop manager strung headlight bulbs together and ran them off a Land Rover battery. And music? Toby Kitchin had a Walkman with two tiny external speakers that could just be heard across the yard. And the dancing? Someone had Dire Straits, someone had Michael Jackson, but Lorna from Aberdeen had tapes of jolly Scottish tunes, just the stuff for partying. Xavier hoped they'd party hard, let off a great deal of steam, burn off the frustration that was seething like Mogga's dreadful beer.

They all came, keen for company, as the dusk *azan* rang out from the mosques. Over the oil-drum grill a goat smoked and frizzled in a Dantean glow. There was a shimmering bustle at the iron gates and a stream of colour flowed into Xavier's yard: the secretaries of every agency, the drivers' and store men's wives in

159

tobes of orange, vermilion and crimson with little slippers in matching hues, their husbands in white robes fluttering about them. The women gathered under the trees like birds of Paradise come down to feed on morsels of goat, and for a while the Europeans sat sociably among them or brought them soft drinks.

But before long Xavier noticed, as in poorly emulsified vinaigrette, a separation. The Sudanese had not moved, but the Europeans had drifted into clumps near the kitchen shed close to Mogga's bucket and the turpentine *arigi*. They were beginning to giggle.

"I have a scheme," shouted Freddy, "to solve all food delivery problems. Screw the truckers; we need pipelines over the desert, Khartoum to Fasher direct. If they can do it for oil, they can do it for food."

"Oil's liquid," observed Rose Price. "How do you pump dry wheat?"

"Porridge!"

"A trans-Kordofan porridge pipeline, a thousand kilometres straight to the villages."

"You'll make this country a junkie."

"So what's new?"

"Cruise missiles!" yelped Toby Kitchin.

"Cruise missiles!" chorused a dozen drunks.

"Take out the warheads, pack 'em with porridge, set the co-ordinates for Kutum, Mellit, splat in the middle of the souk."

"But in Radam al-Souk," tittered Christa happily, "the missile shall fall on the head of my good friend the one shit bastard Mohammed Shattah."

Rose Price felt Sudanese looks turned on them, and was awkward: something was askew in the hospitality. She noticed Xavier and Leila Karim standing aside, watching Nurse Lorna. A tall, heavily-made woman with dark curls and powerful forearms, Lorna was teaching Mr Mogga how to skip and spin through a Gay Gordons. He didn't know that he was dancing the woman's part. Being short, he twizzled merrily under her arm.

"You've got it, Mogga," she approved. "And we finish with a wee polka . . ."

Mogga beamed as Rose came near.

"I love to dance, Miss Rose, even as a child."

"I'm all left feet," grunted Rose.

She looked around the ring of iridescently coloured ladies and saw again that conversation was faltering, that they were eyeing uncertainly the knot of shrill Europeans by the drinks table. Xavier, Rose saw, was biting his lip and frowning.

"Can't you get people up?" Xavier asked Lorna.

"I don't know," she said. "Leila, would the women join in?"

Leila said, "Certainly not."

"If only someone would . . ."

They both peered at the demure flock of secretaries, not knowing what to do. Mogga followed their look.

Fauzi, at the drinks table with his international friends, was ecstatic. They passed the plastic pot of *arigi* and toasted him.

"Best Kwality of Refreshment, Fauzi!" said Toby Kitchin, shiny with sweat. "Fuck, it's appalling, let's get trolleyed."

They slopped oily *arigi* into tumblers with crimson soda to make it palatable.

Fauzi took another himself.

"One hundred years ago," he began, "our Darfur sultan had special police to catch people who drink this refreshment."

"Plus ça change," observed Freddy. Fauzi purred inwardly: ah, they liked to hear his interesting stories.

"In olden days," he continued, "we had some very terrible things in Darfur. There were men in the palace that had two jobs. They were the king's musicians and also the executioners."

"The music here," said Freddy, "is instant death."

"They had water bags of human skin," Fauzi persisted happily. "When there was a new sultan, he calls his brothers and the blacksmith puts out their eyes."

"Charming," said Toby, with an odd sense of discomfort. The expatriates were looking down at the sand, were looking away. But Fauzi didn't notice; he was flushed with the amusing shame of his own people.

"There was special feast each year," he said eagerly, "and for this sacred feast they kill a cow only they don't cook it, they put it in a shed for some days after which the meat is not very nice. Then the princesses must sit in a circle and they must eat every part of this cow without cooking and the chief princess must eat the eyeballs and if they refuse or they are sick, then the soldiers beat them dead. Ha ha!"

"For God's sake," Toby Kitchin muttered into his glass.

The group had fallen silent. Only their postures changed slightly; subtly, they turned aside until Fauzi was outside the ring.

Fauzi's voice merely rose louder.

"I can tell you a very foolish thing about our sultan a long time ago," he cried. "There was a gift came from the King of Egypt and it was a lovely carpet from, you know, Persian people."

"A Persian carpet," someone assisted reluctantly.

"But our sultan does not know what a carpet is so he puts it on himself. He ties it round his middle!"

Behind them came a scuffling, a flurry of white. Rose Price sensed the many-coloured ladies shift, newly alert.

Rose said, "Look at Mogga."

He was in a huddle with the drivers and the store men in their long robes, the watchmen and mechanics in white skullcaps. Mogga had enticed them into the centre of Xavier's garden. Nearby, Toby was fiddling eagerly with his Walkman, and Lorna turned a tape over in her hand, offering it.

"Take your partners," she called, "for a Gay Gordons."

To a plastic trickle of music, they began.

"Heavens!" blinked Rose Price.

"Good Lord," murmured Xavier Hopkins.

"Oh, Mogga," smiled Leila, "*Alhamdulillah*, the praise be Allah's!"

And they laughed happily and stared.

Mogga had seized Daud by both hands, holding them high so that the driver's white robe lifted above his ankles. Mogga marched him forward four beats, turned him and marched him back, one two three four, turned him again and twizzled like a Highland lady under Daud's raised hand. In an instant, a dozen Sudanese drivers and monitors and mechanics had grabbed each other and followed, copying, whooping as the music accelerated and they stumbled and their leather slippers came off and they cared not at all. In pairs they skipped about the garden to the Gay Gordons, pursuing Mogga and Daud, like merry ghosts with their robes swirling white under the sparkling loops of lights in the trees. The women began to clap in time, Leila with them, in delight. Then the expatriates came out of their miserable corner, back among the Sudanese, clapping rhythmically, cheering on Mogga and the boys: one two three four, twizzle. Twizzle again!

"Splendid, Mogga," cried Lorna, "That's it, keep going, again!"

Leila looked from face to face among the expatriates, and saw their relief. She looked at Farida, quietly watchful by the food table, and saw the widow smile slyly. She looked at the secretaries and drivers' wives and saw their disdain for the little black fellow put aside. She saw Mogga scanning the company shrewdly, even as he danced. Suddenly, Leila was frightened for him, and she noticed that Rose Price's smile was clouded also. When their eyes met, Rose and Leila recognised in each other a startled, protective jealousy. They held it for a moment, a nervous, affectionate glance.

"Brilliant," said Xavier Hopkins to himself, "quite brilliant."

It was a good thing, thought Xavier, that Mogga was brilliant, because he was saving people's skins in all manner of ways.

Christa's, certainly, and now Toby Kitchin's.

*

At the outset, earnest young Toby Kitchin had been allocated the town and district of Kutum, to the northwest of El Fasher. It was just ninety-seven kilometres distant, but the way was poor, with patches of black cottonsoil and broad wadis to snare your vehicle; it could take all day, even if you didn't get stuck, and the whole locality was notorious for bandits. Toby had rushed off cheerfully to do his best. He had rented an office, hired staff – an interpreter, a secretary, a cook, a store man – and awaited developments. That was before they had known that food would be coming only to El Fasher. Xavier Hopkins had sent each district officer a message:

Be ready, please. They've signed shipment contracts in Khartoum, the trucking is sewn up. Deliveries expected shortly.

In pretty little Kutum, clustered about a tree-lined wadi, Toby Kitchin climbed the hill to Administration House to inform the authorities.

"The trucks will be despatched from Khartoum and come direct across the desert to the villages," he said, through Malik his assistant and interpreter.

Three officials were scrutinising him; two wore white *jellabiyas* and skullcaps while the third, a puffier figure in spectacles, perspired into a blue tropical suit. They were grouped round a coffee table on low cane-seated armchairs in which they reclined urbanely, a posture expressing distaste for urgency. Only Toby Kitchin sat forward, perched on the edge of his seat. The officials thought him remarkably young to be promising hundreds of tonnes of grain.

"How will they know where to take it?" asked one. "And how much?"

"That'll be my job," said Toby Kitchin with a very sincere smile, "I'm here to ensure that the right people get the food."

The three gentlemen absorbed this. They'd have thought it was their job, naïvely assuming that such matters were the responsibility of local government. Now, apparently, beardless foreign boys took precedence.

"So," urged Toby, "I'll need population figures, as soon as you can manage."

The three gentlemen glanced at each other, nodding thoughtfully. There was, they saw, plenty of room for 'error'.

Toby studied the lists of villages and his team made sketch maps of their whereabouts since many had upped thatch and moved since the last survey. He had them map the town itself. He whitewashed the office, labelled his box files, drafted a preliminary report. All this as he waited to greet the trucks coming across the desert from Khartoum.

He waited, and waited. Then came the bewildering news that only Fasher was to be fed, that Christa and Mogga would be rushing about doing the real business of famine relief while the rest of them must twiddle their thumbs!

Frustrated but determined to be useful, Toby resolved to be patient. And tried to occupy his hours.

Toby Kitchin had decided to fall in love with Kutum. It was the sweetest place in all Darfur. Behind the town were peaks of shattered volcanic debris, black, stark and waterless, home only to bandits. But among the hills ran gorges where underground watercourses defied the drought, and hidden valleys were lush with tamarind and citrus. There, cucumbers would grow, and watermelons that could be carried about the desert as refreshment for the camels. The town wadi was lined with trees so stately you might think they'd been planted as recreational 'gallops' for a monarch. When there was rain, the wadi at evening would be busy with camels drinking, dipping their long necks, and with lorries being washed. On the far bank, *qarad* acacias and snowy clouds of magnolia shaded the thatched quarters of the tribes. On this side were the mud-brick compounds of the merchants, then the town souk in a grove of towering *nim* trees with flickering foliage and a blur of tiny white flowers high overhead. Beyond, a stony track led up Administration Hill to the old colonial headquarters, aloof and apart. There, in past decades, the isolated but omnipotent British administrator had held court, ruling the town solo.

Toby Kitchin did not sit still. He went out and about every day, eagerly. He dearly wished to be accepted by Kutum, though he spoke no Arabic. It was Arab clans who dominated the little town, a dozen tribes at least. But blacks were present also, *zurqa* the Arabs called them. All these various peoples had skins tinged with differing hints of blue, or green or grey-black, or red and copper tones, depending on your prejudices and the slant of the sun. Toby Kitchin felt that, in all this colour, there was surely room for a blackish boy from Colchester.

But when Toby walked out from his office, leaving his staff to their time-filling tasks, he did not feel at ease. Always the scrutiny, always the stares. A merchant riding by would twist in the saddle to examine Toby as he might a stud camel. A knot of urchins would let fly pebbles from catapults. The café proprietor would show him civilly to a stool, would wave a boy to bring spiced coffee, but Toby saw the watch that was kept, the over-the-shoulder mutterings. Where the coffee companions sat in a circle, tall men on joint stools talking the afternoon away, there was something ludicrous about one foreigner – albeit a darkish specimen – perched on a seat in the corner, alone.

Toby yearned to blend in. Himself of a Ghanaian father and an English mother, his soft features had none of the aquiline sharpness of the Arab, but perhaps he could pass as a *zurqa*, even without the chevrons of scarification that adorned the cheeks on many Kutum faces. It was all down to dress. Toby Kitchin acquired, through his secretary, a long *jellabiya* of finely striped grey wool, such as the middling merchants wore, a little skullcap in embroidered cotton and leather slippers. And he went out, late in the afternoon, to take his coffee inconspicuously. But, whereas on previous afternoons he might reach the outskirts of the souk unremarked, might make his way to the coffee booths with little more than nudges and smiles, now the reaction to his *jellabiya* dismayed him. The urchins shouted and the women cackled something about his fashion sense. Groups of men interrupted discussion to call out: *Hey, English! New jellabiya, eh?* Some were saying, *Nice cloth, it suits you!* But Toby couldn't tell. Long before he reached his café, his ears had combusted. He turned for home, and he did not go out in the *jellabiya* again, though humiliation followed him back to the office in the smirks of his staff when they learnt what had happened.

And then he got dysentery, or shigella or giardia; people knew the names but were never sure which was which. Toby's bowels bloated, his shit foamed and reeked and he spent one quarter of every hour in the sweltering, airless latrine out in the yard. His anus oozed blood-streaked mucus, his stomach churned as his own foul gases enveloped him, and his head throbbed. He was so exhausted that he thought of sleeping there in the latrine, to save tottering back and forth. To begin with he felt ashamed in front of his staff, who averted their eyes – but soon he ceased to care.

When Xavier Hopkins heard of young Toby's illness, he responded quickly. He liked Toby; everyone did. Toby was bright and quick, Toby was cheerful and eager to be doing. But he was only twenty-two and looked less, and Kutum was a proud place. Now he was shitting blood and needed help.

"You go, Mogga," Xavier ordered.

The little black spread his hands and demurred gently.

"We are very busy," he said. "Miss Christa has said we must follow every sack."

"It's just for a few days. Bail Toby out."

"Then, of course," smiled Mogga.

So, carrying in his red knapsack a stash of pills and a promise of a visit from Dr Maeve, Mogga went to the rescue.

Exhausted as he was, Toby had mixed feelings on hearing this, for Mogga was very black indeed, and Toby's own claim to colour paled even further in comparison. And there was, he sensed, something about Mogga, something effervescent, something attractive. Toby thought of his own *jellabiya*, and winced. Mogga, he saw, made no effort to blend in at all. It was a curious thing. Mogga was neither European nor Arab nor Muslim black; he was like no one else here – but it seemed not to matter.

Within a week, Mogga had rescued Toby from calamity.

Dear Xavier,

Scribble in great haste coz theres a truck leaving for Fasher. Will fill in detail later. Big hassle in Kutum but think it'll be OK. The problem the sorghum seed sent up by Khartoum, did you know that it is poisonous!!! It's supposed to be, it's treated to stop the farmers eating it. Trouble is, usually they dye it green – not this lot, the sacks not marked at all, what the hell Khartoum at!!! We distributed to fourteen villages last week but they can't plant without rain, so eating it. Tuesday someone in Karnoi died – a child! Major horror and how to stop more?! Wanted to collect it back but no good, Mogga said I shouldn't go to villages because a) I'm still v. weak and b) they're v. angry, could be dodgy, me responsible, foreign etc. Police involved. Anyway Mogga brilliant, defused whole thing. Driving like madman last three days, went to every village council in Kutum District, explained about the poison seed. Mogga's masterstroke: went in a police Land Rover using our diesel. Don't know how he kept the police going – hardly slept – amazing! He paid police something, hope that's kosher. Umm Borro villagers nearly beat him up, police got stroppy waving guns but all sorted. The thing's pretty well blown over – two deaths rumoured - true or not? – should be OK, everyone knows about the seed now. Mogga inexhaustible, totally <u>brilliant</u>! See you soon.

All best, Toby.

But all was not best. Whisper had spread of the death of children. Villagers had seen Mogga with policemen: clearly, there'd been a wrongdoing. Which meant there'd be reparations paid. Villages from Mashaba in the eastern hills to Tondubaya in the far west rediscovered dead children and began to clamour.

Toby Kitchin was pale and washed out, with most of his haemoglobin now fattening the cockroaches in the pit latrine. He sat in his cement office with its slammingly hot tin roof, fending off angry delegations and demands for information from Administration Hill. As the temperature and the tempers rose, Toby became tearful and trembly. He looked so ill that at last Mogga loaded him into the Land Rover with very little protest, and they set off south for El Fasher and Dr Maeve.

Which left Malik – Toby's assistant and interpreter – in charge in Kutum, with not even the semblance of a foreigner's authority and with no grain coming.

*

They were drifting, Rose and Xavier, under the eucalyptus on the banks of Wad Golu, while El Fasher was at Friday prayers. It was a broad colonial reservoir, the work of busy, improving men. But there was no water. Fifteen feet down the sloping bank, the mud was three acres of deep fissures in brown paste. The eucalypts waved and rustled, and the bee-eaters with flushed chests and cobalt wings sped from trunk to trunk, drawing threads of colour in the air.

"What was that American on about," asked Rose, "that Paronian? About Bengal, and your father?"

Should I not have asked, she immediately wondered. Did Paronian open a wound? She had a sudden instant's vision of a mole that she was trying to help, squealing . . . Then told herself not to be silly. Xavier was not helpless, and was by no means blind.

Xavier had stopped, and was gazing out over the scrub.

"It was cheap of Paronian," he said tightly. "My father, yes. He was an Army medical officer in India. Dreadfully young, in '43, when everyone was expecting the Japs to pour over the border and start bayoneting them."

Xavier Hopkins and Rose Price ('the Two Storks', the Sudanese staff called them) resumed their walk under the trees, pensive, not daring to leave the shade. Again the eucalyptus rattled, but even with the breeze, it was frighteningly hot, an *abu farrar*, 'father of axes', a day that would cut you down. To Rose, today, even the idea of water was cool. She walked slowly, her face angular and her legs elongated, her disproportionately short body perched high above and her dusty face sucking at interminable 'Marlboros'. She was thinking, how oddly British, to be pacing in the debris of one former colony speaking of the wartime disasters of another.

Xavier moved distractedly, deep in hand-me-down memory.

"Nobody in Calcutta," he went on, "noticed that the people right amongst them were starting to die. Civilians, peasants, country Bengalis had drifted into town looking for food, scavenging behind the hotels. There'd been typhoons, crop failures, any amount of disruption, but in wartime the Brits weren't paying attention, you see? People had been starving for months but bureaucracy was so slow, the Bengal Government hadn't spotted the figures creeping up. Landless people died first, potters and labourers, carpenters, basket makers. Nobody had money for pots or baskets. Dad began to notice. He got off a train to walk along the platform for his breakfast, and he heard this extraordinary, bleating wail. The whole platform was seething with emaciated people who grasped at him with their clammy hands. He never forgot the sound."

Xavier stopped again, peering at the baked mud dish of Wad Golu. He was wearing khaki drill trousers and a short-sleeved shirt. He looked the part that, as a student, he had himself decried, the athletic young Englishman administering Africa.

"Dad says the dead were like road kill, all over the pavements of Calcutta. There was a blackout of course, and you tripped over corpses on the pavements in the dark. That made Brits take notice, but it was too late. Winter of '43, best part of two million people died. The authorities never allowed the word famine, just 'food distress', and then they tried all the free-market stuff, the same that failed in the Irish potato famines a century before. They'd learnt nothing, not a damn thing. Be ready, Dad says now: look for the warning signs, but read them intelligently. You must read them correctly. If what you do isn't right, it's wrong."

He was talking to himself, his voice fading, recoiling from his father's anger and shame.

"I've tried," he breathed to the trees, "to learn, to think it through and I tell you, what we're doing now, what we've been bounced into, is crap. Again and again we're panicked into nonsensical food deliveries. The least hint of hunger and we muscle in, frantic not to fail again. That's what Paronian was playing on: our guilt at all those famines past. But we don't look, and we don't think. What is going to happen, what I can feel coming, is chaos, utter bloody chaos."

Beyond the trees, Rose saw a gaudy bee-eater riding on the neck of a moth-eaten creature that might have been sheep or goat.

Angry for him, she said, "You, though, you look for the truth. You send someone to the souk every day for the price of animals. You send us out to the villages every day."

Xavier grimaced.

"When Hassan al-Bedawi gives us the permits. That, as Christa would say, is one shit bastard."

He looked at Rose in deep gratitude.

"I do depend on your support, you know."

She was startled. She spluttered:

"Well, we need you to keep a clear head."

"But truly," he persevered, "I couldn't, without you."

It hung between them – until a clung of goat bells gave a merciful excuse for looking across the reservoir.

"They're rather fond of each other," Xavier observed.

Rose followed his look and laughed dryly: "She's twice his height."

On the far side of Wad Golu, Leila Karim shook out a cloth with a rather grand flapping motion, and then passed it down to Farida who crouched on her haunches in the shade, tidying the picnic before ants came. The widow folded the last of the thin, sour *kisra* pancakes that Mrs Karim liked so much and tucked them in a plastic box. She tossed the chicken bones aside and flicked drops of hibiscus juice from the mugs.

Then she looked up. Mrs Karim was speaking, her voice haughty.

"You see that tree, Mogga? The stems are glabrous, the inflorescence has corymbose racemes, and the fruit is tardily dehiscent."

"I don't know what you are saying," protested Mogga.

"Quite," agreed Leila, glancing at Farida snapping lids onto nesting pots. "Nor do our peasants."

"Some people are ignorant," said Mogga, uncomfortable.

"But listen, Mogga," her voice rose excitedly, "this is only half the story. Who knows these plants: me, or Adam Zachariah? The expert with dried specimens in a cabinet or the poor man in a torn *jellabiya* out beyond the wadi? Who can tell you whether a camel will get sick eating those leaves? Who knows which sap cures leather, which leaves make a cool poultice? What do we experts with our inflorescence and our racemes know of that?"

Leila glanced across the wadi to where Xavier and Rose were

now making their way back toward the Land Rover. She frowned:

"Mogga, are these village people starving or not?"

"That is what Mr Xavier is forever asking."

"Mogga!" Leila snapped, "have you seen anyone starving? Have you seen them, skin and bones and lying dead in the village dust? Have you?"

"No," he replied uncertainly.

"But how so?" cried Leila. "The crops have failed two years, the rains have failed; who can buy millet? Who can afford *durra*? But they are not starving, I tell you, not yet. They may starve, they may die next month but not yet. Why?"

Mogga, still sitting cross-legged on the bank, studied her in perplexed silence.

"Because," she went on, "they are eating what Merciful Allah has provided for them in the woods and the wilderness. There, look."

She waved imperious fingers at the scrub. Mogga saw shapeless thorn bushes, thistles and grasses. Between these wandered thin goats half-heartedly marshalled by listless boys.

"There," she declared, "wild food for all the villages. We saw it at Seraf Umra, at Kebkabiya, the women threshing by the road, in the souk selling their berries, their leaves. It is *difra* and *mukheit* and *maikah*. You see that grass which is like evil thistles? *Haskaneet*, and in those thistles there is good food. Adam told me. I shall write it down, Mogga, I shall record it in books before they forget."

"And may I help you?" he jumped up, "with those books?"

Mogga stood dusting his trousers, facing her.

"Miss Leila," he whispered excitedly, "what fine books those books could be."

"Ah," breathed Leila, "it is possible to do something."

They looked out over the dry country that hemmed the colonial pond. The dropping sun had put a faint rose sheen onto the golden grasses. It was a landscape that Mogga would once have called dry and dreary. But Leila's face was shining and therefore Mogga saw how lovely the scene was, not dun and dead but lively, with a thousand connections, patterns, directions and pathways that he'd not noticed. The nut-coloured larks strutted their own routes among the shrubs, rummaging for seed; the swallow-tailed kites burst from the spiny *qarad* trees in predatory gangs and made off over the dunes on special kite-itineraries; the sky-blue rollers, whose plumage was of a downy hue so soft that it seemed to haze at the edges, and the bee-eaters, carmine and lemon; they tied their colours from tree to tree in loops and hoops that bound the busy desert together. Every goat followed clear goat tracks that wound between the *sayal* scrub and the thistly *haskaneet*, while the ground crept with beetles labouring on tiny dusty trails. All was appropriate, hardy and at work, and over it all gazed Leila and Mogga, side by side, afire with business. They were like childhood conspirators; they would put her scheme to Xavier as soon as they were back in town . . .

But there was a storm gathering.

THREE

By night, in bed in Kutum, Malik felt quite disembodied. Toby's assistant lay on the string cot staring up at the darkness, nervous, slim, wrapped only in silence. All bodily sensations – his profuse sweating, his weight pressing through the threadbare sheet onto the rough cords of the *angareb* – all had left him. He felt that he was floating through a very nasty dream.

It had been a bad week for the little town. At the brickworks, they'd set women to stack bricks. For each thousand, they'd paid the women the price of four cups of tea; there had been a fight. Someone had been found with an antique rifle, had been beaten unconscious by police in the street. Raiders had been seen in the rocky wastelands north of town, and the army helicopter had caught them in the open and strafed them – but they weren't raiders at all, just nomads, who died in the sands among their punctured baggage and the smashed bones and exploded bowels of their camels.

For Malik, it had been very difficult. Too many promises were rebounding. He'd promised to pay the Agency staff on Monday, but the bank had run out of notes. He'd offered the staff sugar, which they could trade, but how long would they stay on? He'd promised cash very soon but, that evening, someone had stolen his radio. Tuesday morning had brought delegations of village elders, dignified men politely reminding Malik that they were dying and that the Agency had promised to prevent this. Tuesday afternoon, the clinic for malnourished babies complained that they had no high-calorie mix for 'Allah's special infants'. Malik had promised to send the Toyota pickup to collect some from Dr Maeve but it wouldn't start. On Wednesday the Administration's radio operator had brought a message: be informed, please, that

174

the replacement sorghum seed promised by Toby Kitchin would not be available.

Walking in the souk that evening, Malik had felt the stares, felt himself clamped and squeezed by the people's hostility.

Today, Thursday, a truck had arrived, one small truck, carrying not seed but milk powder for schoolchildren. It was a special donation from Norway. The milk was very old and smelled bad; the headmaster tasted some and spat it out. They tipped a sackful onto a mat by the school gate and a thin, sour dust rose from the powder. Black weevils had found it, and a growing crowd jeered as these weevils wriggled outwards in a ring, fleeing towards the edge of the mat. Men's faces were twisted in contempt for foreign food, foreign aid, governments foreign or otherwise, for college boys like Malik and their promises.

"So," they'd sneered aloud, "What else have you to offer us? Wonderful, is it not, what these educated types can do."

"I promise you . . . !" Malik had cried, his voice wavering. But the elders had turned their white-robed backs on the anxious young man with his green nylon shirt standing by the disgusting heap of dust and insects. They'd stalked away to the souk in a malevolent huddle.

A hot wind was rising. By nightfall the raw cement walls of the Agency office throbbed with heat. In the toilet block Malik washed by candlelight with brown water from a bucket, then tried to sleep.

Far off, a vehicle whined, lurching down into the dry wadi, accelerating across the riverbed, heaving out again. Police, thought Malik, searching for hoarders, or the Army chasing their tails as the bandits made fools of them. But the vehicle turned off the main street, climbed the steep stony lane to the Agency house – and stopped. Now Malik thought: the Army have come for me. He lay still in the heat and darkness, telling his heart to hush.

"Malik?" The voice was female. That also seemed unreal. "Malik? Are you there?"

He heard the steel gate scraping open.

"Sir? The doctor lady is come," his houseboy called. Suddenly, the world was urgently concrete.

"Wait, Doctor Maeve, I'm coming," Malik cried out, "please wait, don't go!"

Medicines! Medicines that Mr Kitchin had promised to the clinic. A delivery, he could make a delivery!

"Malik," said the woman with a torch, "We've driven seven hours, had two flats and dug ourselves out twice. We're most surely staying with you tonight."

Malik backed inside, pumped and relit the lamp. Maeve was slim and handsome with a strong mouth and bouncy black hair thick with dust. A thin flower-print skirt swung about her fine legs. Self-assured and nosey, she surveyed the unfinished cement shop that Toby Kitchin had rented for the Agency's office.

"So, Malik, you're nicely set up here."

Malik peered round in surprise. Behind a crude screen of grey blankets pegged over string, his charpoy skulked. Stinking clothes lay on the floor. Steel chairs, a table, a litter of tools and tins, cardboard boxes serving as filing cabinets scattered about on the concrete: that was it. In his rush Malik had buttoned his shirt by the wrong buttonholes; it hung asquint. He began re-fastening it, pretending to merely toy with the buttons.

The doctor swallowed the water he'd given her.

"Some drive!" she grimaced cheerfully. "I've just flogged my way over from Mellit and way up north to Malha before that, oh, we've been whizzing all over."

Malik blinked: to Malha, two hundred kilometres of the most notorious, bandit-infested road in Darfur!

"Have you brought medicine?" he enquired excitedly.

She purred, "What are you needing?"

"Every medicine!" Malik blurted. She became doctorish.

"What exactly is the matter?"

"Malaria is coming, there is tuberculosis . . ."

"You've tuberculosis? Malik . . ."

"Not I, all the people! The sick are everywhere. These Medical Assistants are helpless, they cry to me daily."

"I see," said Maeve.

"What can we deliver?"

"Not so much."

"Not much?"

"I've some vitamins left, though Malha and Mellit got most of them."

"What vitamins?"

"Oh, now, don't you worry your head about that tonight. I'm here to inspect the health posts. Did you know your shirt's askew?"

Malik blushed furiously and buttoned the shirt again, sick with disappointment.

"We do have food with us," she said kindly. "Have you eaten?"

Waving away his help, she produced crackers, red Libyan jam and pilchards. The driver took his plate out to the Land Rover. The doctor sat at the rickety table, eating with gusto, grinning at Malik. He thought, she drives all day and still has energy, while I am washed-up.

She declared breezily:

"I'd like your company tomorrow."

"Company?" echoed Malik.

"The village health posts. We'll visit the Medical Assistants in the morning, dole out the vitamins, see what else they need."

"They need medicines," said Malik sullenly.

The doctor parried:

"Must assess them first. Any coffee? No matter, I've my own."

He made to stand and light the stove but she was there first, ignoring him.

"The Assistants will not be at their places," said Malik.

"Why so?"

"They are in town, hoping for some food or some pay."

"They'll not be paid if they're not working," Maeve observed sharply, "so you can guide us."

"But I am expecting delegations tomorrow," pleaded Malik.

The doctor frowned.

"Oh? Well, in the morning you can show us the souk, we'll round up the Assistants and return them to their villages."

"Thank you," said Malik. She had no authority, but the Assistants wouldn't defy her, and he'd be relieved to see them go.

"Time for bed." She reached for her bag. Malik wondered where he should sleep. He started tugging the grubby sheet from the charpoy, but she stopped him.

"You keep that. I've a camp bed."

She bent down and straightened holding a pair of Malik's underpants, which she folded, popping them on the end of the charpoy.

Malik did his best not to stare, which his father had taught him was rude.

*

In the morning, he saw in the back of her Land Rover two cardboard boxes, disintegrating and stained where something oily had leaked. Malik took out a large plastic pot. Inside were hundreds of little golden capsules.

"What does it do?" he asked.

"Vitamins," she replied, "retinol, vitamin A, good for the eyes. They've a lot of problems with eyes up north, they're most grateful for this."

He was peering at the label.

"Is it old?" he asked. "There is a date, look, last year . . ."

"Never you fret," Maeve cut him short, removing the pot and popping it back in the box. "I wheedled it out of Khartoum and I'm giving it out to all the kiddies."

They found three Medical Assistants in the souk, drinking glasses of sweet tea in an airless booth of rush matting, balanced on stools with their toes peeping from under the white robes. Dr Maeve stood over them.

"Now," she commanded Malik, "the Medical Assistants can distribute the vitamins. Which is the one who's saying his village chief is unwell? Tell him I'll visit. That'll be diplomatic."

She shooed the Assistants into the back of her Land Rover, telling Malik she'd be back by evening. He watched the Land Rover wallow across the sands beyond the wadi, and then he walked home. Everyone knew he had delivered weevils. He felt the disdainful stares.

The heat grew insidiously on a wind edged with grit. Malik's nylon shirt stuck to his back; it was making his skin spotty, but he had no other. Mid-morning, the farmers' delegation arrived in ill humour.

"Oh Malik, your promises are as worthless as a European's."

Malik flushed angrily: "We brought you sorghum seed," he retorted.

They guffawed.

"Wonderful! You nearly killed us all."

That was just an error, Malik expostulated, and they'd got the seed at least, a free gift from the Agency.

"A gift of no value, the wrong species, Ugandan rubbish."

"It's good sorghum!" protested Malik.

"Good for the blacks of the south, maybe," scoffed a lout in a filthy *jellabiya* whose spittle foamed through black tooth stumps, "It won't grow here, as anyone else would know."

"Anywhere but here they'd have the wit to make it grow!" shouted Malik, incensed. This was another mistake.

"Oh Malik, you insult us as well as starve us? We shall not forget. We'll tell our people what you think of us. Then, we promise you, we'll be back."

They swept out. Malik's staff stared at him in dismay, then downed their pens and departed. He thought they were running away – until he realised that the *muezzin* was calling.

Then the town fell silent, ill-will hanging in the air like dust.

Some time after prayers, Malik's secretary hammered on the steel gate calling:

"Peace upon this house!"

The houseboy did not appear.

"Oh, Malik!" the secretary persisted, less courteously.

The man remained outside the gate, declining to enter, glancing apprehensively downhill.

"You know," he said, "that the chief is dead?"

"Which chief is that?" asked his young employer.

"Of Burush," the man answered. "He has been old and sick all month. But his death, that was today."

The secretary tugged up his robe and departed, stumbling in the ruts in his haste. Malik wondered why he should be told so particularly about this death. The lady doctor was inspecting Burush. What difference that might make, he couldn't tell.

Still the heat grew. In the yard, sitting on the sloping sand by the toilet block, Malik felt bewildered by anxiety and loneliness. The high mud brick walls gave no security: who might that be, scuffling and whispering behind them? Hearing the Land Rover return, he felt a rush of warmth and gratitude to the lady doctor but, as he opened the steel gates, he glimpsed two men staring from the street corner, a third joining them, gesturing at Malik's house.

The Land Rover bumped into the yard.

"We've been all over!" Maeve declared, twirling in to dump her shoulder bag on a chair. "And all the health posts have had their vitamins, that's the little golden capsules you saw, all the kiddies shall get those from the Medical Assistants. Those poor frustrated fellows, they're aching to work and I've promised they shall."

She patted the dust off her flowery skirt and took water from the jar.

Malik asked: "You saw Burush?"

"Surely, and the chief, poor man, lain on his cot in a sweltering hut and flies crawling over his eyes. He's quite poorly."

"Yes," agreed Malik. "He is now dead."

She looked sorry.

"Well, I called as promised and gave him an injection though he was too far gone."

Malik sat down hard, staring open-mouthed. She frowned.

"Now, what's wrong? You want one too?"

"You gave an injection?"

"To show willing."

"He is dead," said Malik, "after the injection."

"Oh dear," she responded breezily, "though I'm not surprised."

"After you gave him an injection, he died," restated Malik.

He jumped up and pulled the steel shutters tight, bolts squealing home. The doctor followed with her eyes, touched by his fear.

"It was just penicillin," she said. "Malik, he was three-quarters dead."

"All dead now!" cried Malik, shouting to her driver to reverse his Land Rover against the high gate.

"What? What are you thinking of?" said the doctor in a whisper.

The sloping yard looked down across town towards the tree-shaded souk. Malik stared that way.

"Oh!" he cried. His tone startled her.

"Malik, are you expecting . . . ?" She tailed off, frightened.

"Coming now," he whispered.

"Who?" She took his elbow and began, "Promise me nothing awful . . ."

But Malik promised nothing, only pointed. Maeve looked past him.

"Dear Lord," she breathed.

Across the little town, a tawny, billowing curtain was advancing. It stretched from the mountains beyond the wadi on their left, to somewhere far into the desert on their right, and from the sandy ground to somewhere hundreds of feet above. At this moment it divided the souk precisely, obliterating one half. The curtain was quite opaque, as thick, as heavy as velvet. It was made of fine yellow dust, millions of tons of dust hanging in the hot air. The desert was up on its feet, and was coming.

It approached silently, smoothly, with the steady purpose of a phalanx of soldiers in leather armour. The dust drew over trees that melted from sight. It devoured houses, and you expected shrieks from inside, but there was only the clatter of a hundred shutters. Malik and the doctor watched, mesmerized. A jeep fled, struggling towards them up a sandy back street with headlights blazing, but the curtain drew over the vehicle and the lights turned bilious before disappearing. On a roof nearby, a hatchway opened and a man appeared. He glanced at the approaching dust, turned his gaze on Malik and shook his fist. Then he was enveloped and gone.

"Allah be thanked." Malik's eyes shone, and he smiled.

"*Thanked?*" said Maeve, astounded.

"They cannot get us in this. Tomorrow we go early, quickly, we go away!"

"Who's wanting to get us?"

But Malik rushed about bolting everything, yelling to the driver who hurried inside. They pulled the doors tight behind him.

"Light the lamp!" Malik ordered the doctor, then recalled that the kerosene was finished. "Candles, in there." He covered the typewriter, files, water jar and his suitcase of clothes. Then he sat down.

"What do we do?" said the doctor, flapping her hands helplessly.

"Please, be comfortable," he gestured to the bed. "That is best. Now we must wait."

The candlelight seemed to curdle. There was silence – until the tin roof began to heave and clang, the shutters straining, squealing in their steel frames. Beneath the door, puffs and curlicues of dust streamed in. It penetrated in little jets through the tiniest chinks. It entered the roof-space, dribbling down through holes in the ceiling where bare wires hung. It found cracks in the solid walls and seeped in. The house seemed to bleed internally.

Malik saw Maeve fumble with the collar of her shirt, trying to pull it over her mouth. He saw that she was scared.

"Malik," she whispered, "shall we suffocate?"

He gave her a tea towel wetted with a scoop from the water jar. The doctor pressed this over her mouth and nose.

"Thank you!" he heard, muffled.

After which, all three remained in silence, sunk in thought. The candles burned away while dust drifts gathered on the floor and a film settled on the room until all was a uniform colour, as though they sat in a sepia world.

The driver said, "Last year my neighbour's children disappeared in a *haboob* like this and were not seen for two days."

"Dear Lord, Malik!" whimpered Maeve.

Malik watched the candle flame wave gently in its halo of dusty fluorescence, and he wished that the storm might last forever. But it didn't, and at dawn Malik, Dr Maeve and her driver left Kutum in a flurry of gears and sand.

*

"It has to be Mogga," said Xavier Hopkins. "Malik can't cope. I'll send Mogga straight back."

Rose Price was listening. Her long, dry-skinned face peered at him seriously.

Xavier gazed out of the window, as though further contributory factors were suspended over the rooftops of El Fasher.

"Mogga knows Kutum. Another expatriate would be too high-profile, would just draw the flak that Maeve . . ."

He wanted to say 'deserves', but he opted for solidarity and silence on that.

"It has to be Mogga," he repeated. "It'll be the only district without an expat. One has to be careful. Local staff are much more vulnerable, piggy in the middle."

He turned to face Rose, who stood silent and gawky in the centre of the room watching him, sipping at a tin cup of water.

"Though he is very black, of course, southern and so on. One has to hope no one takes against a southerner in authority. You like Mogga, don't you?" he added.

"Surely," she replied.

"I sometimes think," said Xavier, "that we've become a little bit dependent on him. Did you ever read *Nostromo*? He's that sort of chap, the one we can't do without."

Rose was peering intently at some important patch of grit on the floor.

Xavier hastened on.

"I mean, he's irrepressibly cheerful, he's sorted us out a few times, and kept people going when they were looking quite wobbly. Christa, Toby . . ."

He almost said, 'and me'.

Rose Price frowned.

"He's excellent," she observed.

It was strangely embarrassing, this praise. They were complicit in squirming.

"I want him to get back to Kutum a.s.a.p," said Xavier. "Do you happen to know where he is?"

*

Through Maweishi souk in El Fasher, Rose Price strides past the *angareb* makers hauling cords tight on new bedsteads. Here too are the charcoal men, some of whom argue furiously with a customer who is heaving two lumpy sacks into a handcart. Across the way, blacksmiths under awnings of sacking make their timeless din, fashioning hoes and daggers and swagger sticks whose leather tips conceal a little blade. Rose, in her yellow T-shirt and shapeless flower print trousers stalks on past woodcarvers, beadstringers, and grain merchants who seem to be selling nothing but buying everything they can. To all of these, Rose Price gives her curt unsmiling nod. It's not them she seeks.

By the town wells where the camels take their evening drink, she sees four youths kicking a donkey. The donkey looks like a sick old man, patches of its hair fallen, its face drawn, its eyes dry and dull. It is starved, ribs plainly visible. It has collapsed under the weight of bulging water skins, and cannot stand. So they kick it furiously, desperately. Their livelihood is the selling of water door to door, but their donkey cannot stand.

Rose walks on.

Beyond the wells she sees – or, at first, hears – a dance. There is a grove of fine old *nim* trees seventy feet high, dark and fissured, the mass of spear-blade leaves ('lanceolate', Leila Karim would have said) casting a broad and even shade. In this shade are men dancing. They are certainly not Arab, neither of the noble nor the corrupt lineages. The Arabs would call them *zurqa*, but they're not Fur, nor southerners like Mogga, but tall and powerful men, very proud, though shoeless and dressed in drab synthetics. They have formed two rings: an inner circle faces outwards, each man clacking two thick white sticks, while about them stamp and shuffle a dozen more.

A crowd is growing.

"Mrs! You like dancing?"

Someone touches Rose on the shoulder, smirking at the dancers. "Falata man, Hausa man, from far far west."

Rose thinks the sneer lacks conviction. The dance is powerful, the circling steady and strong, the stamping forceful; the dust puffs up to cake on the men's faces that run with sweat. Sweat soaks the shirts, darkening each back in broad spades. *Clack clack*, the sticks rattle, *thud thud*, the feet are precise and the faces sure and strong, knowing their dance.

Rose Price sees that Mogga is there, standing on a tree root that gives him a view; he has not noticed Rose. She is about to go to him when Mogga comes down off his root and pushes forward through the crowd. She sees the Arabs' surprise; some begin to take offence, and she realises that for once Mogga doesn't care. He's entranced, he's excited, he has to get nearer to the ring. He has reached the front of the onlookers, and Rose sees that his brow is raised and his eyes bright, his mouth half open. He is leaning forward, his knees slightly flexed. He looks like a long-distance runner waiting for the pistol.

Rose Price understands that Mogga longs to dance. He is poised to join in, to burst in and join the circle of these dusty *zurqa* though he's nothing to do with them and most of them are twice his height. He'll do it, she thinks, good God, he can't stop himself. Oh my Lord, what will they do? Will they all stumble and fall over each other? Will they grab his shirt collar and throw him down? Or beat him with their dancing sticks, pursue him and beat him to death?

Or can Mogga, alone of all people, dance anyone's dance?

She suddenly sees, in his electric poise, her answer.

Mogga has been dancing all along.

The noise, the clacking and stamping intensify, accelerate. She sees the Falata glance at Mogga – they are daring him! – and she sees the little man's legs move a fraction. He flexes. She cannot watch, she begins to turn away . . .

Mogga catches sight of her; startled, he freezes. For a moment they exchange stares and Rose senses that the personal ecstasy is draining out of him. To be replaced by something faintly vocational and hard.

"Mogga," she says, "You're needed."

In his infinite courtesy, he bobs and smiles.

PART FOUR
Hassan

ONE

The future Colonel Hassan al-Bedawi had, from his early childhood, associated Europeans with acrid smoke, ragged trousers and moral chaos.

"Beloved? I'd like to invite some friends," his mother said, one day, at dinner, "to our home."

Little Hassan detected hesitation. Mother had worked herself up to this request.

"What friends?" growled Father, a burly man who sold building materials in Kosti, and who now continued to watch television as he ate. "And what for?"

Mother's tone was mollifying, tremulously gay: "The *zar*, only the *zar* which keeps us poor women happy!"

Hassan, aged just four, had no idea what *zar* was – but the word brought merry scorn from Father.

"Filling my house with shrilling lunatics? Allah preserve us."

"We take turns," cried Mother in a fluster, "All my friends, my little *zar* circle. You want this house shamed? You want us called misers by all Kosti?"

At which Father had bellowed with laughter.

"The only shame is the silliness of women!"

Mother was piqued, but she swallowed her pride, and wheedled:

"Take a day off, go into the desert, go hunting with your policeman friends. It's a long while since you've had some fun."

Father declared this true, at least. The notion grew on him, of laying on vehicles and food for police pals who in return could supply firearms. So Mother would get the house for a day, and she invited all her *zar* circle.

But the preparations took weeks: planning, shopping, cleaning,

189

cooking. Hassan felt neglected. Mother's intimates urged her not to stint on her purchases – at which Father became tetchy:

"Are we entertaining clergy?" he grumbled. "Are we receiving the President?"

"You'd want me to do us proud," Mother purred, "You'd not want me to put on a bad show."

"Show, circus, farce, it's bloody expensive. What's that lot?" He scowled at bulging shopping baskets. "You buying out the souk?"

He turned – and tripped over a large basin of borrowed cutlery that skidded and crashed across the floor.

"Mind out . . ." Mother cried.

"Allah be merciful!" roared Father.

Little Hassan ducked into the bedroom as Mother shrilled:

"Mrs Almaghrabi and her girls and Mrs Hillawi are coming to help any moment. Go to the souk, beloved, find your friends . . ."

"And bring them back," Father retorted, "to drive out the cackling hens."

"Oh!" gasped Mother, "don't even think . . ."

"I'll think and do what I like!"

Father stamped away to the souk and stayed there. Mother thanked the saints.

"Why does he complain so?" she sighed to Hassan. "Does he want us disgraced?"

Mother had always fretted over appearances but still Hassan was startled by the frantic dressmaking that now ensued, the scrubbing of the house, the polishing of windows, the raking of the sand in the yard. Next day, a goat appeared, tethered out by the kitchen with a mournful expression. Hassan offered it fodder.

"Bloody zoo," scoffed Father.

In the yard, Mother set the watchman to dig a small pit.

"What for?" demanded Hassan, mimicking Father's scepticism.

"For little boys who ask too many questions," retorted Mother, counting crockery. She relented and gave Hassan a quick smile: "You'll see. Wonderful things. The *zar*! Now, where's your father?"

Mother moved through the house calling, "Beloved? We're short of the yellow tumblers, they're not expensive . . ." Seconds later, the predictable furious bellow – but the tumblers appeared next day.

The evening before the party, Hassan saw the watchman crossing the yard carrying a steel hammer and a long knife. He ran into the back bedroom to peep. The watchman sidled up to the tethered goat, which regarded him darkly. As the man swung his hammer, the animal sprang aside in terror. The blow glanced off the creature's back and the goat began leaping, kicking, thrashing on its rope while the watchman shouted, waving the hammer furiously.

"Look at that," said a voice behind Hassan. It was Father, watching the fracas with contempt. "I'm not helping him out."

The watchman swung at the goat's head; the animal collapsed, stunned. The man flourished his knife and seized an enamel bowl which filled with blood scummed with dust.

In the kitchen outhouse next morning, the watchman lit a huge charcoal stove while the cook hacked at the goat. Father emerged wearing camouflage trousers, fawn with splodges of pale brown and green. He tucked sunglasses into his shirt, then loaded the lunch hamper onto his pickup.

"Have a lovely day in the desert," Mother simpered.

"If there's no game, I'll be back at lunchtime," he retorted. Mother looked startled. "With the police," he added.

"You wouldn't . . ." Mother breathed.

Father grinned at her and left. Mother let out a long sigh, and then dressed Hassan in clean blue cotton shorts.

"Shirumbay doesn't like dirty little boys," she murmured. Hassan had no idea who Shirumbay might be.

At noon, guests bustled in, women in swirling wraps and diaphanous veils of orange and blue tulle. They had trailed through the baking streets, their faces were patinated with dust and diesel; they dabbed at their eyes with tiny handkerchiefs. They'd brought contributions, nests of aluminium pans with okra stew and sweets. They chattered loudly, twitching at their wispy drapes. The women breezed through to the back yard, entirely ignoring Hassan. Several he recognised but there was a mood on them, a peculiar unladylike excitement that made Hassan keep to the shadows, wary. He wished Father and his policemen would come home. Today, Mother's friends were weird.

There was a *rakuba* at one end of the yard, an awning thatched with brushwood and dense purple bougainvillaea. A lady in green robes sat here upon an armchair of white steel and red plastic. Hassan decided she was rich; she never smiled and heavy gold bangles flopped noisily on her wrist. She'd the pockmarks of old boils on her cheeks, and long hennaed fingers. The ladies danced attendance or settled on a line of chairs in the shade, bubbling with anticipation.

"Greet your aunty!" Mother seized Hassan and dragged him out in front of everyone. "Give these to her."

She thrust at Hassan an unmarked bottle of clear fluid stopped with a cork, and a square gilt tin with a rose embossed on the lid. Hassan tried to deposit them on the ground but Mother held him up.

"Quickly!" Mother pushed him. "Everyone is watching."

Hassan dropped both items, backing away.

"Hassan!"

Flustered, fumbling, Mother rushed toward the rich lady with the bottle and tin. The lady waved a limp hand, Mother opened the tin and the lady took out a cigarette and a lighter. Hassan's mouth fell open.

"Don't stare like that!" shrilled Mother. "Your aunty is *sheika* of our *zar*."

Aunty? This was an aunty? It was no one Hassan had seen before. A smoking aunty! He understood nothing of what was happening. On the floor near 'Aunty' were two drums, wide and low. Hassan wanted someone to play them but there was only talk and more talk, of illnesses beyond all doctors, of sorrows needing a power to sort them: matters for Shirumbay.

Ladies in their filmy chiffon sat sucking awkwardly at un-accustomed cigarettes held in fingers stiff as tweezers. The cigarettes made Hassan uneasy. And what were they drinking? A woman filled yellow tumblers from an unlabelled bottle. Hassan picked up a drink for himself but there was a sudden twittering and a hand vibrant with henna dots stopped him.

"Hassan!" Mother called in a hurry, "there's cordial for you in the kitchen." The odour of the ladies' drink had risen from the glass to make Hassan retch. It smelled like sugared petrol. He retreated beyond the *rakuba* to the shadows of the kitchen outhouse, his fingernails picking at the flaked blue paint of the doorframe.

In the *rakuba's* shade, in front of Aunty on her throne, lay a mat with a hole in its centre over the pit the watchman had dug. Through the hole streamed a sickly smoke that rolled out from under the purple bougainvillaea, drenching the yard with its perfume. Today, thought Hassan, everything is sweet and nasty. A woman moved onto the mat, bowed obsequiously to Aunty, and then picked up a thin green shawl shot with golden threads, spreading it over her head like a cape in a rainstorm. She squatted over the hole, making for herself a little tent filled with fumes. There the woman stayed until Hassan thought she must be cooked.

The child looked uneasily at his mother. She laughed at him.

"Hassan, it's a smoke bath; you want to try?"

Hassan took cover behind the kitchen door. Mother laughed again, gratified by the approving snickers of her friends.

Dismayed, Hassan saw Mother go to the smoke hole, bobbing to Aunty before disappearing under the drape. The child gripped the doorframe in alarm. What if Mother reappeared naked or a dreadful colour? He was no longer so certain of her. He looked round for an escape route across the yard. Beneath the green shawl, Mother coughed – then tossed off the drape and emerged unchanged, giggling to her friends. A belch of sweet smoke rolled towards Hassan who flapped it away. He knew that if Mother took him anywhere near that pit he'd be violently sick.

The ladies took coffee from a tray of chased tinplate that some-one brought from the kitchen. (*All these people can go anywhere in our house.*) They paid, too, laying notes on the tray. (*Why are they paying for coffee at our house?*)

A woman in green fanned a terracotta incense brazier, humming to herself. The gathering fell quiet, attentive. The brazier was lifted and placed in front of Aunty who, with slow and deliberate movements, cast a handful of yellow powder over the coals. A thick, grey-brown pungency billowed up. Aunty leaned forward, hands on her knees and her bangles clanking, letting the greasy smoke lick up over her face. Hassan heard someone say matter-of-factly:

"Shirumbay is coming."

Then Aunty got to her feet and without a word strode into the house. The guests watched bright-eyed. "She's going to the Box," they murmured knowingly.

Mother said, over-loud: "Be good for Shirumbay, Hassan!"

Was it good enough, Hassan wondered, that he kept perfectly silent? To be quite still, he crossed his knees and squeezed his elbows to his side. He longed to scratch his left ankle with the welt of his right shoe but didn't dare.

"Hassan's seeing women as we really are," Mother chirruped anxiously at her friends. "I meant to send him to his uncle's . . ."

"Spirit Shirumbay comes from far away, Hassan," said a lady with a cigarette. "Far away!"

"Shirumbay's mother is Abyssinian," another butted in, "but his father is Italian which is a man from Europe where they all like cigarettes and whisky-whisky!"

Hassan did not understand at all. The ladies smiled indulgently, and then forgot him. They were looking towards the house door. They sighed . . .

For the rest of his life, what came through this door was to be Hassan's notion of a European. The figure sported a shiny brown suit such as gentlemen on television wear when they step from aeroplanes and shake hands. There was a white shirt, a tie of dark green and a brown hat with a black band. It would have been smart, but for two things: the trousers were torn off at the knee, and this 'Italian man' was Hassan's rich aunty.

"Spirit Shirumbay is in her," whispered Hassan's mother.

"Shirumbay, welcome," said the ladies. Perhaps it is a party and this is the joker, thought Hassan. But nobody laughed. They said again, "Welcome, Spirit Shirumbay," in solemn voices.

The Italian-cum-Aunty stepped out solemnly, back under the purple bougainvillaea to her red plastic chair. Someone pushed the smoking brazier closer; Aunty breathed in the oily stink. One by one the ladies bobbed low, taking Aunty by her big black thumb, murmuring requests. Hassan saw now why she was rich. There was a biscuit tin open on the ground; as each guest came before her, each dropped in a bank note. Aunty said nothing. Her eyes were quite empty.

The drumbeats startled Hassan. Two women sat whacking the skins with long whippy sticks, whining a song. Someone was passing out tumblers of the sweet-scented petrol-drink. *As long as I don't have to drink that . . .*

Mother held out a hand.

"Hassan, come now." She took her little boy's wrist and drew him from the shelter of the kitchen towards the *rakuba*. "Greet Spirit Shirumbay, Hassan," said Mother.

The ladies gave an encouraging clap, but the boy grabbed at the wooden post of the *rakuba*. It felt cool and pleasant but was too slender to hide him. Hassan turned sideways to be thinner, to vanish. He saw the wormholes in the wood: *Can't I creep in there?*

"Hassan, come!" commanded Mother, starting to prise his hand from the wood. The boy's legs gave way; he was sliding down the post. He saw the dreadful figure above him, the Italian-cum-Aunty with her knees showing, the black eyes that rolled emptily.

"Hassan, greet Shirumbay politely so he looks after you," Mother snapped as she peeled small fingers off the last-hope post.

Hassan squealed and sat down hard.

"Hassan!" shrilled Mother, "Hassan, you get up!"

She took her son by his skinny forearm and pulled; Hassan's feet skidded and scrabbled on the grit. A belch of brown smoke passed over Aunty's face while Hassan gave high-pitched squeals of terror. His mother smacked at his bottom. Hassan skewed in her grasp, twisted free and backed away.

The ladies began to laugh.

"Eh! You doing this to me?" his mother shouted in mortification.

"Let the little treasure sit with me," said Aunty. Mother stared in astonishment.

"Hassan's so . . . so bad," she stuttered.

"No, he's just little," Aunty reproved, patting her bare knee.

Hassan ran. He crossed the yard, ran down the side of the house, past the watchman dozing on his rush cot, out of the gate and into the roadway. He ran stumbling down the sandy street to the main road, past the blacksmith's souk where the air pinged and dinged with beaten steel, to the transport souk where diesel trucks bellowed and shuddered. He ran to his father's office. But there was only Abdullah the old clerk, perched behind the desk.

"Your father's in the desert with the police," said Abdullah.

He saw Hassan's tear-smudged face and smiled gently.

"Sit down, Master Hassan. Shall I send for a soda? You know what I have heard? Yesterday a Russian gentleman has flown all around the earth, out in space among the stars. What do you think of that?"

Hassan thought nothing could shock him now. Nor could anything make him like foreigners, however high they flew.

*

The lessons of the *zar* never left Colonel Hassan al-Bedawi. Looking back, years later, it still impressed him as deeply offensive, a sinful riot. Spirits and indecency, loud women and Moral Disorder: these were a cancer in his country, and behind it all, somehow, lay Europe.

He grew to be a fastidious young man, slim in build, strong of will but controlled and rigorous. Energy and efficiency propelled young Hassan up through the ranks of the Khartoum police and, in a deft sidestep, to the promisingly discreet fiefdoms of State Security. His work was well organised, very thorough and carried more than a hint of ruthlessness. These talents brought him to the notice of General Mahjoub al-Mansur, the President's aide who, for his ferocity even from his student days, was called 'the Steel Fist'. When Steel Fist was appointed Governor to restore order in the West and to impose the disciplines of *sharia* law,

Hassan al-Bedawi was an obvious choice to accompany him.

Had he heard – enquired Steel Fist – of the tumult in Darfur? How nomads and farmers were at each other's throats?

Yes, Hassan had heard; also that the matter was absurdly complicated. For a start, there were dozens of tribes and sub-tribes jumbled in the province. There were the old Arab clans, the Kababish and the Bani Hussein and many more who claimed descent from Yemen, ancient Arabia and the Prophet himself. There were cattle Arabs, the Baqqara, men who one hundred years before had formed the battalions of the Mahdi. There were nomads and traders, stock breeders and farmers, all of different and fiercely proud lineage: the Hamar, the Mahariya, the Rizeigat and the Bani Halba, the Zayadiya and the Awlad Rashid, the wild Meidob and the Messalit, the uncouth Berti, the Mahamid and the warrior Goran . . . The list was long and intricate, with centuries of feuds and animosities interwoven as a delicate *modus vivendi* of trade, raid and retaliation. In their huge scrubby land they had rubbed along. It was not Hassan al-Bedawi's idea of a society either secure, ordered or moral. But Darfur had 'worked'.

Until the grasslands of the camel nomads began to wither. Now the desert was creeping south, and men whose stock was dying pushed south also into the farmlands of the Fur who tilled the tropical slopes of the Jebel Marra. The camel tribes, even the fierce Zaghawa, would notify the Fur in advance: *Vacate, for we are coming to take your villages and your fields.*

But Hassan had heard that the issue was more complicated still. For some of the fast-riding camel men were Arab, but some were blacks. And while some of the farmers were *zurqa*, others were Arabs. Neither would yield an inch without a fight. Added to which, there were civil wars: one war across the border in Chad, with combatants spilling into Sudan to dodge reprisals. And another war in the far south of Sudan between Christians and Muslims, with all their internecine feuds, that encroached on Darfur as well.

So there were farmers fighting nomads, blacks fighting Arabs, South against North, tribe against tribe and tumult everywhere.

To Hassan al-Bedawi, the zealous Security man, it was a distasteful picture of chaos.

"But do you know" – demanded Steel Fist – "of the Darfur Peace Conference some months ago, when supposedly the tribes agreed to set differences aside?"

Yes, Hassan had heard, thank goodness, since Steel Fist was not patient with Security officers who did not keep up to speed.

"That peace," scoffed Steel Fist, "is already breaking down. They are fighting again, and I shall put a stop to it. I have requested that you accompany me; you are appointed Chief of Security for Darfur. You shall seek out troublemakers, detain and interrogate and keep me very well informed. Between us we shall bring them to heel."

Hassan felt a hard thrill of anticipation. This was his notion of order.

When Hassan al-Bedawi told his wife that he had been appointed to the staff of Steel Fist, she purred with pleasure at the homage she'd be due from her ladies' circle. When he informed her that they would be going to Darfur, living in El Fasher surrounded by the stinking and vulgar Fur, she had hysterics and fled to her mother's house. Hassan left her there for two days while he organised, then fetched her back without discussion. Perhaps she hoped the nightmare had passed, and she entered their home with a light step, as though delighted to be restoring normality. Then she saw his preparations, the files and handbooks, the webbing belt, holster and pistol laid out tidily on the bed, together with his police cane.

She could only whimper: "Dearest . . . ?"

"Start your packing," he instructed her, "We have little time."

He had married Zahra not for her intellect but her family connections. He had wanted these not for his career (he managed that unaided), but for the dignity of his family and kin. During their (efficiently swift) courtship, it had been an additional, pleasant surprise to find that they shared many opinions, not least about the Western Province. To Zahra, far away Darfur was a desert devoid of society, peopled by bandits. Hassan thought much the same, though he preferred the language of the staff college: Darfur was internally unstable, a security risk, jeopardising the integrity of the Nation. When rumour of famine reached Khartoum, Zahra shrilled that the Fur were eating their own babies. Hassan told her not to be foolish, while privately agreeing with his brother officers that short rations would dampen the spirits of the fiery Fur and would be no bad thing. Security meant holding people in check. If they were hungry and lethargic, so much the easier.

Colonel al-Bedawi took up his post in El Fasher, narrowed his eyes and set to work, probing, arresting, interrogating, inflicting a little pain quietly enough to be terrifying. To begin with, the food shortages worked for him. People were nervous, were feeling vulnerable; they broke and talked readily, especially in the high security jail beyond the edge of town. Hassan was therefore piqued to find that there were organisations in the province working to prevent the useful hunger. Worse still, they were foreigners, and they showed astounding disrespect. In the souk, he had a confrontation with a revolting, gawky Englishwoman with pink skin who had taken to drinking tea in public, in the company of prostitutes and of men.

Hassan al-Bedawi enjoyed making the foreigners' lives very difficult. He had only to refuse travel permits, and their enquiries and researches in the desert villages became impossible. Here the Colonel saw a pleasing irony; decades before, certain British officials had used this same device to stop the rural poor receiving an education, simply by preventing them from getting to school. Thus, for weeks, Hassan was deaf to the pleas of Mr Xavier Hopkins. Only a paltry trickle of survey trips was approved.

But, in Khartoum, the Americans prevailed: food was to be sent to Darfur. Hassan was very irritated. Feeding insurgents was hardly his idea of sound strategy, but he was obliged to hold his tongue. When, however, he heard that the food was for El Fasher district only, he could not remain silent. He went to the Governor's first-floor office, where glass louvres opened on the sounds of the souk and a huge ceiling fan stirred two national flags flanking a photograph of the President. Steel Fist gazed out of the window, sipping at a glass of cold tea as Hassan expostulated:

"Sir, this will create envy and disequilibrium. There will be profiteering; black marketeers will flourish."

Hassan already knew of the activities of one Mohammed Shattah, a functionary in this very building. But today Steel Fist was oddly unresponsive.

"Thank you for your opinion, Colonel," he replied curtly. "Such possibilities had not escaped me."

Hassan left the building troubled. Had his superior been overruled? Must even Steel Fist – that stern dark eminence – struggle against vested interests? It made the Colonel profoundly angry to think of the Governor, a man of moral authority, obstructed by the pious self-servers who masqueraded as national saviours in the image of the Mahdi himself. But this, he knew, was how Khartoum worked.

At least, here in Darfur, the Governor had the Army behind him, so Hassan believed. Until Wadaa was attacked. Zaghawa bandits had come by night, reputedly three hundred of them.

Hassan al-Bedawi went to inspect the scene in convoy with a company of soldiers and two trucks from the Sudan Red Crescent carrying food and plastic tenting. They drove out of El Fasher heading southeast, following a wadi for one hundred kilometres through a stark, baked land until at last a rocky hill came into view. At its foot was a smudge of struggling crops and a little town of mud-brick and thatch. The settlement looked strangely unharmed: the morning after the attack, a dust storm had begun, a fine *haboob*. Whole blocks of homes and storehouses had been blasted and burnt, but the wreckage was now swathed in healing drifts of clean yellow sand. Only the charred stumps of posts were visible. The school was just a clutch of blackened and twisted steel chairs in the sand, the building entirely gone.

As the Red Crescent and the Army unloaded, Hassan al-Bedawi began asking his questions. The Zaghawa raiders had opened fire in the darkness from the dunes around town. Using what, asked the Colonel? What had caused this shambles, this destruction?

'Fire bullets', said the people, had set the thatch ablaze. Many townsfolk had been shot but seven had burned to death. The Colonel probed further: 'fire bullets'? Where, he wondered, do desperadoes on camels obtain incendiary ammunition? Or the heavy machine guns to fire it? And what had caused the explosions that had levelled the police post, the school and the souk? Rocket-propelled grenades, perhaps, streaking at short range from the rocky hillside into the sleeping town. But where in the desert do savages obtain rocket-propelled grenades?

He moved through the town, questioning and delving. He left the ruined centre, heading out among the huts of straw in their brushwood compounds. He entered these with a *Salaamalaikum* so curt and stern that the returned *Walaikum asalaam* was already nervous and submissive. In the cool fly-filled interiors, terrified women offered him tin mugs of red *karkadeh* juice in which small larvae twitched, while the men shifted from foot to foot. What do you know, he demanded of everyone. Who did you see? Who did you recognise? What do you know?

But he learned little.

"What about these so-called fire bullets?" he demanded impatiently, "and machine guns? They could not have obtained such things. You're talking nonsense!"

The men said nothing, were too petrified, but they glanced often at the soldiers, now setting up two heavy mortars with a studied lack of urgency.

A shadow passed over Colonel Hassan al-Bedawi. He persisted and probed, and became more and more uneasy. Had the weapons been sold by hungry troopers, or by profiteering officers? He would see them hanged. But, while he could believe it of a few rifles, the idea that RPGs and heavy machine guns were being stolen did not ring true.

He went straight back to the Governor, very cautiously voicing his suspicions. Once again, Steel Fist heard him out in silence, then said merely, "Thank you."

Was that all? No discussion, no request for further updates? Hassan took his leave and brooded, troubled and confused. Was

Steel Fist not as firmly in control of the Army as Hassan had believed? How could that be? When, years before, southern rebels had penetrated Darfur, Steel Fist had taken command of Government forces and had recruited in addition a ferocious militia of Rizeigat horsemen to drive the traitors off with a very bloody snout. Surely if anyone was in control here it was General Mahjoub al-Mansur, who would pound troublemakers with that celebrated Steel Fist.

But Hassan was too disciplined, too scrupulous to ignore the evidence he himself collected. He now had little doubt: the guns came from the Army. Hassan began to watch the soldiers carefully, particularly Steel Fist's immediate subordinates, teasing out their contacts, their strategy. He concluded that they were conspiring to undermine the Governor.

Hassan was not a philosophical man; the notion that chaos could itself be a form of order did not come easily to him. He saw only that the Army was stirring up conflict, even to the extent of arming 'the enemy'. Hassan believed that all guns should be confiscated, that all villagers should be confined to their localities. But the Army liked to shoot anything that moved – and if the populace not only moved but shot back, so much the better excuse.

And now an Army Captain delivered a message that was calculated to enrage. Not orders, of course: Security was not answerable to the military. But the visitor suggested that it was time the foreigners stopped their surveys; they had seen quite enough.

"We feel, Sir," purred the Captain, "that there is nothing to be gained from having these people pry into the way the Republic of Sudan manages its internal affairs."

What you mean, thought Hassan, is that the foreigners might get wind of what you are up to. He felt perplexed: what to do? Was he to defy and expose his own country's Armed Forces? How could he, a mere Colonel, contemplate such a thing? This time, he did not broach the matter with Steel Fist, whose position must be very delicate. But the Governor surely shared Hassan's belief that chaos was an evil to be resisted with all available means.

Didn't he? Perhaps the undermining had gone too far already.

The more Hassan al-Bedawi suspected that his own power was illusory, and the more he feared the Army outmanoeuvring him in the esteem of Steel Fist, the more bitter he grew. He felt an urge to vicious retaliation that he knew was unprofessional.

Hassan now made the startling discovery that Mr Xavier Hopkins shared certain of his opinions. He had assumed that the Agency was a tool in America's scheme to make Sudan helplessly dependent on handouts of US wheat and soya. But when the hapless Hopkins came yet again to beg for travel permits (the man's doggedness was extraordinary), Hassan learned otherwise. For Hopkins implied that he wanted nutritional data because he was sceptical about the existence of a famine.

"Do you mean," queried Hassan, studying the pale Englishman suspiciously, "that you would prefer *not* to be handing out food?"

"Just so!" blurted Hopkins. "Food aid does little good. It distorts local economies, it solves nothing. The World Food Programme is champing at the bit, wanting to flood every Rural District of Darfur with free grain. It's a nightmare."

He stopped, awkward; perhaps this was not the moment to be riding hobbyhorses. The complaint had an over-practised, habitual air about it. The Colonel scrutinised him.

"If you had suitable data," Hassan asked, "could you halt it?"

"I would do my best."

"I see," mused the Colonel, and to Xavier's astonishment issued every travel permit requested. One was for a journey to Kutum.

"Kutum," mused the Colonel affably. "Some awkwardness there over toxic seed. Young Kitchin: he has left?"

"I'm re-assigning him," replied Xavier cautiously.

"And who will go in his place?"

Xavier hesitated.

"I've sent a chap called Mogga," he said casually.

Colonel al-Bedawi's eyes were on him, glinting.

"Have you now."

Xavier began cramming the permits into his briefcase in case the Colonel might think again and snatch them back.

Hassan watched him, thoughtful. Hassan did not think he had ever met this Mogga (he had, at Farida's tea stall) but the southerner had come to the attention of Security several times since an incident at Radam al-Souk, a confrontation over trucking deliveries that had put the authorities in a very poor light. It had been reported to Hassan by his insider in the Governor's office, Mohammed Shattah, a transparently crooked fellow much given to sweating. The *zurqa* had caused further embarrassment by exposing grain hoarders and profiteering prison staff. Hassan did not defend the corrupt. It was, however, his business to chastise them; it was not the business of any *zurqa*.

But, dear God, did it not show him up too? Was he, Hassan al-Bedawi, to be supine and timorous, too weak-willed to take on corruption in the State, while a pitiful little black showed no fear at all?

"One thing before you go."

Xavier, heading for the door, looked round apprehensively.

"If I'm not mistaken," began Hassan smoothly, "you have a British journalist staying with you at present. A photographer, perhaps?"

A rhetorical question: Hassan's agents had logged the man's every move since he'd arrived.

"He's a photo-journalist," replied Xavier suspiciously. "He's from a London paper, we were asked to look after . . ."

"Of course," Hassan interrupted, for he knew all this. "Would you ask him to drop over and see me this afternoon?"

He saw a look of horror on Xavier's face and was amused; really, did they think him a common torturer?

"Just a short discussion," he smiled reassuringly. "Have you sent any supplies down to Wadaa? I think you should. And that journalist too, don't you think?"

"I'll arrange it," replied Xavier, bewildered.

TWO

The first morning of his return to Kutum, Mogga sought to pay his respects to the Chairman of the Rural Council.

He walked up the steep dirt road that wound to the top of Administration Hill. On the stony crest there were no trees, and an arbitrary road was marked out with rocks daubed white that could have been moved fifty yards either way. There stood the Government offices, a colonial H-block, exaggeratedly noble for such a back corner of a scrub country. There was a carriage sweep, a portico, and high windows. The old brick was pitted and pocked, fired and re-fired by the sun that flailed upon the hilltop.

No one guarded the drive; no one stood in the doorway or barred his entry. Mogga entered out of the white sunlight and for a moment could see nothing. He stood still. He could hear, from some distant wing, a very large typewriter striking very slowly. Moving forward a few paces he found himself in a large chamber. The roof was high and three globe lamps hung there; a fourth had gone, leaving only a clutch of bare wires. The floor was of gritty red tiles, their colour turning to brown, one in nine emboldened with a black-stencilled flower. Two massive wooden desks were islanded on the expanse of floor, blotched with ink and stacked with papers over which lay a fine desert dust. On each desk stood a half-empty glass of water with a tin lid painted in crude blue and yellow flowers. There were three low, lazy chairs with seats of woven cane around an octagonal coffee table surfaced with thick brown gunk. On the table there was a triangular tin ashtray – nothing else.

A soft padding made Mogga turn; a bearer in a white *jellabiya* was sliding in leather slippers across the tiles. The man was thin-faced and long-jawed. He gave a tiny bob of his head and gestured

Mogga to the lazy chairs. Mogga sat obediently, as the man left the hall by a door opposite. Silence again, except for the distant slow *thwack* of the typewriter. He looked at the wooden-cased clock high on the end wall, with the maker's name: *Gueurnier, Marseille*. The long hands, as thin as Miss Rose Price's fingers, indicated half-past four. Mogga saw two other fixtures on the walls: in a wooden frame there was a large map under crackled, yellowing varnish. Opposite hung the skin of some large animal, spread-eagled in defeat, its fur so old as to be no colour at all.

The bearer returned cradling in both hands another glass of water with a plain aluminium dust cover. This he set on the table by Mogga.

"Thank you," said Mogga, pointing at the animal skin. "What is that?"

The bearer regarded the skin with a frown, as though he'd not seen it in years.

"A lion," he replied at last.

"A lion," echoed Mogga.

"That," said the bearer more confidently, "was the last lion in Darfur."

Then he left.

Mogga sat peering through the cool gloom at the last lion in Darfur. The lion did not roar, the bearer did not reappear. The sound of the typewriter ceased.

Mogga got to his feet and wandered to the tall rear window of the hall, pushing open the wooden shutter. Outside there was a courtyard and a rusting jeep with four flat tyres. He ambled to the front porch but there was no one there. It was approaching mid-day and the heat was building steadily. Mogga backed inside again. He went to the side door from which the bearer had first materialised and looked along a high corridor painted gloss green to waist height, a flaking whitewash above. There was no one in sight. He took a first few steps down the corridor then hesitated, wondering if cries of bureaucratic outrage or the running of soldiers would greet his audacity. Neither came. Bolder, he moved forward. He passed a half-open door on the left and glimpsed files upon a desk, a standard fan, but no one working. He went on. The next door stood open also, and on this desk stood a type-writer, surely the one he'd heard, a monstrous old thing with a clutch of foolscap carbons sticking out of it, left in mid-sentence.

On he went. Now the corridor turned right and he put his head around gingerly, half-expecting to meet the barrel of a gun. Still the passageway was deserted. On. Two more open doors to left and right, two more offices, a third room quite empty. And then, at the back of the building, a door that was closed, with a small wooden notice and black lettering: 'Library'.

Mogga's father had had a library in the Iwenwe schoolhouse. That, at least, was what he called the shelf over his bed holding the half-dozen broken-spined textbooks he taught from, year after year. There had been a library at Mateki Vocational School also, consisting of a single wooden bookcase in the staff room. Mogga could not resist a library. He grasped the brass door handle as though he were shaking hands with some revered teacher. The door would not open, and for a moment Mogga thought that it was locked. Then it juddered backwards, a pebble trapped beneath. It had not been opened in a good while.

The room was not large, and was lit by two casement windows though the glass was caked with dust and the light much dimmed. Chicken wire had been stapled over the inside of the window frames. Beneath the window was a little writing table, an upright chair tucked in neatly. All around the walls, and in freestanding cases, were books.

Mogga had never seen so many books. All the books he had seen in his life put together would not total one quarter of these. Most were darkly bound in cloth, with a few in leather and a row of official-looking volumes in faded blue paper covers; reports no doubt. There were small yellowing labels with letters and numbers, one for every book though some had fallen off. Mogga spied a label lying on the floor and he knelt to pick it up, wetting it with his tongue and endeavouring to stick it back on, but the ancient gum would not take to the book's dusty spine and it fell again; he placed it carefully on the edge of the shelf.

He began to read titles, and was startled to see that some were clearly Christian: there was a clergyman's life – *Frank, Bishop of Zanzibar* – here in the heart of the Muslim north! But most were works of geography and of history by authors both British and Sudanese. He saw *The Sudan Question* by Abbas Mekki; what question might that be? wondered Mogga; he could think of so many. There was *Fire and Sword in the Sudan* by R. Slatin and *The River War* by W. Churchill: which river? Not the wadi at Kutum, he felt sure. There was *Desert Life* by Mr Solymos and *Ten Little Niggers* by A. Christie. He found several uniform volumes by Mr Gustav Nachtigal but when he pulled one from the shelves he could not understand it at all, neither the language nor even the script, the letters lumpish, black and heavy such as he had never seen before.

He was dazzled, he crouched and touched them, he sat cross-legged on the cement floor and pulled down book after book, blowing off dust, flicking the pages to marvel at the plethora of words before snapping the volumes shut and startling several scorpions on the shelves which scurried into darker refuges. Taking yet another volume at random, he sat carefully, reverently, on the wooden chair.

"Now I am studying in a library," he murmured to himself.

The volume he had picked out was *A History of the Arabs in the Sudan*. Inside, Mogga found that it was by Mr Harold McMichael and had been published in 1922. That was so long ago, surely before his father Samuel Mogga had been born. Mogga ruffled through the pages until he read:

> In person, the Fur are small and skinny with thin legs, small bones and egg-shaped heads. All have a peculiarly rancid smell.

Mogga sat quite still for a moment, then read these sentences again. He was startled: an Englishman writing so rudely, about the people of this very country! Mogga read further.

> Their character is marked by stupidity and low cunning in combination.

Mogga's eyebrows shot up higher than the tufts on his ears. He had never imagined that a book could be harsh and abusive. Why did McMichael think like this?

They are suspicious and deceitful and they instinctively lie about even the most trivial subject rather than speak a word of the truth.

He cannot have enjoyed his stay in Sudan, this person. Perhaps he'd had a bad experience in Darfur, in Kutum even.

They are very ignorant and credulous, hot-tempered, idle and drunken; but they are easily amused and have a distinct sense of the ludicrous.

Well, thought Mogga, that last was true.

Their one ambition in life is to acquire more cattle.

He laughed aloud: true, true! Or if not cattle, then goats or chickens or pickup trucks even, yes he knew this, he recognised the Fur from this. He read on, not noticing the passage of time, or the tiny prickling of dust thrown against the window by the wind.

But when he was at last roused by the call of the *muezzin*, penetrating thinly and distantly into the little library, Mogga had already stopped reading. His mood had quite changed. McMichael lay disregarded on his lap; Mogga was gazing into some inner distance. His face was sombre, and he was rubbing and scratching at the scars on the palms of his hands. He got to his feet, replaced McMichael on the shelves and left the building before he could be locked in.

*

"I realised some most unpleasant things," said Mogga to Leila, who had arrived on tour that afternoon, her Land Rover laden with death-to-locusts and tomato seeds. Mogga's voice was tinged with agitation.

"The first is that Europeans think it natural to say unkind

things about the people here. They do not know that they are
being unkind, they would not understand that they are being
unkind, because they are not really speaking about human persons."

"Was it not a very old book?" inquired Leila, sitting demurely
at the table in his house-and-office, just as Dr Maeve had sat with
Malik.

"Not so old," said Mogga. "A man born then might be alive
now."

"What was the second thing?" she asked.

She saw that Mogga was not himself but preoccupied and
unhappy. He could not return her look, but gazed in the direction
of the door. Outside, her driver Abdurrahman was seated on the
step cleaning the components of a pressure lamp. But Mogga was
not thinking of Abdurrahman. He seemed embarrassed and shy,
as though in a confessional.

"The second thing that you realised?" she prompted.

Another moment of silence.

Then he whispered, "I realised that I agreed."

"You agreed? With McMichael?"

"Not all of it, Miss Leila, but with much! Sometimes I knew
because I laughed, sometimes because I scoffed. Sometimes I
realised that I had read some terrible thing without protest because
in my heart I agreed."

"What sort of thing?"

"Unkind things."

He dropped his voice.

"McMichael says the Fur smell nasty."

"Ah," said Leila, nodding, "that."

"They smell like heavily perspiring goats. And he says that they
are very, very stupid, and not to be trusted at all."

"And you agreed with this?" she wanted to know.

He murmured, "I found some recognition in my heart."

He was examining the cement floor between his knees. Leila
saw, in her friend's eyes, shame and bewilderment and anger. She
could not be sure what he was angry at, but it was clearly not very
far away. She said:

"Do you find that you despise those you came to help?"

"Not despise. But neither do I respect them."

"And you thought that you had worked for them with love in your heart."

"Such was my vanity."

"Though you thought it unusual, that a southern black could come among these ingrates with a charitable heart."

"I admit . . ."

"Another vanity. So Mogga finds that he is not saintly but vain."

"Miss Leila . . ."

"You have seen yourself in a mirror, dear friend, and what could be more pitiless than your own gaze? You suspect that, after all, you are as contemptuous as the most foolish and patronising European."

"Oh," moaned Mogga, "you see through me."

"Only," replied Leila gently, "because it is at you that I choose to look."

He said nothing.

"And I see with some relief," Leila continued, "that you share my prejudices. Let me tell you how we Sudanis loathe each other, since you appear not to have noticed. Do you know what we Khartoum sophisticates think of the Daju of Jebel Marra and south Darfur? We call these countrymen of ours *nas fira'on*, People of Pharoah, meaning evil and violent. Or the Massiriya of Jebel Khares: we call them red-skinned, violent brigands who never heed the laws of hospitality, and are therefore not true Arabs. The Zaghawa are dark, *khodr*-skinned which is a green and sickly hue. They are poor Muslims, they drink *merissa* beer and asses' milk and catch gazelles in snares, certainly not the practice of the noble Arab. The Messalit are worse, are cannibals, we have nothing to do with them. The Zebeda are *surf*, a dirty copper yellow, they are good horsemen but not civilised."

"Oh," mused Mogga.

"Need I go on? We of fine Arab stock have little time for our countrymen, these would-be Arabs. We can despise them without the help of foreigners."

"Ah, foreigners," Mogga sighed, "I am the foreigners' tool, the tool of old empire in Sudan again."

"We are all tools, Mogga," said Leila, "Tools of God and Nature."

But Mogga was on his feet, turning about like a caged bear.

"I thought them such fine persons, this Mr Xavier Hopkins, this Mr Toby Kitchin, Miss Rose Price and Miss Christa Lerche, all! I saw them as redeemers of our tribes who fight and thieve. I was honoured to work among them and to protect them. But now I see that this comparison is itself a sin, a pride, a despising of the poor and innocent who have only struggled to eat from day to day – yes, I see that in admiring these redeemers, I am undone by pride."

"Undone? Oh, come . . ."

But he went on angrily, his voice hard and bitter.

"I say to myself, Mogga, face a fact here: the English send you to deal with difficulties that they dare not face themselves. I am front-line, go-between, pig-in-the-middle. By Sudanis I am despised for my name of a southerner. I am not a noble Arab, not even a decent Fur or Zaghawa, I am barely human to them. But if the foreigners blunder, I am Sudani enough to be accused of treason to Sudan. If things do not work, and usually they do not work, it is Mogga they can blame, it is Mogga they curse."

She looked at him in great concern, her black eyes wide with alarm. She saw that Mogga's face was twisted, his eyes watering, and that he was balling his hands into fists, kneading and squeezing them in turn, again and again and again . . . She seized his right hand and held it strongly.

"Stop that!" she commanded. And Mogga stopped.

He sat again, his face hanging heavy with weariness. He stared down at his own hand clamped firmly in hers. Leila released her fierce grip, and gently opened his fist. When she saw the palm, she frowned: the scar was red and swollen as she had never noticed it before. She believed she could almost see it throbbing.

"Sometimes," he whispered, "my hands grow sore."

For two long moments they sat quite still. Then:

212

"I must leave," he said, "I must leave this work."

"That is nonsense," she began.

"I have had enough," Mogga's eyes blazed, "and seen enough. I have no respect for myself or my employers or the people, therefore I must remove myself quickly."

"You are being absurd," said Leila.

"Absurd? Absurd?" The little man's passions were in flux. "Absurd is working for these Xaviers and Tobys and Roses who aid no one and who I must sort and save when they give poisoned seed to villages and injections to chiefs!"

He gripped her hand, shaking his head from side to side, seeing nothing but a pit that had appeared in front of him, into which he stared with loathing.

"I tell you absurd," he blundered on. "It is a giant of a country so down upon its knees that it can only be saved by England . . ."

But Leila was angry also.

"*You* are absurd," she repeated mercilessly. "A million people face a nightmare."

"I have faced nightmares!" he retorted, "I have seen slaughter, I have seen those I wished to protect shot to pieces. I saw a train . . ."

"That is enough."

She took her hand away, her nostrils flaring with an indrawn breath.

His tirade halted. He peered at Leila, puzzled.

"Have I offended you?"

The slightest softening of her shoulders, an easing of her jaw, of minuscule muscles beneath her lower eyelids – these almost invisible signs signalled to him that she relented.

"Mogga," her low voice soothed him, "even when you thought it came to nothing, there has been a will in your work that has nourished everyone. Myself also, you have aided me in very dark hours."

She held his look. Mogga blushed.

"Forgive me," he said. "I am bewildered."

"I should like you to know that I love you," she said.

Mogga blinked, and blushed.

"I love you for a very fine man," she added.

Mogga sat back in his chair, and his expression became one of melancholy exhaustion.

"Oh, this," he laughed, "to be known for a fine man."

"A lion!" she said.

He smiled sadly: "The last lion in Darfur."

Another silence between them.

Then he stood, saying, "I am a poor host, at any rate. I shall make you some tea. This Abdurrahman outside, he can doubtless hear every word, what must he think."

He pottered to the kerosene stove, was clumsy with matches, had it burning at last.

As he returned to the table, she drew herself more upright and looked at him directly. She was very proud, he saw; her dignified pride was a presence in the room, a stern chaperone. Mogga leaned towards Leila, peering as though he had been shown a wonderful palace in her mind. She returned his gaze with her calm affection, and the moment stayed, for there was nowhere for it to go.

Until, suddenly, her eyes changed, sparkling like a naughty girl's.

"Mogga, may I show you some magic?"

"How, magic?" He looked dubious. "You wish to summon devils, Miss Leila?"

"No, no," she grinned, "you need no camphor against my sorcery. I shall show you the value of money, how indestructible is the Sudan pound."

She glanced quickly round the room. Behind her on a shelf lay a little heap of envelopes, small, flimsy and greyish.

"Mogga, do you have fifty pounds?"

Mogga was not to be overawed.

"Fifty pounds? Of course."

He took his purse from his pocket, holding out the red note that showed a mighty baobab tree and the National Bank.

"Thank you, Mogga," she said with a prim twinkle of amusement.

She took the note from him, bowing graciously.

"The red fifty," she said solemnly. "The baobab signifies safe keeping, because our people store water in its hollow trunk. Did you know, Mogga, such is the permanence of our nation's currency, that this note cannot be burned?"

Now he stared. This was final evidence that she had been in Darfur too long.

"Observe me, please," she commanded.

She was busy with her back to him in the kitchen corner, rummaging for this and that. He wanted to assist . . .

"Sit down, Mogga! Now, mark a little cross upon this note."

He did so, with a blue ballpoint. She placed an enamel plate upon the table.

"I fold your note – so, and so."

She took the envelope and opened the flap.

"And I place your fifty pounds in this."

She slid the folded note inside, then licked the flap, raising her eyebrows at him mysteriously.

"Light me a match, Mogga."

She held the corner of the envelope into the flame. It browned and blackened . . .

"Miss Leila!" cried Mogga, reaching – but she drew back her hand and the flame swarmed up the little envelope.

"Fifty pounds!" he wailed.

The paper was curling and falling apart; Leila dropped it onto the enamel plate. They stared at the smoking remains.

"Miss Leila?" breathed Mogga, "What have you done to my money?"

She was frowning. She poked at the heap of ashes on the plate.

"Oh, Mogga," said Leila unhappily.

"Fifty pounds!" he whispered, astonished. "You have just burned fifty pounds."

Of a sudden, she laughed: "No, wait . . ."

She delved into her *tobe* and waved a tightly folded note at him.

"See, here is your money! Here is your mark!"

His eyes popped and he shouted at her.

"How . . . ? Oh, you! Miss Leila, you!"

He laughed, his eyes ran, he howled with happiness. She reached across the table and cuffed him on the shoulder, shrieking with laughter likewise.

Outside in the dusk, Abdurrahman the driver glanced uneasily at the door through which came such immodest noises. Was the black man leading a Muslim lady into impropriety? Good and dignified Miss Leila? Should he, a mere driver, intervene? The tittering, the whispering . . .

"Abdurrahman," she cried, "Abdurrahman!"

She was laughing. Maybe the black had turned her mind. Abdurrahman, with steady resolve, opened the steel door.

Leila was standing by the table, grinning fit to bust.

"Abdurrahman, Abdurrahman, give us your money!"

The driver began to edge back, out into the darkness.

"No, come in, please, we want to burn your money. Really, are you afraid of a woman?"

He dithered, he glanced at Mogga but the *zurqa's* smile was friendly, his eyes hardly devilish. Abdurrahman stepped gingerly inside and closed the door behind him.

"What money do you have in your pocket?" giggled Leila.

The young man took out a floppy ten-pound note that smelled of camels.

"Thank you!" she sang gaily, tweaking it from his hand. There was an envelope lying on the table.

"Now, you watch, Abdurrahman," said Leila excitedly. "I am going to burn your money."

"Please . . ." began her driver weakly.

"You shall see it magically reappear."

She was folding his money, tucking it into the envelope, sealing it up. Then she lit a match and, before he could protest, she incinerated his salary.

Mogga beamed at them. Walking home from Administration Hill earlier, terribly depressed, he could not have dreamed of such a merry evening. Leila delighted him utterly, and Mogga could not tell what he honoured most: her high serious endeavour in the field or her silliness, laughter and magic this evening.

216

"Miss Leila," he wondered, when Abdurrahman had gone to wash, "where did you learn such a trick?"

"University," she answered. "We had a lecturer from France one year. His lessons were dull but afterwards he taught us French magic."

"Ah." said Mogga.

A pause.

He put out his hand to cover hers upon the table. She did not move.

"Bless you, Miss Leila," said Mogga.

Nor did she take her hand away.

Mogga sighed.

"Please," he said, "sleep behind the screen."

*

At dawn, Mogga woke – and at once his face turned towards the cotton screen behind which Leila rested. Mogga, himself on blankets on the concrete floor, felt deeply grateful that she'd accepted his bed. He blushed, almost laughed aloud, yet his gratitude was a physical, exciting thing. Then came a flood of protectiveness, accompanied by a bizarre and unseemly urge to take Leila her breakfast in bed. He had once read that this was a sophisticated thing to do.

What had woken him, however, was a knocking on the door.

Mogga went to the gate.

"What is it?" said Leila, appearing at his side.

"A message is come," said Abdurrahman expressionlessly.

Mogga smiled cheerfully at Leila. Her fresh green *tobe* was neat enough for giving a lecture to the university, but her hair was unbrushed and hung in a loose queue over one shoulder. Mogga felt dangerously thrilled. He sensed the glances of the messenger, and of Abdurrahman.

"I must go to Administration House," he said.

Leila was distracted, gazing down the steep lane to the corner below. A vehicle, a battered green Toyota Land Cruiser, had slowed as it crossed, pausing for a look. She half-recognised one face, a big man – but the pickup rolled on out of sight.

"Oh?" she enquired vaguely.

"I am urgently called to the radio."

Half an hour later, he was back. He must return to El Fasher at once, he reported, for an emergency consultation, something to do with some vitamins that had been distributed. He had been speaking with Dr Maeve. She sounded very worried.

THREE

He fingered the reports on his desk: angry, handwritten notes from Kutum, from Malha and Mellit, that concerned a fool doctor and out-of-date pills. Colonel Hassan al-Bedawi could recognise a weapon; he knew the sharp cuts that paper could inflict. The reports were potent; for what, exactly, would become clear in due course.

There was a man standing in front of Hassan, sweating with fear, as they generally did; the blades of the ceiling fan turning overhead made visitors think less of cool than of decapitation. This fellow was a chemist from the El Fasher College, and he had sensed the Colonel's foul mood.

"So," repeated Hassan, his voice chillingly even, "our traitor's wife is to bring you posies of desert flowers. How nice. Do you imagine stories like that will earn you your keep from me?"

The chemist licked his lips and shuffled his feet. Really, thought Hassan, I wish my spies had more spine.

"Well?" demanded the Chief of Security.

"She wants me to analyse them," explained the chemist.

"Are you going into perfume manufacture? Is that what our fine University College has come to?"

"It's plants that people eat, the ones they ferment, *kawal* and suchlike."

"So what?" snapped Hassan.

"She wants to know exactly what's in them, chemically."

"And you can do that," queried the Colonel sarcastically, "in your little laboratory?"

The man flushed.

"I can do ash content, I can do crude protein, I can do lipids and some amino acids . . ."

219

"Ah, can you? Excellent!"

"Chromatography I'd have to send to Khartoum."

"Splendid!" the Security Chief applauded mockingly. "And what will our lady friend do with your results?"

"She's going to show them to Dr Shamal – he's the paediatrician at the hospital . . ."

"I know very well who he is," shot Hassan, "that is my job. Continue!"

"She wants to know," the chemist persisted doggedly, "which plants are best for children in a food crisis."

"Why?"

"She'll tell the villagers. She's going to tell them to plant wild foods that survive drought. Then, in bad years, they won't be dependent on the Government."

Hassan al-Bedawi scrutinised the chemist. The fellow was not such an idiot; Hassan was more interested than he'd admit.

The lecturer, a limp little figure in an over-large nylon shirt now wringing with perspiration, was making for the door.

"One moment," barked Hassan, stopping him short. "Where is she now?"

"Mrs Karim? Kutum, I think, gathering specimens." The chemist hesitated. "And visiting the *zurqa*," he mumbled.

When the weasely academic had gone, Hassan admitted to himself that he found the notion of Leila visiting Mogga distasteful. But, having indulged the notion for a moment, he suppressed it utterly. Hassan knew the difference between mere personal distaste and a public offence.

Leila Karim in Kutum: a woman touring the villages, telling peasants how to be self-sufficient, free of Government. Had she asked permission to supplant the State, for permission to instruct the tribes in any matter at all? Was she a Governor, a General, a President, that she gave orders to society? And was she not the wife of a traitor? These were piques to the body politic, and Hassan would slap them down. For he felt a chafing as though small insects had made punctures in his skin, just where the leather belts of his rank and office were sure to rub them into open sores.

The Colonel, his mind in a seethe, returned home grim-faced and thin-lipped. He would bring them all to heel. But when he entered his own well-ordered house, he found that his wife had fled.

"She's gone *where*?" he snarled at the terrified housemaid and watchman who stood side by side, close together in the face of Hassan's fury.

"Khartoum, sir," the girl bleated, "a jet came, SudanAir, and when Madame heard it she said her mother was sick and rushed to the airfield . . ."

The girl stumbled to a halt, dragged down by the preposterous story. Hassan turned a full circle on the spot, as though his wife might be there after all, simpering at this silly joke. But she was not.

He, too, had heard the Boeing. He had always found something incongruous in these huge jets scraping along El Fasher's dirt runway, dust and stones pluming from the fat tyres, scratching the fuselage paint. He turned back to glare at the trembling servants. The watchman said:

"I think she paid cash, Sir."

The Colonel stalked from room to room, seeking an explanation for this shaming, precipitate flight. There were no signs of panic, no indication that she had seized an armful of clothes from the wardrobe. No signs of feverish packing at all. She could not have gone without something, surely.

"She took no bags?"

The housemaid's eyes stayed on his, not out of courage but in petrified fixity.

"Well?" snapped Hassan, "did she not take any bags? I see no sign of packing."

"Sir, she had one ready," the girl whispered, "under the wardrobe . . ."

This last was scarcely audible. Hassan turned away from her lest she see his mortification, for he now visualised the small suitcase, its handle peeking from beneath the wardrobe. He had never thought to ask why it was there. He, the Security Chief.

So, she had fled the barbarities of Darfur, fled the people who eat their babies in a sauce of tomatoes and ground cattle bone. They were savages, of course they were, but one did not run from savages. Home to Mother!

Hassan felt savage enough to spit but, outwardly, he determined to show nothing. Not that it would do him any good. Half El Fasher would know of the débâcle by sunset, probably already did. Those Army men he was determined to chastise, to teach that order and law must be obeyed, they'd be hooting with derision at a Security Chief whose wife ran away.

He would betray nothing, neither fury nor surprise nor dismay nor any weakness whatever. He would impose order, he would be implacable.

He thought of that Leila Karim, her effrontery.

He would be steel, he would be ice.

Ice, in Darfur.

*

Dr Khalid Shamal, a gentle paediatrician with a weary walk, left El Fasher Civil Hospital, principal medical centre of Darfur Province, and went home to do something more useful than labour in a place with no medicines.

In the dusty back yard of his house, on the verandah and sometimes in the street outside, people were waiting for him, dozens of them. They sat or squatted on the sand, mostly women, attempting to soothe and quiet their infants, whispering and crooning, wiping at the slack skin and soiled thighs, peering down as Dr Shamal's houseboy moved about the yard setting out a few oil lanterns, a few candles in jars.

When the young doctor arrived, the crowd stirred. Khalid Shamal always hesitated a moment in his own gateway, astonished by the numbers waiting to be seen, the prospect of several hours more work. Each adult was clutching a numbered card; under their shawls and gowns, each had a handful of Sudan shillings, as much as they could raise from family or friends. Dr Shamal had set a standard fee for consultation, but asked only that people pay what they could up to that fee, because the pharmacies charged dearly for whatever he prescribed. If he prescribed less they might have been able to pay him more. His private clinics were not going to make him rich.

He went to his bathroom, washed his face and hands. He paused five minutes in his inner rooms to drink black tea and eat a little bread and fruit. Then he moved to his desk under the pressure lamp on the verandah, and began.

Only, this evening there was a hiccup in the routine. His house-boy murmured to him that there was a woman waiting – no, not a mother, not a patient: a distinguished person, the lady from Khartoum. She begged a word before the clinic began, she asked his indulgence . . . Khalid Shamal turned his handsome face toward the far end of the verandah and saw, standing beneath the pale green arch and caught in the light of two candles, Leila Karim.

His heart sank.

"I cannot help you," he said.

The dismay that suffused her look was so awful that he thought she would start wailing with grief. He took her arm and steered her indoors, out of earshot of the crowd. She began to berate him:

"Yes, indeed you can, if only . . . !"

He raised a tired hand.

"Please, I would, by Allah indeed I would, I beg you to under-stand . . ."

"I understand," she retorted, "that you have outside a score of sickly children. Every single one would be healthier if they were better nourished, which every single family could manage if they knew more precisely which plants . . ."

"It is not as simple as that," murmured the doctor miserably, shrinking.

"Of course it's not simple!" she ranted. "What do they know of amino acids? Which of them has heard of phosphates and zinc? It is *our* job!"

Leila stopped and peered at him, the contempt in her eyes as loud as the sarcasm in her voice.

"How simple would you like?" she queried.

Now Khalid flushed, and lashed out.

"You think me incompetent? I'll tell you incompetence: that woman giving everyone in Kutum her old pills, her out-of-date junk. Are we somebody's dustbin? Does she think we'll eat rubbish and be thankful? Who does she think we are? Yes, we've all heard: there are staff in our Ministry who can read labels. These are your arrogant, stupid friends, so you tell them!"

He stopped, ashamed of himself. Leila stared at him with her aquiline nostrils flaring and her lips pressed together. Beyond the open doorway, by the dim flicker of candlelight the patients waited. Their eyes never left the doctor and his awkward, time-consuming visitor.

"I have been given to understand," he tried to speak calmly, "that your project would not be favoured by the authorities."

She was studying him minutely, silent only because there was more to come. Dr Shamal looked unhappily at the floor, at his own plastic sandals.

"I have been advised that my clinic here might be closed, declared illegal, unauthorised . . . something like that."

By now he was whispering, lifting his look and indicating the silent, watchful people with his eyes.

"This is the best that I can do for them. This is all I can do."

"Who has said this?" she hissed. "Who!?"

He shrugged, he wriggled, implying that it was no one in particular, that it didn't matter . . .

"Is it Security? Is it al-Bedawi?"

He only sighed the deep sigh of a man with a lungful of poison that he could not shift. She walked out.

And drove straight to the offices of State Security, still lit in their pale, unkind way. Hassan al-Bedawi seemed to be expecting her.

"Sit," he commanded.

He paced about the room, where he had been re-reading those letters from Malha and Kutum in which indignant officials denounced the idiot doctor and her Land Rover full of old vitamins.

"So, here you are," he said, "wasting your energy again."

She started to bargain, she urged, pleaded to be allowed to pursue her project. The Colonel could not expect her to be idle. She was working for her country, she was contributing, a good Sudani. She wished only the betterment of her – of *their* people . . .

She twisted in her chair to see if he was paying the slightest attention. Colonel al-Bedawi stood unmoving, his hands behind his back, gazing at a large map on the wall. Infuriated, she overstepped the mark.

"I find it difficult to see how you, a servant of the nation, can justify suppressing my work. You are depriving the people of what is rightfully theirs. It is a betrayal . . ."

Leila stopped, having noted a slight lift of the Colonel's chin, a hint of a straightening of the spine. Slowly, he turned on her, his brow raised in frigid irony.

"Betrayal?" he replied evenly. "It is not my spouse residing in our high security cell."

He moved swiftly to stand behind Leila's chair. She felt his voice, rapid and slippery, like eels sliding through her poor defences.

"As Dr Othman Karim's notion of his duty is so suspect, my own duty is to keep his wife from folly."

She heard his breath hissing softly in his nostrils. He continued:

"For your husband's sake you should cultivate my mercy, not jeopardise it. Your husband will not be finding our investigations comfortable."

His voice froze her heart, her guts, her muscles. Leila could feel his digit touch her right temple – but in fact it had not done so. She was imagining it, imagining every possible horror, the price he was going to exact for Othman's safety . . .

She was near to panic. She made one last play for dignity.

"My father," she said, "raised me to believe that our talents should be placed at the service of our people."

"Your father," said Hassan al-Bedawi, "was a person of no talents whatever. As for your own . . ."

He moved around his desk and studied Leila's furious-frightened face.

"Your talents are many, but they are in great need of discipline."

She could not look at him, but sensed his scrutiny moving over her whole body like fingertips, as though he was preparing to cut her.

"Now go home," he said.

She left quickly.

As Leila went, her retreating back was observed from the shadows by a massively built man whose sweaty odour Hassan found particularly distasteful.

"Well?" the Colonel demanded curtly. "You've something for me?"

Mohammed Shattah's face was resentful, fearful and shifty all at once.

"I've had word of Army plans for the Meidob," he mumbled.

"Tell me."

Shattah spoke of an atrocity in the making – but as he spoke, he couldn't stop his eyes reaching out through the louvre blinds after the departing woman.

"Perhaps," observed the Colonel frigidly, "you would care to concentrate on your story rather than your unclean thoughts?"

"She," said Mohammed Shattah coolly, "was in Kutum a week ago, sleeping in that *zurqa's* house."

Shattah was now studying the Colonel minutely, watching for his least reaction.

"I am well aware of all that," snapped Hassan. "Who do you think his staff report to?"

But Shattah ploughed on, his eyes fixed to the Colonel's face.

"I saw her coming out of his house, half-dressed."

Hassan al-Bedawi returned his look: between them, a long, hard, silent stare. Ah, Mohammed Shattah was suddenly sure he had understood: the Colonel's rage, his wife fled, the Karim woman who prefers a black . . . In the Colonel's eyes Shattah read a corroding, bitter, squalid jealousy. The man was transparent! Shattah sweated all the more, fearful but exultant.

"Get back to what you were saying about the Army," hissed Colonel al-Bedawi.

*

He left his office. He walked out into the night streets of El Fasher where, though the sun was long gone, the deep sand that had soaked up the day's heat now threw it back, wearying the citizens. As he trudged, Hassan thought of his visitors.

The woman: so utterly unlike his craven Zahra. Hassan allowed Leila's elegant, hawkish face into his mind a moment; he considered her fiery intelligence, he saw her sitting before him, her long hands . . . He suppressed the image ruthlessly, and if a little tremor passed through his body as he walked through the dark, he clamped it down. He had a firm grip on Leila Karim; he put her out of mind.

But not his spy in the Governor's office, that sour-smelling crook. Hassan had the evidence to hang Mohammed Shattah; the man was desperate to deliver something that the Colonel actually wanted, but now he'd produced information that Hassan had dreaded, that wounded him profoundly. It had left a bleeding gash in the Colonel's spirit.

For Shattah had confirmed that Hassan's patron and mentor had deceived him. Steel Fist had lied to him and used him, had misled him entirely. Had no intention of supporting Hassan's stand against traitors in the Army. Had, in fact, the very same policy as the Army: to divide and destroy the Darfur tribes. They had together armed the turbulent factions, had provoked unrest, incited killings and feuds among the tribes to weaken them. And now they would not scruple to stage a slaughter, to blame it on some hapless tribe, to provoke retaliatory bloodletting. All this done with information Hassan himself had supplied! Steel Fist had hoodwinked and humiliated Colonel al-Bedawi, a man who could not even discipline his own wife.

So now the Colonel tramped through the unlit, subdued streets into the centre of a rebellious town whose very shadows murmured resentment. The walking calmed him a little. Hassan gradually felt less like striking with his baton at the face of the first street urchin that came within range. He was possessed by a darker, quieter rage.

When vehicles passed, their headlights revealed flocks of men in white robes striding here and there with expressions of great purpose, but whose intentions were strangely hidden to the Chief of Security. He noted how these men – Fur and Zaghawa and Messalit, all the tribes of incurable rebellion – how they peered back at him, recognising his uniform in the scything headlights. He wondered how close he was, once the vehicle was gone and the night closed in again, to having a knife stuck through his ribs, or his head broken with a swinging cudgel by a figure that would flit away down a black lane.

But Colonel Hassan al-Bedawi had no fear. He had a resolve on him, and he was hurrying through the dark towards the souk and the house of Xavier Hopkins. He would deliver information that he expected would surface in the Western press quite swiftly. He would oblige Hopkins to send a witness north, to fetch first-hand evidence of what the Army was about. And Hopkins, because he was surely looking to save his Programme, would do as he was told.

PART FIVE
Nomads

ONE

He entered Xavier's dark garden without ceremony. The Chief of Darfur Security moved swiftly towards the pool of soft yellow light under the trees where Xavier Hopkins sat reading letters. Startled, Hopkins got to his feet as though expecting the Colonel to pull out an automatic pistol and destroy him.

"There is some information," said the Colonel, "which you should know."

"Please . . ." began Xavier, gesturing towards a chair, squirming to find his manners wrong-footed. Colonel al-Bedawi remained standing.

"It concerns the relief programme," he said, his voice rapid, quiet but utterly clear, "and the Army."

"Ah," sighed Xavier.

"If I told you that military elements are using your food . . ."

"It's not mine," Hopkins began, but the Colonel over-rode him. ". . . using it to create disorder?"

"That," murmured Xavier, "would of course be unacceptable."

The Colonel was turning slowly this way and that, peering through the darkness at the high compound walls as though there might be listeners perched there.

"You say, military elements . . ." Xavier prompted. He was puzzled, fearful, and bizarrely excited: was this ferocious Security Chief an ally after all?

The Colonel dropped a brown envelope onto the low table on which rings of coffee jostled gobbets of cold candle wax. He said:

"You have just found an envelope, delivered anonymously to your house. How it got there, who can tell? But were you to pass that envelope to your London reporter, he might be intrigued. Has he not already heard whisper that the Army is diverting food to certain unarmed villages, while supplying munitions to others nearby from whom food has been inexplicably withheld? Wouldn't he like to find evidence of that? He might wonder, don't you think, about the effects of such imbalance, in a warrior society on the brink of collapse."

Xavier stared. The Colonel continued, as he spoke, to peer about into the night.

"Well, Mr Hopkins? What do you imagine? One tribe rich in food but defenceless, its neighbours hungry and heavily armed. The poor are terribly vulnerable to rivals who these days are well armed – astonishingly well armed."

Xavier looked in alarm at the envelope, then back. Good God, he thought, the man standing before him had surely just committed professional and personal suicide. He noticed that Hassan was immaculately dressed, his uniform pressed, belts and shoes polished to perfection. This appealed to the fastidious in Xavier Hopkins. Being well groomed on the eve of apocalypse was something in which one might take pride. One might also recognise the trait in others; one might even feel a certain kinship.

He waited for his visitor to speak again – which at last the Colonel did, in that same low voice.

"Give me your word that you will not divulge this conversation to others."

This was an order.

"Certainly. But, why are they doing this? There'll be mayhem. Do they *want* a famine?"

A feeble bleat. In the lamplight, the Colonel's face twitched, a picture of anger and humiliation.

"Mr Hopkins, this is a province of unruly savages." The icy voice began to break and shake with fury. "For as long as we can remember, they have been rebelling against all and anyone. If Darfur starves, Khartoum will be delighted."

"But it will be chaos . . ."

"Don't you know," sneered the Colonel (though he himself had realised this only today), "that chaos is the tyrant's friend? The famished tribes won't have time for rebellion, they'll be far too busy cutting each other's throats and stealing the bread from the babies' mouths. Such a people will be helpless; one regiment will hold them down."

"And you?" retorted Xavier, appalled at the picture and resentful at the lecture, so that he spoke with undiplomatic aggression. "What is your role? I suppose you'd like the tribes to starve also?"

Was it the flickering light, or did al-Bedawi wince?

"That, Mr Hopkins, is no idea of order that I could ever share. That is a travesty of order, a betrayal of Security."

The Colonel looked away. As the moment of silence between them lengthened, Xavier sensed the deepening mutual sympathy.

"The question for you, Mr Hopkins, is whether you should have any part of such a situation – whether you should be here at all."

The Director felt sick. *I have played the part of a silly elf.*

Al-Bedawi turned to go, then seemed to recall something.

"I've had reports," he said, "that your doctor has distributed a large quantity of out-dated medicines. She's handed them out all over the north, Malha District, and Mellit and Kutum also. Local officials are none too pleased. Did you approve that?"

Xavier felt an anxious chill.

"No," he protested. He'd wring Maeve's stupid neck.

"It is just as illegal to distribute date-expired drugs in this country as it is in your country, Mr Hopkins. Does your doctor consider that Sudan's laws may simply be ignored when they are inconvenient? Extraordinary, don't you agree. I would call this both professional negligence and an infringement of her – in fact, of your entire organisation's – visa conditions."

"I'll sort it out," began Xavier. "I'll send a team out, we'll collect the stuff straight away. Do you know where . . . ?"

"Send your *zurqa*," Hassan cut him short. Xavier looked startled all over again. The Colonel took from his pocket a folded piece of paper.

"A list of villages, of settlements. These are where the medicines have gone."

"I'm sure the doctor has a record of where . . ."

"No!" snapped the Colonel. "She does not know. Matters have

moved on, the vitamins have been dispersed. My reports tell me that your doctor's medicines have reached every one of these small places and they must be retrieved, every pill or capsule."

"I'll see to it," reiterated Xavier. He could not fathom this Colonel. Did Security really care so very much about pills? Was there nothing more?

"You give this list to that man, Mogga. He's good at tidying up problems, and he does what he's told. Do you still have your English journalist with you? You will send him also."

"I'll suggest it . . ."

"The photographer goes too, Mr Hopkins!"

It was almost a shout. Xavier blinked and said nothing; Colonel al-Bedawi seemed to draw breath.

"In that envelope," he said more calmly, "he will find also a photography permit for the north. Tell him to use it, to take with him plenty of film, to take many pictures of anything he happens to see. Get them up north to Malha, Mr Hopkins, quick as you can. Tell them to open their eyes."

With that, Colonel al-Bedawi slipped away into the night. Xavier placed the letter in his briefcase, and then paced about his garden with an anxious frown.

But in the morning, when he drove to the Resthouse, he heard that the fearless London correspondent had left El Fasher at dawn. He was on a jeep heading out of Darfur, east for El Obeid, Khartoum and a plane home. Whatever it was in the north that the Colonel wanted seen, it would not be photographed by the London press corps.

*

Everyone, thought Mogga, was being very kind to him this morning.

Dr Maeve said, in a voice too busy, "Just remember, Mogga: if the medicine's caused any problems, I can be up there in a trice."

"Thank you," said Mogga.

He saw Xavier Hopkins' horrified look, and the doctor catching this and fleeing indoors, mortified. The Director turned to Mogga, livid, muttering furiously.

"Just get the bloody pills back, will you? You have the list? There's a list of villages . . ."

His voice tailed off; Mogga thought, how anxiously the Director is now regarding me. Xavier Hopkins was distressed, Mogga saw; it showed in his rigid immobility. He was red in the face but then he would be, standing out in the open in the office yard on a day like this, an *abu farrar*, 'father of axes'. Mogga hoped that Xavier would soon return to the shade.

On all sides, Mogga noticed, people were watching his departure. Standing a few feet aside, Rose Price also was uncommonly still as she peered intently at Mogga. By the door of the Meeting Room, Toby Kitchin was talking to Christa Lerche urgently, excitedly – as he did about everything – but when they saw Mogga, they fell silent and stared. From the radio room meanwhile came a broken jumble of Arabic voices but the operator disregarded these, for he too was peeking out at Mogga. A pickup halted in the lane, its engine dying. Nyala Freddy, flicking the hair off his eyes, walked into the yard – then stopped, watchful, alert to something uncomfortable. From the thatched *rakuba* by the gate, Fauzi and the watchman studied Mogga as though they'd never seen him before, or had not realised his celebrity, or were surprised that he was still alive.

Mogga saw all their discomfort and smiled kindly.

"I have everything," he said, patting the little red nylon knapsack.

But as he started towards the gate, the Director called out:

"Hang on a tick, Mogga."

Xavier disappeared into his office, reappearing seconds later with a solar light, a tough grey plastic panel with an array of photovoltaic cells on one side and a neon strip at the edge. It was equipment the Agency issued to expatriates only.

"You might find one of these handy," cried Xavier, hurrying to put it into the little man's hand.

Mogga looked at the lamp, pleased if faintly bemused.

"Good, good, thank you very much," he said in his usual busy way.

He beamed at Rose Price, turned past the grey aluminium of the upturned boat and bustled out of the yard to the Land Rover where Adam Zachariah hurried to join him. In the shade of the watchman's *rakuba*, Adam had been praying, mumbling *Ya Sin*, verses for a safe road.

"Let us travel quickly," Adam now urged. Mogga saw his driver's eyes flick to left and right in apprehension.

"We shall have a pleasant journey," Mogga remarked cheerfully.

"It is better not to be overtaken," retorted Adam, starting the engine.

As they moved off, another Land Rover swung into the road-way by the office. Leila Karim stepped out, and looked momentarily after Mogga's vehicle as it pulled away.

By the gate, two Arab youths were hauling at the lashings of a donkey's pack frame from which hung black water skins, glistening but empty and limp. They had sold all their water to Xavier Hopkins.

"*Zurqa*," said one of the boys, jutting his chin theatrically after Mogga's car. "The black man goes to hell, because he lodges where she-devils make strong wine."

Leila said sharply, "That is nothing to do with me," and went into the compound.

They left town, Mogga and Adam, to the north-north east, skirting to their left a stony waste broken by small hills, slagheaps of sharp stone, and ridges that lay stretched like exhausted creatures with broken spines. Nothing could live among those rocks but lizards, little green scorpions and the camel-spiders that by night would spin in tarantellas on the hot grit. None would shelter there but raiders, squinting over rifle sights. Far to the east, the desert swelled and subsided in gentle downs.

They drove steadily, past a village of thatched cones standing among rings and whorls of thorn hedging, but the wind had got at the huts, had toppled some, and there was no one there. Where the road divided, a building stood, high gable ends of yellow mud brick and a tin roof, still bright, with little windows where wooden shutters swung loose. A police post, thought Adam, or a prison. It stood alone on an open tract of hard ground, unshaded.

"Look," said Mogga cheerily, "even here, a school!"

On they rushed through the burning noon. Adam Zachariah's leather charm cases dangled from the driver's mirror, knocking against the glass. On to Mellit, over the *naka*, the hard-packed desert soil, on and beyond to the north.

*

"But what must he do there?"

She was pale. Looking at Leila, Xavier Hopkins felt her fear.

"He simply has to collect up all these wretched vitamin pills that are out of date, that should never have been distributed. Just gather them in, bring them back."

"Why must it be Mogga?" Leila breathed.

"Because Security cleared him to go," replied Xavier. He was saying nothing about Colonel al-Bedawi's night visit.

"Why Mogga?" Leila came again, merciless, probing into Xavier's eyes.

"Probably because he's good at his job!" Xavier retorted, thinking unkind thoughts about the rest of his team. He saw Leila scowling, and demanded crossly:

"Do you have some particular concern with Mogga?"

She flushed.

"Why would he be some particular concern of mine?"

She seemed confused. She went back out of the gate and stood gazing abstractedly down the street.

"Are we to hurry after him?" enquired Abdurrahman, who had just lifted the bonnet to cool the engine.

Leila spun about, furious.

"Who? Who are we to run after?"

"The *zurqa* . . ." Abdurrahman muttered.

"And I should scurry after this person?" demanded Leila, fists clenched. "Drive me to the prison. I must take a note to the prison."

But, once parked outside the prison beyond the town perimeter, she did not know what to do. She sat in the Land Rover before the windowless red-brown high walls thinking: *In there is someone I am supposed to love and revere. But I cannot see him, and I cannot feel him. And at this moment he does not touch me.*

From the guard post, they watched in mild surprise. They knew her well; it was unlike her to dither.

From her satchel Leila took a notebook and pencil. She turned to the centre fold and studied the surface of the paper, blank save for faint blue-green rulings. She could feel Abdurrahman waiting to see her write, for he could not write himself. She hesitated – and felt her driver thinking, why has she come here, if she has nothing to say to her husband?

She pencilled, 'I honour you . . .'

She tugged the page free of the staples, folded it and wrote neatly on the outside: Othman Abd al-Karim, 'servant of the truth'. Then she considered honour and how little Othman received in this place, and she wrote 'Dr' in front of his name. She opened her door, moving round the front of the vehicle until she faced the guard post. She surveyed the high steel gates, the walls, the razor wire, the men with automatic weapons watching indifferently. She wanted to believe that her presence here in front of the prison and the guards was a meaningful witness, a true defiance. But in her heart she had no passion with which to confront them.

She was back in the Land Rover so swiftly that Abdurrahman blinked; he must have missed her walking to the guard post with her letter . . .

"Drive quickly, into town."

The young man saw a flicker at the corner of her eye.

"Go!" she commanded.

They came to a cement roundabout at the edge of town. The vehicle slowed.

"Where now, Miss Leila?"

"I . . . Over there. I must think. Stop there a moment."

He turned off the engine, waiting, sensing a struggle. Once or twice she seemed about to speak – but nothing came.

Until there was a tap on the passenger window, a harsh, insulting rap, like a passport inspector or a customs man.

"*Salaamalaikum!*" grinned Mohammed Shattah, heavy and sweaty and in her face. "Nice time at the prison? Saw you come into town. How's your *zurqa?*"

"What are you talking about?" Leila replied, refusing to look at him.

"What am I bloody talking about, listen to her!" He was leering shamelessly now. "Your little southerner, the one you're always mooning about with, while your traitor husband is banged up."

"Drive," snapped Leila to Abdurrahman.

"Your *zurqa* with the ridiculous hair, the one all the *khowajiyah* women are screwing because they're desperate . . ."

"Drive!" She slapped her hand on the dashboard.

"Where to?" begged Abdurrahman, flustered.

"After her boyfriend," jeered Mohammed Shattah. "Is he circumcised? You know, the one I'm going to castrate . . ."

She slid the window shut with a wrench that hurt her fingers as the car jolted forward through a pothole and up the street.

Mohammed Shattah laughed after her.

"Go to the devil!"

Just what she was doing, he thought: going to the devil, a fine Arab mare served by a nasty black goat. He thought of Colonel al-Bedawi's jealousy, and he purred. He thought of disposing of that squalid little southerner and of getting back into the Colonel's favour at a single blow. He thought of heading north.

*

On Xavier's desk the reports clamoured, also the accounts, the interim this and provisional that, but the ink was furry where it had sunk into cheap foolscap and his eyes were drifting out of focus. This plethora of words helped nothing. The terms were too narrow, the questions too petty, compared with that devastatingly simple challenge put in his mind by Colonel Hassan al-Bedawi.

Should we be here at all?

What is the highlight of our Programme at this moment? It is

Mogga scurrying about the desert gathering up pills, the pathetic fragments of a medical débâcle. Food distribution in El Fasher District was a shambles but on his desk was a confidential memo from Khartoum: the Americans were now pressing for food distribution to be extended across all Darfur.

He could not remain still. He felt suffocated, and moved out into the middle of the room, sitting briefly on one of the crude wooden armchairs but that felt worse, was too low, as though the weight of everything was bearing down. He stood again, lifted the tin lid from his water glass, took up the glass . . . But he did not drink; he merely gazed into it distractedly.

Thirst. Drought. The very words made Xavier nervous, made him wonder if he had sufficient drinking water in his car to survive the half-mile drive across town to his home. Everything hung upon the rains, so the outside world supposed: another terrible drought in Africa, millions imperilled. But wise men could cope with drought; the desert people had coped for centuries. It was only the unwise, the ill-advised, the bamboozled, the silly elf who failed, who could not flex and adapt. Peering into his tepid drink, Xavier Hopkins thought once more of the miserable Hicks, apoplectic with frustration in Khartoum as he laboured to turn ten thousand disheartened Egyptian peasants into something resembling an army. In despair, Hicks had resigned but had been talked round, trapped in his own foolish, stubborn honour.

Again and again, so Xavier recalled, Hicks had mistrusted his own judgement. He had known full well that Darfur and Kordofan were turbulent with rebellion and in the Mahdi's power; an expedition to recapture them could not succeed. And yet he had led that expedition. He had known that he had grossly inadequate military intelligence, useless maps and suspect guides, and yet he had led his reluctant army out into the trackless scrub. He had seen clearly that his amateurish European officers were no match for the situation, that his troops were a rabble and his staff way out of their depth, and yet he had marched. He had known that he could not maintain a line of communication and supply from Khartoum, and yet he had led ten thousand into the woods. He had newspaper reporters in Khartoum – O'Donovan, Power, Vizziatelli – telling him that the expedition was doomed before it departed, and yet he set off, and those same reporters went with him in spite of being certain of coming disaster.

And here we are in turbulent Darfur, thought Xavier Hopkins, with erratic communications, plagued by broken supply lines, and out of our depth. The only difference is, our reporter has fled.

Why, in 1883, had Hicks so fatally persisted? Had he become so obsessed with his farcical preparations that he had forgotten rudimentary strategy? Had he put such faith in machinery – the battery of Nordenfeldt guns, the one million rounds of ammunition – that he had ignored the absurdity of trying to march an army in square formation through thorny waterless bush? Had he feared the angry scorn, if he withdrew, of his colonial paymasters in Cairo and London? Or had he, once embarked upon a plan, been simply too stubborn to change?

And here we are in parched Darfur, Xavier Hopkins mused, still peering into his not-very-clean glass of water, trusting in trucks and trains and Land Rovers, radios and airlifts. Here am I, with a desk laden with troublesome detail, struggling to be prepared for the coming disaster, not looking at the broader strategy. Here we are, afraid of what they'll think of us in Washington and Rome and London. Here we are, too damn proud to admit that we have made no difference to anyone except as scapegoats. What, in my position, would General William Hicks Pasha have done? He'd have stayed, and led everyone to annihilation. Hicks would have forgotten the one question that really mattered: should we be here at all?

So Xavier Hopkins, historian and Field Director, reached his own resolution.

He opened his briefcase to stow the reports he intended to ignore, and saw again Colonel al-Bedawi's letter to the departed London journalist, undelivered and unopened. He sent a driver to return it to Security, with a polite note of explanation.

TWO

"His release is entirely at my discretion. You know that."

Hassan's arrival in Leila's house felt hurried, unplanned. He was tall, this Colonel; he looked down on her and, to emphasise his dominance, seemed to lean forward slightly, to loom over her. She could feel great tension in him controlled by ferocious will, and sensed that his muscles were poised as though on hair triggers, ready to snap. Small patches of sweat darkened his olive green uniform; not the sweat of a flabby, exhausted man, but indicating something charged, an energy held in check, like the soft hissing of a primed machine.

Today, though, there was an agitation about him that she had never seen before; he did not seem so entirely controlled.

"Security in this province – political security – is my charge, mine alone. You understand that? It rests with me. Not with the police, not with the Army."

The Colonel turned quickly, agitatedly about the room. The sand scraped under his boot; Farida had not yet swept, and was now in the kitchen keeping well out of sight.

Leila said, "There is nothing more I can do."

She didn't want this fierce officer in her house. He had driven himself, had brought no escort. She didn't know why he'd come or where this conversation was going. She tried to close it down by sitting on the *angareb*, peering at the floor.

"What *have* you done," he asked sardonically, "for your husband?"

"I don't know what you mean," she replied feebly.

"No? A good wife could have been more assiduous in working to free her spouse."

"The lawyer wouldn't travel!" she began to protest. "I go to the jail daily."

"But you've never been inside. We keep that jail for prisoners who make us truly cross. Can you imagine conditions in there? The heat, the scorpions lodged in those mud walls, the diet?"

"I take food."

"Oh? I'd say your husband was losing weight rather fast. I'm sure that you take delicious meals, such as are rarely seen in a guard room, but what steps do you take to ensure that these delicacies reach your husband?"

"Steps . . . ?" she parried weakly.

"You don't pay the guards?" There was an audible smirk. "You don't offer anything else? What other sacrifices don't you make?"

She looked round for something to strike him with.

"Surely you're not too proud?" he taunted, "After all, though we have *sharia* here and you are a married woman, you let yourself be seen out and about with a *zurqa*."

Oh, Mogga, again Mogga, held against her!

The other was studying her, inspecting her eagerly, as though in a hurry to put her to use: she felt like a slave girl in the market. She made an effort to lift her face and look out toward the kitchen.

"Let me call Farida for refreshment . . ." she began.

"Don't!" he snapped, his voice low and hard. "I have an urgent matter to put to you. A proposition. A deal."

She felt a sickly shiver pass through her, like the first touch of malaria. A disagreeable smell suddenly filled her nostrils; she did not know if it was the Colonel, or herself, or the fear between them. He was about to demand something that she surely could not survive giving.

"I have something here for your very good friend Mogga," said the Colonel. "I ask you to take it to him. That is all."

She couldn't trust him, she must not trust him!

"Mogga is away," Leila began, "he has gone . . ."

"I know very well where he has gone," al-Bedawi cut her off, "just as I know that you would be after him like a shot if you could."

There was a moment's silence as he let her absorb this. He continued more quietly:

"I know where the *zurqa* is because I sent him, as I now send you."

She made to speak, but the Colonel ignored her.

"I also sent that idiot English photographer but he has run away, did you know? He was a bloody fool and a coward and he has gone. I therefore require the *zurqa* to do the Londoner's work. This is what you are to take."

He held out to her a bag of dark brown cotton in which something small and heavy made awkward bulges. Leila took it gingerly. The Colonel remained silent, so she unrolled the bag and looked inside.

"Why?" she asked.

"Because there are things to be seen and recorded, that's why. Do not ask me more. Can the *zurqa* operate a camera?"

"I've no idea."

"Can you?"

"I think so. My father often . . ."

The Colonel laughed dryly.

"Your many-talented father."

Leila bristled: "You should speak with Mr Hopkins . . ."

"I am speaking to you."

His voice was quiet, but the control was faltering. A shrillness underlay each word.

"I do not care," he said, "about vitamin pills. There is something else I want him to see. And to report."

"What?" she said, bewildered.

"Never you mind. He will know it when he sees it, and if he visits the places on the list he has, he *will* see it. You leave at once, understand? You show him how to use the camera, you tell him to give the films to Hopkins to go to London. You understand? The films go to London! You speak to no one about where you are going, and you relate this conversation to no one. You will instruct your driver to obtain fuel now, immediately, and take the road for Mellit and Malha this afternoon; you've a good chance of catching up."

He looked away.

"In return," he said, almost incidentally, "I shall release your husband. There is an Islander flight to Chad, possibly in two or three day's time. Do what I say, and I shall put him on that flight."

Again, she thought how anxious Hassan looked.

"Dr Karim shall carry a letter for me," he said.

*

It was mid-morning before Xavier Hopkins learned that Leila had had driven out of town with Abdurrahman the previous evening. Xavier had seen the fuel storekeeper return a ledger to the office shelves.

"Who were you issuing to?" the Director asked casually.

The store man pulled the ledger back down from the shelf and presented it to him without a word. Xavier glanced at the last entry, and frowned.

"Leila? A full drum of diesel? What for? Why didn't you refer this to me?"

"The lady was in a hurry," replied the man expressionlessly.

"What sort of a hurry?"

"Going north," said the store man, "to Malha."

Xavier frowned harder.

"Malha? Does she have a Security permit?"

The store man shrugged. Leila had shown him no permit; she had not needed one, because a Security man had come to the fuel dump with her. Of this, the store man said nothing.

Someone else might have spoken, but remained silent. The widow Farida was in trouble. She never enquired after the doings of her pitiless in-laws, who had reclaimed poor dead Farah's wealth and left her near-destitute. But Mohammed Shattah she could not avoid, for he came to the house to take rent from Fauzi and herself and to leer at her. He'd come two days before, a rancid odour pouring off his skin and a lurid excitement in his eyes. He'd pushed into her hot brick room and pressed up against her, his stinking, suffocating weight pinning her against the wall, his strong hands clawing, oblivious to the whimperings of *Mama!* from the girls outside – until they all heard the tinny clang of the top gate, and Fauzi coming home.

Shattah released her, and smoothed his clothes.

"I'm away to Malha," he breathed, as though he'd just remembered. "I'll see you when I get back."

He went swiftly out of the gate, his movements always silent in spite of his bulk. In the lane outside stood a green Toyota pickup in which waited a small man with a strangely elongated face, looking remarkably like a rat.

*

Mogga told Adam Zachariah: "We must report to the police."

Adam said, "We could be done and gone before they need know we are here."

Mogga replied, "Let us not make their lives harder."

To which Adam could only bite his lip.

They had paused, late afternoon, at a hill crest. There was a small town below them, a straggling starfish of five dusty roads leading out from a colossal tree. Lining each road was a ribbon of baking little brick houses in wide, treeless walled compounds. Mogga saw that, set high into each compound wall, there was a brick privy reached by steps, with a heavy wooden door opening at cart-height over the street outside. They had been proud and civic once in this desert place, and had organised night-soil collection.

A police sergeant stood outside his office, watching them approach; Adam Zachariah wondered if the man was waiting, was expecting them. As they drew near, the sergeant shouted something at an urchin playing nearby. The child glanced at the Land Rover, and then scampered round a corner.

In his stifling room opening directly off the street, the sergeant sat at a carved and ink-stained wooden desk with a sloping top, a schoolroom desk. He pored over Mogga's documents, noting the details in an achingly slow hand on grey sheets of foolscap.

He looked up.

"Tomorrow you will go with a guide."

"Thank you," said Mogga, glancing at Adam Zachariah, "but we need not trouble you. My driver here knows the area well, and we have maps . . ."

"You will go with a guide," the policeman repeated. "I am to appoint him."

Adam thought: *on whose instruction?*

The officer fixed hard and penetrating eyes on Mogga.

"Do not think to go without this guide."

He rose and went to the open street door, looking about outside and calling to a skinny man with teeth at every angle and a frightened look.

The sergeant gestured at the newcomer.

"This is the Public Health Officer," he said. "He will take you to the Resthouse."

"But I know . . ." began Adam Zachariah.

"Go with this man," said the policeman.

The Public Health Officer opened the front door of the vehicle and pushed his way in alongside Mogga and Adam.

"Go," he ordered.

"Yes," said Mogga agreeably.

They drove deeper into town, to the star at its heart where the five roads met under the great tree. In the middle of the way, a grey-brown bulk lay swelling in the heat. It was a dead mule, its abdomen stretched tight by the hot gasses within. In the tree, glittering eyes and beaks waited.

"That is a public health hazard," the Public Health Officer declared, "but who will do anything about it?"

They reached a brick wall, thirty yards long, which seemed to be sinking into the sand intact, like a scuttled ship. He pointed.

"Here."

He stepped down from the vehicle and at once walked away, leaving them.

There was a Resthouse, a block of two rooms with cement floors, unshuttered windows, no doors on the hinges. One room was empty; the other contained three wooden beds and three steel chairs. Set in the outer wall at the back was another of the high brick latrines. When Adam opened that door, a rustling stench hit him squarely and he backed out.

Mogga saw his dismay.

"Adam," the little southerner began brightly, "we shall make our home here tonight. It will be cool and quiet and safe."

"I shall bring the Land Rover in," sighed Adam, going to pull wide the steel gate.

The light faded; the sky was yellow, then pink and mauve, then the grey-blues of evening. Stars appeared. They dragged two beds out onto the sand, and two chairs. From the Land Rover they brought their grey blankets, then fetched the kerosene stove, the plastic sack of bread, onions and tins of fish.

"Tea first," said Mogga cheerily. "We have all evening to cook."

But at that moment they heard the *muezzin*. Adam unrolled a green and black plastic mat and began to pray.

Mogga propped the solar panel in the sand; its glow was pale, flickering slightly as in a fever. He sat down with an enamel basin, water, a tin of mackerel and the sack of bread. When he had just begun tearing up bread, the gate juddered, and a quiet procession came into the yard: a youth and two women, led by the Public Health Officer, finding their way across the uneven ground by torchlight. They carried a broad tin platter with a cover of woven straw, and a basket and a nest of three pots in yellow enamel.

The Health Officer indicated the ground by the solar light.

"There," he muttered.

The youth and the women knelt, and the boy swept the sand with his hand, smoothing the place in deference to the guests.

"*Asha*, your evening meal," he said quietly.

They set everything out before Mogga.

"*Barak Allah*," whispered Adam Zachariah, "God bless you." But already the visitors were on their feet, were gone.

Thin slivers of camel meat in a sauce of tomato and beans. Wild cucumbers. Radishes, fried chicken and small boiled lemons. *Dukn* grain soaked in tamarind. Sheep's milk. *Kisra* pancakes.

"They have honoured us," said Mogga.

"They have offered us hospitality, as every Believer is commanded," reproved Adam Zachariah.

*

At the town of Mellit, trailing in Mogga's wake, Leila came that same evening to the official Resthouse and found a man in an unbleached cotton shift and tyre-rubber sandals who slithered out at the sound of her vehicle. He had seen no other Land Rover, he mumbled apologetically. Leila studied the face, the huge flapping wrinkles that hung over his eyes; she would have been surprised if he'd seen anything.

"You must ask at the police post," he declared suddenly, perking up.

"Yes . . ." said Leila, non-committal.

"I shall take you," announced the old man, making towards the vehicle, anticipating a ride.

"Do not trouble yourself," Leila said hurriedly. "We know the way."

She climbed back in.

"They have gone ahead," said Leila. "They are hurrying, they will have no time for Mellit. They are far beyond, making for Malha."

"Miss Leila," said Abdurrahman, "It will be dark soon."

"We go on."

"Surely you must rest . . ."

But she made him drive another hour until they came to a meandering dry wadi and ran the Land Rover cautiously along its bed one hundred metres. There they could park out of sight between two *hashab* gum trees and sleep, Leila locked within the vehicle, Abdurrahman on the roof. At dawn they were off again, after Mogga.

*

At breakfast, Adam Zachariah said: "Before we depart, I wish to visit a man in this town. A cousin. He knows everything here. He knows if the Kababish are raiding, and if there is water in the wells. Let me go now."

249

Leaving Mogga in the compound, he drove back through the silent streets, past the soon-to-explode mule.

The cousin was a camel breeder who sent herds for slaughter in Egypt. He was a man of the desert and lived at the far edge of town beyond the last brick compound, his mats on the sand and his flocks of goats milling nearby. His face was desiccated and cracked like a dry lake; his hair was a stack of tight black curls. His teeth jutted like a camel's, with a long nose to match.

"The Kababish and Meidob have been quiet," said the cousin, "for weeks now, but everyone can see that there will be a fight soon. There are too many grudges unpaid. Someone is making trouble. They have obtained ammunition, we don't know where."

He eyed Adam Zachariah piercingly, as though some abstruse family honour were at stake.

"Is that why you've brought spies in your wake? To find out?"

"What is that?" blinked Adam.

"A Toyota came in last night: two men, one a really big oaf, the other a little creep, like a rat. We know that sort of person: Government officials, some shit. They were at the police post."

Adam thought, this is the end of the trip, Mogga must see sense, they must by no means go out into the desert. But when he arrived at the Resthouse, he was startled to see another white Land Rover drawn up outside, its bonnet lifted for cooling. When Adam entered the compound, he saw Leila Karim and Mogga standing face to face. Her expression was a twist of urgency and anxiety, her hands held tight before her. Adam thought, she is about to seize hold of him.

But Mogga was wreathed in smiles. He saw his driver and called out:

"Adam, you see? Miss Leila has joined us. She has brought me important packages and we shall proceed together, it is an opportunity! We shall gather some plants for our great work. And in every place that I must collect these pills, we shall enquire after the names and the goodness of plants also. Here's a piece of fortune, Adam!"

The young driver told himself: *I could stop them. If I said aloud that this was an absurd folly, I could stop them.*

"So, you will accompany us?" enquired Adam, as neutral as could be.

Leila looked to Mogga, saw his radiant smile.

"I will," she affirmed. "I shall come in your vehicle."

At which Adam Zachariah felt a strange chill.

"But your vehicle?" he demanded. "We can take both, it will be safer . . ."

"It is best that Abdurrahman waits for us here," said Mogga, glancing toward the shadows where Abdurrahman lolled on the sand.

"So," queried Adam, "where are we going? Where are these villages? Sir, you have not yet told us the names."

"Ah, nor I have," agreed Mogga. He took the list from his breast pocket and read it out.

Adam's eyes wrinkled in astonishment.

"Jebel Issa? It's a mountain, who lives there? El Harra? A ruin! Who lives at El Harra? Why are you going to such places? Qalti Tawin? It's a water pool in the rocks! Maybe a family or two with their camels come there some days, no more."

Mogga said, that was where the medicine was believed to be.

"But there's nothing there!"

Leila asked, had not the list come from Colonel Hassan al-Bedawi? It had, said Mogga.

"We must go," he added, "where the Colonel sends us."

At which, everyone fell silent.

Adam pulled Mogga to one side, murmuring urgently to him of men in a green Toyota. Mogga only nodded, as though it were all quite proper.

"I'm sure they have their duties."

A curt voice from the gate: "*Salaamalaikum.*"

"*Walaikum asalaam!*" Adam Zachariah responded.

Through the gate came a small man with hunched shoulders, a low forehead and a jutting narrow chin.

Adam stared at him: *A little creep, like a rat.*

Mogga called cheerfully:

"Good morning!"

"I am your guide," said the rodent newcomer, and again a chill went down Adam's spine.

"Welcome," beamed Mogga.

"I am to ensure that you bring your medicines to show to the Sergeant of Police."

"Everything will be done properly," Mogga assured him.

Adam Zachariah was thinking: *Mogga said nothing about medicine to the police. How does this Rat Man know about medicine?*

Mogga, however, was friends with everyone this morning. He took the Rat Man's paw and shook it vigorously.

"You are most welcome," he repeated. "We shall make a most jolly party, Adam."

"We leave at once," said the Rat Man.

*

"I've asked you all to come in," said Xavier Hopkins, "because I've an announcement to make." He spoke with exaggerated care and in measured periods. "An important and rather difficult announcement."

His audience – all the staff that he'd been able to round up from the field at twenty-four hours' notice – were jammed into the meeting room, peering at Xavier through the gloom and toying with pens. Outside, the daylight burned white. Overhead, the hot roof was ticking.

"I've received word," their Director continued ponderously, as though to hold down his unruly feelings with weighty speech, "of developments in the Government's handling of the current food crisis. I'm not going to spell it all out, but the nub of it is that I am convinced our position here is untenable, politically, professionally and morally. I have this morning radioed Khartoum informing them that I am closing the Programme."

A complete silence. The sixteen people in the room stared at him intently, waiting for a punch line or denouement to the party trick, a neat explosion perhaps, with purple smoke.

"With immediate effect," added Xavier.

There was a bang, of sorts. Nyala Freddy had been leaning low over the table, readying his pencil over a spiral-bound pad. He now sat back in his chair so hard that his knees caught the underside of the table, lifting and juddering it. His lank hair swung like tetchy little snakes in front of eyes wide with defiance.

"Have I misunderstood something here? I was under the impression that there was about to be one hell of a famine . . ."

"That looks possible," said Xavier.

"A famine which we, as a humanitarian agency, as supposed famine relief experts, are here to deal with?"

"That was the plan," the Director conceded.

"In which case – pardon my Arabic, Xavier – what the fuck do you mean, close the Programme?"

"The point is," Xavier reiterated, knowing that he'd get no sympathy whatever, "the present situation is unacceptable."

"Damn right!" exploded Toby Kitchin, clutching the table's edge with both hands.

"The poor ones have nothing," began Christa, "and it is our duty . . ."

"No," Xavier interrupted. "It's not our duty. Not *our* duty. It's the Government's duty, the Government of Sudan's . . ."

"But they cannot," retorted Christa in her most relentless gear, each word even in tone and spacing and inflection.

"They can," replied Xavier, "but they won't. That is what I now see. That is what all the evidence now makes clear. The Government of Sudan does not wish to prevent this famine."

"The Government," echoed Christa, uncomprehending, "does not wish?"

"The Government wants a famine." Xavier was icy, marvelling at his own clear resolve. "They actually want a famine, because it suits them and the Army very nicely."

He saw in his young team's eyes only bewilderment. So, he would make them see.

"It suits them because Darfur is a turbulent, unruly place which is a thorn in the Government's arse. A stable, strong Darfur is dangerous to Khartoum. Any number of revolts have started from here and the Government won't risk another, not while it's got the war in the south and a fractious capital. The Darfur tribes united would be an utter disaster and Khartoum far prefers them to go hungry, prefers them to be at each others' throats, prefers them emaciated, starving and weak on their feet. Do you understand? They *want* a famine, but we are not going to be any part of it."

"But people have begun moving into town, into camps and shanties, they'll start to die . . ." began Nurse Lorna, shaking her head like some honest old carthorse.

"Quite possibly," replied Xavier.

"You're saying everything we've done has been a failure . . ."

"Not a failure. Just irrelevant."

He knew that they despised him, and at last he didn't care; at least, never again would they think him weak. He saw in their faces the anger building, he sensed their wounded self-esteem turning vicious. He looked around the room for an ally, and saw only Rose Price frowning and nodding.

But Nyala Freddy would have none of it:

"Irrelevant!? Damn that . . . !"

"Nothing we have done, or will do, makes the slightest bit of difference," persisted Xavier levelly, "except to legitimise a criminal government's scheming."

"Well, I must say . . ." Lorna was puffy with umbrage.

"I think," said Christa, slow and bitter, "that we have worked hard, like professionals."

"Of course you have," Xavier parried coolly, "and it's because we are professionals that we go."

"We've worked our fucking socks off, when the bastards would let us!" wailed Toby Kitchin.

"Exactly," replied Xavier, "when they'd let you. Only when it suited them. And now that things are really breaking down, it will suit them just fine to have a bunch of foreigners neatly to hand to blame for everything. Don't you understand? All right, it's taken me weeks to see it, but that is the point. We're stooges, we're fall guys, we're here for one reason only, which is to allow the Khartoum regime to get away with starving their own people. Will you all, please, get your heads around that basic fact."

Silence again.

He continued, quieter.

"The evidence is incontrovertible, and I will not allow our position to continue one day longer. We are pulling out at once, all of us, as soon as we can be flown out of here. I am sorry to say that for many of you it means your contracts will be terminated in the very near future, but you were employed strictly on an 'as required' basis. Very probably the situation in Chad will require your attention instead."

Twenty minutes later, Xavier Hopkins stood in his office sipping cold tea.

"Thank you," he said to Rose Price, "for your support."

She couldn't tell if this was sarcasm or not.

"I said nothing," she began.

"That was most helpful," he replied.

"But will Head Office let you close this down? Won't they just recall you for consultation?"

"They won't dare. I've told them the security situation is collapsing and that I cannot guarantee the team's safety. Oh, it's temporary, I know; they'll send someone else soon enough; I can't prevent that. But for a while . . ."

He stared out of the window across the compound, to where the aluminium hull gleamed.

"You know," he said, his voice brisk, "the West has the most absurdly limited notion of suffering. All Europeans can think of is famine. That's not what concerns Darfur; they know about hunger, they've been hungry since the dawn of time. They tighten their belts, find more berries and sit it out. It's not famine which appals them, it's destitution and moral collapse and dishonour and suchlike, that's what matters . . ."

His meditation was interrupted by an extraordinary noise: a rhythmic thumping bang accompanied by shouts, manly European shouts: *Fuck! Fuck! Fuck!*

Xavier and Rose went to the wire-netted window. There was Nyala Freddy, kicking a Land Rover and shouting. The Sudanese staff watched from a respectful distance, as though they'd known all along that this would happen.

THREE

The Rat Man sat unspeaking in the rear of the vehicle. There was haze again, like driving into a mild hangover. The vehicle rattled ceaselessly. Under the wheels was a crust like grey scurf on the desert. If you tried to pick up the flakes, they fell to dust.

Mogga was upbeat as ever.

"We are whizzing along!" he called boyishly, "the road is open before us."

But Adam Zachariah only looked apprehensive, while their guide showed no sign of having heard.

The road divided; they paused. To the east, the Meidob Hills were a silhouette, a maze of gorges where a tribe of infamous raiders hid. Adam was uncomfortable, more nervous with every moment. He remembered a good friend of his, Farah ibn Mashoud, shot with a high velocity rifle on the road from Nyala to El Fasher.

"We go that way," Adam replied, pointing along the wadi towards a long, low broken crest like a string of rock castles. "The Teiga flats, Qalti Tawin on the far side."

But the Rat Man spoke out at last.

"We cross the wadi," he announced, waving his hand to the trail that dropped down the bluff to the riverbed.

Leila looked again at her map.

"No," she began, "that is a long way, two sides of the triangle. To Qalti Tawin we can go direct . . ."

"You cross, and go here." The Rat Man jabbed at Adam's shoulder, pointing him to turn north.

Leila and Adam looked at each other, Leila fuming at the discourtesy, Adam in simple alarm. But Mogga said amiably:

"I am sure you are right. What would the reason be?"

"It is better," said the Rat Man.

"Adam . . . ?" Mogga indicated the wadi crossing.

Adam Zachariah, sullen, turned the Land Rover down the bluff.

A few hundred yards beyond the wadi crossing, they reached a gentle turning incline. There, for just seconds, Adam had a view back towards the wadi – and he glimpsed another vehicle, a green Toyota pickup. It had not followed across the wadi but was moving quickly along the bluff, away to the northeast in the direction they should have gone. The shorter route.

If they are going to Qalti Tawin, thought Adam Zachariah, they will get there first. But would Mogga see the point? No, today, Mogga could see nothing.

Next there came a gorge, and relief from the sun.

The road dropped through a dramatic cut in the scarp and the light softened. The sequestered air held cool moisture.

"Let us take refreshment," said Mogga.

They stood in the trees' shade and drank hibiscus juice from a small plastic drum. Their ears settled from the road's roar, and they began to notice the birds: bee-eaters, Abyssinian rollers of deep indigo, a pair of Nubian woodpeckers wearing grey coats but with caps and jaws of scarlet. Mogga looked this way and that, entranced. The gorge was teeming. In gullies and ravines, a tumult of twittering came from safe havens in the tangles of vine, wild cucumber and flowering columbine, while from above swung the neat work of weaverbirds. Fifty yards off was a great plume of magnolia. Underfoot, the sand was fine and glistening like powdered titanium. It had a hint of firmness, as though it had not long been wetted. There were clear prints of robbers, the ferenc foxes.

Adam was praying. The Rat Man sat silently on a rock, drinking his hibiscus, observing Mogga.

"Such loveliness," said Mogga to Leila. "Do you know the names of every plant we can see?"

She laughed gaily.

"Am I an encyclopaedia?"

"You are a deep well of instruction," he averred. "It makes me so happy to think of classes to come."

She lowered her eyes thoughtfully, and then gave him a look of the tenderest melancholy.

"How are your hands?" she asked.

"Today," he beamed, "they are very well."

But Adam, who had now climbed onto a boulder, called, "Look at the clouds!"

They were darker, and closer.

"We must not be caught in a watercourse," said Adam.

Mid-afternoon, they were scudding over *naka*, hard soil that glittered with silicates. Then came black shale and pockets of iron-flake where the desert was rusted. They continued due north, climbing steadily into starker lands. Now the crust was replaced by countless pebbles rolled against their neighbours until smooth and oval. The pebbles were spaced and spread evenly as far as the eye could see, like a grainy photo. In all that empty space, thought Adam, you could not lie comfortably down to sleep; there would be no rest. Next there was lava detritus, and packed gravel. Furrows in the ground showed where once it had rained, but now the Land Rover was burning up, the dust that came in through the vents singed and scoured their skin and made it raw. On such a day, the tribes say that the sun is the liver of the sky, smoking with pain.

Away to the north, the sky was darker, almost purple.

"You see?" said Leila, "You see that? Someone is getting wet at last."

Twenty minutes later, they came to another, broader wadi crossing. They must traverse 200 yards of watercourse where the sand was deep brown with the debris of shrubs, crumbled to dust. Thorn trees stood out, their aspect strange. The level of sand about the trunks was too high, where alluvium swirled about them in a rising embrace.

Adam Zachariah contemplated the route, the surface.

"Is it good?" asked Leila. "Is it firm enough?"

Adam shrugged: "*Inshallah*."

He drove forward steadily, and at once they felt the surface sag and crack beneath the heavy vehicle. But on they went, willing the ground to bear them up, clenching their fists. After eighty yards they reached a slight rise in mid-river, an island just a few paces across, and all let out their breath, grinning with relief.

"All right!" laughed Adam, putting the vehicle into gear again and moving gently down the slope for the next stretch.

The front wheels, striking downwards, broke through and plunged into greasy silt.

"Eh!" growled Adam Zachariah, and Leila gasped.

The forward gears only pushed the vehicle in deeper, down to its front fender. Reversing merely spun the wheels. There they sat, pitched forward.

"Oh dear," murmured Mogga, while the Rat Man frowned.

Adam opened his door and peered resignedly at the dark paste beneath them, at the place where his front axle cap would have been visible were it not six inches underground. He went to the rear and dragged out a shovel.

"I dig first," he said to the Rat Man clinging to the steeply sloping back seat, "then you."

The digging did not go well.

They took turns, the three men, and the sweat ran freely. They jacked the wheels up, gathered brushwood and stuffed it underneath. They put their shoulders to the front wings and strained, while the spinning tyres sent plumes of dirt all over them. Leila Karim sat demurely on a log, and watched and willed. Nothing worked.

"Someone will assist us," Mogga was sure, "for we have much to do."

"We must wait for another vehicle," said Adam Zachariah crossly. "God knows who will come this way. If we had taken the main road . . ."

He looked accusingly at the Rat Man, wondering if he knew which vehicles had been permitted to come this way.

But the Rat Man was staring along the wadi bed.

"There is a vehicle over there," he said, thoughtfully.

They all squinted into the sun.

"It's a truck," said Adam Zachariah.

One hundred yards downstream was a grove of small acacias,

twisted cruelly, split and contorted. Half-hidden among them, a yellow ten-wheeler stood. It had begun the crossing, like them gaining high ground in mid-river. There, it had stopped. It was quite out of scale, almost as tall as the little trees. There wasn't anyone to be seen. It was simply there among the trees, with its long bonnet raised.

Without a word, they walked towards it across the grey-brown crusted mud. As they approached they saw that the truck's load was another, smaller vehicle, a white pickup whose cab windows peeked timidly over the sides. There was also a stack of cooking oil in boxes. From the flanks hung bags of water, and long sand ladders for placing under the wheels in troublesome drifts.

Down the yellow flanks and over the sand ladders ran streaks of dried blood, stark on the yellow paint. The blood had poured down from the truck's top edge, as though someone had been shot while climbing in to hide.

"Oh dear," said Mogga lamely. He glanced at Leila who held her hand over her mouth. Her eyes were big, but she did not flinch.

The Rat Man walked quickly back to the Land Rover, his face pale. He stood looking in the opposite direction, not moving.

"They have taken some parts away," said Adam, peering into the engine under the curiously open bonnet.

"But there is nobody here at all," observed Mr Mogga, "not even any dead. What has happened?"

"Let us go on," said Leila.

"Yes, yes," cried Mr Mogga, "On we go!"

Adam Zachariah stared in disbelief.

"You want to go on?"

"Of course." Mogga's face shone with conviction, as though the murders proved some crucial point. But Adam jabbed towards the blood-streaked truck.

"What about this?!"

"There is no one here," replied Mogga. "They are elsewhere now. No need for concern."

He seemed to possess a weird calm, as though from some

261

superior knowledge or understanding they had missed. Adam despaired: what could that possibly be? And then Leila chimed in.

"Yes, Mogga, let us continue at once," she said.

"There, Adam, a lady commands."

You're both mad, thought Adam.

Leila murmured, "We have far to go."

Adam protested, "But we are stuck!"

*

A draught of cold air swept through the chicken wire that enclosed the Resthouse verandah. It was sudden and unexpected; it made them wince. The daylight changed from a white so intense as to be painful on the eye, to a grey bruised with purple.

Toby Kitchin sang out, "Rain!"

They crowded out into the yard, peering at the sky in all directions.

"Good news," declared someone briskly, "for the sorghum."

"Joyous!" crowed another, unconvinced. The farmers might rush out to plant in the wetted desert only for the rain to vanish, leaving another consignment of seed germinated, then toasted. Such rain was not to be trusted. Then they recalled that they were all to leave very soon; to them, rain mattered not a damn.

"It'll be heavy," remarked Rose Price, looking at the clouds.

It was so heavy it hurt, smacking onto thin cotton shirts with stinging force. The team shuffled back into shelter but the rain followed them, hitting the ground so hard that it bounced and flew in through the chicken wire to land in a gobbet of grime. Drops clung to the wire and careered down the zigzags.

They were suddenly, uncomfortably cold, and taken aback by the dark weight of cloud. They shivered; they were not accustomed to this. As one, the team went to their suitcases – shut tight against the all-penetrating dust of Darfur – to find warm clothes.

Rose Price, in a green cotton jacket, tucked her long thin legs under her on the bed, spread a warm towel across her knees and lit a cigarette. She sneaked glances at her colleagues pulling on fleeces and long trousers. She thought, they share a notion that they don't care to voice: if it rains across Africa, if the crops in Chad are watered too and famine averted, what shall become of the famine team? She saw how each expatriate looked about warily before going to their knobbly, knotted string bedsteads to sit with their backs against the wall, peering out at the lakes beginning to form in the back yard.

Rose thought, how small, how young they look, in a little rain.

The mesh door flapped and banged open: Nyala Freddy, shouting as ever.

"The souk's flooded and the town tank's awash, I tell you, the *fula's* filling, just like that!"

"Let's go boating," said someone.

When, towards dusk, Xavier Hopkins came to the Resthouse, he found no one there but the cook who giggled: *Fula! Fula!* He drove to the centre of town, and saw a crowd gathering by the Agency's blue Bedford truck on the *fula* shore. He stepped out of his vehicle, smelt the rich stink of storm drains stirred by rainwater, saw the townspeople gazing out across the tank, and saw on the water the grey aluminium boat circling aimlessly in the rain with his own staff, his team, his international agents of relief, waving paddles, splashing and shouting, a *Narrenschiff*, a spectacle of fools. A few stuttering neon signs from the souk blinked in gaudy green, red and mauve over the lake, lighting his people in harlequin reflections.

*

At dusk, the trees of the wadi lost definition, the colours sighed away, the flash of lurid vermilion in the sky died to a cool wash. Only the Land Rover, nose down in the mud, its tail high on the island behind it, retained its bulk and its pale gleam.

They huddled on the bank by a fire of plentiful driftwood, while every flying and biting thing in the province came looking for them. They wrapped themselves in whatever thin jackets they had, turning their collars high, but the gnats and mosquitoes swarmed about them until their faces felt puffy and their hair crawled. They took grey blankets and draped these over their heads, only to feel sharp pricks as sand fleas found their ankles. They ate in near silence, the Rat Man declining to share anything but the hot tea. Then exhaustion seized them. Adam Zachariah tried to be comfortable cuddling a log. The Rat Man curled up like a wood-louse upon the dirt. Only Mogga and Leila remained upright, side by side, letting the smoke drift over their faces to discourage the insects that piped gleefully.

Mogga sensed Leila tremble.

"Miss Leila, you are cold," he said.

"No," she asserted, just as a new shiver seized her. Mogga began to take the blanket off his shoulders.

"Do not offer me that," she insisted, "I shall not accept that."

Mogga studied her silhouette. He half-stood and shuffled closer to her. He sat so close that each felt the touch of the other's hip. She froze.

"Two are warmer than one," he murmured, "if I do not offend you."

His voice was sweet and simple. She could hear in it neither guile, nor pleading, nor doubt. She relaxed a little – and immediately the shivers returned. Mogga lifted the blanket on his arm and lowered it about them both, his arm across her back, drawing her closer to him. He remained like this, very still, for a long minute during which he saw out of the corner of his eye that her head tilted forward and she looked down.

"Thank you," she whispered.

A second later he felt the very slightest change in her body, almost imperceptible and yet a transformation: she had softened and leaned towards him.

They remained in silence while the quality of the night altered, heavy darkness settling about them. The orange fire put up a show of defiance against the night, a mouse shaking its fists at a cat. Beyond the circle of its glow, the blackness was as thick as a rich slime seeping up from the wadi. As time passed, there came another change: as the rainstorms moved about the country, the haze left the air and the stars came out in their bright battalions. A breeze got up, and the trees and grasses rustled and shushed. The wind lifted the fire and Mogga fed it driftwood. They heard night creatures calling: a fox barking; a sudden kerfuffle and mortal screech as a wildcat met with its dinner; the hooting of a hyrax from an outcrop of rock.

Still Leila did not move, but remained shaped to his flank. Mogga wondered if she would speak to him. He wanted to hear her voice, so he trawled for it.

"In the country of my childhood," began Mogga softly, "there were many rivers, and so full of life. When I came here to the desert, I thought it hard to be without rivers. But I was not looking closely. You recall Adam's story at Seraf Umra? That the rainwater from the mountains runs underground to hide from the sun, so that the river flows a metre below the surface of the sand."

"It was in Kebkabiya that he told us," whispered Leila.

"Ah, was it so?" replied Mogga dishonestly; he had made the error on purpose, to tempt her reply.

"He said," continued Leila, "that if one digs in the wadi, the hole will fill with water and the water with fish."

"Is it true? Fish from out between the grains of sand?"

"In our country," said Leila, "we need some marvellous things."

"Imagine it," Mogga responded, "the marvellous river that is flowing past us a metre down, here where we think there is only clinging dirt."

"And the fish passing through it."

He heard the smile in her voice.

"An unseen river of life!" he laughed happily. "That is our Sudan, Miss Leila. We are stuck up to our axles and baked to a crisp but still we are washed by that secret river. We see only desert and danger, but there it flows."

"*Alhamdullilah*," she breathed, "God be praised."

God be praised! sang in Mogga's heart. He pulled her a tiny bit closer.

They're mad, thought Adam Zachariah, peeping at them between his arms clasped about the log. *Save us, they're mad and dangerous.*

An hour after dawn, they saw newcomers.

An ancient Austin Champ, oxide red and open, carrying two men in sunglasses and white turbans. As it reached the opposite bank of the wadi, some seventy yards in front of them, the Champ came to a skidding halt, slewing arcs of gravel from its tyres. It was as though the driver had not seen the watercourse, or was intent on something closing from behind.

The two men sat motionless, surveying the wadi. First they scrutinised Mogga, Leila, Adam Zachariah and the Rat Man, now lined up expectantly on the mid-river island. Next, they studied the Land Rover, nose down in the riverbed. They could be seen discussing it, working it out in low, rapid voices as though spirits were listening from the acacia groves.

Then, slowly, the Champ edged forward, down the slope and onto the crust. It did not sink, but came on steadily, breaking through but maintaining enough momentum to keep afloat, like a rusty water-skier in slow motion.

"Well, it's lighter, that antique," growled Adam in chagrin, "there's nothing to it, not even a top . . ."

A few yards from the island, the driver of the Champ revved hard, hitting the slope with a bang, bouncing wildly onto higher ground. To their astonishment, he did not stop. With a sideways glance at them, he attempted to drive past, to leave them there.

"Hey!" shouted Adam, in outrage if not panic.

"Wait!" cried Leila.

"One moment!" bellowed Mogga.

"Stop!" commanded the Rat Man.

The driver would have taken no notice, would have slithered and roared away, had not his chosen route suddenly presented him with a fallen tree. He slammed on his brakes, thumped the tree, attempted to reverse – and stalled. The Rat Man, showing an undreamt of turn of speed, sprinted the fifty-yard gap and closed in, talking hard. Adam saw him take something from a pocket – a paper, a document – and thrust it under the man's face, with instant effect. While Mogga, Adam and Leila watched, the Rat Man gave orders.

Then he came back to the Land Rover.

"He will not stay long; he is afraid. But he will pull us back onto the island."

"Thank God," murmured Leila.

"So he damn well should," huffed Adam.

"How kind," smiled Mogga.

With a stiff short rope of oily sisal, it was done. The Champ and the Land Rover stood tail to tail on the island.

"*Alhamdulillah*, now we can go back together," announced Adam, hugely relieved, "the sensible way, to the junction and back to Malha before some murderer . . ."

"We go on," said the Rat Man, pointing over the wadi, "that way."

"Forget that!" exclaimed Adam Zachariah furiously.

"Certainly, Adam," said Mogga gently, "our mission is barely begun."

"It's impossible, it's crazy! We'll sink again. And there are bandits, and raiders. These people know, by God!"

He flapped a hand towards the Champ.

Mogga laughed, kindly but serious: "Oh Adam, come now . . ."

"Why didn't they want to stop? Don't tell me they're not running. It's suicide . . ."

Mogga studied him, searching and saddened.

"But Adam," Leila was emollient, "we rely on you."

"It's lunatic!" Adam's voice rose shriller, frustrated and frightened. "There's fighting, there's people with guns everywhere now, out for food and money, no one is safe. And you, a woman . . . ! What if there is an ambush, by God? I think there could be an ambush."

At this, the Rat Man peered at him questioningly.

Leila smiled confidently at Mogga.

"You have no fears, do you, Mogga?"

But, to her bewilderment, Mogga bowed his head.

"I believe that Adam is right."

"*Alhamdulillah!*" their driver yelped.

"It is no place for a woman," said Mogga, "not this desert, not in such times. I was foolish to let you accompany us."

She was dumbfounded, she was livid. She found her hard professional tongue and she lashed Mogga.

"Mogga, I am grown up now, and I am known to have a head on my shoulders. I do not need telling when a thing is safe for me."

Mogga shook his head. "I am ashamed that I brought you. I should have known at Malha."

The Rat Man watched every move, his small brown eyes flicking from one to the other.

"So, you side with Adam now?" She was incensed. "You give up?"

"Not at all," said Mogga. "You must go back to Malha with these people. Adam is quite right: return is the only option."

"Quite right, by God!" Adam shouted, "Back we go."

"Only, I go on," said Mogga.

Leila's mouth fell open, but Adam Zachariah called out triumphantly:

"You can't drive!"

"True, I cannot," acknowledged Mogga. The Rat Man was suddenly excited and apprehensive. Mogga nodded at him.

"I believe that this gentleman can."

The Rat Man said, "Yes."

"Him?!" Adam was appalled, was incredulous.

"You know nothing about me!" hissed the Rat Man. "For your information, I can drive any vehicle in this desert."

For a rat, he was being loquacious. He turned to Mogga, tossing his head emphatically.

"All these return to Malha at once. We take the Land Rover and we go on, you and I only."

"So be it," smiled Mogga, with a wonderful finality.

It left Adam bewildered and hurt: he had done his best, and now he was supplanted. It left Leila quite faint, and she laid a hand on Adam's shoulder for support. The colour went from her face.

"What is it?" Mogga was alarmed. "Are you unwell?"

"No," she murmured, "not unwell . . ."

268

"Oh, I should never have allowed . . ."

"Mogga!" She looked up. "Please, now, come with me."

She took him by the arm, leading him aside, then turning on him.

"Do you suppose you are my nursemaid?"

"No," he sighed, "but I brought you into danger."

"I am at liberty to leave," she hissed, "so why am I not at liberty to stay?"

Mogga peered at her in dismay.

"You are not expected, you are not required . . ."

"Not required?" she interrupted. "You say I am redundant?"

He tried to be conciliatory.

"It is not your role, Miss Leila."

"Role be damned!" she spat. "They have a role for you, all right."

"Who has, Miss Leila?" he enquired respectfully.

"In Fasher, all those Directors and Administrators and Governors, they've a role for you: victim, scapegoat, whipping boy and fool!"

"Why should they whip me?"

"Because they are frustrated and helpless and must whip someone to stop themselves feeling entirely pathetic. I cannot believe you don't see it!"

"Who is helpless?"

"All of them! This Steel Fist, this Xavier, these village chiefs, these trucking bosses, this everybody. They can do nothing, so to feel better they will whip someone like hell – you! Because you are not one thing or another, not Arab, not local, not foreign, you will do. You are the cow's cunt, Mogga, neither meat nor leather!"

He blinked and blushed: "Miss Leila . . . !"

"Yes, the cow's cunt is what you are."

She turned her flushed face downstream as her eyes began to glisten.

"Ah, Miss Leila," began Mogga, dismayed – but she wailed.

"What makes you do this? You do not have to do this!"

"It is my duty," he replied simply.

"Duty?" she moaned. "Duty to whom? There is no one worth . . ."

She did not finish.

She turned back to him. There was no pretence; her face streamed.

"My dear friend," she began, shaking her head. Mogga reached out and took her hands.

"Now then, now then," he urged. "This is too much, too much really. I merely go to the desert for a day; you make too much of it. You can plan for my return."

"Planning?"

"We must begin our work, our book! The day I return, we must compare notes. You have so many notes already, needing only to be put in order, and you can give me orders to go out and make enquiries. We shall compile and assemble it all, till we can publish. Then we shall have done something for our Sudan! What are we to call it, Miss Leila? Have you chosen the title? *Sudanese Plants and their Uses? The Vegetable Wisdom of Sudan?* What shall it be?"

She murmured, "I have not thought."

"Ah, you must think, think very hard. Let that title be loud and clear, declaring what we are – which is not the cow's cunt."

He laughed aloud. The waiting clutch of men watched them curiously. He brought her gently back to the vehicles, one hand resting upon his own, as though processing: one might almost have applauded. As they approached the Champ, Adam Zachariah opened the door and Leila took her place in the front seat. The original passenger climbed in behind her. The driver of the Champ took his place.

For an instant, no one else moved. The Rat Man looked enquiringly at Adam Zachariah who returned it darkly. The Rat Man held out his hand. Adam hesitated – then held out the key, dropping it into the Rat Man's palm. Adam gave Mogga a reproachful scowl, then took two bags from the Land Rover, Leila's and his own.

Then they went away over the riverbed.

Mogga and the Rat Man watched them go, standing in silence together. Unconsciously Mogga scratched at the palms of his hands, which were itching.

*

"Chad! Let's hit Chad!"

That's what they'd do; Chad would be their making and saving. There was trouble in Chad, proper trouble, with refugee camps, malnutrition, airlifts and everything frightful and fitting. They were needed there, the whole team.

At the Resthouse, there was a whirl of packing. The Islander would come for the first of them today. With the seasons of famine they would move on, true nomads.

Xavier Hopkins began the work of dismantling.

At the workshop, he told the Lebanese manager to pack as much diesel into the Land Rovers as possible and despatch them to Khartoum before dawn.

"We'll keep one here. The rest can be used in the Red Sea Hills."

"But why before dawn?"

"So the Army don't get them. I'm not having that."

At the hospital, Dr Khalid Shamal was interrupted on his ward round by a respectful murmur from an orderly. There was a truck at the door, laden with boxes.

"You can have it all," said Dr Maeve. "We're leaving. Mind you use it responsibly, now."

Dr Khalid Shamal was too well-mannered to spit.

"What is in the boxes?" asked Khalid hopefully. "Is it medicines?"

"Baby scales, spirit sterilisers, UNICEF growth charts."

Dr Shamal already had a cupboard full of UNICEF baby scales and growth charts, and a score of WHO sterilisers without any spirit.

"No medicines?" he enquired again.

"Twenty-seven thousand paracetamol," replied Dr Maeve, "enough for one hell of a headache."

At Seed and Tools, Fauzi was enjoying pleasant daydreams.

He had decided to get married: it was that simple. He had been observing the young widow with whom he shared his compound, and her three girls. He had noted that she was very personable, very hard working and exceedingly poor. The children seemed pleasant and what could be more charming, after the day's responsibilities, than the play of girlish fancy? Their mother's circumstances were dire, and he could hardly imagine Farida refusing a fellow like him. Her first husband, poor Farah, had been a likeable chap but by no means as well-educated, as smart, as cosmopolitan as himself. No, thought Fauzi, Farida was in no position to refuse.

He had marched across the compound and put the matter to her baldly.

Farida had stared at him in such astonishment that Fauzi had been slightly offended.

"I should point out," he remarked, "that I have a highly responsible position with the foreigners. I am Supervisor of Seed and Tools, Grade Four."

Farida was speechless for a moment. Then she blurted out that she was honoured, and would give him her reply tomorrow.

Fauzi, thoroughly pleased with himself, was further gratified to receive a summons to Head Office.

"Now you will see," he informed the toothless watchman, "I daresay I am promoted again. Logistics, perhaps: it may well be that I am to undertake Logistics."

"Nnnng baaah gmmm," remarked the old man.

But when Fauzi came before Xavier, he was politely given his notice. He was told that he would receive one month's termination pay, and was instructed to surrender all the seed and tools to the Sudan Red Crescent, who would be coming to collect.

Rose Price, meanwhile, was sitting on a bench on the office porch, sucking her Libyan 'Marlboro'.

"Rose?" began Xavier. "Will you stay on in Chad? They could use you, I'm sure."

She puffed again, wrinkling her eyes in her sun-dried face, before returning gruffly:

"Will you?"

"No," said Xavier. "Frankly, I think I've done with aid work, with being a salaried nomad. I've other things to do."

Rose Price sat up straighter, lifting her chin as she studied him.

"Oh?" she queried, "such as?"

He had to think a moment, as though even visualising another country was an effort.

He said, "I'd like to go back to college."

He was abstracted, frowning. Rose said:

"What of Leila and her husband? They'll be isolated."

"Well, perhaps . . ." Hopkins began to reply, but Rose was suddenly standing and facing him, full of alarm.

"Where's Mogga? What of him? What'll he do?"

"I can't speak for Mogga," Xavier responded weakly, knowing that she was about to demand more answers.

"But he knows none of all this. He's out collecting that stupid woman's pills, he has no idea what's happening. He'll come back to find everyone gone!"

"I'll be here a little while."

"But what will he *do?*" She was almost stamping her feet.

"Well, that's up to Mogga. He's a free . . ."

"No," exclaimed Rose Price, "Mogga's not free at all, he's trapped here. With us gone they'll be gunning for him."

Xavier looked more and more uncomfortable.

"He's not responsible for anything."

"But they'll hold him responsible! They'll go for him; God knows what they'll do. When we run off, he'll be all that's left."

"We're NOT running!" Hopkins exploded. "We're leaving on a point of very firm principle."

She dropped her cigarette, stamping on it, her ageless grey eyes seething. She hurried from the room.

FOUR

They turned due west again, leaving the Mewadag Hills behind them. The Rat Man drove fast, saying nothing, and in the passenger seat Mogga was obliged to grip the edge of his seat and the grab handle of the door. For an hour they crossed flatlands spattered with thin scrub and *siwak* trees, their hazy blue leaves and smooth, grey-green trunks all thickly coated with dust that the rain had gobbed on, leaving a pattern like scales on the bark. Then the rocks began to gather, the outriders of a massif. Soon came low ridges running alongside the road. They were soft stone, red, yellow and white in horizontal strata, eroded into fantastical blocks.

"Like a castle!" Mogga smiled to the Rat Man.

The Rat Man said nothing, but drove on steadily. Mogga thought that, with each passing mile, the Rat Man looked more haunted.

The ground changed colour, darker, more sparkling, full of quartz and schist.

"Shall we reach the *qalti* soon?" Mogga tried.

The Rat Man jutted his jaw straight ahead, but Mogga saw his eyes flick urgently about the landscape. He even looked in his mirror as if, in this wasteland, there might be traffic.

Which there was.

Ahead of them, a pocket caravan of mules trotted, a man and five women all comically tall above their mounts. They rode with long sticks across their laps, flourishing these at other animals with sacks and bundles lashed to the pack frames. They must have heard the Land Rover behind them, for suddenly they left the trail and trotted hurriedly to the south, urging their beasts with kicks and sticks. Where were they going? In that direction Mogga could see nothing but barren hills, flat-topped and steep-flanked.

"They are returning to their farms and their homes," he offered, unconvinced.

Still the Rat Man did not answer. They were pulling away from the mule caravan when a tyre blew out, tearing itself to rubber rags and flapping madly inside the Land Rover's wheel arch.

The Rat Man brought them to a halt.

"Oh dear," said Mogga.

They sat in silence. The Rat Man remained motionless, his grip still tight upon the wheel. Mogga twisted in his seat to look at him, but the Rat Man's gaze was drifting, slewing reluctantly towards Mogga as though he was terrified to meet his passenger's eyes.

"Are you perhaps unwell . . ." Mogga began half-heartedly.

The Rat Man seized his door handle, threw the door open and leapt out as if electrocuted onto the hard dirt. He landed awkwardly, Mogga saw, stumbling, twisting his ankle, but in an instant started into a painful run out across the desert. He was in pursuit of the caravan. The riders heard him shout and they glanced back, not slowing their beasts. The Rat Man waved his arms, closed on them, ran alongside the man pleading with him until, with frantic looks back towards the Land Rover, he scrambled onto a mule.

Mogga watched him go, astonished and not astonished. What else would a Rat Man do?

The caravan bustled into the distance, trailing a thin dust-screen.

Mogga stepped down also.

He looked at the shredded tyre, its tattered remains pinched between the wheel and the stony ground. He looked through the window at the two spares jammed alongside the diesel drum. But he didn't know how to do it – and besides, he couldn't drive.

He looked about: at the scarps to the south; at the sands to the east behind him, apricot in the sinking sun; ahead at the blue-grey pebbles and the distant volcanic cones. How far distant he could not tell, for that way the haze was deepening.

He began to walk. Ahead of him would be the *qalti*, a pool among the rocks, and people surely. On he walked, following the trail towards the conical hills. Here were no trees, only a rust-coloured dirt broken by clumps of coarse grass and thistles. A hot breeze made the grasses bob, and bowled along seeds and shreds of leaf. He stopped and peered at the ground. There were tyre tracks that appeared from nowhere and vanished again, but the prints were already blurring as sand trickled into the impression. He could not say if they were new or old.

Mogga marched on towards the ravines where the rock pool Qalti Tawin was hidden, his head fuzzy in the heat and his feet burnt by the grit surface. The lining of his mouth was papery and his tongue was beginning to swell with thirst. He thought, if I spoke now, my words would sound like the thick babblings of an idiot. His march slowed. He wiped the insistent drizzle of sweat from his eyes, feeling that the heat was folding itself tighter and tighter about him – until he stumbled and fell.

Mogga twisted, sprawled and skidded, his arms outstretched and his hands scraping painfully, heel and knuckle on the sharp dirt. Winded, he lay immobile some moments, moving only to lift his head. He could do that, at least; his neck was not broken, though after the jarring fall he'd imagined that it might be. He peered very closely at the pebbles under his face. His cheek stung, and when at last he sat up and put his hand there, he felt grit and blood together. He attempted to stand, and almost fell again. His right shoe had split, the thin heel doubled under. He straightened it and tried to walk, but the flapping thing almost had him down again. He took out his handkerchief and tied it about his foot to hold the sole in place. Then he could hobble onwards, though every hundred yards or so he had to stop and retie.

In the late afternoon, to his complete surprise, he came to a depression in the plain that he'd not suspected until he was upon it. It was just before the foot of the hills, a mile or more across, the bowl of an ancient shallow lake or swamp, he thought, where no water had lain in centuries. It was crowded with thorn trees, quite dead, so devoid of the juices of life that they could have been petrified. They gleamed grey-white, glistering with the silicates embedded in them by the wind. They leaned and teetered at wild angles, some stretching and clawing upwards, some cracked and tumbled. Though the hot wind swirled between them, nothing stirred.

Mogga stumbled down the track that descended into the forest of tree corpses. He tottered forward, he picked up momentum, he began to run, lurching and limping in his wounded shoe, sending stones flying as he came pell-mell among the trees. At the first pool of shade, he plunged forward. And lay again.

He sat with his back against a tree trunk and surveyed the dead forest. No birds moved, no lizards, nothing. If he ceased breathing, the silence was complete.

He was struggling to focus his mind. He was beginning to mumble. The palms of his hands were throbbing.

On the ground before him, he saw a track, tiny prints of paw or claw, winding busily under the splintered end of the fallen tree. He studied the tracks: they appeared new, sharp, not yet blurred or blotted by the wind. The little prints went in pairs, and in each pair, one print overlaid the other, perhaps a rear foot catching up the forepaw. He'd seen this before, somewhere distant, but he couldn't recall . . . He wiped at his face to see better, clearing one eye but putting grit into the other.

The light was changing, the haze replaced by a gleaming darkness. It made Mogga nervous. He felt that something was coming for him.

He thought: *I must keep moving. If I stop here, I shall be turned to stone, as the trees are.*

He sought in the crevices of his mouth for a hint of moisture, for a last active salivary gland to lubricate his tongue. He eased a finger between his lips that were now cracked into battlements and deep embrasures. He tried to stand – but was too weak. He thought, everything here is quite dead. Perhaps I too am beyond saving myself, beyond my last powers.

More to prove the point than to escape, he put his hands against the stony bark of the tree behind his back, and pushed. The base of his spine pressed painfully against the wood, while the heat-thickened blood slurped through his brain. He pushed once more till he was upright, then staggered, caught and steadied himself against the tree trunk. As he did so, a terrific roar burst all about him, overwhelming him, while the light changed to a penal grey.

The rain hit him. It fell as though in a lump from the sky, as though all the rain hit the ground together. Instantly, Mogga was cold, chattering and shivering. He threw his head back and the rain hit his eyes. He closed his lids and held his head further and further back until his neck hurt, his mouth as wide open as he could stretch the cracked lips. He tore off his shirt, then his trousers also, shivering wildly as he spread the cloth over the tree trunk. In seconds everything was drenched, and Mogga seized first his shirt and then his trousers, sucking greedily at the fabric before spreading it again for more. He stood in his shabby grey under-pants sucking at the clothes in a downpour that mortified his flesh.

A few minutes later, the rain eased and then stopped. Trembling, Mogga leaned against the tree trunk. He stopped sucking at his shirt, tried to calm himself, to let go of his shivering.

The ground was steaming, slowly at first, in wisps. Then the sand smoked steadily, plumes rising from pockets of rainwater in the lee of fallen trees. Moments before, Mogga had trembled and shaken with cold; now he was steamed alive.

And the earth split.

All about him, crevices opened and out of these climbed termites in thousands of thousands. They had little red heads and swollen bodies from which wings trailed, and as they dragged themselves hurriedly out into the sunlight they spread these wings and stirred them and twizzled into the air in slow gyres past Mogga. They were so delicately charming in the air, but so cumbersome on the wet sand. Those that did not fly at once were set upon; almost as soon as the nests broke open they were surrounded by ants, the voracious *qarasa*, dark predators who snapped and seized. A termite might be overwhelmed by three or four *qarasa* in the very door-way of the nest, until they dropped together back below ground like the damned dragged down by devils.

Mogga stared in wonder; he knew this sight so well, yet he had not seen it since leaving the red humid south where on hands and knees he had watched the mud split and the termites twirl up just so, till New Mother lifted him clear of the nipping ants. It was the same here; the wonder was just the same.

Now, to Mogga's amazement, the sand itself changed colour: it took on a crimson tinge that ran and ebbed in swirls. He looked closely, and saw countless tiny red spiders with velvety circular bodies that milled in swarms like a delicate carpet. Then he saw that he must watch his feet, for next came dozens of brown scorpions marching about masterfully with their hot tails in the air, seizing ants and spiders too. Even on the dead trees there was new, living colour, for thousands of grasshoppers had appeared, as long as a finger, mostly a soft grey-green but some tinted with blue and violet, with red at their knees and elbows and bulging grey eyes. Where they had come from, Mogga could not imagine, for what food was there here? But they clicked and leapt and flew south and he followed their strong, certain flight away across the fallen forest.

At last, from behind roots came the owner of the paw prints; a bustling, snuffling hedgehog that peered at the throng of insects, then scurried forward snapping to left and right like a guest at a grand buffet. Yet, however many ants the hedgehog snaffled, however many spiders the scorpions devoured, however many termites fell into the ants' clutches, always another crowd appeared from nowhere. Mogga was awestruck, dumbfounded at the relentlessness, the species that rushed to throw themselves into the paths of their ancient predators, dying or consuming as they had always done, generation on generation.

At his feet, the banquet went on. Mogga began to chuckle: there was more than enough for everybody to eat everybody! He lifted his face, he grinned a cracked grin at the swirl of red and green about his feet. He was beaming with pleasure, he spoke aloud, he cried out in a laughing voice:

"Leila! Oh Leila!"

He wanted her to see this, to witness with him the ebullience of life and to name it for him. So now, in the dead forest that seethed with life, it was her he named.

"Miss Leila!"

Tears of joy sprang on his sore, sun-stiffened gritty black face, while he sighed and sighed again.

Mogga perched upon a tree trunk, watching the creatures go about their sudden lives. The light was changing again; dusk was in the forest, was well advanced. He glanced up and saw that the sky had cleared, sluiced clean by the rain. From between the volcanic peaks, the crescent moon rose startlingly.

He buttoned his wringing shirt that was colder than nakedness, and was about to pull on the trousers too when he remembered the scorpions and looked down; the remnants of his shoe were gone. He slipped off his underpants, then with a sharp stone and his teeth tore from them two thin strips. He used these strips to tie the pants in a bundle about his foot.

So Mogga walked through the moonlit forest.

He had been moving between the trees for a time he could no longer gauge. The trail, that was merely a shadow, wound and twisted among the petrified groves. Often he believed that he had lost it, but always they seemed to meet again. He neared the edge of the forest, where the way rose up towards the rocks ahead. He was almost out, and believed that he could see clear ground. He was going slowly, cautiously, stooping to retie the cloth about his foot, though the scorpions appeared to have gone to their beds now.

Then, just before him moved a creature that did not sleep, a sombre bulk that at first he could not interpret. It heard or scented his approach and turned, so that now he understood the high back, the droop in the neck: a camel, loose in the forest.

Wary (camels were not creatures from his world), Mogga drew nearer. The animal saw him and gave a low moan. Some distance to his left, he heard an answering sound: deep animal pain. He glimpsed another bulk on the ground, inelegant, askew, its neck waving weakly as it tried to rise. The moonlight was probing through the forest at other shapes on the ground that he did not understand, dark lumps and chaotic scraps of black.

He came forward among them. They were scattered among the silver-grey dead trees all about him: animals, people, dozens perhaps, surrounded by wrecked baggage. He peered closely: there were men, women, children also, lain in peculiar postures on the sand, some face down with their arms and legs straight out, others on their backs or unnaturally twisted. They did not move or moan; they were silent and perfectly still.

Gingerly, Mogga stepped between them, keeping a little distance, as though a hand might reach out to seize his leg. He looked now at a huddle that would have been a family group: man, woman, an infant lying between them, their protection inadequate. Mogga examined them closely in the raking silver light that cast strong shadows, such that every fibre in the rough woollen packs was distinct and sharply focused. But he could distinguish few wounds. The eyes shone from faces on which the moonlight put a soft metallic gleam, a patina that smoothed away death. The corpses were cool and tranquil; Mogga thought them beautiful. He felt no fear now, only tenderness. He thought to make them more comfortable and moved among the groups, bending over the most contorted, straightening their limbs.

But when he pulled himself up straighter, more analytical thoughts marred the peace. He saw now that there were burns on flesh, on bags; a nomad woman's riding canopy was scorched away leaving only rags on the fractured remains of the wooden frame. He saw boxes shattered, splintered and crushed. He saw a camel whose rear quarter had been blasted off by some horrific power. He saw craters in the sand and far-flung fragments of packs, or perhaps of people.

This was more than an ambush of rival tribes, though they'd be blamed. There had been explosions here; there had been bombs or maybe rockets, from the rocks or from the air? In his mind's eye he glimpsed uniforms, predatory and closing. He envisaged the caravan in open ground between the forest depression and the hills' protection, jolted and shocked by a first strike, racing for the shelter of the trees but caught by the attackers, cut down even there. He could feel the sky juddering, could hear the rotors smashing the air down.

Mogga felt weary. His hands ached painfully and he struggled to think. He moved apart and sat down in a small clearing, looking back at the humped shadows. A devouring had happened here, life-consuming life as always in the desert, as Mogga knew there had always been across the world. What had happened here was just that which had seemed excellent among insects. Men consumed each other's lives, goods and power, and grew stronger by this; women died or prospered, fattening on resources taken by force. It was the same: between ant and termite, between tribes and nations, gangs and armies.

Between horsemen and families burning in a train.

There was nothing to be done: what intercession could make a difference, or halt the devouring? What sacrifice or effort? And yet there would always be a species of folk drawn into such hopeless labours as inevitably as termites burst from crevices and small spiders carpeted the ground red.

He knew that he was one such, and that when he was devoured nothing would be altered by it. In his head, he cried in bewildered fury: *Miss Leila! Why?*

He thought of the far south, of his mother and the Acholi girl who had been so unhappy but had for a while cheered his father. He thought of the brilliant parakeets and cordonbleus by the river, and the women dancing as they walked. He thought of the children on the class log under his father's tree, of the eager students at the vocational school. Good things, he remembered.

But then it was his young carpenter Marcello, his foot stuck out across the path through the millet. And the Arab, Tariq, in his blazing shop. These visions froze him. The previous dusk, he had called upon Leila to witness the creatures. Now, he alone was the witness.

Mogga lay upon the damp sand, curled up like a hedgehog and slept.

*

Mustafa the half-wit dragged open the steel gates. Leila detected a new nervousness in his servility, a looking at her sideways, a readiness to flee. She thought, the old fool never expected me to return. Perhaps he thinks I'm now a *jinn*. When Abdurrahman had edged the Land Rover into the narrow courtyard, Mustafa would once have been eager to dust and sweep out the vehicle. Now he stood aside, suspiciously watching the driver walk away.

Farida gestured towards the kitchen in gentle reproach: Leila had come without warning; she'd given her young housekeeper no chance to make dinner.

"There is no food," said Farida apologetically, "and no charcoal."

Leila looked round the yard, under the *rakuba* and through the open doorway to the inner rooms. There on the blue concrete ledge beneath the chicken-wired window was a plate with a mango and a small serrated knife.

"I am not hungry," replied Leila. "Fruit will be sufficient. Come back in the morning, Farida. Send Mustafa now to the souk for fuel, then he can go to the mosque."

It was mid-afternoon. The watchman mumbled, nodded and set off. Farida gave Leila a hesitant look, as though wishing to ask something – but really, why should Mrs Karim be interested in her offer of marriage? It was not as though Farida had much choice but to accept. She took her child and departed also.

Leila opened the water jar that stood oozing by the door and scooped out a drink. She sank into a steel-tube chair under the *rakuba*, thankful for silence, letting the noise of travel drain from her. Later, she would wash the stains from her body also.

She sat waiting.

After some while, she heard a vehicle draw to a halt outside and the engine cut. A door was closed. There was no call of greeting, no *Salaamalaikum*. A foreigner? Xavier Hopkins, perhaps. She did not move.

"You should have returned yesterday," said Colonel Hassan al-Bedawi tersely, without formalities. "Where have you been? Did you deliver the camera? The *zurqa* has it?"

A tremble went through Leila from head to foot. She visualised the camera, lying even now in its bag in Mogga's Land Rover, in the stowaway under the passenger seat. She'd entirely forgotten to show Mogga how it worked.

"He has it," she said.

The Colonel studied her. He stood before her with a stillness that was not relaxed. His uniform, dun-coloured, seemed stiff upon him. His hands hung by his side like weights, lifeless except for the curling and uncurling of both little fingers. He leaned slightly forward, over her, for in her weariness she had not risen.

"So," he said, "what will you do now?"

She was startled to think she heard a curious tenderness in his voice.

"Do?" she murmured vaguely.

"The English are leaving," he informed her. "They are running. They will not even return to Khartoum and depart with dignity but are fleeing direct to Chad, some of them today. Even now they are at the airstrip. The Islander is here."

He was studying her, seemingly puzzled by her lack of reaction, as though there was some obvious implication that she was not grasping. And then he smiled slightly, for he had seen Leila momentarily tense and, as suddenly, turn pale and limp. Yes, she had remembered: the Islander, and her husband.

She struggled to sit upright, fighting for air.

"Is he . . . is my . . ." she began.

But Colonel Hassan cocked his head at the air, at the breeze that blew from the west across the town, bringing a new sound: a rich mechanical roar. It had started suddenly, rising to a strong baritone that continued on a level for perhaps a minute. The man and the woman listened, watching each other. Then the note soared, changing to a snarl as, on the airfield a mile distant, the pitch of the propellers altered to grab at the air, and the aircraft surged down the stony runway. Then another change in tone as the Islander tilted and lifted its head into the dusty sky.

"Your husband, Dr Othman Karim, is on his way to Chad."

For a second her heart rose in hope – but was it true, this Colonel's say-so? Her husband airborne, spirited away from harm? Her guilty heart shrieked with alarm: what if Othman Karim was merely sitting in his cell in his dull despair, entirely ignorant of the deal? What if Othman was at this moment lying stunned with his face kicked bloody on the guardroom floor? What if Othman were no longer alive, perhaps had not been alive for weeks? Leila saw how Colonel Hassan looked down on her with a face that said, *Now you see what I have done. Now you will acknowledge my power, now you will be grateful and obedient.* She read it in his eyes: *Let us test your obedience again.* She read something new, like the dark heat in a waiting forge.

She tried to stand, to rise with dignity and strength of purpose to face him as an equal, but her legs were weakened with apprehension and hours of travel, and as she tried to straighten she wobbled and lurched.

"I must have water," she breathed, faint with terror and disgust, teetering towards the tall earthenware jar. As she reached it, she sensed the man close behind her, reaching out for her even as she was about to fall, grabbing at her.

Her left hand flailed at him and her right knocked the mango and its saw-toothed knife from the window ledge onto the floor. Her legs gave way and she sprawled on the cement, knocking the side of her head on the blue ledge as she went down on her back, crying thickly as her skull struck the ground, yet she rebounded to a sitting position, her left forearm slithering on the grit, pushing her up. The man was astride her, his legs apart and one foot between her feet as he bent to reach down for her, the dun fabric of his uniform trousers stretched under his crotch. Fear and nausea winded her, and into her stunned and muddled brain blazed a light like arc lamps on a scene which night after night had ruined her sleep: a little girl surrounded, forced down on her back with her legs spread to shrilling music and women's shouts: *Bring the little bride! This is your special day!*

She felt under her hand a serrated blade, and she was thrashing and cutting and hacking while she shrieked into the noise of an aircraft passing overhead.

Then she passed out.

*

"Leila Karim . . ."

The voice was weak, but not far away.

"Leila Karim . . . help me."

The voice was spent.

She opened her eyes. She was lying on her side, her brain swirling and pounding, her hip bruised from her fall. Giddy, she could not lift her head. But she saw, on the far side of the room, a figure sitting against the wall. She thought, the floor is dirty, we have chairs . . . She focused a little better, raised her head, then managed to pull her feet round and to raise her own back till she rested against the wall, one leg straight out and the other folded awkwardly beneath her. The nausea billowed again and she retched, her head dropping forward, terribly heavy. She took deep breaths, pleaded with her racing heart, and lifted her face.

Opposite her, she recognised her sister Khamisa, propped like herself against the cream-painted wall except that Khamisa had both feet straight out. From between the outstretched legs there spread a sea of crimson, a tide of arterial blood that widened and advanced towards her, its rolling front edge lifting the dust from the floor as it came. Khamisa's face was full of surprise, of outrage, of bewilderment. To Leila it was all quite familiar – save that, for some reason she could not grasp, her sister was not in her new red dress with little black camels about the hem, but wore a dun-coloured uniform.

*

Not so many hours after, Mogga was woken by daylight, already warm. With barely a look at the silent battleground, he walked past and onto the track beyond.

The way rose up from the ancient lake floor to the foot of the hills. He looked west, and the trail blurred into the distance. Somewhere there it turned north towards the saltpans of Al Atrun in the Libyan Desert. He looked back the way he had come, over the dead forest. Very far away, something bright blinked at him and in an instant his heart lifted, was touched by hope, and sank again, for the flash was sun striking his own vehicle, his Land Rover, so many hours of walking in the past.

Before him, a complex of volcanic cones and lava flows. There was a narrow gorge curling in between the peaks, and there was a quality of rub and wear about all the surfaces, down to the pebbles on the ground, hinting at centuries of visitors. It was the entrance to Qalti Tawin, the natural rock cistern. At the realisation, Mogga's thirst came back hard, and hunger too.

As ever, he went forward, among the boulders and into the gorge. He trudged with his one foot shod and one wrapped in rags, along a flat sand floor between steep sides of swelling, rounded rock, the hardest-looking stuff he'd ever seen, glinting with quartz. The gully closed and Mogga stepped up onto the sloping granite where the way was scarred by generations of Arabs and their animals torn between terror and eagerness at the scent of water. Mogga climbed and climbed, until he looked down into the deep, shaded arena where the rains pooled on impervious strata between steep volcanic walls.

It was deserted.

At first he could see no water. He came forward, feeling the sandy floor, heavy and saturated. Then he noticed a rock spur and, in the shadows behind it, a pool. He clambered onto the spur, gazing down into the black water perhaps three feet below him. He could not reach it with his mouth; barely could he reach it with his hand. He had no leather bucket, as the Arabs carried. But he took off his remaining shoe, lay flat, stretched and scooped and caught up a drink. He sucked at it urgently, dipped again, drank. Then he lay, still and exhausted on the rock, peering down.

He heard a soft scraping sound behind him, shoes on grit. Too weary, he did not move. He had been startled, but a moment later this gave way to resignation. He noted, gratefully, that the throbbing pain in his hands had ceased. He waited.

The scrape came again, close by. Mogga caught a sudden stink of rancid perspiration. In the water, which was still lapping from the dip of his shoe, he saw a new reflection: two figures standing, one looming large, one furtive. He puzzled at the apparitions that swayed and stretched fantastically as the water moved. The bigger one seemed to lift something irregular and heavy over his head.

The blow came. Mogga slithered and tumbled forwards, his blood streaking the rock, staining the pool.

*

There was to have been a book, Father. You'd have been pleased. You saw me as an engineer or a surgeon; you never thought of plants. Maybe they didn't seem to you part of the modern age, but it would have been a fine book, the science of Sudanese food plants, all achieved here in Sudan. I was to have done this with a *zurqa*. It could have helped, some lives might even . . .

The *azan* was being called from the mosque; the interminable call to prayer and yet more prayer. She heard, over the yard walls, the coarsely amplified voice of the *muezzin* scraping out from the loudspeakers: *Come, put your soul in order, in readiness for the night.* It was not a man these days, just a tape; such had been the contribution of technology to modern Sudan.

What I have in fact achieved is quite other. After all those wise words from you, my Father, those exhortations, those visits we made, after all those years of study, I have reached an end. This is the culmination of my life's work; it certainly terminates my labours, here in Sudan. What is it, Father, that I have accomplished for my people? I have slain the Chief of State Security in Darfur. I daresay it is a very fine thing to have done.

There was a hedgehog – she could just see it from where she sat motionless under the *rakuba* – a little brown hedgehog snuffling and rustling in the debris of palm leaves that lay in a shady corner by the kitchen shed. It would be looking for grubs, for insects, for snakes' eggs. The indomitable Sudanese hedgehog. Mogga liked them.

He is in there, against the wall, staring out through the chicken wire with dull eyes, and his blood is all across the floor of my house. This achievement is mine alone. I hope Othman gets to hear of it.

*

Mogga had been found by a family of Meidob, who had arrived at the *qalti* half dead of thirst. They had rushed to the water among the rocks, frantic to quench their own and their camels' need – and had seen a corpse floating in the pool. They had managed to loop a rope onto him and haul him clear. Disgusted, frightened too, they had been obliged to drink from the pool in which he'd floated and into which his blood had run, and to water their animals there also. They'd had no choice; there was no other water for them. They'd seen a truck coming south from the saltpans of Al Atrun, and had sent the corpse to Malha.

Rose Price had come to the old, doorless brick Resthouse with Adam Zachariah. There, in the still heat of late afternoon, she'd seen Mogga lain out upon a worn canvas sheet on the cement floor.

"Has he any family?" demanded the police Sergeant. Rose said she thought not. Mogga had come to Darfur out of the ruins of the south.

"Then there is no one to be informed, and you must take him away from here," the Sergeant concluded, hoping they would forget the fine Land Rover that was reported to be standing abandoned in the desert.

"We must bury him now," insisted Adam Zachariah. "It is the only thing."

Rose Price nodded.

"Here," she said.

"He does not belong here, he is a *zurqa!*" shouted the

Sergeant, before he realised how unseemly this was and restrained himself.

"It must be here," repeated Rose Price, her voice thick and gruff with travel and cigarettes and weariness. She did not look at the Sergeant.

"Then do it yourselves."

The policeman went striding out of the resthouse gates before they could make some awful request of him.

"We shall need men to dig," said Adam.

Rose stared down from her gawky height at the poor, swelling thing on the canvas. She saw that Mogga's head was covered in clotted blood, and sand which looked so sore, abrading the raw wounds on his skull.

"Will you find a water boy?" she said to Adam Zachariah. "We must wash him."

"We cannot lay our hands upon him!" protested Adam.

"You do as you wish," she replied without anger, "but find me water."

So Adam Zachariah went in search. When he returned, Rose was still there, sitting on a steel chair near the door of the hot, reeking room, with Mogga. She was motionless; for a moment Adam thought her as lifeless as the little black man.

The donkey boy stood with his animal outside the gate, afraid of the *jinn* of a bloated dead *zurqa*. He would not enter, but pointed. From the sand drifts by the wall of the compound, a crescent shape projected. Adam pulled out an enamelled basin that was too battered even for the frugal Arabs. He knocked the dirt from it, then held it out for water.

"Stay," he commanded the boy, "We shall need more."

He heard the opening of the Land Rover door. Rose Price was pulling something from her bag: a shirt or towel perhaps. She looked expectantly at Adam and the driver gagged, close to vomiting: did she expect him to bathe the corpse?

"Bring the bowl," said Rose gruffly.

Adam passed through the doorway with the heavy container, blinking at the dimness. Rose Price knelt by Mogga's shoulder and

Adam placed the bowl by her, the small impact causing a hollow note that swirled around the circumference as the cloudy water swayed to and fro, slopping a small pool onto the floor.

Rose Price lowered a clean T-shirt into the water, twisted out the cloth and began to wipe Mogga's face. But the wet sand rolled and stuck and scratched the black skin. She stopped and looked at the mess; her hands held out the wet shirt, helpless. Adam Zachariah saw that she was trembling, and that down the pale, dry skin over the bony cheeks were rolling tears, more and more tears. She shook, her jaw quavered and she was very ugly. She looked round at Adam, her eyes awash.

"Mogga is dead," she wailed. "Oh, Mogga is dead!"

Appalled, Adam Zachariah came beside her, kneeling at Mogga's head. He lifted the wide bowl of water and held it over the *zurqa's* face. Carefully, he tipped the dish and poured a stream onto the forehead, so that the sand rinsed through the tufts of hair over the ears and onto the heavy canvas sheet. Rose Price dabbed at the dead face, though her own was in more need.

Beyond the northern edge of town stood a majestic *nim* tree, eighty feet high with deeply fissured brown bark and a rich canopy of jagged leaves forever moving sedately in breezes one could not feel on the ground below. The calm and steady movement, always the same whether the day was still or there was a dust storm blowing – this steady, gentle waving consoled all those who came to a burial. There was still a scattering of tiny white flowers in the high branches, like a light sprinkling of sugar crystals visible at dawn or dusk. But in such a dry season the *nim* tree was husbanding its deep water, and the flowers were few, while the fleshy fruits had lost their glowing orange sheen earlier than they should, and were brown and wrinkled. The tree had been planted – who knew when – to shade the cemetery. Near but not among the Muslim dead, Mogga was lowered into the ground.

The burial was observed from a short distance by the Sergeant, the Public Health Officer and, from a low and scruffy dune, by a dozen town urchins who stared at the tall, thin foreigner in a pink T-shirt and loose flower print trousers. This person's hair was short, the face bony, and the figure undistinguished by anything but height. The urchins realised, however, that this was a *khowajiyah*, a female. They regarded the scene warily, poised to remove themselves smartly should the *khowajiyah* show signs of approaching them. Fortunately, there was also a proper Sudanese who seemed to control her and move her about, for he drove her Land Rover and gave sensible orders to the two local men in white who'd done the digging.

The sand was heaped over Mogga, with a layer of rocks to keep off the dogs. The diggers were paid, and they drifted back towards the fringe of brushwood huts buffering the mud-brick settlement against the sands. The Sergeant and the Public Health man departed also, neither gesturing nor speaking to Rose Price or Adam Zachariah.

"Damn you," muttered Rose Price, "damn you, damn you," fumbling for a cigarette. But her curse did not carry, and Adam was restarting the engine.

Finis

POLYGON is an imprint of Birlinn Limited. Our list includes titles by Alexander McCall Smith, Liz Lochhead, Kenneth White, Robin Jenkins and other critically acclaimed authors. Should you wish to be put on our catalogue mailing list contact:

Catalogue Request
Polygon
West Newington House
10 Newington Road
Edinburgh EH9 1QS
Scotland, UK

Tel: +44 (0) 131 668 4371
Fax: +44 (0) 131 668 4466
e-mail: info@birlinn.co.uk

Postage and packing is free within the UK. For overseas orders, postage and packing (airmail) will be charged at 30% of the total order value.

Our complete list can be viewed on our website. Go to www.birlinn.co.uk and click on the Polygon logo at the top of the home page.